PLAYERS

By the same author

Mind's Eye

White Devils

PLAYERS

Paul McAuley

SIMON &
SCHUSTER

London · New York · Sydney · Toronto

A CBS COMPANY

First published in Great Britain by Simon & Schuster UK Ltd, 2007
A CBS COMPANY

1 3 5 7 9 10 8 6 4 2

Simon & Schuster UK Ltd
Africa House
64–78 Kingsway
London WC2B 6AH

www.simonsays.co.uk

Simon & Schuster Australia
Sydney

A CIP catalogue record for this book
is available from the British Library

Hardback ISBN-13: 978-0-7432-7617-7
ISBN-10: 0-7432-7617-5

Trade paperback ISBN-13: 978-0-7432-7618-4
ISBN-10: 0-7432-7618-3

For Georgina
and
For Stephen Jones,
this sliver of dark

1

Late Tuesday afternoon, the Robbery Unit of the Portland Police Bureau, Detective Sergeant Ryland Nelsen called Summer Ziegler into his office. He didn't ask her to sit down, so she stood in front of his desk, straight-backed in a cream blouse and black skirt, waiting for him to finish studying a custody report. She'd dressed for a court appearance that had eaten up most of the day, and she'd been working late, finishing paper-work. She wished now that she'd gone straight home at the end of the shift, because she was dead certain that her boss was about to hand her yet another petty errand.

He took his own sweet time with the report, reading both sides, saying at last, 'Do you believe in karma, Detective Ziegler?'

'As in fate?'

'As in be sure your sins will catch up with you.'

'I believe it would make our work a lot easier if karma caught up with all the bad guys.'

Ryland Nelsen dropped the report on his desk, leaned back in his chair and laced his hands behind his grey buzz cut. 'Cast your mind back to last December. You arrested a young woman name of Edie Collier.'

Summer thought for a moment. 'She tried to boost a couple of cashmere sweaters from Meier and Frank, the store detective challenged her, she made a run for it. I was cruising the area, helped chase her down. She got thirty days' county time plus two years' probation.'

'She got county time for shoplifting? All my arrests should go up before that judge.'

'She was already on probation for another shoplifting offence, plus she had a bunch of priors. She pled guilty at arraignment and the judge told her he was going to give her a short, sharp shock, stick her in jail over Christmas in the hope it would straighten her out. But I guess it didn't.'

Summer also guessed that Edie Collier must have gotten into something much more serious than shoplifting if she had come to the attention of the Robbery Unit, which investigated thefts involving use of a weapon or threats implying the presence of a weapon; mundane property crimes like shoplifting were handled by uniformed police and precinct detectives.

'I don't know if it straightened her out or not,' Ryland Nelsen said. 'I do know that a couple of fishermen stumbled across her in woods way the hell south of here, near Cedar Falls. Know where it is?'

'I've driven past it.'

'On the I-5, like me and a million other people. Anyhow, Edie Collier was badly injured from some kind of fall, and she died before the paramedics could get her to hospital. The local police are treating it as a suspicious death. They identified her from finger-prints and found out that her last known address was in Portland, and their Sheriff put in a call to the Chief's office, asked if some-one in the Bureau could inform her parents and persuade them to make the trip to Cedar Falls for formal ID and disposition of the body. And, well, the request bounced down the chain of command to the officer who last arrested her.'

'Me,' Summer said, with a falling sensation.

'You,' Ryland Nelsen said, pointing his forefinger at her and cocking his thumb gunwise. 'During your time in uniform, were you ever asked to do a next-of-kin notification?'

'No, sir. We left that kind of thing to detectives.'

'And just three weeks ago you got your detective's badge . . . See what I mean about karma?'

'I'm beginning to get an idea.'

'Breaking the bad news is never easy,' Ryland Nelsen said. 'And in this case, if it turns out to be manslaughter or murder . . .'

He paused, waiting for Summer to complete the thought.

She said, 'The parents will be suspects. I'll need to take some-one with me, in case they say something relevant.'

'I'm certain the Cedar Falls police would handle it themselves if they thought her parents had anything to do with her death. But having someone there to witness what goes down when you break the bad news, it's a sensible precaution. Do you have anyone in mind?'

Summer's mentor, Andy Parish, had rolled out an hour ago, at the end of the shift. Only Dick Searle was still at his desk, but he was busy, his phone caught between his shoulder and jaw while he typed something into his computer, and Summer barely knew him – they'd exchanged about a dozen sentences since she'd started work in the Robbery Unit. She could ask Ryland Nelsen to help her out, of course, but she didn't want her boss standing at her back and believed that she was expected to show some initiative. Well, the custody report she'd typed up after she'd arrested Edie Collier was on the desk right in front of her. Although it was upside down, she could read Edie's home address easily enough, and an x'd box further down the form confirmed that it was the address of her parents . . .

She said, 'Her parents live out by Southeast Foster. I have a friend in the precinct who can help me out.'

'Sounds like a plan. Don't think that I'm handing you this because you're presently lowest of the low on the thirteenth floor, by the way. It's because you knew the girl. Are we clear on that?'

'Yes, sir.'

Summer was pleased and apprehensive. Pleased to be given a chance to prove her worth; apprehensive because she knew that this little job could be trickier than it seemed. She remembered exchanging words with Edie Collier's stepfather outside the courtroom. He hadn't been a big guy, but he'd definitely had a bad attitude.

She said, 'Do you know what she was doing out in the woods?'

Ryland Nelsen shook his head. 'Let the local police worry about that. All you have to do is inform her next of kin of the unfortunate circumstances, and aim them toward the Sheriff's office in Cedar Falls. Okay?'

'Yes, sir.'

'Personally, I don't believe in karma or predestination or the rest of that bullcrap,' Ryland Nelsen said. 'But there's definitely an appealing neatness to this, don't you think?'

2

Edie Collier's mother and stepfather lived in Felony Flats, a run-down neighbourhood in southeast Portland crammed with drug labs and ex-convicts. Summer Ziegler rode there in a cruiser driven by her friend Laura Killinger, who brought her up to speed on Southeast Precinct gossip before asking her how she was enjoying detective work and whether she'd solved any good cases.

Summer said, 'They haven't let me be the primary on anything yet. The kind of thing I've been doing, I spent yesterday afternoon tossing the hotel room of this addict who'd held up a convenience store. He had one change of underwear and about a hundred stacks of newspapers and back copies of the *New Yorker.*'

Laura said, 'The *New Yorker*? You definitely get a better class of criminal in Central Precinct.'

Summer said, 'I don't know if this guy had ever read any of the stuff in his room, but I do know he was dumb enough to pull a knife and wave it around when the clerk didn't open the till fast enough, put himself down for ten years' state time. I had to look through every one of his newspapers and magazines, to see if he'd hidden anything incriminating in them. All I found was a couple of used needles – he probably stuck the proceeds of his robberies straight in his arm.'

Laura smiled. 'It's not as glamorous as it seems, huh?'

'I'm trying to get used to turning up after everything is over. Also, I'm amazed by the amount of paperwork. I knew there would be a lot, but we seem to spend most of our time on it. Writing up witness statements, processing preliminary complaint reports and supplemental reports and evidence submission slips, building case files . . .'

'So that's why you're dressed like a secretary.'

'Very funny. I was in court today, giving evidence about a case from four months back. Remember the bar-room argument between two brothers that ended in a stabbing?'

'Was it the one where the doer fled the scene on his motorcycle, and spun out on the Fremont Bridge, right in front of a cruiser?'

'That's it. He's claiming self-defence, but the prosecutor told me he has three good witnesses who say otherwise. Not to mention the brother.'

The court had been running late. Summer had sat around in a corridor for half the morning, and then for an hour after lunch, and when she'd finally been called she'd spent less than ten minutes on the stand, confirming that she had been the first officer on the scene and had given first aid to the victim, explaining that he had been conscious and alert and had been able to tell her what had happened.

Summer remembered kneeling beside the victim on the barroom floor, pressing a clean dishcloth against the wound in his belly to staunch the flow of blood, remembered his angry gaze and the way he'd grabbed her wrist when he'd told her that he'd been attacked by his younger brother during an argument over a watch he had inherited from their father. She'd called it in, discovered that the brother had just been in an accident and had been arrested for DUI. She'd arranged for him to be brought back to the bar, where she'd presented him to the detectives who had just arrived to investigate the attempted homicide.

She said to Laura, 'I never thought I'd say it, but I'm beginning to miss the action on the street.'

'It'll always be out here,' Laura said. 'The same old same old, no end to it. All that's changed since I last saw you is I've added another five pounds around my hips.'

Laura Killinger was a chunky woman in her early thirties, blonde hair twisted into a thick braid that hung halfway down the back of her uniform jacket. She and Summer had worked together as rookies in the North Precinct. After Summer had transferred to Central and Laura had moved to Southeast, they'd continued to meet up every so often for drinks or to play squash, or to go target-shooting at a range owned by a retired cop. They were good friends who felt that they could say anything to each other.

Summer told Laura, 'You have to stay away from those doughnuts.'

'Don't I know it. But just about every day some honest citizen drops off a box at the desk to show how much they appreciate the good work of Portland's finest. It would be churlish to turn one down.'

'Churlish?'

Laura was a crossword fiend, and liked to work obscure or exotic words into the conversation.

'To behave like a churl, which I believe is some kind of old-time farm worker. Speaking of which, how are your co-workers treating you, you being a shit-hot, hotshot young detective and all? I hear that when you reported for duty, your commanding officer said that he could smell the Lycra in your superhero costume.'

While most cops in the Portland Police Bureau spent at least seven years in uniform before trying out for detective, Summer had made the grade after only five. She knew that she needed to prove her worth to her new colleagues, veterans who didn't much bother to hide their belief that she was an inexperienced officer who'd been fast-tracked because she was the kind of presentable young woman favoured by senior officers more interested in good PR than in clearance rates. It hadn't helped that the *Oregonian* had run a brief story on her promotion, emphasizing her relative youth and rehashing the story of how she and two other cops had won Life Saving Medals after grabbing a would-be suicide straddling the railing at the mid-span of Broadway Bridge.

Summer said, 'What it was, Ryland Nelsen asked me if I was *wearing* Lycra. I'd just left his office after reporting to him, and he came to the door and asked casually – like Peter Falk playing Columbo? Asked me, was I wearing Lycra under my nice new suit.'

'Sexual harassment, no question,' Laura said.

'One of Ryland Nelsen's patented gotchas was what it was. I was standing there like an idiot, trying to figure out what he meant, with the other detectives in the unit grinning at me — they knew what he was up to. Then he asked me if I'd ever outrun a speeding locomotive or jumped a tall building with a single bound.'

'Or had you ever been mistaken for a bird or a plane.'

'That's a good one, he forgot to ask that. I said something dumb, like, "I don't know about a locomotive, but I'm definitely slower than a speeding bullet," and he told me that he was glad to hear it, because the Robbery Unit was no place for super-heroes. Any time he smelled Lycra, he said, I would be in trouble.'

'Funny guy. So when you're done with the Robbery Unit, where else do you plan to put your superpowers to good use?'

In the Portland Police Bureau, new detectives spent their first year rotating through three different areas of assignment.

Summer said, 'I've put in for gang enforcement and homicide, but just about everyone wants to work homicide.'

'So they'll probably give you child abuse and sex crimes instead.'

'Because I'm a woman?'

'Because you know how to talk to people. Because everyone knows that if some drunken son of a bitch has locked himself in his house with his wife and kids, you're absolutely, positively the person who can talk him out of there.'

'I only did that the one time.'

'Shit, girl, everyone knows you're the uncrowned queen of domestic disturbances. What are you going to do in homicide? None of those dead bodies can talk back to you.'

'No, but witnesses can. And the point of my rookie year, as my mentor reminds me every time I bitch about the paper-work, is that I'm supposed to be learning all kinds of new skills.'

'This mentor of yours, is he cute?'

Laura had just come out of a divorce, and was, as she put it, on the prowl again.

Summer said, 'Andy Parish? He has a cute moustache. He's also forty-eight, happily married, and already a grandfather.'

'I can go for older men. I remember having this terrific crush on my English teacher at high school.'

'Stop by some time and I'll introduce you. Andy will be more than happy to show off photographs of his brand-new grandson to a fresh victim. There are a couple of cute-ish guys on the thirteenth floor, but in my opinion not cute enough to break the fraternization regs.'

Laura poked the onboard computer that sat between her and Summer, checking for new updates from the dispatcher. 'If you're still allowed to fraternize with mere uniformed police, we could go cruising some time. Hit Binks or the Horse Brass Pub, play pool, drink beer, and check out the action.'

'I think I'll take a rain check.'

'Still not over your lawyer guy?'

'*I'm* over him – it's my mother who's still heartbroken. She really was hoping he was the one.'

'So if you're over him, come hunting with me.'

'What it is, I need to get on top of my new job. And I guess I'm not quite ready for the singles scene again.'

'I don't blame you. It's brutal out there,' Laura said, and made a left turn. 'This is the street you want. One hundred fourteen, right?'

'Right.'

They crawled along until they spotted it, a shabby cinder-block bungalow behind a chain-link fence. After they had stepped out of the cruiser, Laura said, 'How do you want to work this?'

Neither of them had done a next-of-kin before. The closest Summer had come was assuring a woman injured in a head-on collision that the paramedics were looking after her boyfriend, while the boyfriend sat dead behind the wheel of his car with the engine block where his legs should have been.

She said, 'I guess I should do the talking.'

'No problem.'

'It shouldn't be, unless the mother or stepfather turn ugly.'

Before driving over to the Southeast Precinct, Summer had checked out Edie's stepfather, Randy Farrell, on the computer, and confirmed her suspicion that he had a record. White male, black hair, brown eyes. Five foot seven, one hundred forty pounds – not a big guy, but he had thirty pounds and a couple of inches on her. His D.O.B. made him fifty-four years old. No scars or other identifying marks, no FBI number . . . Most of his crimes were minor – housebreaking, receiving or attempting to sell stolen goods – and he'd been given plenty of second chances or through plea agreements had received probation instead of jail time, which made Summer suspect that he was some detective's confidential informant. But he'd served time in the gladiatorial arena of state prison at Salem after having been convicted of conspiracy to rob, and with no less than three charges of assault to his name it looked as if he was quick to use his fists. She remembered that he'd sat right behind his stepdaughter in the courtroom, arms folded across the front of his denim jacket, hair lacquered back from his temples, sucking on a permanently sour expression; remembered how he'd bulled up to her in the busy corridor outside the courtroom after Edie Collier had been sentenced, asking her how she liked sending a young girl to jail, turning on his heel and stomping off after she'd advised him to take it up with the judge. Randy Farrell's wife, Edie's mother, had a record of violence, too: threatening behaviour and several charges of assault, including one on a high-school teacher that had gotten her a year's probation, plus one charge of public drunkenness and three DUIs; her driver's licence had been suspended after the last, two months ago.

Anticipating trouble, Summer was happy to have Laura at her back as she walked up to the bungalow. It was dusk now. Lights were burning in a couple of the bungalow's windows, but Summer had to lean on the doorbell for more than a minute before she saw movement behind the three stepped panes of frosted glass in the front door. When it opened, Summer straightened her back and held up her badge, saw from the corner of her eye Laura move her right hand towards the Glock holstered on her hip. But the man who stood in the doorway was a skinny scarecrow, barefoot in a dressing gown that hung open over a T-shirt and boxer shorts, his face sallow and sunken and sporting the makings of a black eye. It took Summer a long moment to recognize in this ruin the man she'd faced down outside the courtroom just six months ago.

He stared at Summer without seeming to recognize her, stared at Laura, and said, 'Whatever you're selling, I don't need it.'

Summer asked if she could speak with his wife.

'What kind of trouble has she gotten herself into now?'

'She isn't in any trouble that I know of, Mr Farrell. Could you have her come to the door?'

'Lucinda ain't in any fit state to talk to the police. Why don't you come back tomorrow?'

'It's about her daughter, Mr Farrell. If she can't come to the door, you should let us in. We need to talk with her.'

Randy Farrell's attitude, a junkyard dog defending its turf, evaporated. 'This is about Edie? What happened? Is she hurt, in hospital somewhere?'

'Let us in, Mr Farrell. We need to talk to your wife.'

'Oh Jesus,' Randy Farrell said, and closed his eyes for a moment.

Laura said, 'We don't want to talk about this out here, Mr Farrell, in full view of your neighbours, and I'm sure you don't want to either. So why don't we go inside?'

'I guess,' Randy Farrell said, standing aside. 'But I should warn you, Lucinda's more than half in the bag, and she ain't taking prisoners.'

Summer and Laura followed him down a narrow hall stacked with cardboard cartons. The air was hot and close, and stank of cigarette smoke and greasy cooking.

'In there,' Randy Farrell said, with a wave of a hand towards an archway filled with the flicker of TV light.

Lucinda Farrell slumped on a plastic-covered couch, a blown-up bear of a woman in a pink sweatshirt and grey sweatpants, clutching a tall glass half-full of ice cubes to her bosom as she watched Oprah on the big TV across the room. A fifth of vodka, a gallon jug of orange juice, a washing-up bowl heaped with popcorn, and an ashtray full of cigarette stubs crowded a bamboo coffee table. When Summer stepped into the room, Lucinda Farrell looked at her and said with shrill but forceful scorn that cut through the laughter and applause of Oprah's audience, 'I got nothing to say to any cops, so why don't the both of you march straight on out of here.'

Randy Farrell said from the archway, 'Take it easy, why don't you? They got something to tell you. About Edie.'

'Edie? Fuck her. Fuck you too, for letting in these fuckers.'

Summer switched on the ceiling lights and in the sudden glare crossed the room and punched off the TV and took a position directly in front of the woman on the couch. Laura was standing just inside the archway, ready to block Randy Farrell if he tried to cause trouble. Summer said, 'How about we start over, Mrs Farrell?'

The woman stared at Summer. Bleached hair dry as straw stuck out around her pugnacious face. 'My daughter ran out on me four months back. Anything she did, it isn't my problem, she's over eighteen now. So how about you say what you got to say and get out.'

Summer waited a beat, making it clear that she was doing this in her own time. 'Mrs Farrell, your daughter was found badly injured this morning, in woods near a town by the name of Cedar Falls. I'm very sorry to have to tell you that she died on the way to hospital.'

'Jesus Christ,' Randy Farrell said softly.

Lucinda Farrell leaned forwards and with the frowning concentration of a small child sloshed a good three fingers of vodka into her glass. She added a splash of orange juice, sucked down half the drink, and said to no one in particular, 'So that's that.'

'Mrs Farrell, the Sheriff's office in Cedar Falls would like you to make a formal identification—'

The woman flapped a hand. 'She was dead to me when she left this house. I told her so, she said she didn't give a fuck, and she hasn't been back since. So why should I give a fuck now?'

'You need to do the right thing by your daughter,' Summer said.

'I already done all I could by her,' Lucinda Farrell said flatly, and drained the rest of her drink.

Summer tried to talk her around, but the woman retreated into stubborn silence, clutching her glass in her swollen paws and glaring at a spot somewhere beyond Summer's left shoulder. At last, Summer said, 'I'll come back tomorrow. We'll talk about this again.'

'Switch on the fucking TV on your way out. I wanna see Oprah ask Demi Moore about her toyboy.'

Summer ignored her request, and in the hallway asked Randy Farrell if Edie's biological father lived in Portland.

'He died in a car accident way before I met Lucinda. Edie kept his name, but if she has a father – Jesus, *had* one – it would be me.'

Summer said, 'I'll have to come back tomorrow, Mr Farrell. I have to talk to your wife again.'

'Won't do any good.'

'The local police need her to ID her daughter. It's a formality, but it has to be done before they can release the body. And at some point your wife will have to think about funeral arrangements.'

Randy Farrell shook his head. 'Lucinda meant what she said about Edie being dead to her. She never once tried to find her after she ran off, never once visited her when she was in jail . . .'

'Talk to her, Mr Farrell. Tell her that she needs to do the right thing by Edie. I'll come by tomorrow morning, see if she's changed her mind.'

'When Lucinda sets her mind to something, that's it. Edie was the same way.' Randy Farrell looked at Summer and said, 'How she ended up, out there in the woods. You have any idea how she got there?'

'I'm sorry, Mr Farrell. It isn't my case.'

Before setting out for the Southeast Precinct, Summer had called the Cedar Falls Sheriff's office and talked briefly with Denise Childers, the detective in charge of the case. The woman had been friendly enough, but hadn't given anything away.

Randy Farrell said, 'She didn't have any reason to leave

Portland I knew of. You should ask her boyfriend what she was doing out there.'

When Summer had been given this job, she'd believed that she wouldn't get much out of it. If she messed up, she would confirm Ryland Nelsen's unvoiced suspicion that she was a hot-shot promoted beyond her experience and capability. And if she did okay she'd probably be landed with every next-of-kin notification the Robbery Unit had to deal with: it was the kind of dirty, thankless task that male cops liked to pass on to their female colleagues because, according to them, women had better people skills. Now, though, she felt a twinge of interest and said, 'Do you have a name and address for this boyfriend?'

Randy Farrell stared past her for a moment, then said, 'I think it was Billy something.'

'Do you have a last name? An address?'

Randy Farrell shook his head. 'I never met the guy, and I only talked to Edie one time after she took up with him. She told me she and him were living out of his van. I wasn't too happy, hearing that, but she said she was doing fine.'

'When did she leave home?'

'First week in February, after she and her mother had a big bust-up.'

'And she ran off to be with her boyfriend?'

Randy Farrell shrugged.

'How long had she known him?'

'Let's put it this way, I'd never heard of him before she ran off.'

'Does he have a job?'

'I wouldn't know.'

'They were living in his van. Where did they park at night?'

'Somewhere over near the airport I think.'

Laura said, 'I'll ask the guys in the Northeast Precinct to keep a look out. Mr Farrell, do you know if they had a regular spot where they parked at night? Up in Piedmont, maybe? Maywood Park?'

'Somewhere near the airport, that's all I know.'

'How about you tell me something about this van,' Laura said. 'Make, colour – anything at all.'

'Like I said, I never met him, and I never saw his van either.'

Summer said, 'Take your time, Mr Farrell. Anything you can remember could be a big help.'

'I remember that she was happy, when I saw her. She had plans, she was thinking of going back to school . . . What will happen to her if no one takes care of her?'

Summer said, 'If no one claims her, the state will serve as sponsor.'

'Yeah, that's what I thought. And they'll bury her in a cardboard coffin without a marker. She doesn't deserve that.' Randy Farrell paused, then told Summer, 'I know who you are. You're the one arrested Edie just before Christmas. You were in uniform then, but I don't forget a face. Listen, it's okay, I'm not blaming you for what happened to her, but how about cutting me a break?'

'If you want to help Edie, Mr Farrell, you should persuade your wife to go make the ID.'

'You need someone to make the ID? How about you take me to Cedar Falls,' Randy Farrell said. 'I'll take care of whatever arrangements need to be made, too. I have money.'

'Perhaps I should come by tomorrow and talk to your wife again.'

'It won't make no difference. But I want to do right by Edie, even if Lucinda doesn't.'

Summer saw that the man was genuinely upset. 'I'll tell the police in Cedar Falls about your offer, Mr Farrell. That's the best I can do right now.'

'I was like a father to her, you understand? I helped raise her for more than ten years, I want to do right by her now . . . You tell them that. Also, you should explain that I have cancer of the liver and I can't drive on account of my medication, the side effects. I get these blackouts. So you tell them, if they want someone to ID her, either you take me, or they'll have to come get me.'

Summer took out one of her cards and handed it to him. 'If you remember anything you think might be useful, anything at all, give me a call and I'll pass it on to the detective in charge of the case. But right now, Mr Farrell, maybe you should go look after your wife. I think she's more shaken up than she lets on.'

Outside, Laura Killinger hitched up her Garrison belt and said, 'Edie Collier was brought up by those two, and all she had on her sheet was shoplifting? She must have been some kind of saint.'

Later that evening Summer's mother said, 'Who do you think did it? Her mother, her stepfather, or both of them together?'

Summer said, 'Actually, I don't see either of them doing it.'

'You think this boyfriend has something to do with it?'

'It's possible.'

'If he exists,' her mother said.

'You think Randy Farrell made him up? Why would he do that?'

'To divert your attention from the obvious suspect. Lucinda Farrell claimed that her daughter hadn't once come back home after she'd run off. But what if she had? You have a mother and daughter who don't get on, the mother drinks heavily, she has a bad temper, she was convicted of assaulting a teacher . . . Suppose she attacked her daughter in some kind of drunken fit? She beats her so badly that it looks like she's killed her, and she and her husband dump the body in the forest. They drive off, but the girl isn't dead. She comes around, but she's hurt, she can't find her way out of the forest, and she ends up walking in circles or in the wrong direction until she collapses.'

Summer said, 'Stranger things have happened, but Cedar Falls is two hundred miles south of Portland. It's a long way to go, to dump a body.'

'It would explain why Randy Farrell didn't want you to talk to his wife. It would explain Lucinda Farrell's reaction to the news of her daughter's death. And isn't it true that nine times out of ten in a murder case, the victim knew the person who killed them?'

'Yeah, but in most domestic homicides you find the doer standing over the body. Or sitting in the next room, watching TV and drinking beer. One time, a friend of mine found this guy working on his roof, nailing shingles with the hammer he'd just used to kill his wife after she'd told him to stop what he was doing and take her shopping. It's possible that Lucinda Farrell killed her daughter, that she and Randy Farrell conspired to get rid of the body. But why was Edie Collier found so far from Portland when there are plenty of places where you can dump a body right here in the city? The rivers, one of the parks . . . or any back alley or vacant lot, come to that.'

Summer and her mother, June, were sitting at the long pine table in the shabbily comfortable kitchen of June's house, where Summer had been living ever since Jeff Tuohy, her lawyer guy, had moved to Washington, D.C. and she'd had to move out of the apartment in The Pearl that she couldn't afford to rent on her own. Summer was eating a late supper, spaghetti in a marinara sauce that she'd picked up from the local Italian place, a glass of red wine. Her mother was working on her third gin and tonic, smoking a cigarette, and playing at detective. She was a professor at the University of Portland, an anthropologist who specialized in pre-Columbian Native American littoral communities. A tall woman in her mid-sixties, with a handsome, lined face, grey hair held in a loose ponytail by a large wooden clasp, she was wearing blue jeans and a baggy blue sweatshirt that had belonged to her husband; she'd taken to wearing his clothes after he had died of a heart attack last year.

June Ziegler, the daughter of an English war bride who had married a US Army captain and emigrated to the States after World War Two, liked to cook an English Sunday roast once a month, followed every twist and turn of the real-life soap opera of the British Royal Family, and devoured old-fashioned mystery novels set in English country houses, with intricate clockwork plots that were resolved when the detective gathered all the suspects in the library and showed them how clever he was. Although she still voiced her disapproval at Summer's choice of career five years after the fact, the one thing she and her daughter could talk about without getting personal were the stories Summer brought home from work.

Now June blew a plume of smoke at the ceiling and said,

'Perhaps the Farrells have some connection with the place where their daughter was found.'

Summer smiled. 'They beat her up so badly that they believed they'd killed her, and then they were overcome with a fit of sentimentality, and took her to a favourite spot?'

'When people are stressed, they often return to familiar territory.'

'It's more likely that Edie Collier took off with her boyfriend on some crazy jaunt, wandered into the forest and got herself lost.'

'Assuming there *is* a boyfriend.'

'Or maybe she was hitchhiking and chose the wrong vehicle to climb into, managed to escape after some kind of assault, and *then* got lost.'

'Perhaps the mother or the stepfather grew up in Cedar Falls.'

Summer said, 'The thing is, neither of them can drive.'

'Lucinda Farrell lost her licence and Randy Farrell told you he wasn't allowed to drive because of his meds. It doesn't mean that they *can't* drive.'

It was a good point, annoyingly enough.

Summer watched her mother mash her cigarette stub into the ashtray, and said, 'When are you going to give those up?'

'I hope I haven't yet reached that point in life where I have to think of giving things up.'

'You'll reach that point a lot sooner than you think if you keep on smoking.'

'It's a good deal less dangerous than associating with criminals every day.'

'I associate with a better class of criminal now that I'm a detective,' Summer said, remembering Laura Killinger's remark. 'I could even shake hands with some of them without having to put on gloves first.'

'I forgot to mention, I met Ed Vara the other day. He asked after you.'

'Your lawyer friend?'

Summer was instantly wary, wondering if this was leading up to yet another of her mother's attempts to get her back in contact with Jeff. He'd phoned Summer a couple of times after he'd moved, and she knew that he'd phoned her mother once or twice too, but as far as she was concerned their relationship had been heading for the rocks long before he'd decided to move to Washington, D.C.

Summer had met Jeff Tuohy when he'd been working for the Public Defender's office – Jeff had political aspirations, and it was a good place to earn brownie points. They could talk to each other about their work, and Jeff was easy on the eye, smart and funny, and touchingly idealistic. But he was also ferociously ambitious, and by the time they'd taken the big step and moved in together he was working sixteen hours a day, leaving the housework and cooking to Summer. And then, because of volunteer work he'd done for a congresswoman's successful election campaign, he'd been offered a job on her permanent staff. Summer hadn't been ready to give up her job in Portland, move clear across the country and get married, become a homemaker . . . she'd already had enough of cooking and cleaning for him. Jeff had offered to turn the job down, but Summer had known that his heart was set on it and that if she'd asked him to stay their relationship would have lasted about one more week. So that had been that for Summer and the lawyer guy, but Summer's mother still nursed a small hope that they would get back together, and every so often she gave it an airing.

But what June Ziegler said now was, 'Ed told me that he's looking for a contract investigator.'

'I thought he mostly took civil-rights cases. What does he need an investigator for?'

'I thought you might like to discuss it with him.'

'I have a job.'

'Doing paperwork and running trivial errands.'

'That's exactly what contract investigators do. They're fact-checkers and skip-tracers. They sit at their desks and comb through phone books and databases.'

'The reason I mentioned it, Ed's coming over for dinner Saturday. Don't look so alarmed, darling. My English colleague is coming too, and some other people.'

'I guess I can give him the names of some recently retired cops who might be interested.'

Her mother shrugged, and lit another cigarette.

Summer said with fond exasperation, 'I'm not your little girl any more.'

'Of course you are. And if you don't mind me giving you some advice, I think you should talk to the Farrells' neighbours. Perhaps they saw the girl recently. Or perhaps her parents took a long car trip a few days ago.'

Summer used a heel of bread to mop up sauce. 'That's what I'd do if it was my case. But it isn't. It belongs to the Cedar Falls Sheriff's office.'

'So you're going to forget all about it because of some non-sense about jurisdiction?'

'Not exactly,' Summer said. 'As a matter of fact, I've already talked to the detective in charge of the case. What I have to do now is figure out how to get Randy Farrell to Cedar Falls.'

3

On the way to confront his boss, to find out just how badly the man had screwed up while he'd been away, Carl Kelley surprised one of the security guards in the trophy room. The guy had no right or reason to be there. A computerized system allowed or denied residents, guests, visitors and employees access to different parts of the mansion's towers and outbuildings according to codes in the electronic bracelets everyone had to wear. The security guards who manned the main gate and patrolled the perimeter of the estate were allowed into the gatehouse, the kitchens and the staff dining room, that was it, but here was the new guy who'd started work just last week, Frank Wilson, wandering around a room reserved only for those with the highest privilege rating.

The trophy room took up much of the ground floor of the main tower: adobe walls hung with the heads of cougars and antelope and pronghorn deer; leather armchairs, low tables and zebra-skin rugs scattered around the central open-hearth fireplace, with its platform of rough stone and its copper hood that was as big as the vent of a Moon rocket. Carl stood just beyond the open door, a wiry middle-aged man wearing a short-sleeved white shirt and black cargo pants, an athletic bag slung over one shoulder. The security guard, Frank Wilson, was bending to look at things in low alcoves, leaning close to things on shelves, turning now as Carl walked across the room towards him.

'This is some place, huh?' Wilson said, with a quick, false smile.

'I hope you didn't touch anything,' Carl said. 'It takes for ever to reset the system.'

Each collectable and piece of art was tagged with an RFID

chip, a little printed circuit that sent out a coded signal when pulsed with a specific radio frequency. It was possible to bring up a virtual schematic of any room in the mansion and see the pieces standing in place like chess pieces on a board. If anything was moved by so much as an inch, its icon would turn red and started blinking; if it was carried off, the computer would lock down doors and trigger the alarms.

'I was just looking, is all,' Wilson said. He was a good six inches taller than Carl, and wore a light blue shirt with black epaulettes that matched his pants. A nightstick, a radio and a five-cell flashlight were hooked to his belt.

Carl said, giving it right back to him, 'Did you see anything that took your fancy?'

'I bet you're wondering how I got in here. What happened, I was checking the lights along the driveway,' Wilson said. He pulled a voltage tester from the back pocket of his pants and showed it to Carl. A pair of eights was tattooed on the knuckles of the middle and ring fingers of his right hand. 'Maybe you noticed some of them haven't been coming on when they should. Anyhow, I saw the main door was open, I thought I should check it out, and I found the door to this room open too.'

Carl said, 'It's a funny thing, but the main door wasn't open just now.'

'I guess I must have shut it when I came in,' Wilson said.

The man was still smiling, but something had hardened in his gaze. It took Carl back to the army, and to the orphanage before that. Two guys sizing each other up, neither ready to back down.

He said, 'That door won't open for anyone who isn't supposed to be here. I got to be somewhere, but first I'll have to let you out.'

Carl let Frank Wilson walk ahead of him, across the trophy room and through the doorway into the double-height foyer beyond, the man looking left and right, checking out the stuff in glass-fronted steel cabinets, in niches cut into the pink adobe. Pieces of Japanese armour mixed up with scratch-built fantasy pieces. Cases of knives and knuckledusters. Human skulls modified with sagittal crests, fangs, bony spines or frills. Stairs curved to the left and right, and high above hung a kind of chandelier of welded steel and a couple of dozen TVs, old-fashioned cathode-ray tubes without casings, circuit boards and bundles of wires open to the air, the TVs facing in different directions, showing different scenes from *Trans*, the computer game that had paid for all this.

Wilson said, 'He sure has a lot of stuff. Like a museum, uh?'

'This is my favourite piece,' Carl said, stepping over to a niche under the sweep of the left-hand staircase, where a ceremonial sword rested on two pieces of black oak, its curved blade pulled halfway out of its red lacquered scabbard, a red tassel hanging at the end of its pommel. 'It's Korean, three centuries old.'

'It's nice,' Wilson said without any enthusiasm, clearly wanting to get out of there now.

Carl said, 'They used it for executions. I tried it out myself once, on a dog. Sliced through the neck-bones like they were butter.'

Wilson didn't have anything to say about that. Carl stared at him for a moment, then walked towards the tall castle door. Its lock sensed the chip in his bracelet and clanked open; he ushered the security guard through it and led him around the base of the main tower. The other two towers, one truncated, left unfinished when the money had run out, loomed above thickets of bamboo. Carl pointed to the tree line at the top of the ridge beyond, black against a darkening sky where a few stars glimmered, and told Wilson that he should get back to where he belonged – if he didn't know about it, there was a stairway that led straight up to the gatehouse, he'd find it a quicker route than using the driveway.

Adding casually, 'Oh, by the way, what did you do time for?'

'I don't follow.'

'Don't bullshit me, son. I saw those jailhouse tattoos on your fingers. Two eights, that's white-power code for HH, isn't it? HH: Heil Hitler. What did you do time for? Where did you do it?'

Frank Wilson tried and failed to meet Carl's cold stare. 'That's none of your business.'

'When I find someone who's done time wandering around where he isn't supposed to be, taking an interest in my boss's possessions, you can bet it's my business.'

'You think I was looking to steal some of that shit?'

Yeah, it was just like the army, except this guy with his jail muscles and stupid frown was a pushover compared to a beered-up squaddie backed by a dozen braying mates.

Carl said, 'What I think is that you were somebody's bitch when you were in prison. Was he black? Did he share you around?'

'You're crazy.'

'You're big, but he was bigger, am I right? What was it like, him bearing down on you every night?'

Wilson gave Carl a mean, angry look and took a step forward, his balled fists half raised. 'Say that again, you little fuck.'

Carl pulled the brand-new captive-bolt pistol from his athletic bag, stuck its muzzle six inches from the bridge of the man's nose.

'I'd advise you to back off right now unless you want a new hole in your head.'

Wilson's eyes crossed as he tried to focus on the pistol. With its grained plastic grip and fat chamber it looked like a science-fiction ray gun. He said, 'Next time I see you, you better be carrying a real gun.'

'You run along now, Mr Wilson. If I need to talk to you again, you'll know all about it.'

Carl watched the man walk off along the path to the stairway, past spotlights shining among stands of bamboo and imported black granite boulders. Some time in the very near future, Carl thought, he would be having a crunchy conversation with Patrick Metcalf, the manager of the company that supplied the guards. Ask him why he was employing a former convict, ask him how that former convict had managed to get inside the main tower without the proper bracelet. If the cops didn't turn up first, that is, asking awkward questions about a dead girl . . .

It never rains but it pours, Carl thought, and went back inside the tower and took the little elevator up to the library, where his boss, Dirk Merrit, was waiting for him.

The library, like the trophy room, the media centre, the baronial dining room, and the master bedroom, took up an entire floor of the main tower. There weren't many books in it, and they were either decorative, like the great medieval Bible chained to an oak lectern carved with the likeness of a skull-faced angel, or totemic: *catalogues raisonnés* of Francis Bacon, Hans Belmer, Diane Arbus, Joel-Peter Witkin, and other masters of the human grotesque; medical dictionaries, directories and catalogues; a complete run of *The Journal of Plastic Surgery*; and a slew of books on transhumanism, futurology and life-extension techniques that publishers had sent for publicity quotes (Dirk Merrit always gave them). Most of the books were kept in two big glass-fronted steel cabinets, purchased second-hand from St Vincent's Hospital in New York, that had once stored surgical instruments. Elsewhere in the big room was a projection TV with leather armchairs ranged in front of it and a cocktail cabinet and popcorn maker off to the side, a suit of armour fantasticated with spikes and flanges, freestanding cabinets containing antique knives, hunting bows and crossbows and guns, globes of the Earth and the Moon and Mars, and a glass-and-steel desk the size of a small car that faced a bank of twenty TVs. A sixteenth-century Flemish tapestry depicting men and hounds hunting a boar through a winter forest was spread across the wall behind the desk. And hanging above all this was a full-scale replica in cherrywood and canvas of Leonardo da Vinci's famous flying machine, its hinged batlike wings fully spread, their tips less than a hand-span from opposite sides of the room's poured-concrete wall. The pilot in its cradle wore Dirk Merrit's face and had been much modified, keeping pace with the many modifications that Dirk Merrit's plastic surgeons had performed on their client.

The man himself sat in a carved oak chair with a high back that was crested with carved spikes, giving it the look of a throne. His new best friend and personal doctor, Elias Silver, was unwrapping the cuff of a blood-pressure measuring kit from his left arm. Silver gave Carl a sour look as he approached.

'Carl,' Dirk Merrit said. 'Here you are at last.'

He was wearing his favourite kimono, a green silk antique three hundred years old, and sat straight-backed in the chair, very tall, very thin. An imperial bearing. At first glance it looked as if he was wearing a mask. Then you realized that the mask was his face. Some people couldn't look for very long at Dirk Merrit. At what he had done to himself. At what he had become. Others stared with frank amazement or disgust at the high buttresses of his cheekbones, the bat-ears, the forehead and shaven scalp ridged like a scallop shell. Carl, who was as intimately familiar with the rich variety of the human form as any surgeon, hardly noticed.

'We were wondering where you were,' Elias Silver said.

'Driving straight up the I-5 from Los Angeles with no sleep,' Carl said, staring at the doctor until he dropped his gaze.

When his finances had redlined six months ago, Dirk Merrit had fired his cordon-bleu chef and kitchen staff, his personal trainer, his English butler and a round dozen gardeners and maids. And then Elias Silver had turned up one weekend as a house guest and had never left, making himself useful by supplying Dirk Merrit with cocktails of drugs, and pandering to his obsessions about transcendence, about evolving beyond his ordinary human origins and living for ever.

Dirk Merrit said, 'Elias has been showing me a new design for my ears. He's very keen on a novel technique for culturing cartilage. You use stem cells grown on collagen templates, any shape you want.'

Carl set his athletic bag at his feet, straightened up and folded his arms. 'There's this thing we need to talk about. In private.'

'I hope it will not take long,' Elias Silver said. He was packing his equipment into an aluminium briefcase. A short, over-weight man with a cap of hair dyed snow-white, he had the fussy manner of someone much older than his thirty years. His glasses were tinted ice-blue. The nails of his small soft white hands were immaculately manicured. He was wearing one of his trademark collarless jackets, bright yellow, buttoned all the way up the front. Closing his briefcase with a brisk snap, he told Carl, 'Dirk has been in video conference with his financial advisers for most of the afternoon. His blood pressure is slightly elevated. He needs to rest.'

'You shouldn't feed him all those speedballs,' Carl said.

'As a matter of fact, I've just given him a milligram of Ativan.'

'Yeah, and what else?'

'Perhaps you would also like an Ativan. You seem a bit hyper.'

When he talked to someone, Elias Silver had a habit of addressing the air about a foot to the side of their face. He was doing it now, and as usual it annoyed the shit out of Carl.

Dirk Merrit, his head moving back and forth as he followed the conversation, said cheerfully, 'You boys really must try to get along better.'

'Don't stay up late,' Elias Silver told him. 'And try that tea I recommended.'

'It tastes like stewed grass.'

'It will help you relax.'

When Elias Silver had left, Carl took an envelope from a pocket of his cargo pants and upended it over a side table, spilling credit cards next to a big glass jar in which a pair of conjoined human foetuses floated in straw-coloured alcohol.

'Goody,' Dirk Merrit said. 'Did Mr Grow give you any trouble?'

Erik Grow was the inside man at Powered By Lightning, the company that owned and maintained *Trans*. Dirk Merrit had been the majority shareholder until his financial troubles had begun to bite and the Bank of America had ordered a major reorganization of his assets. Erik Grow provided current passwords and other useful information from *Trans*'s subscription lists, supplied cloned credit cards from a Russian connection, and with Carl's help was planning to rip off his employers in the very near future.

Carl said, 'He was his usual sweet self. You should only use each of these once. A cash transaction, an online purchase or whatever. Once and once only, then destroy the card.'

'I haven't forgotten the drill.'

'I want to make sure, because there are a lot of things that you *have* forgotten. Keeping your pilgrims for at least a week before doing anything to them, that's one. Never doing anything on your own, and never, ever doing anything on your front doorstep, that's two more. And then there's the promise you made before I left.'

'Oh, are we getting into that now?'

'Of course we bloody well are.'

The shit had hit the fan early that morning. Carl had been in his motel room in Los Angeles with a girl from his favourite agency, enjoying some well-deserved R&R after collecting the credit cards and setting Erik Grow straight, when Dirk Merrit had called. The man had been shrill and agitated, saying that he'd misplaced one of the packages, ringing off, not picking up when Carl called him back. Carl, guessing straight away what had happened, had got rid of the hooker, booked out of the motel, and headed straight back to Oregon. He'd been stuck in heavy traffic south of Sacramento when Dirk Merrit had called again, much calmer now, telling him that the police had recovered the package, but that it wasn't a problem because it had been damaged beyond repair. In that moment, Carl had been half-minded to turn around and let the man take what was coming to him. But he wasn't ready to walk away from a score that could set him up for the rest of his life, and there was also the small matter of the photos and video footage documenting their first collaboration. Dirk Merrit had insisted that they each hide copies somewhere safe: insurance that would, he'd said, ensure that they could trust each other absolutely. Until he was ready to take down Powered By Lightning's subscription service and make a run for it, Carl had to do his best to keep Dirk Merrit out of the hands of the police – and that meant he had to deal with this latest mess.

He said now, 'You'd better begin at the beginning. Which one was it, girl or boy?'

'The girl. And don't worry – she's dead.'

'You let the *girl* get away from you?'

'It was bad luck. An accident.'

Carl had long ago learned to control his anger, but sometimes his control faltered and strong impulses seized hold of him, slow black lightning rolling up his spine and exploding inside his skull, filling his mind with violent images. Feeling that lightning now, flashing on Dirk Merrit's bone-white face broken and bleeding, falling away beneath remorseless blows, he snatched up the big glass jar from the table, lifted it above his head and smashed it to the floor.

Saying quietly, in the echo of the crash, 'You think that was an accident too?'

Dirk Merrit didn't flinch from Carl's hot gaze, saying, 'You're angry. It's entirely understandable.'

Carl kicked at scraps of fish-white flesh and gleaming shards of broken glass. The sweet reek of ethanol filled the air. 'Want me to show you just how angry I am?'

'I believe you have already made your point, Carl. That particular specimen cost me twenty-five hundred dollars.'

'Take it out of the wages you don't pay me any more. Where did it happen, this accident?'

'The meadow on the ridge, at the southern edge of the estate.'

'Christ. Couldn't you at least have driven her a couple of miles away from where you live? From where *I* live.'

'I wanted to do it on my own land. It seemed important . . . And besides, suppose someone saw me driving along the public highway?'

Dirk Merrit's financial advisers had forced him to sell that particular parcel of land last year, but Carl let it slide. 'When did you do it? Day or night?'

'Night. That was part of it, you see. I've never done it alone, and I've never done it at night.'

'No one saw you? No one followed you?'

Carl was worried about Elias Silver, that sly sneak.

'It was after midnight.'

'You took her out there, you padlocked her to a stake.'

'Mmm-hmm.'

'You were wearing your ski mask, you told her you were

going to kill her, you triggered the charge that blew the padlock open, and she ran for her life.'

'I did everything the way we always do it.'

'No. No, you didn't. You did it on your own, and you let her get away. What happened, did you have a problem with the ultralight?'

'I didn't use the ultralight. It was night, and I'm not *that* crazy. I gave her a knife and I released her. I was going to give her a head start.'

'You were going to chase her on foot and you gave her a knife? What were you thinking?'

'It was to give her a sporting chance,' Dirk Merrit said. 'I had a knife too, and my crossbow. And my night-vision goggles.'

'All right. You gave her a knife, you blew the padlock. She ran off into the forest, and you lost her.'

'Not exactly. Well, she did run into the forest. I had some fun chasing her in circles, and then I took a shot. But I missed, and she ran straight over the edge of a drop, fifteen, twenty feet straight down. One moment she was there, the next – poof, gone. Imagine my surprise. By the time I had found a way to the bottom there was no trace of her.'

'But she turned up the next day. Someone found her.'

'And she died before they could get her to hospital. So you see, it all worked out in the end.'

'Unless she said something before she died. Something that'll lead the cops straight to you.'

Dirk Merrit shrugged inside his green kimono. 'If she'd said anything incriminating, the police would already be here.'

'The medical examiner will have done an autopsy on her by now. Christ knows what he found.'

'She was naked, and she spent most of the night wandering around in the woods after she got away, so I don't suppose the medical examiner will have found anything significant. Listen to me, Carl. What happened to her after she got away isn't important, but the fact that she got away in the first place . . . Have you ever heard of what they call the fortunate accident? Of serendipity? It's an integral part of creativity. You're looking for one thing, or you aren't even looking for anything in particular, and you stumble on something that's perfect for your needs. It happened all the time when I was creating *Trans*. And that's what this is. A fortunate accident. It's opened my eyes. It's changed *everything*. It frees me up to move into an entirely new arena.'

'Listen to me,' Carl said. Despite his lack of sleep, his anger, and his conviction that everything was about to come crashing down, he was fully in control of himself again, a fat white hum filling his head. 'Listen to me, and listen hard. This isn't like your fucking computer game. Something has gone badly wrong, and you can't go back and try again until you get it right. The girl escaped. Maybe she died before she could say anything, but right now the cops will be trying to figure out who she is, and how come she happened to be wandering around in the woods without a stitch on. So don't get the idea that this is over. Don't go thinking that the cops won't be snooping around here, that they won't come up here to ask you some leading questions. Because they will.'

Dirk Merrit shook his head. 'The police won't be interested in me – I'll tell you why in a minute. The thing is, Carl, the bottom line, I have complicated needs. You satisfy many of them, I'm happy to admit that. But you can't satisfy them all, and I don't expect you to understand all that I need any more than I would expect . . . a dog to appreciate colour television.'

'I'm not your dog. Dr Elias Silver, yeah, I can see that. But don't you ever forget what *I* am.'

'The dog thing, Carl, it's a simile. Dogs can't see colours. They lack the cones or rods or whatever. Some kind of cell in their retinas that we have and they don't. Elias would know, I'm sure. The point is, what we do together is fine fun. It's strong meat. But I can't live on meat alone. I need a varied diet.'

The point was, Dirk Merrit believed that he was cleverer than he actually was. In the past couple of years, as he'd bled away his fortune on his house and his appetites, his ego had ballooned like an aneurysm. He believed that he had evolved beyond the reach of any human agency, believed that he could do anything he wanted, and his cycles were getting shorter because his trophies and videos were no longer enough to feed his fantasies and recreate the excitement of his games.

Carl said, speaking out of the white hum of his great calm, 'I think you should lie low for a while. Wait until things cool down after this "fortunate accident" or whatever it is you want to call it.' He pulled the captive-bolt pistol from his athletic bag and held it up. 'Know what this is?'

Dirk Merrit cocked his head. 'Why, Carl. I do believe that you're trying to make a dramatic point.'

'It's used in slaughterhouses to kill animals.'

Carl had carried something similar in Africa, an old-fashioned model that used a shotgun cartridge to fire a nail into the brain of the animal – and could also do some serious damage to the kneecaps and hands of prisoners who refused to talk right away. This version used a cylinder of compressed carbon dioxide to fire a captive bolt. He'd bought it in an agricultural supply store on the outskirts of Sacramento, after Dirk Merrit's second phone call.

Dirk Merrit smiled. 'You want to teach me a lesson by dispatching our latest pilgrim like an animal. For you, Carl, this is quite subtle.'

'One shot through the forehead, an inch of steel straight into the brain, lights out. No fuss, no noise. Unlike a regular gun, you can use this in that basement without the risk of going deaf. I think we should kill him there, wait until it gets really dark, and dump his body in the lake.'

'If it comes to that, I have a silencer for my Colt that would do just as well. But while I agree that we need to get rid of him as quickly as possible, I'm not going to slaughter him like some broke-back horse. No, we will deal with our pilgrim in the usual way. Tomorrow, or the day after at the very latest. Can you arrange it by then?'

'Are you serious?'

'Any other course of action would be dishonourable.'

'What's honour got to do with it? The kid was trying to rip you off.'

Dirk Merrit leaned forward. Light gleamed on his ridged

scalp. His eyes, capped with black contact lenses that covered the entire ball, glittered like fresh-cut coal. 'That's exactly why we're going to put him to the hunt. He deserves nothing less.'

'No way. If they find him, they'll connect him with the girl. Or with the game.'

'How many have they found so far? Just two. And even if they do find him, even if they do connect him with the girl, so what? They can't connect the girl with me.'

'I can go down there right now and do him, nice and clean, quick as anything. Inside an hour, it'll be as if he was never here. It'll be as if he never existed.'

Dirk Merrit shook his head again. 'It would be an insult to him, and it would also be a sign of weakness. Of panic.'

'It's necessary. Like cleaning up after an accident.'

'I know you mean well, but I will honour this boy. With you or without you,' Dirk Merrit said, staring straight at Carl. 'And don't think of sneaking in there and doing him behind my back. I changed the lock.'

Once Dirk Merrit got like this, there was no reasoning with him. Well, Carl thought, he needed to keep on the right side of his boss for a little longer, and they had to get rid of the boy anyway . . .

He said, 'I suppose as it's already set up, we might as well go ahead with it.'

'Exactly.'

'But you can't leave the body. Not this time. We'll have to get rid of it.'

'No, it must be like all the other sacrifices. I will have his heart, and our friends of the air will have the rest.' Dirk Merrit's smile was showing most of his sharp teeth now. 'Don't look so worried, Carl. This business with the girl, I believe there is a way to put the blame on someone else. Let me show you something that was just now on the local TV news, and then I'll explain what we need to do.'

4

The detectives of the Portland Police Bureau kept bankers' hours, eight to four, but Sergeant Ryland Nelsen liked to start work before the shift began so that he could check out the custody and investigation reports that had been filed overnight and distribute them among his detectives when they reported for duty. When he arrived at his office on the thirteenth floor of the Justice Building on Wednesday morning, seven-fifteen, he found Summer Ziegler waiting for him with two cups of coffee and a paper sack of assorted doughnuts. He studied her for a moment, poker-faced, then said, 'I hope this doesn't mean you ran into trouble with that simple little next-of-kin notification.'

'It isn't a peace offering or an apology, sir. It's more in the nature of a bribe.'

'Let's talk in my office.'

This time he asked Summer to sit down. She explained that Lucinda Farrell had refused to have anything to do with her daughter, but the stepfather, Randy Farrell, had volunteered to go to Cedar Falls. 'I talked to the detective in charge of the case, told her about the situation. She's happy to let him make the ID.'

Ryland Nelsen took a sip of coffee. There was a dusting of powdered sugar on his tie. 'He wants to do it, the DIC is happy to let him do it. What's the problem?'

'Randy Farrell isn't allowed to drive. He has cancer, and his medication gives him blackouts.'

'His wife doesn't want to make the ID, but why can't she drive him?'

'Like I said, she flat-out refused to have anything at all to do with this. And in any case she lost her licence after one too many DUIs.'

'I believe there's a bus service goes all the way down the I-5 to California, stopping off at points in between.'

'The guy's pretty sick. Also, Denise Childers, the DIC, is anxious to talk to him.'

'You spoke to her?'

'Last night, after I spoke to Randy Farrell. She believes that he can give her some useful background information about his step-daughter.'

Summer paused, but Ryland Nelsen didn't say anything.

She said, 'I could run him down there and be back by the end of the day.'

'Do you know what the unit's clearance rate currently stands at, Detective Ziegler?'

'I think it's around fifty per cent.'

'It's closer to forty, and even counting you I'm two men short. How do I know this isn't some scheme you've cooked up because you're bored with the very useful work we do around here?'

'I'm trying to do my best by the dead girl, sir. And a long drive with a felon who has a history of violence against women is hardly a holiday.'

There was another pause. At last, Ryland Nelsen said, 'Let me talk to Detective Childers.'

Summer waited at her desk. Grey mist hung outside the windows. It was seven-thirty, and only one other detective was at work, over in the northeast corner occupied by the Homicide Unit, his feet up on his desk as he talked on the phone. After five minutes, Ryland Nelsen came out of his office and said, 'Can you handle this guy on your own?'

'I believe so.'

'You better be sure. I can't spare anyone else.'

'He won't give me any trouble. He wants to cooperate.'

'You'll have to take one of the Bureau's clunkers instead of your own car. Your insurance won't cover police work. And make sure you report to me first thing tomorrow morning.'

Before they set off for Cedar Falls, Randy Farrell insisted on showing Summer that his wife had passed out on her bed. It was a queen-size, and Lucinda Farrell took up most of it, lying there fully clothed in the dim overheated bedroom, reeking of alcohol and snoring open-mouthed.

'She took the news bad, in her own way,' Randy Farrell said softly. He closed the door of the bedroom and told Summer that he had a thousand dollars in cash and wanted to use it to pay for Edie's funeral. 'You think that will cover it?'

'You'll have to talk the funeral director, Mr Farrell. Are you ready to go?'

'I have to take my pills first.'

It was a straight shot down the I-5, through the Willamette Valley to the beginning of Oregon's banana belt. It started to rain soon after they set out, but forty miles south of Portland the sun broke through, lighting up a ragged chasm in the clouds, probing farmland on either side of the freeway with slanting fingers of light. Randy Farrell spent the first part of the trip zoned out in the back seat of the Police Bureau Taurus, waking only when Summer turned off the I-5 at Springfield for a pit stop at a Wendy's. After picking over his plain burger and fries, he disappeared into the men's room. Ten minutes later, Summer went to look for him and found him out back by a Dumpster, sucking on the last half-inch of a tightly rolled joint.

'I'm licensed to use it,' he said, giving her a defiant look. 'It helps control the nausea I get after I eat. You don't believe me, I have a registration card my doctor gave me.'

'I don't need to see your card, Mr Farrell. I'll wait by the car until you've finished, but don't be too long.'

After they had set off again, Randy Farrell explained that he'd been diagnosed with liver cancer three years ago, the doctors had cut a tumour as big as a goose egg out of him. He'd gotten better, but four months ago the cancer had come back worse than ever, had spread to his bones and his pancreas. He didn't have long to live, which was why he wanted to do right by Edie. Also, he said, he loved the girl as if she was one of his own. He'd been a son of a bitch when he was younger, beating up on his girlfriends, even beating his mother once, but marriage and helping to raise his stepdaughter had grounded him. He'd even quit drinking after his last stretch in the joint, but not before the damage had been done.

His confession was well rehearsed and laced with jargon he'd probably learned at Alcoholics Anonymous meetings and cancer support groups. But he seemed sincere, telling Summer that Edie had loved to read, English had been her best subject at school and she would have studied it in college if she hadn't grown wild and gotten into trouble with the police. Telling her that Edie had loved a little black cat she called Edgar Allan Poe, that Edie had sewn her own clothes from patterns, and she had been a really good artist, too. Edie and her mother had never gotten along, Randy Farrell said, but he hoped he had been some help to her. When he'd seen her that one time after she ran off, she had been full of plans; he'd given her money to buy something smart so she could try to get back to school, train for an office job. Meanwhile, she'd been waitressing in a short-order place. The manager took a kickback straight from her basic pay because she'd been on probation and he could violate her back to jail any time he wanted, but she had been making that up on tips.

'Everything was going right for her, except for that no-good boyfriend.'

'Have you remembered anything more about him?'

Before driving to the Farrells' house Summer had phoned around Portland's five precincts in case Edie Collier's boyfriend had reported her missing, but she'd had no luck.

Randy Farrell said, 'I saw them together once, by accident. I was on the floor above them in the Lloyd Center, looking to buy something for Lucinda's birthday. I saw Edie with some young guy outside the multiplex there.'

'Did you get a good look at him?'

'When I spotted them, like I said, I was on the floor above. By the time I had ridden down on the escalator they'd split. Went to see a movie, I guess.' Randy Farrell was quiet for a moment. Summer glanced at him in the rear-view mirror. He was look-ing at something inside his head and the corners of his mouth were turned down. Saying at last, 'I just realized that was the last time I saw her.'

'When was this?'

'Two weeks ago to the day. I got Lucinda a crystal dolphin. She loves shit like that. Edie didn't even send a card, I'm sorry to say.'

'That was the only time you saw Edie's boyfriend?'

'If the guy she was with was her boyfriend, yeah.'

'What did he look like?'

'I didn't really get to look at him.'

'Well, was he white or black?'

'White.'

'How old would you say?'

'I guess about Edie's age. Maybe a little older, it's hard to say.'

'Edie was eighteen.'

'Nineteen next month.'

'So this boyfriend, Billy no-last-name, was eighteen or nineteen.'

'Maybe a little older. I didn't get a real good look.'

'How tall was he?'

'I was pretty far away.'

'Taller than Edie? Shorter?'

'Maybe a head taller. He had black hair, too, shoulder-length.'

'What he was wearing?'

'Jeans, I think. Blue jeans. And a big plaid shirt, some kids wear them like a coat over their T-shirt? Like that. And he had a briefcase too. Apart from that, he looked like any of those kids who hang around Pioneer Square.'

'What kind of briefcase?'

'What do you mean?'

'Was it metal or leather?'

Randy Farrell thought for a moment. 'I guess it was more like one of those cases you carry those small computers in. You know, with a shoulder strap.'

'A laptop computer case.'

'I guess.'

'Did you get a look at his face?'

'I only saw him from behind.'

'Shoulder-length black hair, blue jeans, a plaid shirt. And a computer case.' It wasn't much, but it was something. There couldn't be too many street kids who lugged around a laptop computer – or, at least, its case.

Randy Farrell said, 'Edie told me they were in love. She showed me this cheap ring he bought her. Way she talked you could see she thought he was Mr Wonderful, but don't you guys say that in a murder case the first suspect is the one nearest the victim?'

'I don't have an opinion one way or another, Mr Farrell. It isn't my case.'

But Summer was wondering if Edie Collier's probation officer or the manager of the place where she'd worked as a waitress would know anything about her boyfriend – his last name, where to find him. She wanted to ask him what Edie had been doing two hundred miles south of Portland; she wanted to ask him if Edie had ever visited her parents after she'd left home. Meanwhile, she decided to push Randy Farrell a little, see if anything popped out.

'Hey, Mr Farrell? I was wondering about something. How did you get that black eye? It's turning into quite a shiner.'

'I walked into a door,' Randy Farrell said, a little too quickly. Adding, 'The drugs I have to take, they make me dizzy. I'm always falling over. And I bruise easy these days, too.'

'I couldn't help thinking that Lucinda might have had something to do with it. She has quite a temper, doesn't she?'

'She has her troubles.'

'She didn't seem too troubled by the news about Edie. I mean, she was troubled by the fact that we'd disturbed her enjoyment of Oprah, but not by the actual news.'

'You saw how she was this morning. She was troubled, in her own way.'

'I saw how she was last night. Has your wife ever hit you, Mr Farrell? It's nothing to be ashamed of if she does. Guys hitting women, everyone knows about that. Especially you. But women hitting guys, it's not as uncommon as you'd think.'

'What I did, that was a long time ago. Not that I'm not ashamed of it, but I'm a different guy now.'

'If you say so, Mr Farrell.'

'What is this, you think I had something to do with how Edie died? Man, that's cold, even for a cop. Plus she was found all the way out here in the fucking country, and I can't even drive.'

'Take it easy, Mr Farrell,' Summer said. 'We weren't talking about Edie. We were talking about you and your wife.'

'You have no right,' Randy Farrell said. He was sitting back now, looking sulky, hunched inside a black nylon jacket zipped up to the neck. Like a two-thousand-year-old kid who'd been caught with his hand in the cookie jar.

Summer said, 'One time when I was in uniform, I was called out to investigate a domestic disturbance. This truck driver, a man who looked like a cross between a Hell's Angel and one of those TV wrestlers, six foot four, two hundred and fifty pounds, had been set on fire by his wife. Who was maybe half his weight soaking wet. It turned out she used to beat up on him all the time. She hit him with skillets, she stabbed him with scissors, kitchen knives . . . It went on for years until he ended up in the emergency room with second-degree burns over half his body. There's a tendency to think that women are passive, that they aren't violent. And it's true that they usually don't get into bar fights or road-rage incidents. But women battering their spouses or their partners, Mr Farrell, you'd be amazed how often it happens, and how often the guy covers it up.'

Randy Farrell didn't say anything. His pride had taken a big hit, and he had gone into a sulk.

Summer let the silence stretch. The one-lunged Taurus, an ex-rental company rust-bucket with over a hundred thousand miles on the clock, was being overtaken by everything else on the road: cars and trucks and RVs, a pickup towing a trailer with a big white speedboat on it, a pickup with a German shepherd sitting on the loadbed right behind the cab. Summer overtook a string of tractor trailers labouring up a long curving grade and the tractor trailers overtook her on a flat stretch a couple of miles later. Steep slopes thick with Douglas firs rose up either side of the freeway.

'Tell me something, Mr Farrell, did your wife ever hit Edie?' Summer was watching him in the rear-view mirror. When he shrugged, she said, 'You told me last night they were rowing all the time when Edie lived at home.'

'That doesn't have anything to do with it,' Randy Farrell said forcefully.

Summer wondered if he was genuinely angry, or if he was becoming nervous because she was getting close to something that he wanted to keep hidden.

She said, 'How I see it – you can jump all over me if I'm wrong – your wife doesn't have Edie to hit any more, but she still lashes out. She hits you because you're too sick to defend yourself.'

Randy Farrell didn't say anything, staring straight at her when she looked at him in the rear-view, a stare that had something raw and unforgiving in it.

Summer decided that it was time to back off. 'Like I said, there's nothing to be ashamed of, Mr Farrell. Maybe I can help find you counselling, if you want it.'

He shrugged.

Summer drove for a little while, then said, 'Just one more thing. Why do you stay with your wife when she treats you so badly?'

Their gazes met in the rear-view mirror again. Randy Farrell said, 'You tell me, where else could I go at this point in my life?'

5

Carl Kelley braced Pat Metcalf Wednesday lunchtime, when the
security company manager arrived at the estate for his weekly
inspection. Walking straight up to him, saying, 'I want a word.'

'Make it quick. I'm running late.'

They were standing beside Metcalf's black Range Rover in
the parking lot by the gatehouse, with a view down the valley to
the tall narrow vee of the dam and the lake spread behind it, the
ruins of the old lodge and holiday cabins on one side, forest on
the other. It was a warm, sunny day. A hawk was circling in the
stark blue sky.

Carl said, 'I'll come straight to the point. I found one of your
guys in the mansion last night, wandering around the trophy
room.'

'Yeah, Frank Wilson told me about that,' Metcalf said. 'He
also told me you threatened him.'

'He was pricing Mr Merrit's possessions like an auctioneer.
What are you going to do about it?'

'He found the door open and checked it out. Why should I
do anything?'

Pat Metcalf was a heavy-set man with an untidy mop of hair
dyed black, wearing a sport jacket over a white shirt and bolo tie.
He'd been a senior detective in LAPD's Vice Unit until he ended
up on the wrong side of an assault charge after beating up a
working girl and putting her in a coma because she wouldn't
give him a freebie. That had been ten years ago, but he still pos-
sessed a cop's bullish arrogance and made it clear that he
considered Carl to be some kind of untrustworthy freeloading
lowlife. Saying in passing, 'I've got your number, buddy.' Or,
'Don't think I don't know.' Or, 'You and me, anywhere, any

time.' Eye-fucking him with belligerent contempt. Daring him to try something.

Metcalf was giving Carl that look now. Carl gave it right back, saying, 'Did you know that Frank Wilson has done time? I don't suppose you do, or you wouldn't have hired him.'

'I interview a guy for a job, I can't ask him was he ever arrested. That's a straight violation of Federal law – invasion of privacy. I can't ask him if he's ever been a mental patient either, or if he's gay or has HIV.'

'Frank Wilson is sporting a prison tattoo on his hand. He was definitely convicted for something,' Carl said.

'So?'

'So that story about finding the door open was a load of bull-shit.'

'I told you, the guy got lost.'

'Which reminds me of the other thing that bothers me. Here's a bloke wandering around the trophy room, claiming to have wandered in through an open door. But why was the door open in the first place?'

'Maybe there's a problem with your system. If I were you, I'd get it fixed,' Metcalf said, and made a move to go past Carl.

Carl said, 'Either the system was broken, or Mr Frank Wilson got hold of a bracelet that allowed him entry into a part of the mansion where he had no business being. Maybe I should look into that.'

'What do you want me to do? Fire his ass?'

'That's what I'd do.'

'Yeah, but you don't have to find halfway decent guards who'll take wages that're less than they can earn flipping burgers. And you know what? I'd rather employ someone who's done jail than some crazy queer dripping with the virus.'

'If all your employees are like him, maybe we'd better find another security company.'

'If you're not happy with the service my company provides, why don't you raise the matter with Mr Merrit? Oh, but I bet you already ran to him with your paranoid little story, and he told you to forget about it. Is that why you're sore?'

'I'm pissed off because there's been a breach in security and you aren't taking it seriously.'

'There hasn't *been* any breach in security,' Metcalf said with exaggerated patience, 'so quit bothering me with this weak shit about conspiracy to rob or whatever. Stick to your own job, whatever the fuck it is, and keep your nose out of my business.'

Carl let the man walk past, then said to his back, 'Who mentioned anything about a conspiracy?'

Metcalf didn't take the bait, but walked away across the parking lot towards the gatehouse, a grassy mound with a fieldstone-and-glass frontage. Carl went the other way, down a steep stairway towards the two and a half towers that rose up from a bench cut into the side of the valley. Feeling pleased and happy for the first time since he'd got back from Los Angeles. He was certain now that Metcalf and the security guard, Frank Wilson, were planning to rob Dirk Merrit. It fitted together nice and neatly. The ex-cop had realized that the imminent bankruptcy of one of his company's clients provided the perfect opportunity for some asset-stripping: no one would pay too much attention to items that went missing before insolvency lawyers took charge of the mansion and organized a proper inventory. So he'd used contacts from his former job with the LAPD to reach out to a thief who needed to make some quick cash; someone who, if he was anything like the thieves Carl had known back in England, spent his spare time studying auction catalogues and antiques magazines to keep up with market prices. No better man to appraise Dirk Merrit's stuff, work out what was worth snatching . . .

It all fitted together very nicely indeed, and Carl was going to make good use of it. Pat Metcalf had been hassling Carl ever since he'd moved in, and Carl had been worried that the ex-cop would be a problem when push came to shove. Now he had the perfect excuse to take Metcalf down, and he'd have to get on it right away. Dirk Merrit had very nearly fucked everything up by trying to play with that girl on his own, and although the plan to put the finger on someone else actually seemed to be working, Carl had a feeling that it wasn't going to go away as easily as Merrit believed it would.

All right. Start with Frank Wilson, get the man to confess on tape that he and Metcalf had been planning to rip off some choice goods from the mansion. Get rid of him, get rid of Metcalf, then play the tape to Dirk Merrit and tell the man it was done and dusted. After that, Carl would be able to get on with his own thing, free and clear. He'd do it as soon as they got back from the hunt. No one would miss Frank Wilson, and no one but Metcalf's Filipino girlfriend and his ex-wife and daughter down in Los Angeles would miss *him*. By the time the cops got around to looking for the two men, Carl would be long gone. Wilson, then Metcalf, then all the rest. No point in waiting a minute longer.

Thinking of all the fun he was going to have in the next few days, Carl walked across the driveway to the smaller of the two finished towers, which contained the storerooms, the kitchen, and accommodation for the house's staff. Louis Frazier, the cook, was sitting in a lawn chair on the loading dock, smoking a blunt. A big man with dark brown skin, a red handkerchief tied gangbanger-style around his head, looking up as Carl approached and saying in his soft, sleepy voice, 'It's way past lunchtime, man. We're closed for the afternoon.'

Carl ignored him, walked up the winding stairs to the big kitchen on the second floor. He was fixing a sandwich at the stainless steel counter when Louis Frazier ambled in, taking a final hit from his blunt, dropping the wet roach into the sink at the end of the counter and saying in a pinched voice, 'You see the TV news?'

'I don't watch TV,' Carl said.

He was wrapping his sandwich – ham and cheese on rye – in foil. He planned to spend the rest of the day in the barn, checking over the RV and ultralight, getting ready for tomorrow's road trip.

Louis blew out a huge volume of smoke. 'Man, don't be leaving the lid off the mustard jar, it'll get all crusty round the rim. That young girl found buck-naked in the woods near here, the one who died before they could get her to hospital? The *po*lice –' Louis hit the first syllable hard, he always put some Southern jive into his voice when he was stoned '– just now fingered some crazy white man for it. It's the top story on the local TV news right now. On CNN and Fox too.'

'I told you,' Carl said. 'I don't watch TV.'

But he knew all about the arrest. A few hours ago, he'd swung past the place where he'd planted the evidence last night, had seen police vehicles parked along the road and a swarm of deputies and detectives on the property. Later on Dirk Merrit had told him that someone had leaked the story to the media, the man full of glee at this latest proof of his criminal genius.

Louis Frazier said, 'According to the latest reports, the sicko was keeping her as his sex slave or something. I thought the city was bad, but the things these country folk get up to . . .'

Carl took a pickle from the catering-sized jar, started to wrap it.

'Know what the man ordered a couple of nights ago? Beef carpaccio. I said, beef what? He told me to look it up. Turns out it's raw beef, sliced thin. So what I did, I cut slices from a frozen fillet, soaked 'em in olive oil with a squeeze of lemon juice, added some toasted pine nuts and Parmesan cheese. If I say so myself, it turned out pretty damn fine.' Louis rolled the tip of his tongue around his smile and said, 'Things you learn here, huh?'

'You have a point to make?'

Louis gave Carl a sleepy look. 'Take a chill pill, my brother. We're just talking. Having ourselves a conversation.'

'I'm fixing lunch,' Carl said. 'You're the one who's making all the noise.'

He was wondering if Louis Frazier, another ex-con – two years' state time for attempted extortion, who knew what else he'd been into? – was part of Metcalf and Wilson's little conspiracy, or if he suspected that the dead girl had something to do with Dirk Merrit and was fishing for information, trying to find out what Carl knew.

Carl Kelley had always found it hard to work out how other people felt, to understand the sly signals they passed back and

forth, the aggravating kaleidoscope of their moods and motiva-
tions. When he'd been a kid, after he'd got into serious trouble
with the last of his foster-families, he'd stolen one of his psychiatric assessments and read that he 'exhibited the lack of affect and
spontaneous gesture typical of true sociopaths. He has learned to
imitate expressions associated with ordinary human emotions,
but in my presence everything he says and does is calculated, and
he is in a constant state of alertness, carefully monitoring my
every word and expression. This state of constant vigilance is
exhausting but necessary; his greatest terror is of ridicule, and I
believe that it is this which powers his rage.' Carl had relished
every word of the report. It was a confirmation of what he
already knew: that he was a wolf among sheep. But Christ, it got
really tiring sometimes, pretending to be an ordinary person,
figuring out what was going on behind other people's faces, the
meanings hidden inside their endless chatter.

Like now, with Louis Frazier, who was saying, 'I know you
behave like you a monk, like you taken a vow of silence, but
there's nothing wrong with making conversation, man.
Conversation helps the wheels of civilization go round nice and
smooth. How about passing those pickles? I got the munchies.'

Louis came around the counter when Carl didn't move, fished
a pickle from the jar and took a big bite from it. Saying, as he
chewed and swallowed, 'Know what else the man wanted?
Sushi. I told him, you're gonna have to send out for that shit, had
to give him some smoked salmon in the end, with fennel and
horseradish. You're planning one of those trips again, ain't you?'

Carl looked at him.

Louis smiled. 'I knew it. Know how I knew?'

There was a rack of stainless steel kitchen knives about a foot
from Carl's right hand. He had to step on the impulse to shove
one through Louis Frazier's Adam's apple.

Louis said, 'It's because the man always gets a taste for the raw
before a trip. I guess it must put him in the mood.'

'The mood for what?'

Louis took another bite of pickle, used his thumb to wipe
juice from his chin. 'Hunting, of course. And whatever else it is

you two boys get up to when you're alone together out in Mother Nature. Man, don't look at me like that, I'm jiving you. What is it this time? Deer? Mountain goats? Maybe just for once you could bring some of it back, help me stock up the freezer.'

'I don't think you'd like it,' Carl said, returning Louis's smile. Showing all his teeth.

6

Cedar Falls was a sprawling town cut east to west by the Umpqua River and north to south by the cantilevered lanes of the I-5. Summer Ziegler followed the long curve of the freeway exit down to a four-lane boulevard lined with motels and gas stations, drove across a concrete bridge that spanned the sluggish river, and bumped over a single-track railroad that ran along the western edge of the town centre. The train station had been converted to a bank. There were several blocks of shops and restaurants and small businesses; houses straggled up the steep side of the river valley towards a bare crest crowned by radio, TV and microwave antennae.

The Macabee County Sheriff's office occupied two floors of the town's Justice Building, a four-storey slab of concrete and tinted glass that shared a block with the Macabee County Juvenile Correctional Facility, the city hall, and an imposing Greek Revival courthouse. The detectives' bullpen was on the third floor, a long room cluttered with pairs of back-to-back desks and rows of filing cabinets. On one side, offices, interview rooms and holding cells; on the other, tall windows and a nice view across the town towards the river. This was where Summer Ziegler and Randy Farrell met Denise Childers, the detective in charge of the investigation into Edie Collier's death. Denise Childers introduced them to her partner, Jerry Hill, told Randy Farrell that she was very sorry for his loss, and started to explain that although the Sheriff's office in Macabee County didn't have the resources of a big city like Portland, on the whole they managed pretty well.

Jerry Hill said, 'What Denise is trying to tell you is that we turned this case from an accidental death to a kidnap/homicide *and* brought in the doer, all inside of twenty-four hours.'

Summer said, 'Wait a minute. Someone *kidnapped* Edie Collier?'

Randy Farrell said, 'You know who this guy is? You arrested him?'

He spoke so loudly that a woman working at a nearby photocopier turned to look at him.

'Hold on there, Mr Farrell,' Denise Childers said, shooting an annoyed look at Jerry Hill. 'Let's not get ahead of ourselves.'

'If you arrested some creep for this, I think I have the right to know about it,' Randy Farrell said.

'All I can tell you is that we've arrested a man, but we haven't charged him yet,' Denise Childers said.

She was slightly built and in her early forties, wearing blue jeans and a suede jacket, shoulder-length auburn hair clipped back from her pale face. It was the kind of face, Summer thought, that looked out at you from Depression-era photographs of migrant workers, from earlier photographs of pioneer families posed in the doorways of their sod cabins. Careworn but tough. Determined and forthright.

Jerry Hill said, 'The guy we like for this is a local boy. I arrested him yesterday over another matter, and this morning we came across some stuff that ties him to Edie Collier.'

A burly man in his forties, with a cap of dry, blond hair and the hectic complexion of a dedicated drinker, Jerry Hill was wearing blue jeans too, with a blue short-sleeved shirt, and a burgundy-knit tie spotted with old grease stains. A Sig-Sauer .38 rode on his right hip. Summer felt overdressed in her grey pants suit and her good black purse slung over her shoulder.

Randy Farrell said, 'What kind of stuff?'

Denise Childers said, 'I'm sorry, Mr Farrell, but we can't go into that at this stage.'

Jerry Hill said, 'We haven't questioned him yet, which is why Denise is being so cautious. But believe you me, he's square in the frame. He's going down.'

Randy Farrell was bewildered and angry. Blood flushed his sallow cheeks at the hinges of his jaw. He said, 'You knew that

Edie was killed, you found the fucker that did it, and you didn't tell me?'

'I'm telling you now, aren't I? And watch your language, sport,' Jerry Hill said, smiling at Summer. 'There are ladies present.'

'How did you expect him to react?' Summer said.

She'd taken an instant dislike to Denise Childers's partner. Jerry Hill appeared to be the perfect example of the kind of macho old-school cop who made a lot of noise about having no time for political correctness or snotty-nosed college kids who believed they were better than police who'd learned their trade on the street, the kind who made sure that suspects banged their heads when they were put in the back of a car, who believed it was a fine joke to ask a female colleague how they were hanging.

Denise Childers said, 'It was my call, Mr Farrell. I thought it would be better to speak to you about this in person. We're just as anxious as you are to get at the truth, and I promise you that we are going to do our best by Edie. That's why we'd appreciate it if we could talk to you about her.'

Jerry Hill said, 'Just a little Q&A. A man like you, I'm sure you know the drill.'

'Oh yeah,' Randy Farrell said bitterly. 'I know the drill.'

Summer said, 'Remember that you're here for Edie, Mr Farrell.'

Randy Farrell turned on her. 'You knew all along that she'd been murdered, didn't you?'

'I know as much about this as you.'

Summer had offered to help the investigation into Edie Collier's death when she had talked to Denise Childers on the phone last night, suggested that she could try to track down the girl's boyfriend, ask him what he thought Edie might have been doing in Cedar Falls. She'd been hoping that she could turn Ryland Nelsen's errand into something meaty, something that would prove to the other detectives in the Robbery Unit that she had the right stuff, prove that she could do her job without someone looking over her shoulder, give her career a nice push. But that was blown out of the water now.

Denise Childers suggested that they should find somewhere private to talk, and led Summer and Randy Farrell to one of the interview rooms. The usual scarred table and chairs, a window blanked with blinds, and a video camera up in one corner, an amenity that Portland police weren't allowed because the City believed that videoing interviews would violate citizens' rights.

'Take a seat, Mr Farrell,' Denise Childers said. 'Is there anything I can get you? Soda, a coffee?'

Randy Farrell sat down cautiously. 'A Coke would be nice. Diet. I can't take the sugar any more.'

'Why don't you go get him a cold one, Jerry?' Denise Childers said, and turned a chair to face Randy Farrell's and sat down with her knees almost touching his.

Summer took a chair on the other side of the table, admiring the way the woman had established her authority.

Denise Childers said, 'Once again, let me say that I'm sorry for your loss, Mr Farrell, and that I appreciate you coming all this way. How you can best help me out right now is to tell me about Edie. Where she was living, where she worked, who she was seeing – anything you think might be useful to us.'

'I already told her,' Randy Farrell said, pointing at Summer with his chin.

'I'd appreciate it if you could go through it with me, for the record,' Denise Childers said, taking a notebook from a pocket of her jacket.

She was patient and meticulous, drawing out Randy Farrell on every point, making notes in a rounded hand. Summer prompted him to tell the story about how he had spotted Edie and her boyfriend in the shopping mall. Jerry Hill, leaning by the door with his arms folded across his chest, watched impassively. It took half an hour. At last Denise Childers closed her notebook and thanked Randy Farrell again, told him that the information he had given would greatly help the investigation.

She added casually, 'By the way, is the name Joseph Kronenwetter familiar to you?'

'Is he the guy that killed Edie?'

'Have you ever heard the name before?'

Randy Farrell shook his head.

'Did Edie ever mention it to you?'

Randy Farrell shook his head again. 'She never mentioned this place, either. I don't know what she was doing here.'

'That's something we'd very much like to find out too,' Denise Childers said.

From his sentry position by the door, Jerry Hill said that he would take Summer and Randy Farrell to the hospital, get the chore of identifying the body out of the way. That was the word he used: chore. When Denise Childers gave him a sharp look, he said amiably, 'You go ahead and write this up. I promise to take good care of them.'

As he drove Randy Farrell and Summer through the town in his cherry-red Dodge Ramcharger, Jerry Hill explained that Denise Childers was a good detective who liked to do things by the book, but sometimes the book got in the way of ordinary human decency. He, on the other hand, didn't have a problem with letting them know about the latest developments in the case; in fact, he said, he considered it to be his Christian duty to enlighten them.

'Denise spotted what she thought were marks made by some kind of shackle on one of the girl's legs. When the ME confirmed her guess, all of a sudden we were looking at a potential kidnap/homicide. We started canvassing the area yesterday afternoon, and that's when I had my lucky break,' Jerry Hill said, smiling at Summer.

Randy Farrell said, 'You found this guy. Kronenwetter.'

'It's better than that,' Jerry Hill said. 'Yesterday evening, I paid him a visit to ask him the questions we were asking everyone in the area. Mr Kronenwetter is known to us from various incidents involving trespass and poaching, and he's done jail for assaulting a police officer. When I banged on the door of his shack, you can bet I had my pistol drawn and a couple of deputies at my back. The guy comes out reeking of whiskey, he's shouting all kinds of wild nonsense, and he has a handgun stuck down the front of his pants. I arrested him for threatening a police officer, brought him in, booked him. When he went up before the judge for arraignment this morning, he was sent to the county jail for psychiatric evaluation, and around the same time we get a phone call telling us to take a look in his cellar. Which is where we found a set of leg-irons, the girl's driver's licence, her social security and library cards, her dress, and panties with blood on them that that we're gonna send off to Eugene for DNA typing.'

'Son of a bitch,' Randy Farrell said.

Summer, riding shotgun beside Jerry Hill, turned to Randy Farrell and said, 'Are you all right hearing this?'

Randy Farrell ignored her, asked Jerry Hill who had made the phone call that fingered this creep, he'd like to shake their hand.

'Some guy who didn't leave his name,' Jerry Hill said. 'We figure a neighbour. Joe Kronenwetter pissed off just about every-one unfortunate enough to live close by him. We went straight to the county jail and explained to him exactly how much trouble he was in, asked him if he had anything to say for himself. He didn't say a word, just kept shaking his head and moaning. He wouldn't even talk to the public defender. We left him there to be evaluated by the shrink, and to think about just how much trouble he's in. When the District Attorney has finished the paperwork, we'll bring him in and charge him and go around it again.'

'Son of a bitch,' Randy Farrell said again.

'Don't you worry, Randy. Even if he keeps up the crazy-man act we have enough to put him away for a very long time.' Jerry Hill aimed his grin at Summer. 'So tell me, detective, you ever get this much excitement up in Portland?'

The morgue was in an annexe behind the medical centre, con-nected to the main building by a short corridor with wide double doors at each end. In Portland, relatives and friends iden-tified bodies at one remove, via a TV screen. In Cedar Falls they did it the old-fashioned way, in a small white-tiled room with the body lying on a gurney and covered from head to feet in a stiff blue sheet. When the attendant folded back the top portion of the sheet from the dead face, Randy Farrell said at once, 'That's her.'

Summer recognized Edie Collier too, remembered driving past Meier and Frank in her cruiser and spotting the department store's detective, an ex-cop by the name of Tom McMahon, chasing the girl through crowds of Christmas shoppers. Summer had cut in front of her at an intersection, had been handcuffing her when Tom McMahon had come puffing up. In a drab little office in the basement of the store, Edie Collier had watched with calm indifference as Summer went through her shoulder bag; Summer remembered finding a paperback of Billy Collins's *Nine Horses* among the usual debris, the pages much underlined and annotated, remembered asking Edie Collier if she was a poetry fan, trying to make some contact. But the girl had barely shrugged, her gaze as luminously untroubled as a madonna's when Tom McMahon had told her that the store would be pressing charges. In court, she'd pled guilty with the same serenity, lost in some private world while the judge told her that her priors and the fact that she'd been arrested for shoplifting while on probation for the same offence suggested to him that she should spend Christmas in jail – it would be her chance to think about the course her life was taking and get straightened out.

Randy Farrell, sitting right behind his stepdaughter in the courtroom, had leaned forward to whisper something to her before she was led away; she'd smiled and touched his hand as if to reassure him that she would be all right. Now he brushed back stray strands of hair from her dead face, and with the tender gesture of a parent tucking in a sleeping child adjusted the sheet to hide the beginnings of the crudely stitched Y-shaped autopsy incision. There was a rose tattooed on the ball of her right shoulder, a banner lettered *Billy* in Gothic script curled around its stem.

After five years of policing the streets of Portland, Summer had developed calluses on her soul; most of the time, she did her work with the tough-minded pragmatism of a doctor triaging battlefield casualties. She had good days, she had bad days, and while she hoped the good outweighed the bad, she'd learned that keeping a tally brought nothing but grief, and she tried her best not to take home what she saw on the streets. But she'd also learned that some cases hooked the heart. Edie Collier, raised in a chaotic household with a violent drunk for a mother and a stepfather in and out of jail, was exactly the type who would end up as a victim on a mortuary gurney. Summer had encountered dozens like her down and out on the streets of Portland. But now, looking at the girl's dead face, turned a delicate shade of green by the fluorescent light of the viewing room, Summer felt a hook dig deep, and knew that this was one of the cases she would never forget.

'You have to see this.' Jerry Hill lifted up the other end of the sheet, exposing the dead girl's legs to mid-thigh, and pointed to the two parallel welts above the knuckle of her right ankle. 'This is how we figured out she'd been chained up someplace.'

'Cover her up,' Summer said, with a flash of anger.

Jerry Hill shrugged, let the sheet fall. 'I thought you would be interested. I mean, it's why we started looking for the son of a bitch that killed her.'

In the corridor outside the viewing room, Randy Farrell asked if he could use the restroom. When they were alone, Jerry Hill told Summer, 'It often hits men worse than women, don't you think?'

'He has cancer,' Summer said, 'so why don't you ease up on him?'

And immediately regretted it – it was as if she had betrayed an intimate confidence.

Jerry Hill studied her over the top of his sunglasses. He was standing a little too close to her, and was wearing too much Canoe.

'I checked old Randy's rap sheet,' he said. 'Pretty impressive, isn't it? If it wasn't for Joe Kronenwetter, I would have been asking him some hard questions about his stepdaughter. I don't pretend to know why you're so hot on defending him, unless it's something to do with that famous Portland liberalism.'

'I'd say it was common courtesy,' Summer said.

Jerry Hill nodded to himself. 'Yes sir, if I didn't have Joe Kronenwetter locked away, I'd be taking a very close look at

Randy Farrell. That black eye he's sporting – he could have got it in some kind of struggle. Listen, how about you wait here for your friend while I go outside and make a couple of phone calls.'

When Randy Farrell came out of the restroom, looking bloodless and shrunken, Summer told him that he'd done fine, but he shook his head and he said that he wasn't finished yet, he had to find out how to get Edie back to Portland. Summer talked to one of the ME's assistants, who gave her the name of a funeral parlour that would make the appropriate arrangements once the body had been released. Then she walked Randy Farrell to the parking lot, where Jerry Hill was waiting for them in his Dodge Ram.

He took his time on the drive back to the Justice Building. Keeping well under the speed limit, stopping at intersections to let other vehicles go through ahead of him, stopping at a drive-through coffee shop and spending five minutes bantering with the waitress before placing his order. He told Summer that Cedar Falls was a fine little town – if she was considering staying overnight he could show her a barbecue place that served the best steak in the county, plus he knew of a motel he could recommend. It was basic but comfortable, and cops got a discount there, if she knew what he meant.

Treating her to his shit-eating grin, relaxed and confident, an alpha male on his home turf. She wondered how many women he'd managed to talk into taking a room at this motel of his. She saw him turning up an hour or so after she'd checked in, saw him standing in the doorway with a bottle of something or other and a couple of glasses, saying he thought she might want some company . . . And told him she planned to be back in Portland by the evening.

'I wouldn't count on it,' Jerry Hill said. 'I'm gonna need to talk to Randy again.'

'I've already told you everything I know,' Randy Farrell said.

'We'll see about that,' Jerry Hill said. His beeper went off and he checked it and put on a little speed, sounding his horn as he sped through an intersection, saying, 'Unless you want to leave Randy behind, Detective Ziegler, it very much looks like you might not be getting back to Portland tonight. Think about that motel, why don't you? I'll be happy to fix you up.'

'I bet this is a fun town,' Summer said, 'but I really do have to get back to Portland. I think we should ask your partner if she thinks it's necessary to talk with Mr Farrell again.'

'She's welcome to sit in on the conversation. You too,' Jerry Hill said, swinging his big pickup into the parking lot behind the Justice Building. Saying with mock innocence, 'Oh my, what do we have here?'

A TV van was parked amongst the black and white cruisers and civilian vehicles, and there was a small commotion at the rear entrance of the building. Two deputies were arguing with a smartly dressed woman and a man with a video camera up on his shoulder, while two more deputies helped a big shaggy-haired man in shackles and an orange jumpsuit clamber out of the back of a cruiser. Summer realized that the prisoner must be Joseph Kronenwetter, and turned in her seat to tell Randy Farrell to stay right where he was. But he was already clawing at the handle of his door, and Jerry Hill caught Summer's arm when she reached for him, saying, 'Let the poor guy have some fun.'

'Get your hands off me,' Summer said, and jumped down and chased Randy Farrell across the parking lot.

He was running flat out. One of the deputies, a woman, got in his way and tried to grab hold of him, and they whirled around in an awkward tangle. He smacked her in the eye with an elbow, she lost her footing and sat down hard, and he dodged around her, throwing wild punches and kicks at the prisoner, yelling that he was going to kill the fucking son of a bitch. Then Summer slammed into him and drove him against the side of the cruiser, grabbing hold of one of his wrists and wrenching it up behind his back, pinning him there while a burly deputy handcuffed him and two more deputies hustled the prisoner away, the reporter shouting questions, and the video camera sucking it all in.

7

Charles F. Worden, the Sheriff of Macabee County, was a scrawny guy in a navy-blue suit and club tie, with a puff of blow-dried white hair and the pinched expression of a man who'd eaten something that had gone bad on him. Perched on his leather-covered swivel chair behind his big desk, he fixed Summer with a severe gaze and told her that Randy Farrell would spend the night in custody, and stand before the judge tomorrow morning to answer to a charge of assaulting a police officer.

'As far as I'm concerned it's done and dusted, but seeing as you're a guest in my town, detective, I'm willing to hear you out.'

Summer was determined to give it her best shot. She was still angry about the mean trick Jerry Hill had pulled, and she felt a touch of guilt, too. She'd tried to do the right thing when she'd brought Randy Farrell to Cedar Falls, she felt responsible for him, and now he was being processed for admission to the holding facility on the fourth floor of the Justice Building.

She said, 'Mr Farrell had only just come from identifying his stepdaughter's body when he was confronted with the man accused of kidnapping her. It never should have happened, sir, and given the circumstances I don't think that Mr Farrell should be punished for his reaction, wrong though it was.' She paused, and when Sheriff Worden didn't say anything, she played her ace. She didn't like doing it, but felt that she had no choice. 'Also, he's suffering from terminal cancer. Think of the bad publicity when the press gets to hear about that.'

Sheriff Worden's pinched expression deepened into a scowl.

'I'm sorry to hear about the cancer. But your Mr Farrell is a low-life recidivist with a string of convictions for violent crime who isn't even a blood relative of the victim, and he assaulted one of my deputies, a *female* deputy, in front of a TV camera. In case you missed it, let me tell you that the footage was on the local news, right after a report on the positive developments in the Collier case. This is a friendly town, Detective Ziegler. A nice town. A *quiet* town. We don't like it when people come here and cause trouble.'

'Mr Farrell didn't come here to cause trouble, sir,' Summer said. She was finding it hard to stay calm. 'He came here to identify his stepdaughter's body, at the request of one of your detectives. There was only trouble because he was brought back from the morgue at the exact same time that Joseph Kronenwetter arrived from the county jail.'

'Are you implying that this was some kind of set-up, Detective Ziegler?'

That was exactly what Summer wanted to say, but she knew that it would be pointless to make a direct accusation against Jerry Hill. 'All I'm asking, sir, is for a little leniency.'

'I have already shown leniency, Detective Ziegler, in that I have decided not to make a complaint to your superior officer about your negligence.'

'My superior officer already knows what happened, sir. He isn't happy about how things turned out either.'

It hadn't been an easy conversation, but Ryland Nelsen, after hearing Summer's version of events, had agreed that she should stay overnight in Cedar Falls and attend Randy Farrell's arraignment the next day.

'I bet he isn't happy,' Sheriff Worden said. 'And I can understand why you and him don't want this to come to court, given your duty of care towards Mr Farrell. But justice has to take its course, detective. I'm afraid you're going to have to take your lumps on this one.'

Summer thought that the Sheriff's prissy smile, his wet underlip sticking out, made him look like the turtle her brother had kept as a pet when they'd been kids. She gave it one last try, saying, 'This isn't about me, sir. It's about a sick, grieving man who made a silly mistake.'

'Like I said, I understand your position. And I hope *you* understand why I can't let this slide. Cedar Falls has a fine reputation as a place where families and retired folk can feel safe, where visitors can enjoy our fishing, hunting and white-water sports without fear of the kind of crime that bedevils cities like Portland,' Sheriff Worden said, flapping a hand towards a wall hung with photographs of himself shaking hands with celebrities. Bruce Willis and Demi Moore before their divorce. Dolph Lundgren in a white wetsuit. Sylvester Stallone. Chuck Norris. Clint Eastwood. In every photograph, Sheriff Worden wore the same brown shirt with gold braid on the shoulders and a gold star pinned to the chest, and the same rigid smile.

'I have a duty to protect that reputation, and to reassure everyone that my department is on top of every aspect of this unfortunate case. As a matter of fact,' Sheriff Worden said, patting his springy puff of white hair, 'I have a TV interview in ten minutes, with our NBC affiliate. Is there anything else I can do for you?'

In the small dark observation room off the detectives' bullpen, men clustered around a twenty-inch colour TV set on a scarred table. They made way for Summer when she came in. The TV was displaying the feed from the video camera in the interrogation room. While she had been waiting to see Sheriff Worden, Summer had watched Denise Childers trying to break through Joseph Kronenwetter's sullen silence. Now, one of the men told her, 'Jerry's been giving it his best shot, but he's had about as much luck as Denise.'

The view was angled down on Joseph Kronenwetter. He sat on a steel chair at a small table, the wrist of his right arm locked in the handcuff bolted to the table's frame. His shaggy head was bowed, his long white beard folded against the chest of his orange jumpsuit. Denise Childers sat across the table from him while Jerry Hill stalked around the edges of the room, his voice blaring from the TV's speaker.

'Let's go over this one more time, Joe. You have the poor girl's dress, you have her ID, you have a whole stash of her belongings down in your cellar. You have her driver's licence. Here it is, in case you forgot about it,' Jerry Hill said, picking up a plastic evidence bag from a corner of the table and thrusting it under Kronenwetter's downturned face. 'You remember this, Joe? You remember the girl in the itsy-bitsy photograph? I'm sure you do. Okay. You have the dress, you have the driver's licence with her name on it and her fucking picture. What else? Oh yeah – how could I forget? You have her social security card and you have her library card. Look here, for the Multnomah County Central Library, made out to Edie Collier. Same girl whose picture is on the driver's licence.'

Summer thought that he was hamming it up, having fun, playing with the man rather than trying to play him. Jerry Hill liked his games, all right.

'And last but not least, we have her panties,' Jerry Hill said. 'Right now, some technician in a room full of those expensive machines you see on *CSI* is taking a good look at the blood on them. But we both know whose blood it is, don't we?'

Kronenwetter stared down at the table. His cuffed hand clenched and unclenched; otherwise he did not move.

Denise Childers leaned across and put her hand on his, told him that he would feel a lot better if he told them exactly what had happened.

One of the detectives standing with Summer in the observation room said, 'Man's going into a fugue. They won't get anything useful out of him now.'

Summer asked if Kronenwetter had said anything at all.

'Not one word after he told the public defender he didn't need a lawyer because he was innocent.'

Another detective said, 'First time Jerry had a crack at him, he was raving about a monster in the woods. Claimed it had been stalking him, blamed it for the poor girl's death.'

'*He's* the monster,' the first detective said. 'Or anyhow, he has a monster inside his head.'

Jerry Hill was standing behind Kronenwetter now, his hands

on the man's shoulders, his face tilted towards the camera. Showboating, Summer thought, with a quick flare of anger.

'Maybe you could explain to me,' Jerry Hill said, 'why you kept her panties, but not her bra. Oh, but I guess she wasn't wearing a bra. We've had a good stretch of hot weather, and I bet that when you caught up with her, all she had on was this thin cotton dress and her little black panties. Is that why you went for her, Joe? Pretty young girl, the sun shining through her dress, showing up her smooth body and her little titties?'

'Go easy,' Denise Childers said, but Jerry Hill ignored her.

'Did you get hard for her then, Joe? How about it? Am I right or am I right?'

Kronenwetter was staring at the table, his long hair hanging loose around his face.

'Fugue,' the first detective said.

On the TV, Denise Childers said, 'We need to hear your version, Joe. Why not help yourself and tell me all about it?'

Jerry Hill said, 'Here's how I see it, Joe. I'll lay it out for you, and any time you think I got something wrong, you just jump right in and tell me. Okay? Way I see it, you're driving along, and you see this pretty young girl standing by the side of the road, holding out her thumb, looking for a lift. She's wearing nothing but a flimsy dress and she's a young, good-looking girl, you can see the shape of her body through that thin material. So you do what any red-blooded man would do. You stop your truck and you tell her to hop in. So far, you haven't done anything wrong, but now she's sitting right beside you in that thin dress, you can smell her, and she smells so good you want to eat her up. You live by yourself out in the country, I bet a week might go by without you talking to anyone, much less a delectable peachy-fresh girl like this. She got into your truck of her own accord, in that thin little dress, she's talking away, maybe she's leaning at the window letting the wind blow her hair back and you can smell her and you want her. You ache for her, don't you? Any man would, right?'

Watching this on the little TV, Summer realized that Jerry Hill wasn't interested in getting Kronenwetter to confirm or deny the story. No, the son of a bitch was making sure that he got his version of events on record.

Look at him now, smiling up at the camera, saying, 'So you make a move. And then she's screaming, and you panic and somehow or other you knock her out. And when you've done that, you've crossed the line. And crossing the line frees you up. You can do anything you like. So you take her back to your cabin – or no, maybe first of all you pull off the road and drag her out of the truck into the ditch and you have her right there, don't you, Joe? Because you can't wait. Because she's so young and fresh.

'And afterward, you know you can't let her go,' Jerry Hill said, his voice getting louder. 'So you take her back to your cabin, you drag her down into your cellar. You rip off that thin little dress and those black panties, and you chain her up. You keep her down there, naked and chained like an animal. We know you did, Joe, because we found the leg-irons you used. And you know what? Those leg-irons have her blood on them. The very same blood we found on her dress and on her panties.'

Kronenwetter shook his head violently, hair whipping from side to side, his teeth bared in a grimace, his eyes squeezed shut.

The noise he made was shrill and raw, like razor-wire ripped from his throat.

Summer felt as if someone had dropped an ice cube down her back. One of the detectives said, 'Jesus.'

On the TV, Denise Childers said, 'Maybe we should take a break.'

Jerry Hill caught hold of a handful of Kronenwetter's hair, winding it around his fist, pulling back the big man's head, leaning down to speak in his ear. 'You picked up that little girl from the side of the road. You kidnapped her and you held her prisoner and you raped her. How many times? Five? Ten? Twenty? You did all that, and then she got away and what did you do? Nothing. Because you just didn't care. Because you thought you were so fucking powerful there was no way you would get caught. Or wait, maybe you *wanted* to get caught. Is that it? Is that why you left her dress and her driver's licence and her library card and her panties down there in your cellar? Is that why you left the fucking leg-irons there? Is that why you're blubbering now, you piece of shit?'

Kronenwetter's mouth worked inside his beard and he gave a wordless cry, so loud that everyone around Summer jumped. On the TV, Jerry Hill had let go of Kronenwetter's hair, and the man was shaking his head, shouting.

'It wasn't me! It wasn't me! It was the monster!'

8

Joseph Kronenwetter clammed up after his outburst. While Denise Childers and Jerry Hill took turns to pick at him, he stared down at the table and at one point started to cry, making wet snuffling noises and wiping his nose on his sleeve, this prophet-bearded wild man weeping like a scared little kid. When it became clear that he wasn't going to say anything else, he was sent upstairs to the holding cells, and Summer booked herself into a Travelodge. She phoned her mother to tell her that she wouldn't be coming back that night, and then had to explain why. Telling her mother how Jerry Hill had excused himself to make a couple of phone calls at the morgue, how he'd dawdled on the way back until his beeper had gone off, how Randy Farrell had attacked Joseph Kronenwetter in front of a TV reporter and cameraman and been arrested, about her unsuccessful conversation with Sheriff Worden.

'I can't prove it,' she said, 'but I have to wonder if Jerry Hill called the county jail to find out what time Kronenwetter was due back at the Sheriff's office, and if he didn't call the TV reporter too.'

'You think he set up some kind of confrontation?'

'It's possible.'

'Well, why don't you ask him?'

'You think I should call him out, like in the Wild West? His Sig-Sauer against my Glock, I guess it might be interesting.'

'My little girl, and her unhealthy fascination with guns.'

'I guess it doesn't really matter why or how it happened. All I can do now is stand up in court for Randy Farrell and hope for the best.'

'It isn't your fault,' her mother said. 'Mr Farrell is old enough to know better.'

'He may be a scumbag with a hair-trigger temper, but he really does care about what happened to his stepdaughter. He came all this way to do right by her, and he didn't deserve to get slung in jail.'

Summer was still angry about it, angry and upset and more than a little ashamed. For one thing, she'd brought Randy Farrell to Cedar Falls and felt that she had a duty to protect him. For another, Jerry Hill had blindsided her. He'd set up the confronta-tion between Randy Farrell and Joseph Kronenwetter right in front of her, and she hadn't realized what he was doing until it was too late. Not only that, but she couldn't figure out why he'd done it. Maybe it had been nothing but plain meanness, just because he could. But he'd already had his fun with Randy Farrell when he'd sprung the news that Edie had been kid-napped, so she couldn't help wondering if he had some other reason.

Her mother said, 'Let me talk to Ed Vara about this. He has a lot of experience with cases of police provocation and entrap-ment.'

'Randy Farrell might appreciate some help if he is committed to trial. But right now, bringing in a Portland human-rights lawyer would be like throwing gasoline on a bonfire.'

Her mother said, 'You think I'm interfering.'

'Have you ever been to Cedar Falls?'

'I've passed by it any number of times.'

'It's a nice little town. Old-fashioned. Most businesses have those red, white and blue cards declaring support for our troops, and most of the pickups and cars have yellow-ribbon stickers on their bumpers. The Republicans have a storefront office right in the middle of Main Street, pictures of elected politicians on one side of the window, pictures of locals serving in Iraq on the other. The Democrats, on the other hand, have this kind of shack perched on a steep slope at one end of a parking lot.'

'In other words, it isn't Portland.'

'Let's put it this way: I bet anyone who lives here and voted for Kerry kept quiet about it. I'll find out how much trouble Randy Farrell is in tomorrow, at the arraignment. If they decide to prosecute, then he'll probably appreciate some *pro bono* help. But let's wait and see how it falls out.'

A little later, Summer was perched on the end of the bed in her room, watching the TV news with less than half her attention and eating take-out Chinese, greasy fried rice and Kung Pao Chicken that tasted mostly of burned onion, when her cell phone rang. It was Denise Childers, wondering if Summer wanted to get together for a drink.

'I kind of feel that you got a raw deal today. Also, I want to apologise for not telling you about Joe Kronenwetter's arrest before you arrived.'

'No problem. I guess you wanted to catch Randy Farrell off guard when you told him about Joseph Kronenwetter, see how he reacted in case he had anything to do with what happened to his stepdaughter. And I was an unknown quantity: you couldn't be sure that I wouldn't have let something slip if you'd told me what you were planning to do.'

'Something like that. Except Jerry kind of messed it up.'

'He's a loose cannon, isn't he?'

'There's a lodge about ten miles north of town, the only place in Macabee County that serves a half-decent Martini. Let me buy you a drink as a thank-you for bringing Mr Farrell all this way.'

Summer applied Denise Childers's directions to a map she got from the motel's office, and pulled up outside the main building of the lodge thirty minutes later.

It was set in ten acres of wooded grounds tucked into a curve of the Umpqua River. Wooden cabins were strung along the river bank and scattered amongst Douglas firs and white pines. The log-and-stone main building had a lobby with polished pine-plank floors and lodgepole-pine columns. Denise Childers was in a booth in the small dark bar off to the side of the busy restaurant, nursing a dirty Martini. She'd let down her hair and put on lipstick, but she was still wearing the scuffed suede jacket and blue jeans – she had probably come here straight from work.

Summer bet that her badge, beeper and gun were in the big leather purse that sat on the low table in front of her, along with all the other stuff that police had to haul around – handcuffs, flashlight, vinyl gloves, notebook and at least two pens, pepper spray . . .

After the waitress had come over and Summer had ordered a Beefeater Martini with a twist, Denise said that she couldn't stay long. She only had the sitter for a few hours and she had another matter to attend to before she went home.

'You have kids?'

'A daughter, twelve years old. Rebecca.'

'That's a nice age.'

'It is right now, but there's turbulence on the horizon – she's starting to obsess over *American Idol* and boy bands.'

'Uh-oh. I guess real boys are next.'

Denise smiled. 'She's going to be a heartbreaker. Plus, she's ferociously determined to become famous. If I'm not careful, I'm going to end up being the mother of the next Christina Aguilera.'

The waitress brought over the Martini. It was pretty good, crisp and cold. Summer and Denise made small talk about Summer's recent promotion to detective, about how she was trying to find her feet in the Robbery Unit. Summer had plenty of questions she wanted to ask, but Denise owned the case and clearly wanted to sound her out first. Asking her now how she'd gotten into police work, was there a family connection?

'Not really. My father's family has a long tradition of military service, maybe that counts for something. My father served in the army for a couple of years after he finished college, he was on a scholarship, but after he met my mother he quit the army as soon as he could.'

Summer still felt a tug at her heart, talking about her father less than a year after his death. Her parents had met cute, just like in the movies. May, 1971, her mother and three girlfriends had been driving to Washington D.C. for an anti-war demonstration, had stopped for a coffee at a Howard Johnson's and had spotted Sam Ziegler at a neighbouring table, in his army uniform. He'd been on his way to Washington too, where he worked as an aide for a five-star general. Summer's mother confronted him, they'd talked and exchanged addresses, one thing had led to another, and they had gotten married the next year, after Sam Ziegler had served out his hitch in the army.

They spent the early years of their marriage dragging their books and LPs and two small children from campus to campus as they chased a variety of low-grade college and university jobs up and down the East Coast, buying furniture and clothes from thrift stores, clipping coupons from newspapers, driving third- or fourth-hand vehicles to stretch their minuscule income. After ten years of this nomadic existence they settled in Portland, where June won tenure at the university and Sam held down all kinds of odd jobs, from running a jazz café to helping organize the move of Howard Hughes's Spruce Goose from Long Beach to Portland's Evergreen Aviation Museum, while slowly restoring their tumbledown Victorian house in Laurelhurst, a couple of blocks from the park. He taught himself carpentry, learned by trial and error how to put in wiring and plumbing. A couple of years ago he'd used money left him by his father to buy a plot of land in a lovely, lonely spot in the Columbia River Gorge, and had started to build a house he'd designed himself. That was where he had suffered the massive heart attack that had killed him, last August.

Summer told Denise Childers, 'How I joined the police wasn't exactly straightforward. First of all, I dropped out of university. I lasted just six months – I discovered that I just didn't want to do any more school work, I'd split up with my high-school sweetheart . . .'

'I married mine. Big mistake – we were divorced inside of a year.'

'He's the father of your daughter?'

'No, I met Becca's father a couple of years after my first divorce. This was in Seattle. I was born here in Cedar Falls, but my family moved to Seattle when I was a little kid. My second husband was a car salesman. I wanted to replace my junker, and ended up marrying him instead. We muddled along for a few years, there was a pretty good patch after Becca was born, but then one day, out of the clear blue proverbial, he upped and left for Alaska. Turned out he hated selling cars, he really wanted to be a lumberjack. We got a divorce a few years back so he could marry some Russian girl off the Internet, I could care less. At least he pays regular maintenance for Becca: there's good money to be earned felling trees up in Alaska, and no tax to pay on it. So you dropped out of university, but how come you joined the police?'

'I spent a few months working as an au pair in England, did some volunteer work in a homeless shelter in San Francisco, and ended up back in Portland, working for a charity that helps street kids. I dated one of the detectives in the Runaway Juvenile Unit for a couple of months, went on a ride-along one day, and that was it, I knew that I wanted to give the police a try. So I went back to college and took a psychology degree, and here I am.'

'I got into police work by a roundabout route too,' Denise said. 'I had to find a job after my second husband left me, so I became a traffic warden. One of my friends put me on to it. It wasn't a great job, especially in winter, but it paid the bills. Then my father retired, and he and my mother moved back here to start a bed-and-breakfast business. I was visiting them one time and saw an ad in the local paper about the police exam. I took it, I passed, I moved here. I was a deputy ten years before I made detective. The pay's not all it should be, but my daughter has her own pony, and she can walk home from school without me having to worry that some pervert will snatch her or try to sell her drugs. Not that we don't have our share of problems.'

Denise told Summer that although there were plenty of well-off people who had retired to the county or owned second homes there, and Cedar Falls made good money from the timber and tourist trades, there was a good deal of poverty in the rural sections. There were plenty of homeless kids surfing friends' couches and floors; some even camped out in the woods. There was friction between the local chapter of Hell's Angels and homegrown gangbangers. There had always been a problem with marijuana farmers using plots hidden in the forests – the

DEA and Customs had permanent offices in the Justice Building – and now, as in Portland, there was a full-blown crisis over crystal meth. A super-lab in an old farmhouse a few miles north of Cedar Falls had been busted just last month, the fourth that year. Meanwhile, bad guys travelling along the I-5 on their way to somewhere else regularly hit gas stations, motels, fast-food joints and convenience stores; every Thanksgiving and New Year's Day there was a rash of suicides in motel rooms or local beauty spots; and the detective squad worked a dozen or so home-grown murders a year.

'Mostly domestic, but sometimes not,' Denise said. 'Last year, for instance, there was a double homicide and a siege that lasted twelve hours – a couple of teenagers took hostages after a passing patrol car spotted them attempting to stick up a supermarket.'

'So this place isn't a Norman Rockwell painting.'

'Not exactly. Don't judge us by Sheriff Worden.'

'I guess you heard I talked to him.'

Denise brushed back a wing of her hair with the back of her wrist and took a sip of her Martini. 'The sheriff is old-fashioned police, a pillar of the community. We have a local newspaper comes out every week. Most weeks you can find a picture of him on page two, schmoozing with some celebrity visiting the town, and he'll probably be on page five or six too, in black tie at some charity ball or picnic. Last year he used Homeland Security money to put in CCTV along Main Street and metal-detectors in the local high school. He's good at politics, which counts for a lot here, but a real live case like this sends him into a spin. Did you catch him on the TV news, explaining that the Sheriff's office had moved swiftly to deliver justice, and all was well?'

'He more or less gift-wrapped Joe Kronenwetter for the press, didn't he?'

'He surely did.'

Summer waited, certain that they were getting around to what Denise really wanted to talk about.

The woman took another sip of her Martini and said, 'How

the case started, I was the primary because I caught the fisher-men's nine-eleven. I took along a young guy name of Jay Sexton. We reached the scene a couple of minutes behind the paramedics. They had Edie Collier on a stretcher they'd humped all the way through the woods. She was wrapped in one of those thermal blankets, and they were putting a drip in her arm. She was awake, but she was going into shock. She kept saying that she felt like she was falling, and the paramedics kept yelling at her to stay with them. In the middle of all this, I managed to ask her what had happened, but all she said was, "Where's Billy?" I was holding her hand when she said that, and she looked right into my face.'

There was a brief silence. Denise Childers had developed a thousand-yard stare; Summer knew that she was remembering the scene.

Denise said, 'At some point Edie had taken a heavy fall. She'd broken her left wrist and banged up her head; it turned out she was bleeding inside her skull, what they call an epidural bleed that was causing pressure on her brain. The paramedics did their best by her, got her out of there as quick as they could in the air ambulance, but she died before they could get her to hospital.'

Another silence. Summer and Denise sipped their Martinis.

At last Denise said, 'Well, we found out who she was after we ran her prints through AFIS. We pulled her sheet off NCIC and talked to her probation agent, found she'd missed an appoint-ment Friday and that she'd last been seen at the place she worked Thursday.'

Summer said, 'So she was kidnapped some time after she left work early Thursday evening.'

Denise nodded. 'And was held somewhere before she man-aged to escape. How Jerry got involved – as soon as we realized that Edie must have been kept prisoner somewhere we started canvassing everyone in the area. Jerry busted Joe Kronenwetter on some bullshit charge, and then we got an anonymous tip that led us to the stuff in Kronenwetter's cellar.'

'He told me all about it.'

'I bet he did. Anyhow, I was still primary, but Joe

Kronenwetter was Jerry's collar, so we ended up working the case together.'

Summer said, trying to move things along, 'Jerry Hill got lucky, you think Kronenwetter is guilty, so why are we here? Not that I don't appreciate the hospitality.'

Denise said, 'Did you see the interview with Kronenwetter?'

'Part of it. Is that a regular thing here, showing interviews on TV to whoever wants to watch?'

'It's Sheriff Worden's idea. He thinks it encourages the good old team spirit.' Denise looked straight at Summer, a frank open gaze. 'Brutal, wasn't it?'

'I guess Jerry Hill isn't what you'd call subtle.'

'Jerry's the cartoon version of a hard-living, hard-drinking cop. Forty years old, three broken marriages, any number of girlfriends. The guys call him Slick, he likes that a lot. He's a practical joker, mostly harmless stuff like filling the car of a newly married couple with inflated condoms, that kind of thing. And he has a reputation for getting into scrapes, has a whole bunch of war stories he likes to tell after a few beers. He nearly got busted last year, after he was caught screwing the wife of a tourist who'd been put in a coma after a couple of the local yahoos beat up on him. Jerry and the woman were going at it in the linen closet . . .'

Denise gave Summer a wry smile, eyebrows raised. Both women laughed.

'Put Jerry in a room with a high-school kid with a bad atti-tude,' Denise said, 'he'll get the kid to confess in a couple of minutes. Joe Kronenwetter, though, is in a pretty fragile state. He moved back here after he was discharged from the army because of mental-health problems − the psychologist who examined him at the county jail believes that he's a borderline schizophrenic. I told Jerry that we should be patient, draw him out . . .'

Summer waited, knowing that Denise was trying to find a way of saying what she wanted to say without bad-mouthing a colleague.

'Here's the thing,' Denise said. 'Jerry is convinced that Joe

Kronenwetter kidnapped Edie Collier. Sheriff Worden and the District Attorney agree with him. It's a nice, simple story, a clean bust, another chapter in the legend of Jerry Hill. But I have to confess that I have problems with it. Kronenwetter is a loner with a reputation for eccentric behaviour, and while he's been in trouble with the law a bunch of times, it's mostly been for harmless stuff. There have been complaints from his neighbours about use of intimidating language and his habit of sneaking around their places and rooting through their garbage. Marijuana plants were found on his land a couple of times, but he denied all knowledge of them and charges were dropped. Also, he's a known poacher. He's paid several fines for trespassing, and he lost his hunting licence a few years back after he pled guilty to shooting a deer out of season. Then he posted notices all around the boundary of his property last year, warning that he'd mined the place. Of course he hadn't done any such thing, and he would have been let off with a warning if he hadn't gotten into an altercation with the deputies who took the notices down. He got a fine and two weeks in jail, that's as bad as it got until now.'

'The man's definitely troubled, but kidnapping a girl would be a big step up for him.'

Denise nodded. 'What I think, he may have been keeping the girl in his cellar, but it wasn't his idea to put her there. Either he had help kidnapping her, or he was looking after her as a favour for someone else. Let's get past the tip-off, the question of how the anonymous caller knew Edie Collier's stuff was down there in that cellar. Also, let's get past the question of why Joe Kronenwetter was keeping her down there in the first place. Bottom line, I still don't know if she was snatched locally, or if it was in Portland or somewhere else in between.'

Summer remembered Jerry Hill smiling up at the video camera as he told Kronenwetter his version of how Edie Collier's kidnap might have gone down.

She said, 'My first thought is that she must have been snatched in Portland. She was on probation, she had a boyfriend and a steady job, it looked like she was trying to get her life in some kind of order. According to her stepfather, she had no reason to come out here.'

'That was my first thought too,' Denise said. 'Trouble is, Joe Kronenwetter hasn't been outside of the county since he quit the army and moved back. And his truck is held together with baling wire and spit – I don't think it would have survived a round trip to Eugene, let alone Portland. So either he snatched her all by himself, which means that it probably happened here, or else someone snatched her in Portland, brought her here, and asked him to look after her. Maybe this so-called monster he mentioned. Someone he's too frightened of to give up to us.'

Summer said, wondering where this was going, 'But you have no idea who this so-called monster could be, or why he snatched Edie in the first place.'

'There are a bunch of unanswered questions. For instance, there's the question of how Edie ended up where she was found. It's a long way from Kronenwetter's cabin, no way she could have made it there by herself. She must have been taken there, or somewhere nearby, but why? And how did she get so busted up?'

'You have good evidence that she was being kept in Kronenwetter's cellar, but no idea how she got there, or how she ended up in the woods.'

'Our new public defender is a young guy eager to make his mark. He'll be all over this case, and I'm not looking forward to taking the stand and having to explain that I don't know the answers to most of his questions. He'll be defending your Mr Farrell tomorrow, by the way, I should have mentioned that up front. Stop by the court before the session begins tomorrow, around ten, and I'll introduce you. Mark Kirkpatrick. He's from old money, but he's basically one of the good guys.'

'I'd like that.'

Summer briefly considered asking Denise if she had any idea why Jerry Hill had gone to so much trouble to set up the confrontation between Randy Farrell and Joseph Kronenwetter, but decided that it wasn't the right time.

Denise said, 'You can bet that Mark will pick at every one of those holes. Especially how Joe Kronenwetter could have gotten hold of Edie Collier in the first place. I was wondering whether this boyfriend of hers might know something about it.'

Summer smiled. 'I was wondering about him myself.'

'When we talked last night, on the phone, you said you'd be willing to help out.'

'I'm still willing.'

'That's good, because I have a couple of favours to ask,' Denise said. 'First off, I'd like to take you up on your offer of finding out whatever you can about this boyfriend, this Billy no-last-name. What he does, who he associates with . . . You know, the usual stuff. If you could track him down and bring him here, I'd love to sit with him and have a long talk about Edie Collier.'

'Is this an official favour?'

'If you mean, am I going to get Sheriff Worden to ask your boss if he can give you some time and resources to chase up any leads, then no, it isn't exactly official. As far as the sheriff's concerned, the case is down. Nothing to see, time to move on. Otherwise I'd go up to Portland myself.'

'I guess I can talk to Edie's probation agent when I get back, and ask around at the place where she worked. But I'll have to clear it with my sergeant first, and he's already pissed because I'm taking an extra day down here.'

'If it's going to cause problems . . .'

'I'll find a way around it,' Summer said. 'I have my own reasons for wanting to help out.'

Denise smiled. 'Jerry and his little practical joke being one of them, I bet.'

Summer smiled too, relieved that Denise had brought it up. 'If you mean the dust-up between Randy Farrell and Joseph Kronenwetter, then yes.'

'You probably don't know it, but Jerry is good friends with the TV reporter who just happened to be there when your Mr Farrell and Joe Kronenwetter pitched up at the same time. Right now he's probably telling his buddies down at the Hanging Drop, the cop bar, all about it.'

'I already had a pretty good idea that he'd set it up,' Summer said, and explained about the phone calls Jerry Hill had made at the morgue, his beeper going off on the way back to the Sheriff's office. 'It isn't just about that, though. I want to do right by Edie Collier, and I think there's a lot more to what happened than your sheriff wants to believe.'

Denise said, with a sad smile, 'It's a real heartbreaker, all right.'

There was a silence. Summer saw Edie Collier's face plain, her serene indifferent calm, and knew that Denise was seeing her too.

Summer said, 'You said you had a couple of favours to ask. If finding Edie Collier's boyfriend is one, what's the other?'

'I'm going to visit someone who might shed some light on the nature of Joe Kronenwetter's monster, and the question of why Edie Collier ended up where she did. I was wondering if you wanted to come along.'

9

Dirk Merrit was sitting at his big desk in the library, his white, angular face steeped in the glow of the computer's flat screen, his right hand twitching a cordless mouse as he scrolled across a set of architectural plans. On the other side of the dark room, the plasma TV and the bank of smaller screens around it were all showing the same looped clip, sound muted, taken from the local TV station's evening news: a wasted-looking fellow in black lunging at a much bigger man in an orange jumpsuit, the picture jolting as the camera was caught in the mêlée, showing a confusion of feet, a blur of indistinct motion, settling on a woman in a grey pants suit throwing the man in black against the side of a police cruiser, pinning him there while a sheriff's deputy hand-cuffed him. Each time the clip jumped back to its beginning, light and shadow swung across the walls like a flock of birds turning on the wing.

Carl Kelley, walking across the room through television light, knew that Dirk Merrit could hear the ticking of his combat boots on the poured-concrete floor, but the man waited a full minute before dismissing with a click of the mouse the plans he had been scrutinizing – the plans for the mansion – and swinging around in his chair. After Carl had explained that he'd overhauled and fuelled up the RV, and packed the ultralight into its trailer, that everything was good to go, Dirk Merrit said, 'Tomorrow, at dawn.'

'It's your party.'

'I have the feeling that you're still angry because I choose to honour the sacrifice rather than give in to expediency.'

Carl didn't want to get into that again. 'How's he doing?'

'He's angry, too,' Dirk Merrit said. 'He threw his dinner at the wall and stood there in the dark with his fists raised. I believe he was hoping to get into a fight. He's a feisty boy, Carl. We're going to have a lot of fun together.'

'The quiet ones usually run better.'

'We'll see.' Dirk Merrit gestured at the rack of TVs. 'Do you know what that's all about?'

'I imagine the big bloke in orange is the one we framed.'

'Looks suitably crazy, doesn't he?'

Carl shrugged.

'I do hope you'll be over your sulk tomorrow,' Dirk Merrit said. He sounded amused.

'I just came up to report that everything is ready. If there's nothing else, I'd like to turn in, seeing as how we have an early start.'

'The fellow in black, he's the girl's stepfather. The woman, there . . .' Dirk Merrit turned back to his computer, moved the mouse to the menu bar at the bottom of the computer screen, clicked on an icon. Across the room, the action froze on the TVs. 'She's a detective from the Portland Police Bureau. Do you think it signifies anything?'

'She probably brought the stepfather here to ID the girl's body.'

'I think so too.' Dirk Merrit clicked the mouse again and the sequence ran on, the detective shoving the stepfather against the side of the cruiser and pinning his arms while a sheriff's deputy handcuffed him. Dirk Merrit saying, 'She's rather feisty too, don't you think? I bet I could have a lot of fun with her, in the right circumstances.'

Carl didn't say anything. When the man was in this kind of mood, nothing you said to him would make any difference.

'There's another clip I can't be bothered to show you,' Dirk Merrit said, lounging back in his chair, touching his smile with his steepled fingers. Each finger was tipped with a black claw shaped like a rose thorn. 'Sheriff Worden pouring oil across the shallow waters of his troubled little pond, telling the world all about Mr Joseph Kronenwetter. Everything has worked out very well, don't you think?'

'You've been lucky so far,' Carl said. 'But the police could still turn up something, or realize they got the wrong man.'

'Mmmm. As a matter of fact, Denise Childers, the detective who came here a couple of days ago is paying me another visit tonight,' Dirk Merrit said, smiling at Carl. 'Oh, but I forgot. You weren't around.'

Carl stepped on a flutter of alarm. 'What does she want?'

'I don't know.'

'You didn't ask?'

'It didn't seem like a good idea to show interest.'

'Christ. Well, what did she want when she came here the first time?'

'She asked me a few questions about the poor girl who died so tragically in such mysterious circumstances. Nothing specific, the police were making calls on everyone in the area, they hadn't yet received the phone call that led them to Mr Joseph Kronenwetter. I told her I knew nothing, and she went away.'

'Christ,' Carl said again. 'And now she's coming back.'

Dirk Merrit's smile grew. 'She'll be here in fifteen minutes. What do you think I should say to her this time?'

As they drove along a winding two-lane blacktop, giant Douglas firs rising into the darkness on either side, Denise Childers told Summer about Dirk Merrit, the history of his family.

Dirk Merrit owned a ten-thousand-acre parcel of land originally purchased by his great-grandfather, Alfred Merrit, in 1908. Alfred Merrit, owner of the biggest timber mill in Macabee County and one of its richest men, had dammed the small river that ran through his new property to create a lake, and had built a rustic-style camping lodge beside the lake where his family spent two months each summer. After Alfred's death in 1932, his oldest son proceeded to squander the profits of the timber business and run it into the ground, but his youngest son, John, who had inherited the parcel of land, proved to have better business sense. He demolished the summer house and built in its place a lodge whose fishing and hunting amenities and scenic walks and rides soon attracted the rich and famous from all over the West

Coast. The lodge burned down in mysterious circumstances in 1955 – it was rumoured that the fire had been started by John Merrit's daughter, who was committed to an asylum soon after-wards – and although it had been quickly rebuilt it no longer attracted the fashionable set. By 1971, when Dirk Merrit had been born, the lodge was hemmed in by tourist cabins, two campgrounds, and a park for motor homes. Powerboats thrashed up and down the lake where once movie stars and sports stars had fished for rainbow trout.

Dirk Merrit inherited the place after his parents died in a motor accident in the early days of the new millennium, just after he invested the money he'd made during the West Coast's information-technology boom in the development of an online computer game, *Trans*. He closed down the lodge, its camp-grounds and RV park, and began to build a home that was a faithful recreation of one of the keeps in which the rulers of *Trans*'s post-apocalyptic fantasy, the overlords, lived. And at the same time he began to rebuild himself.

'He's had more plastic surgery than the Bride of Wilderstein,' Denise said. 'He's trying his best to become one of his game's overlords – about all he lacks are the wings. Whenever he's asked about that he always says the same thing, that he'll get a pair of wings as soon as someone figures out how to do it, and mean-while if he wants to fly he'll use a plane like everyone else. He used to be on chat shows all the time, talking about the future and immortality and supermen. I can't believe that you haven't heard of him.'

Summer had been brought up in a household that didn't own a television. She'd never been able to understand how Jeff, her lawyer guy, could spend an entire Sunday evening zoned out in front of the mulch that passed for entertainment on the boob tube. It was like switching off the oxygen supply to your brain.

She said, 'I'm not a big fan of chat shows. So he's rich, he's weird . . .'

Denise said, 'He used to be rich, but he's had some serious money trouble recently. Also, he was at the edge of an unsolved double murder in Los Angeles a couple of years ago. The victims were Don Beebe, the guy who helped design the computer game, and Beebe's wife.'

'Merrit was a witness, a suspect – what?'

'He was interviewed, but he was never in the frame. Don Beebe's body was found in a rented apartment with all kinds of gay porn, leather gear . . . The detectives working the case favoured the idea that Beebe picked up a male prostitute who killed him and stole his car, drove to his house to burglarize it, and killed Beebe's wife when she caught him in the act. But they never picked up anyone for it, the case is still open, and it happened just after Dirk Merrit had been forced to sell his controlling interest in the game he and Beebe designed together. I know what you're thinking,' Denise said, 'it's just one of those things, a coincidence, nothing more. But here are a few more coincidences. First, Edie Collier was found just a couple of miles from the southern edge of Merrit's estate, beside a creek that runs back into it. If she had been following that creek downstream, the way people often do when they're trying to find a way through the forest, she could have started out from somewhere on Merrit's land. Second, back when Merrit and Joe Kronenwetter were at high school together, Kronenwetter worked two summers at the resort run by Merrit's parents. And third, remember I told you Kronenwetter had a record of trespassing and poaching? It turns out that one of the people who made a complaint against him was Dirk Merrit. Also, and I know this sounds like nothing, but still, Joe Kronenwetter was raving about monsters when we had him in the box, and after all his plastic surgery Merrit looks like something that's just stepped off a UFO.'

'If you think that Merrit has something to do with what happened to Edie Collier, should we be talking to him right now?'

Summer knew that in most investigations the suspect was the last person you interviewed. You talked to witnesses and friends of the victim, you assembled evidence and chased leads, you thoroughly checked your suspect's background and did all you could to strengthen your case, and only when everything was in place did you invite him into the unfamiliar and intimidating surroundings of a precinct building for a friendly little talk. Not only was Denise's case so weak it almost wasn't there, she was bringing it to the man instead of bringing him in, and Summer couldn't help wondering if she had some kind of personal grudge against him.

Denise said, 'Some cases don't fit established and accepted practice. Sometimes you have to push the envelope. Besides, as far as Merrit is concerned, we've arrested and charged Joseph Kronenwetter for the kidnap and unlawful death of Edie Collier. It's all over the TV news. So why wouldn't he want to talk to us, help clear up a couple of loose ends?'

Summer smiled. 'You want to stir things up a little, see what happens.'

'I want to make absolutely sure that the right person goes down for what happened to that girl. Don't you?'

'That's why I'm here.'

'Good. Now, how I think we should play this, we'll tell Merrit we're doing a follow-up on Joe Kronenwetter's arrest, ask if he minds answering a few questions for background information, and we'll see what he has to say.'

'He's bound to ask me why I'm here. How much should I tell him?'

'Go along with whatever he says, see where it leads.'

'Hope he trips himself up.'

'The thing is, the man likes to talk. Two days ago, before we had the phone call about Joe Kronenwetter's cellar, we were canvassing everyone in the area. Mr Merrit and me, we had an interesting conversation about the possibility that someone could have been chasing Edie Collier through the forest. He told me I should watch this movie, *The Most Dangerous Game*. I looked it up – it's about a crazy millionaire who hunts people through the jungle. Maybe it doesn't signify. The man likes to drop hints, play head games, let on that he knows more than he's saying. But it's one of the things I want to follow up.'

'So he's one of those guys who thinks he's smarter than the police.'

'Uh-uh. This guy, he thinks he's smarter than *everyone*.'

There was a steel-bar gate across the main entrance to Dirk Merrit's estate, the gate and the high fieldstone walls on either side of it lit by floodlights on tall poles. Denise buzzed down the window of her car, leaned out and pressed the button of the intercom that sat on a post, gave her name to the person who answered and said that she had an appointment with Mr Merrit. The gate drew back and Denise and Summer drove through, stopping at a pole barrier a little way beyond. A man in a rent-a-guard uniform examined their badges, then handed them black plastic bracelets and started to explain that they must be worn at all times, that they gave only limited access to the mansion . . .

'You gave the exact same speech when I was here the last time,' Denise said. 'How about just letting us through?'

'Mr Merrit told me to tell you he's in the trophy room. It's on the ground floor of the big tower,' the guard said, and lifted the pole.

Denise and Summer drove down a road that switchbacked between trees and outcrops of rock, a sharp bend suddenly revealing a narrow valley blocked by a tall wedge of white concrete, stark in the floodlights burning along its top. Straight ahead, halfway up the side of the valley, was a broad shelf where three towers stood, also floodlit.

Denise said, 'That's the dam, and that's Merrit's house – if you can call it a house.'

It was like a fairy-tale castle, Summer thought, or a trio of old-fashioned rocket ships. The tallest tower was easily a hundred and fifty feet high, with a little glass dome glinting at the top – yeah, just like a spaceship. The other two towers were shorter; one looked half finished, ending in an uneven crown of rebar. Arrow-slits and round windows shone at different heights in their smooth tan walls.

Denise parked her Jeep Cherokee behind a black Mercedes

SUV at the foot of the tallest tower. She and Summer got out and buckled their bracelets to their wrists. It was very quiet. A steep wooded slope rose on their left towards the black sky. The other two towers were spotlit beyond rocks and stands of bamboo. Although Summer was amused by the obvious theatricality of this spooky setting, she felt a tickle of apprehension as she followed Denise to the smooth flank of the tower, where a castle door swung open silently, a touch straight out of some dumb horror movie. The foyer, pinched between a pair of curving staircases and lit by the lurid flicker of a cluster of TV sets that hung overhead like a chandelier, narrowed to a big steel door that, like the castle door, swung open when Denise and Summer walked towards it, revealing a large room with leather couches and armchairs grouped around an open fireplace in the centre. There were all kinds of objects in niches and behind glass in the adobe walls, clusters of animal heads hung above them, and a tall man stood on the far side, his back to Summer and Denise as he studied or pretended to study a flat-screen TV that was showing some kind of cartoon, a *Mad Max*-style warrior jogging along a ruined street towards a cluster of broken skyscrapers.

The man's hands were clasped behind him, dead white against the green silk of his robe – no, it was a kimono, Summer realized, that big red target on the back was a chrysanthemum. The tall collar of the kimono was turned up so that she couldn't see his head; its hem ended just above his knees. His shanks were as pale as his hands, and as hairless as a mannequin's.

He kept his back to Summer and Denise as they approached. 'Detective Childers, so nice to see you again,' he said. 'Congratulations on the arrest, by the way. It's good to know that our police are so efficient. Or should I say so lucky?'

His voice was a light baritone, as engaging as a chat-show host's.

'It was a little of both,' Denise said. 'This is—'

'Detective Summer Ziegler of the Portland Police Bureau,' Dirk Merrit said, and turned in a sudden flare of green silk.

Summer's first thought was that it was a cheesy move that he must have practised a lot. Her second was that he was wearing a mask. Then he smiled at her, and it was as if a red wound had opened in his stiff white face.

'You're visiting Cedar Falls with the poor dead girl's stepfather. I hope his very public scrap didn't get you into trouble.'

'It's nothing I can't handle.'

Merrit's face was all planes and sharp angles, like a skull that had been shattered and reassembled in slightly the wrong way, or a Pharaoh's mummy brought to life. Skin stretched dead white over his ridged brow, his high cheekbones. His smile was full of teeth filed to points. His eyes were red: pupils like drops of blood. All this framed by the green silk of his upturned collar.

'You've been following the case, Mr Merrit,' Denise said. 'Any particular reason?'

Dirk Merrit ignored her, smiling at Summer, saying, 'This is my trophy room. Souvenirs of happy times, my favourite weapons. I thought you might be interested in seeing it.'

Summer said, 'You have a lot of animal heads. Did you kill them all?'

She found that she was able to look at him. It actually wasn't too bad, not like looking at the victim of an automobile accident or a fire, at something you felt could happen to you if you were unlucky enough. It helped to think that he had done it to himself, like one of those old-time freak-show acts. She wondered if she should ask him about his missing wings.

'Of course I killed them myself,' he said. 'Mostly right here on my property, although I have to admit I went off-piste for a few rarities, like the cougar over there.'

Dirk Merrit pointed across the room. He had black nails – no, they were more like claws.

'I shot him on a permit in Fremont National Forest three years ago. I found a freshly killed deer, and knew he would return to it, so I built a treestand and waited. I had to wait all night and most of the next morning, through a fresh snowfall. But he came back and I took my shot and hit him squarely in the chest. It killed him at once.'

Summer played along. 'You must like hunting very much, sir.'

'We are all of us descended from hunters, Detective Ziegler. It's part of our nature. The ill-mannered, ignorant and plain stupid try to legislate it out of existence, but they'll never succeed. You may as well attempt to legislate against love, or hate.'

'I see you have some zebra-skin rugs.'

'The rugs are souvenirs of a safari in Africa. I'm thinking of going back, actually. There's a place in Namibia where you can hunt any big-game animal you desire. Lions, tigers, rhinoceroses, gorillas . . .'

'Tigers in Africa?'

'Oh, they import all kinds of animals. You can stalk them through the bush using whichever weapon you favour. I favour a crossbow for big game. What weapon do *you* favour, Detective Ziegler?'

Summer said, 'I'm not a hunter, but isn't a crossbow an unusual choice of weapon?'

'It's a very pure form of hunting – you only get the chance of one shot, so you must make absolutely sure that it is the kill-shot. You say you are not a hunter, but isn't that why you are here?'

Dirk Merrit was amused, and seemed to believe that he was in complete control.

Summer said, 'Maybe you could show me the crossbow. The one you used to kill the cougar.'

Both Denise and Dirk Merrit looked at her. Then the man turned and walked around the central fireplace to a set of tall glass-fronted cabinets. He opened a door, lifted out a crossbow, and carried it back to where Summer and Denise stood. It was bigger than Summer had expected, modern and very definitely lethal, with a pistol grip and a skeletal stock. Dirk Merrit rested it on his forearm, explained that the bow part was called the prod and the prod was attached to the table or deck, that both the prod and the deck were made out of carbon-fibre composite, the weapon had a draw weight of one hundred fifty pounds and loosed a twenty-inch arrow at a velocity of two hundred feet per second.

'You can attach a telescopic sight, but I never use one. The lethal range is less than a hundred yards, and I prefer to get as close as possible. I admit to being something of a purist. For instance, I use a goatsfoot lever rather than a powered winder to draw the string.'

Dirk Merrit explained that the arrow generally killed someone not by shock but by massive haemorrhage, so it was necessary for the marksman to have a good working knowledge of the anatomy of his prey, and to be able to think in three dimensions when placing his shot.

'You might say that it is not so much a shot as a lethal incision.'

Summer said, 'Some*one*?'

Dirk Merrit stared at her and she stared right back. The air between them seemed to hum. On the TV behind him, the *Mad Max* warrior was hacking his way through tangles of creepers that were more or less the same colour as Dirk Merrit's bloodcapped eyes.

Summer said, 'You said "some*one*", not "some*thing*".'

'Mmmm. Did you know that it's forbidden by Papal edict to use the crossbow against Christians?'

'Are you saying that you only shoot Muslims, Mr Merrit?'

'If I did, I'd hardly be likely to tell you, would I? Even in the current political climate.'

His smile was back in place, but he seemed wary now, no longer quite the master of his domain.

Denise said, 'Maybe you can tell me if you've been hunting anything recently.'

'As a matter of fact, I'm in the middle of planning a little trip. That's why, regretfully, I can't spare you as much time as I would like.'

'Why we're here,' Denise said, 'we'd like to ask you a couple of questions about Joseph Kronenwetter. You know who I'm talking about?'

'Of course. He was the poor crazy person who kidnapped the girl who so unfortunately died. He was on the TV news just now,' Dirk Merrit said, smiling at Summer. 'As were you, Detective Ziegler. From the way you threw that fellow against the van, you're stronger than you look.'

Denise said, 'We need to check up on a few things, talk to people who knew him. It's purely routine, filling in his background and so on.'

'Unfortunately, I can't say that I really knew him at all.'

'You were at high school together.'

'I was at high school with a lot of people. Mmmm, but I do remember that he was some kind of sporting hero. Personally, I wasn't interested in that kind of thing. I was thinking about the long term, even then. High-school sporting heroes enjoy a few minutes' fame, but after that it's a long slide into obscurity. At best they end up as car salesmen or cops. At worst, alcoholics or drug addicts or murderers.'

'Also, I believe that Kronenwetter worked here when this used to be a resort – eighteen, nineteen years ago.'

Dirk Merrit shrugged inside his kimono. 'A lot of people worked in the old resort, Detective Childers. During your last visit, in fact, you told me that your parents worked here.'

'Yes, they did, back in 1963. Joe Kronenwetter worked here much more recently, the summers of 1987 and 1988. I was hoping you might remember him, since you're both the same age, and went to the same school. You didn't ever hang out together?'

'I didn't "hang out" with the help, Detective Childers.'

'Maybe I could show you a photograph of Mr Kronenwetter, refresh your memory.'

'As I said, I saw the man on TV. I must say, he looked the part . . . Do you think he abused the girl sexually?'

'Why are you interested in what he did to the girl?'

'Well, he'd been keeping her in that squalid shack of his, and she was naked when she was found.'

Denise looked at Summer and said, 'I don't know about you, but in my experience, I get a man in the box, I'm interviewing him, and he starts coming on to me, making sly remarks, commenting on the way I look? He's either a rapist or some kind of pathetic peeper or weenie-wagger.'

Dirk Merrit was still smiling, but not as much. It was hard to read the stiff mask of his face, but Summer thought that he was putting an effort into his smile now, trying to maintain his composure while thinking of a smart comeback.

After a moment, he said, 'I suppose that as detectives you must try to keep a professional detachment. But you're also women, and a crime like this . . . well, it must be especially upsetting.'

Denise said, 'Do you have a special interest in rape or sexual abuse, Mr Merrit?'

'We're talking about this poor girl, aren't we?'

'You brought up the topic of sexual abuse, Mr Merrit. I'm wondering why.'

'Idle curiosity.' His smile was coming back. 'My particular interests are on a somewhat higher plane.'

'Such as? If you don't mind sharing them with me and Detective Ziegler, that is.'

'Oh, such as immortality. Did you ever stop to think that there are people alive today who might never have to die?'

'Let me show you this photo of Joe Kronenwetter, see if it refreshes your memory,' Denise said, reaching into her purse.

'As I said, I've already seen him on TV.'

'This is from back when he was working at your parents' resort,' Denise said, pulling an eight-by-ten black and white photograph from a manila envelope, handing it to Dirk Merrit. 'That's him, on the school hockey team. He's on the far left.'

Dirk Merrit studied or pretended to study the photograph, then shook his head. 'I'm afraid it rings no bells.'

'Take another look.'

'He looks like a typical high-school jock. Not the kind of person I would count as a friend, then or now,' Dirk Merrit said, handing the photograph back to Denise.

She said, 'More recently, you filed a complaint against him for trespass.'

'Did I? I'll have to look it up. Or better still, ask my lawyers.'

'I'm surprised you don't remember. It was just eighteen months ago.'

'Every Fall I have trouble with hunters wandering onto my estate. They always claim to have missed the notices posted along the boundary of my property.'

'Mr Kronenwetter was definitely a hunter. Do you think his taste could run to hunting young women? I'm thinking of that movie you mentioned.'

'He sounds more like a poacher,' Dirk Merrit said, and turned away from Denise and Summer and clicked his sharp black nails against the TV screen. 'You see this pilgrim? *He*'s a hunter, on a quest to find treasure buried deep in the ruins of post-apocalypse Los Angeles. A hunter like you, Detective Childers, or you, Detective Ziegler.'

'I've never hunted,' Summer said.

Dirk Merrit turned towards her. 'Of course you have. You chase felons you believe to be guilty. You stalk them and you catch them and cage them. I would suppose that there is a sense of achievement in that which is similar to the satisfaction of a hunter.'

Summer gave him her best dead-eye look and said, 'I don't think we're in any way alike.'

'I think it would be quite an honour to be hunted by you, detective,' Dirk Merrit said. 'And it would be quite an honour to hunt you, too.'

'Is that a threat, sir?'

'It was intended as a compliment. Now, is there anything else you need to ask me, detectives? It's late, and I have an early start tomorrow.'

Back in the library, after the two detectives had left, Dirk Merrit told Carl Kelley, 'That went very well.'

'You gave them a show, all right. Thing is, they didn't come here to be entertained. And they didn't come here to ask a few routine questions, either.'

Carl had watched it all on CCTV, the man playing up to the two women, the women watching him with stony expressions that gave nothing away.

Dirk Merrit said, 'So why did they come here? Enlighten me.'

'They think they're onto something. Something you said, something they saw . . . And they'll be back again, too. They won't stop at this.'

Dirk Merrit shook his head. 'Joseph Kronenwetter has been arrested and charged, and in due course he will be tried and convicted. This was a last hurrah on the part of Detective Childers. If she continues to harass me, Sheriff Worden will shut her down.'

'Yeah? What about the one from Portland?'

'She was a sparky little thing, wasn't she? I meant it, by the way, about hunting her.'

'While we're on the subject of your hunts,' Carl said, pouncing on the opening, 'I reckon you should definitely think about rescheduling your spot of fun.'

'Nonsense. Everything is in place and I'm really looking forward to it.'

'The police could be watching you. If they follow us, or stop the RV for some reason, pull it over—'

'They have the man who did it, Carl. It's over.'

Dirk Merrit had to be high on something. Some potion or pill of Elias Silver's.

Carl said, 'They have the man you framed. There's a difference.'

Dirk Merrit ignored this point, saying, 'I'm really looking forward to Nevada. The first time we worked together was in Nevada, and now we're going back. It'll be like a reunion.'

Carl said, 'The first time, it was over by Wheeler Peak. The place I picked this time is nearly three hundred miles to the north and west.'

'Whatever. We'll do him tomorrow, and then you'll need to scout out somewhere new,' Dirk Merrit said, and clicked his mouse again.

Across the room, the rack of TVs flooded with red light. All of them showed the same picture: a man with an unlikely muscular build in leather harness and a kilt jogging through the levelled ruins of a city.

Dirk Merrit said, 'Remember him?'

Carl was getting a very bad feeling. 'He's the partner of your latest sacrifice. The one in Brooklyn. The one you said you weren't interested in. The one you said would give up after he was left on his own.'

'Because he was younger and more inexperienced, yes. But he has managed to reach the ruins of Los Angeles after all. He's been beaten back three times, but he is persistent and clever. He's a stayer after all. If I don't do anything, I do believe he'll reach the oracle soon. And if he has the password that gets him past the oracle, or if he can guess it, he'll be one step away from the source of those valuable trinkets Mr Hunter Smith likes to sell on eBay.'

'So put the wolves on him,' Carl said.

The wolves were a bunch of players in a Romanian click farm, paid by Dirk Merrit to defend the Los Angeles basin from intruders.

On the TV screens, the muscular man jogged past a row of dead palms. Their shrivelled fronds were etched black against a swollen red sun.

Dirk Merrit said, 'His game profile suggested that he was the junior partner. But now I've had to revise my opinion. Not just because of what he has achieved on his own: I've read the emails he exchanged with our sacrifice, too. He's a prodigy.'

'I thought you'd given up trying to crack that laptop.'

When Carl had kidnapped the latest pilgrim and his girl-friend, he'd brought the guy's laptop back too.

'It was quite a clever little bit of encryption. But, as it turns out, I'm cleverer,' Dirk Merrit said complacently. 'I read every one of this player's emails, and he's easily the equal of his partner. Which means that he's equally worthy of my attentions.'

Christ. Carl really didn't want either the distraction or the risk of setting up another hunt right now. Until he had the password that gave access to the hack in the game's subscription service, he needed to keep Dirk Merrit out of harm's way.

He said, 'You have one out of two, and since this kid is on the other side of the continent—'

'Don't worry, Carl, I'm not going to send you after him. However, I am giving some serious thought to letting him get past my wolves and then sending him a congratulatory email and an airline ticket.'

Carl felt a twinge of black lightning. 'Before I came along and started mixing things up, you did two in a row in exactly the same spot, in the Alvord Desert.'

The Alvord Desert was a flat, windy salt pan in eastern Oregon, ideal for the kind of sport that Dirk Merrit enjoyed.

'And you still give me a hard time about doing them in the same place, even though we went on to do two in California.'

'Different parts of California. And there was the one in Alaska between them.'

'Mmm.' Dirk Merrit moved his tongue around the wet red cave of his mouth, savouring the memory like a fine wine. 'I crashed, and she damn near got away. That was a *lot* of fun.'

'The point is,' Carl said, his patience almost exhausted, 'if I hadn't come along to advise you, you'd have kept using the same spot in the Alvord Desert until your luck ran out. I've been choosing random victims, and choosing different places where you can deal with them. I've been keeping you safe. And now you want to do not one but two kids who have a direct connection to you, when after what happened to that girl you should be keeping a low profile.'

'It's quite possible that he could manage to get past the wolves, and then I *would* have to do something, wouldn't I? And besides, as my dear old dead daddy used to say, a job half done is no job at all.'

10

When his mother came back from work at half past midnight, Daryl Weir was still up, still deep in *Trans*. A slender, athletic black boy who looked a lot younger than his sixteen years, he was sitting cross-legged on a corduroy beanbag in T-shirt and boxers, hands folded around his customized controller, his face about a foot from the screen of his computer. The screen was the only source of light in the small, stuffy bedroom. It showed a solidly built man in a leather kilt and a harness hung with all kinds of kit marching at a steady pace down a ruined street, cradling an AK-47 in his muscular arms.

The man in the kilt was Daryl's avatar, a fortune hunter with the handle Seeker8. Daryl was watching him from the usual player's viewpoint, a few yards behind the back of his head, and steering him with his left thumb. The street stretched away across a parched plain gridded with low ruins and overgrown with a scrub of leafless bushes and a scattering of giant cactuses with crooked arms raised in surrender against a technicolour sunset. When he heard his mother call his name through the closed door of his room, Daryl hunched a fraction of an inch closer to the screen. He really didn't need any distraction right now, not when Seeker8 was still a long way from the next save point and night was coming on fast.

The front door of the tiny apartment opened directly onto the living room, with the main bedroom and the bathroom off to the left, and the second bedroom, Daryl's, and the kitchen off to the right. As Seeker8 marched along at an unvarying pace down the middle of the street, past the rusted shells of cars, low mounds of rubble, and street lights leaning at different angles, Daryl heard through the thin plasterboard wall the solid clunk of the refrigerator opening and closing, and knew that his mother was pouring herself a glass of chocolate milk. In a moment the TV would come on; when she got back from her night work, cleaning bank offices in Manhattan, his mother liked to relax in front of the TV with a comforting drink, a White Russian or iced chocolate milk spiked with vodka, before going to bed. But instead of the sudden blare of the TV, the door behind Daryl clicked open, and his mother said, 'Sweetie, you still up?'

Daryl had once fixed a bolt on the inside of his bedroom door, but his mother had raised so much fuss he'd removed it the next day. He said without looking away from the screen, 'I'm working. Talk to you later, okay?'

His mother stepped into the room. 'Where's your friend? Didn't you have a friend along with you?'

'He ain't in the game no more.'

'You had a camel, too. It looked something like a camel, anyhow.'

'The camel died. A snake bit it.'

That had been two weeks ago, soon after Daryl and his online partner, Ratking, had worked their way through the various tests, puzzles, and mini-adventures in the dusty town that was the gateway to the desert, and set out for the treasure hidden in the ruins of Los Angeles. Ratking's avatar had been left behind six days and three save points ago. Daryl had logged on at the usual time and found Ratking's tall, leathery avatar standing there in his black duster, his sniper rifle slung over his shoulder, swaying slightly from side to side in what seemed to be an unbreakable trance. Ratking hadn't answered any of Daryl's increasingly urgent emails, and at last Daryl had sent Seeker8 to face the perils of the ruins of Los Angeles on his own. Since then, he'd made a great deal of progress towards Griffith Observatory, where the treasure was supposed to be hidden, but Ratking still hadn't come back on those emails, and Daryl was beginning to worry that his partner had pulled some kind of trick on him.

Behind him, his mother said, 'Don't be playing that too long now.'

'Mom, *please*. I have to concentrate. If I don't get to this save point by sunset, I'll have to start over.'

The avatar marched on at his even, relentless pace, slowing only at intersections, glancing left and right, marching on. Daryl was watching every part of the screen for any hint of movement, occasionally switching to a cinematic viewpoint that showed from high overhead Seeker8 trudging through the street-grid of the ruined city. All the while Daryl's thumb kept the left joystick lightly pressed forward; all the while Seeker8 marched on tirelessly. In the upper right-hand corner of the screen, read-outs showed his health and armour status; in the lower left-hand corner, a little insert showed a map of his immediate surroundings. Straight ahead, to the west, was the blinking blue square that indicated the save point; scattered around and about were red dots that indicated the presence of other players. Warewolves, all of them, the fierce, jealous guardians of this part of *Trans*.

'I don't know why you don't get him some wings,' his mother said.

'Then he wouldn't be a fortune hunter no more. He'd be an overlord.'

Daryl had explained it to her about a billion times. Overlords, the more-than-human rulers of the game's post-apocalypse world, used a combination of political strategy, single combat, and staged battles between armies of slaves to expand their territories. They could win huge fortunes and acquire all kinds of treasure, but they didn't have the flexibility of fortune hunters like Seeker8, who could form alliances with virtually any other player and roam anywhere, searching out the treasures and weapons and secret pathways that everyone in the game needed or coveted.

His mother said, 'If your man had wings he could fly himself right out of there.'

Every so often she tried to take an interest, always at the worst possible time.

Daryl said, 'There are blood bats and these monster eagles all over the place. If he tried to fly, they'd tear him to pieces. And I don't want to leave, remember? I want to find out what's hidden here.'

Twisted shapes reared up against the horizon – the wreckage of downtown Los Angeles. The next save point was under what was left of the nearest skyscraper. Daryl had to reach it before the sun set and swarms of deadly desert creatures crept out of the basements and underground car parks and sewers of the ruined city.

His mother said, 'You're chasing after this thing you think is worth so much. You think I don't remember what this is all about, but I do.'

'I don't know exactly what it is or what it's worth. But it's definitely hard to get to, so it has to be worth an awful lot,' Daryl said.

He hoped that she wasn't going to start in about getting a job after quitting school, instead of sitting here all day playing games. The last time, he'd told her that finding and selling stuff in *Trans* was a real job that made him real money, she should be grateful he wasn't slinging dope on some corner, and she'd slapped him across the face, shocking both of them. His brother, DeLeon, had been shot dead on a dope corner three years ago.

But all she said was, 'Don't stay up too late,' and drifted out. A moment later, TV voices started talking to each other in the living room.

Daryl could make out the twisted spars and struts of the ruin of the nearest skyscraper now. He nudged the joystick and his avatar began to jog, raising a waist-high trail of dust. Things that he knew were not birds circled lazily around the torn crown of the skyscraper, silhouetted against the burning wreckage of the sunset.

He leaned forward, the controller smooth and slick and hot in his hands. He was moving through a vast lattice of shadow thrown across desert scrub, dodging around heaps of tumbled masonry and thickets of brush, looking for cover. When something flickered over him, he blipped to the cinematic view and saw the black shapes of blood bats – each one big enough to carry a man to their nest of bones, where they would suck him dry – making swooping passes above Seeker8, turning around and around, dropping lower and lower with each turn. He blipped back to the back-of-the-head viewpoint, looked left and right, saw two slabs of masonry leaning against each other, making a kind of tent, and piled on speed. A blood bat hurtled towards him and he targeted it, fired a burst from the AK47, and blew it in half. Then he was off again, hurtling towards the darkness under the leaning slabs – and something smashed into him. He tumbled head over heels in a cloud of dust, and things fell on top of him. Daryl selected his knife and pistol and slashed and shot blindly, but there were too many of them, settling on him, feeding on him, and the red line of the health bar slid rapidly towards zero and the screen flashed and blanked and he was dead.

Seeker8 was dead.

His goddamn mother.

Daryl wiped his sweaty palms on his T-shirt and worked his head from side to side to unkink muscles in his neck, rolled his shoulders. He sat there for a long minute, dumb with exhaustion, his mother's TV mumbling in the living room and the thin wail of a police siren rising in the night beyond the open window, crying to itself somewhere in Brooklyn. At last he shivered and came back to himself. He reached for his mouse, fired up his web browser. Maybe Ratking had answered his latest email. Also, if he was going to do this all over again he needed to arrange to meet his good friend Bernard, tap him for a little chemical enhancement.

11

Summer set out for Joseph Kronenwetter's property early on Thursday morning, just after sunrise. She figured that it would take about twenty minutes to drive there. If she gave herself an hour to snoop around, she would still have plenty of time to get back to Cedar Falls and meet with Denise Childers and the public defender before Randy Farrell's arraignment.

Although she'd only been with the Robbery Unit for three weeks, Summer had helped to investigate enough crimes to know that usually the procedure was as straightforward as filling in the forced-choice tick boxes of a custody report form. You gathered available evidence, talked to the right people, and discovered the mistakes that, hopefully, led straight to the doer. Of course, you weren't going to solve anything but the simplest slam-dunk if you didn't have the talent, instinct, and experience to spot the telling anomaly, to riddle from the confusion of a crime scene the signature that linked a suspect to other crimes, and to work out if a witness was merely confused or was a lying son of a bitch with something to conceal. And you also needed, among other things, a grounding in forensic techniques, a working knowledge of police information databases, proficiency in writing up search and seizure warrants, and the ability to stand up in court and stay cool when the defence lawyer not only tore into your evidence but attempted to prove to the jury that you were an incompetent and almost certainly corrupt sack of shit unable to spot a clue if it fell on your head from the roof of the Mark O. Hatfield Courthouse.

But underpinning every investigation was the patient and meticulous acquisition of information, something that Summer had practised and honed in her years in uniform, writing up incident reports as the primary responding officer for every kind of crime from fender-benders to suspicious deaths. Now that she had promised to help Denise Childers, and after last night's excursion to Dirk Merrit's estate, she realized that she didn't know half as much about this case as she should, and nothing at all about its circumstances. She believed that taking a look at the place where Edie Collier had been kept prisoner would help her get up to speed, and besides, she had to admit that she was simply curious about where and how Joseph Kronenwetter lived.

She drove with her notebook wedged under her thigh, folded to the page on which Denise had written directions. The four-lane highway climbed through sharply folded foothills. Green pasture, ranch-style houses and red barns, squared-off stands of trees moulded to the contours of hilltops. Several dozen RVs in a big field bordered by live oaks. Horses grazing behind split-rail fences. The highway narrowed to two lanes, and soon afterwards Summer turned south along a county road, passing through a little community, Argyle, that was no more than a general store and a handful of houses strung along the road, crossing a steel truss bridge painted apple-green and heading into a dark, steep-sided river valley. Trees crowded along the edge of the road on the left; more trees stepped down to the river on the right. Summer lowered the Taurus's window, savoured the cool, faintly antiseptic air blowing past the car. The river, a tributary of the Umpqua, was dashed with long riffles of white water where it ran swiftly over rocks. A pair of fishermen were unloading their equipment from the back of a pickup truck parked on the shoulder of the road.

Immediately after a concrete bridge carried the road above a bend in the river, Summer turned right onto a gravel fire road and drove past a campground in the deep shade of Douglas firs and white pines. The trees thinned out as the road began to climb. Summer glimpsed fields, a scattering of small houses and trailer homes, hitting her brakes when she saw the black and white cruiser parked across the beginning of the track to Kronenwetter's place.

After Summer drew up behind the vehicle, the deputy took his time climbing out. The brim of his Smokey the Bear hat set low over his eyes, he checked Summer's badge and had her sign the Crime Scene Attendance Log fastened to his clipboard, told her to keep out of the shack because the crime-scene people were coming back to do some more work. She drove down an uneven stony track, Douglas firs rising thickly up a steep slope to her left and an orchard of gnarled and unpruned apple trees to the right. And there, beyond the orchard, was a clapboard shack with a tar-paper roof.

Perched on the stone foundations of a much larger house, the shack was surrounded by a cordon of yellow crime-scene tape strung on wooden stakes hammered into the hard dry ground. The structure had once been painted blue but most of the paint was gone, and what was left was peeling away from wood weathered silver-grey. An old-fashioned outhouse stood behind it, a half-moon cut in the rough boards of its door.

Summer stepped over the crime-scene tape and walked all the way around the shack, peering through its grimy windows but seeing only shadows, finding a trapdoor next to a stack of split logs, its bolt fastened with a padlock as big as her fist. She sat on her haunches and studied the padlock for a long minute. It was an American Standard, its chrome blistered by weather. She wondered if it was Kronenwetter's, or if the Cedar Falls police had put it there in case reporters tried to get into the cellar. She'd have to ask Denise Childers.

Beyond the shack, the track hooked past a tall mound of blackened rubble crowned with weeds. An old Ford pickup and an even older John Deere tractor were parked side by side on a stand of hard, oil-stained dirt. There was a Confederate flag sticker in a corner of the rear window of the pickup's cab. Down by the stream, a strip of ground had been levelled and ploughed. Rows of tomato plants and lettuce and string beans behind a rabbit-proof fence of nylon mesh, a tangled hedge of corn plants, a gasoline-powered water pump connected to a hose that snaked off through a thin line of ash and elder trees to a shallow creek. Beyond the trees, across a stretch of weedy pasture, a white chip gleamed in fresh morning light – the roof of a house.

Seeing this, Summer knew at once that Denise had been right about one thing. If Edie Collier had broken out of Joseph Kronenwetter's cellar, there was no good reason why she would have made her way through thick forest to a spot some ten miles away and a couple of thousand feet higher, not when she could have had headed for the neighbouring house or followed the fire road to the highway. If she'd been kept here, she must have been taken somewhere else before she escaped. Maybe Dirk Merrit's hints about hunting people weren't so fanciful after all. Maybe he knew something about Kronenwetter, and was having fun feeding it to the police bit by bit. Or maybe he and Kronenwetter were hunting buddies . . .

Summer walked back to the shack, studied the padlock again, saw something she'd missed the first time: fresh scratches on the lock plate, around the rim of the keyhole. Crouched there, with the sun warming her back and grasshoppers beginning to wake all around her, she thought about the mysterious caller who'd told the local police to check Joseph Kronenwetter's cellar, and felt a small stab of cautious pleasure, like a hunter finding a hoof print in the mud by a pool.

Joseph Kronenwetter's neighbour was a widow by the name of Rhonda Cannon, a sensible, sharp-eyed, garrulous old bird in jeans and a man's shirt. She had no objection to answering Summer's questions, telling her that she had known Joe Kronenwetter from birth, it was a darn shame he'd turned out the way he did.

'He was a nice little boy, tow-haired and cute as apple pie. He got into a few scrapes with the law when he was a teenager, but it wasn't anything serious, and he straightened up after he joined the army. His father, now, he was a drinking man. That's how they reckon the house burned down, he passed out one evening with a lit cigarette in his hand. It was just after Christmas, in the middle of a snowstorm. My husband – he was still alive then – saw a light flickering through

the falling snow, and realized the Kronenwetters' place was on
fire. It took the fire trucks more than an hour to arrive, not that
it would have made any difference if they had turned up right
away: the house was already alight from top to bottom when
my husband spotted it. It was one of the strangest sights I've
ever seen in my life, that house throwing yellow flame and black
smoke into the night and snow coming down all the while.'

'Joseph Kronenwetter was in the army at the time.'

'Yes, ma'am, getting ready for the First Iraq War. He was
given compassionate leave when his parents died in the fire,
came back for the funeral, stood straight and tall in his dress
uniform by his parents' grave, and then he went right back
to Kuwait to fight Saddam. He's the only one of his family
left. He had an older brother that died in a traffic accident, and
there's a sister who upped and went to live in Los Angeles, no
one knows if she's alive or dead. Anyhow, either the deaths of
his parents hit him hard or something happened to him in
Kuwait, but when he quit the army and came back here you
could see at once that he was a changed man. He'd never been
what you could call talkative, but when he came back he
didn't hardly care to pass the time of day. He was drinking
heavily, he grew his hair and shambled about in ragged clothes
like he was some kind of hobo, and when he did talk to you
it was most often to sound off about how people were out to
get him.'

'What kind of people?'

Rhonda Cannon looked away, shrugged. 'Oh, it was just nonsense. He said that people were hiding in the woods and
watching him, nonsense like that. I paid it no heed.'

Summer said, 'I know you don't want to speak ill of your
neighbour, ma'am. But anything you know about him could
help us understand why this happened. It might even help him.'

'I can't see how, seeing as you have him locked up.'

'It might help get him the right treatment.'

After a pause, Rhonda Cannon said, 'It really was mostly nonsense. The kind of stuff you find in those supermarket papers,
how the government and the UN are accumulating files on

everyone, secret messages in TV programmes and bar codes . . . One time he claimed that the blacks and liberal media, the universities and whatnot, were conspiring against true American values. He tried to give me a book that he said explained it all, but I told him I would appreciate it if he kept that kind of trash talk to himself, too, and he didn't bring it up again. I don't think he really believed any of it – he was just looking for something that would explain the way he felt.'

'Do you remember the title of the book?'

Rhonda Cannon shook her head. 'Like I told him, I didn't care to look at it. I guess Joe could seem threatening if you didn't know him, but if you stood up to him and told him not to be foolish he'd usually take it the right way. Not that he didn't have some demons. When he got into trouble with the police last year I hoped that jail would shock him back to his senses. And he *was* a lot quieter after he came home, but I guess it didn't take.' Rhonda Cannon paused, then looked straight at Summer and said, 'That poor girl, I hear he's been charged for her kidnap. Was she the only one, or were there others? I ask because of you coming all the way down here from Portland.'

'As far as I know, she's the only one.'

'That's something, I suppose, although what happened to her was bad enough.'

'Did Mr Kronenwetter have many visitors?'

'Not that I know of.'

'You didn't see anything unusual in the past week? Vehicles parked by his property, anything like that?'

'I was away over the weekend, visiting my sister and her family on the coast, out by Port Orford. But I don't recall seeing anything out of place before that, or after it, either. Not until all the police arrived.'

'What about two nights ago?'

'Tuesday night? No, I don't believe so.'

Summer pointed towards the line of trees at the boundary of Joseph Kronenwetter's property. 'You didn't see any lights shining over there, a vehicle, anything like that?'

'Just after Joe was arrested?' Rhonda Cannon thought about it, said, 'I don't believe so. I watched TV and fell asleep in front of it like I tend to these days, and went to bed at ten or there-abouts. If there was a disturbance, I missed it. Now *last* night, a carload of teenagers drove up the road bold as you please, but the deputy watching Joe's property sent them on their way. We had TV reporters come by here yesterday, too, but that was when the police were poking around all over the place.'

'Apart from that there's been no trouble? No other visitors?'

'Not to my knowledge.'

Summer was thanking the woman for her time when the noise of an over-revved engine made them both turn. A cherry-red Dodge Ram was speeding down the dirt track towards the house ahead of a banner of dust.

Rhonda Cannon said, 'Friend of yours?'

'Not exactly.'

Summer realized that the deputy must have called in her visit. The big pickup fishtailed to a halt, dust blowing past it, and Jerry Hill swung out of the crew cab and swaggered over, saying loudly, 'I understand you've been doing some sightseeing, Detective Ziegler.'

'I haven't compromised the scene, if that's what brought you all the way out here.'

Jerry Hill hooked down his sunglasses and stared straight at her. 'No need to worry about that any more. The case, it's *down.*'

Summer said, 'Then why are you here? Did Kronenwetter confess?'

Jerry Hill smiled. 'Way better than that. The freak hanged him-self last night.'

When Summer met with Denise Childers, in a coffee shop across the street from the County Courthouse, she got the story of Joseph Kronenwetter's suicide all over again, more or less as Jerry Hill had told it. Kronenwetter had been ranting and raving, generally making a nuisance of himself, and he had been isolated in a special cell. Guards had checked him at regular intervals. At eleven p.m. he couldn't be seen through the spyhole, and the guard had unlocked the door and found him slumped against the corner of his bed. He'd torn the leg of his jumpsuit into strips, made a noose, tied it to the bedhead, and hung himself while sitting down. And he'd left a message clumsily scratched on the wall by the bed.

I didnt mean 4 her 2 die

Jerry Hill had taken enormous pleasure in telling Summer about this death note. And all the way back to Cedar Falls his Dodge Ram had ridden the bumper of her Taurus, its wide chrome grille filling the rear-view mirror even though she had slowed several times to allow him to overtake.

'It's being treated as a dying man's confession,' Denise Childers said.

She was wearing a black skirt suit and a crisp white blouse; her sharp face was softened by lipstick, blusher, and a touch of green eyeshadow. She was, as she'd put it, going to be the eye candy standing next to Jerry Hill and Sheriff Worden while they explained why everyone could sleep safely in their beds again.

Sitting across from Denise in yesterday's underwear, her shoes dusty, grass seeds caught on the cuffs of her pants, Summer said, 'Has it changed your mind about the case?'

'Worden and the public prosecutor reckon that we don't need to take it any further. One half of me agrees with them. The guy killed himself and left that note out of genuine remorse, and that's the end of it. The other half, though, can't help thinking that he was involved in something bigger.'

'I noticed that the trapdoor to the cellar of his shack is padlocked. I was wondering if it's his padlock, or if someone put it there after he was arrested.'

'The trapdoor on the outside?'

'Yeah. I didn't go inside.'

'That one's his. And if you're wondering how Edie Collier could have escaped from a cellar locked on the outside, there's another trapdoor inside the shack. Or more likely, she got away from him when he took her someplace else for whatever reason.'

'There are scratches around the padlock's keyhole. As if some-one had used a set of picks to open it.'

Denise was very still for a moment. 'Are you sure?'

'Not one hundred per cent. But the marks are fresh, and I don't think they were made by a key.'

'So what you're saying . . . Someone could have sneaked in the night before last? Do you have any idea why?'

'Jerry Hill arrested Kronenwetter Tuesday evening, but he didn't check out his shack until the next morning.'

'That's when we got the tip-off.'

'So if someone wanted to set up Kronenwetter, they could have dumped the incriminating evidence in his cellar after he'd been arrested and locked it up again, and the next morning made that phone call, told you to go look down there.'

On the way back from Dirk Merrit's mansion last night, Summer had asked Denise if anyone had made a voiceprint from the tape of the famous anonymous phone call. 'You could com-pare it to a tape of Dirk Merrit.'

'There isn't a tape because it wasn't a nine-eleven call,' Denise had said. 'And the call didn't go to the front desk either, but to one of the phones in the office. The secretary who took it said it sounded like the British scientist. You know, the one in the wheelchair? He was on *The Simpsons*.'

'Stephen Hawking?'

'Yeah. My guess is that whoever placed the call used a vocoder or something like that to disguise his voice.'

Now, Denise thought for a moment, then smiled and said, 'What I should do is get one of the crime-scene people to check out the shack again and take a close look at that padlock. And maybe I should ask Dirk Merrit where he was and what he was doing Tuesday night, too.'

Bringing it straight back to her crazy millionaire.

Summer had worked up another scenario out at Kronenwetter's place. She wanted to run it by Denise, and said, 'I noticed a Confederate flag sticker on the back window of Kronenwetter's pickup, and his neighbour mentioned that he talked about some kind of conspiracy between African-

Americans and the liberal media. Maybe it doesn't add up to anything, but I'm wondering if he was associated with white supremacists.'

Denise's smile went away. 'What are you driving at?'

'Around Portland, quite a few of the people involved in the crystal-meth industry are either white supremacists or bikers who like to fly the Confederate flag. I know you have people cooking up crystal meth here because you told me about a super-lab that was busted last month, so I'm wondering if Kronenwetter had connections with people like that. Maybe he hooked up with them during his recent time in jail.'

'There's nothing about crystal meth in his file.'

'You also told me that marijuana plants had been found on his property.'

'A couple of times, but nothing ever came of it. As I recall, they were in clearings up in the woods – we weren't able to prove that Joe had anything to do with them. You think this could have something to do with drugs?'

'I think it's possible,' Summer said. She'd put it together while driving back to Cedar Falls. 'Suppose Edie Collier's boyfriend came here on business, looking to get a deal on marijuana or crystal meth—'

'From Joe Kronenwetter? Whatever he is, he isn't a drug dealer.'

'From friends of his. The boyfriend brings Edie with him, but the deal goes wrong somehow. Kronenwetter's friends kill the boyfriend, but Edie escapes.'

'And somehow loses her clothes in the process.'

'It's not a nice thought, but maybe they wanted to have some fun with her. The next day she's found barely alive,' Summer said. 'She tries to tell you what happened to her boyfriend, but she dies before she reaches hospital. Kronenwetter is arrested for waving a gun at Jerry Hill, and the bad guys decide to plant evidence in his cellar, put him in the frame and bring the investigation to a quick close.'

'Why does it have to be friends of Kronenwetter's?'

'It has to be someone who knows him – who knows he has a cellar.'

'I like the idea that someone planted evidence in Joe Kronenwetter's cellar, but it could just as easily have been Dirk Merrit as these hypothetical drug-dealing white supremacists of yours. Merrit denies knowing Kronenwetter, but I'm sure he does. And Kronenwetter was raving about a monster, not about drug dealers.'

'If Edie Collier was involved in some kind of drug deal, it would explain why she ended up here.'

'How she ended up here, it could be one of a million reasons,' Denise said. 'Maybe the boyfriend did come here, looking to get a good deal on some country-grown drugs. Or maybe Edie had an argument with him and decided to get out of town and hitched a lift with the wrong person. Or maybe, and this would explain that note he left, Joe Kronenwetter snatched her, and gave her up to Dirk Merrit so the man could have some fun hunting a real live human girl.'

Which was one of the ideas that Summer and Denise had talked about last night, on the way back from the interview with Dirk Merrit.

'Bottom line,' Denise said, 'we don't know enough. Until we do, we can sit here and spin all kinds of ideas, and never get any nearer the truth.'

'So I definitely need to talk to the boyfriend. If he's still around.'

'I think it would be a good idea. You try to find out what the boyfriend was into, I'll follow up on that padlock, and I'll also try to find out what Joe Kronenwetter got up to in jail last year, just in case.' Denise looked at her watch. 'But right now I gotta run – Sheriff Worden will have my hide if I miss that press conference. I'll take you over to meet Mark Kirkpatrick first. Bring that coffee along if you want.'

Summer had drunk only half her cup; she knew from experience that too much coffee before a court session would put unwanted pressure on her bladder. She pushed it away and said, 'I'm done.'

The public defender, Mark Kirkpatrick, was a tall, handsome

man not much older than Summer. He had a tennis tan, about an acre of white teeth, an expensive black suit, and the kind of easy charm and confidence that only old money can buy. Sitting next to him on a bench outside the courtroom, giving her account of Randy Farrell's attempt to assault Joseph Kronenwetter, it occurred to Summer that he was exactly the kind of lawyer her ex, Jeff Tuohy, had aspired to become.

When she'd finished telling him her story, Mark Kirkpatrick thanked her and said, 'That's very useful – it pretty much tallies with what Mr Farrell told me.'

'Did Mr Farrell tell you about his cancer?'

'I called his doctor in Portland. He faxed over an affidavit, but I'll only use it if it looks like he'll be getting a jail sentence.'

'Is that likely?'

'Not as long as he hangs his head in court and apologizes with sufficient meekness.'

'I'll be happy to testify to Mr Farrell's general good character and concern for his stepdaughter if you think it will help.'

'I hope Mr Farrell's character won't become an issue, given his extensive criminal record. What I'm going to do is have him plead guilty, and then I'll ask the judge for a word. Judge Foster is a reasonable woman, and although I feel like a heel saying this, Joseph Kronenwetter's suicide is a big plus, frankly. Everyone in town wants this nasty mess forgotten as quickly as possible, so I doubt very much that Mr Farrell will have to stand trial. He'll get a fine and a conditional discharge and you can take him home.' Mark Kirkpatrick shot his cuffs and glanced at his watch, a stainless steel Rolex, picked up his immaculate oxhide brief-case, and stood. 'Thank you for your time, detective. By the way, where are you parked?'

Summer stood too. 'Across the street.'

'I noticed a couple of reporters hanging around the front steps, so you might want to bring your car around back. The guard will show you where you can park. That way, when Mr Farrell is discharged into your care, you can get away without any embarrassing entanglements.'

The lawyer's boyish grin showed most of his even white

teeth. Summer wondered if she was supposed to swoon into his arms, then told herself to stop being mean, it wasn't his fault that he reminded her of Jeff. Who when she first met him had the thrifty habit of touching up his fraying shirt collars with correcting fluid, but could probably afford good hand-made suits of his own now that he was part of Washington D.C.'s inner circle.

She sat at the back of the wood-panelled courtroom and watched things go down pretty much as Mark Kirkpatrick had predicted. A line of shackled prisoners shuffled in, mostly wife-beaters, petty thieves and hung-over drunks, all of them wearing orange jumpsuits with 'Macabee County Correctional Facility' stencilled in black letters across their chests and backs. Randy Farrell was hunched between a wincing teenager and a dignified black man with a shaven head. When he noticed that Summer was looking at him, something hardened in his face and he looked away.

The court officer, a balding man wearing an ancient Colt in a worn leather holster under his paunch, ordered everyone to rise, and the judge appeared from a door behind the bench like a figure in a medieval clock. Randy Farrell's case was first up. Mark Kirkpatrick said that his client wished to plead guilty, and asked to approach the bench. He had a brief whispered conversation with the judge, stepped back. The judge fixed Randy Farrell with a sharp stare and told him that assault on an officer of the law was a serious matter, but given the circumstances and the recent tragic events she was minded to mitigate the sentence to a fine of five hundred dollars and a suspended sentence of a hundred days. The prosecutor made no objection, and the judge banged her gavel and moved on to the next case.

After that, everything moved with the smooth dispatch of a well-rehearsed execution. Randy Farrell was released into Summer's custody, and after he had changed into his own clothes in a restroom and paid his fine at the cashier's desk Summer drove him out of the parking lot and through Cedar Falls's one-way system to the I-5.

Although no one followed them, Summer had the feeling that a hundred years ago they would have been tarred and feathered and ridden out of town on a rail. She let Randy Farrell sit up front next to her, but he hardly said a word on the long trip back to Portland.

12

The Black Rock Desert, Nevada. The sun a fiery nail hammered high in the wide blue sky; hot wind blowing threads of alkali dust across the playa towards bare mountains rippling behind glassy layers of heat haze.

Carl Kelley was standing in a thin wedge of shade at the rear of the big RV, wearing a baseball cap, an unbuttoned denim shirt and black combat pants, sipping from a bottle of spring water, and watching with edgy and uncharacteristic impatience as Dirk Merrit's ultralight stooped and turned and climbed a couple of miles away. The buzz of the ultralight's rear-mounted prop sounded like a bee at a window, rising and falling as Merrit harried the sacrifice to and fro across the dry lake bed, taking his bloody time about it.

The RV, a Coachman Cross Country SE finished with ten coats of hand-rubbed black lacquer and customized from stem to stern, was an ideal way of transporting sacrifices to remote sites where Dirk Merrit could act out his fantasies. The sacrifice could be kept trussed and gagged on the bed in the main sleeping compartment; Dirk Merrit liked to stretch out his unlikely length on the modified recliner behind the big, comfortable driver's chair. And because people who own RVs often attach all kinds of leisure equipment to them, no one looked twice at the trail bike hung on the rear rack, or the Cumulus motor glider folded on its twenty-foot trailer.

The volume of the walkie-talkie clipped to Carl's belt was turned right down because he was tired of listening to Dirk Merrit's breathless whoops of glee, and he didn't bother to follow the action with the pair of Bushnell field glasses hung around his neck because he knew from all the other times how it would go. If the sacrifice stood its ground, Dirk Merrit would fire shots around it until it ran; when it ran, he chased it and dive-bombed it and took pot shots until it was too tired to run any more, and then he landed and dispatched it with his crossbow.

All in all, it was an expensive, complicated, and dangerous way to get your rocks off, and Carl had lost all patience with it. Also, he felt a squirt of acid in his blood every time the flimsy little aircraft swooped low. Dirk Merrit took unnecessary risks because he thought he was smarter than anyone else and was going to live for ever. Carl would be glad enough to see the back of him, but it wasn't quite time for him to die. Soon, but not quite yet.

Carl had come into Dirk Merrit's orbit a little under two years ago. He'd been working as a guide for a safari outfit in Namibia, lying low after a spot of bother in Uganda had brought him to the attention of the International War Crimes Tribunal in The Hague. The job with the safari outfit hadn't been anything much – escorting millionaires and business executives around the bush, leading them to some poor sick lion or elephant that had been bought from poachers or some dodgy zoo and doped up before it was released, so that they could dispatch it with brand-new high-powered rifles that they'd probably never use again. After only six months Carl had been ready to pack it in and move on, had been thinking of signing up under a new name with a private security outfit in Afghanistan or Iraq. Then Dirk Merrit had turned up.

He'd been so very different from the usual customer – younger, crazier, charismatic. The night after he'd dispatched an arthritic, half-blind lion, he'd asked Carl if there was any chance of some real action. Poaching, say. And so, for a flat fee of forty thousand dollars, Carl and a buddy from the good old days had taken Dirk Merrit across the border into Botswana, where they'd helped this lairy gang of poachers bag an elephant. Afterwards, Dirk Merrit had asked Carl if he'd ever heard of *The Most Dangerous Game*, later on showing him on a portable DVD player this ancient black and white film about a white hunter and girl being stalked through the jungle by a crazy millionaire until they managed to turn the tables on him. Carl had told him that the best way to do that kind of thing was to give your victim a knife and a head start, motivate him with the idea that he might escape. He'd also told him a couple of well-rehearsed stories about the fun he'd had in Uganda, thinking nothing of it: it was the kind of bullshit people traded back and forth in a bar with the right kind of company, after the right kind of fun. But two weeks later Dirk Merrit had called him from the States and offered him a job.

It had worked out pretty well, at first. Carl didn't consider himself an employee. It was more a teacher/pupil thing, and Dirk Merrit was an apt pupil. Carl had plenty of fun cruising up and down I-5, selecting and snatching suitable sacrifices, getting them ready for Dirk Merrit. But the man was changing. It wasn't just the plastic surgery, although the last couple of bouts had been pretty extreme. He was growing more impatient, more paranoid, more impulsive, taking risks when he didn't need to, flirting with disaster. Also, he was running out of money. He'd spent too much on his house, on himself, on his obsessions. After he'd been forced to sell his interest in the company that ran his beloved computer game, he'd begun to complain about losing control, by which he meant losing the financial muscle to do whatever he wanted. As if to compensate, the period between hunts had been growing shorter and shorter, and even before the nonsense with the girl and the discovery of that security guard scoping out the stuff in the trophy room, Carl had realized that the wheels were coming off the wagon. Sooner or later Dirk Merrit was going to get himself caught or killed.

Carl couldn't just walk away – if those incriminating videos and photographs stored in the safe of Dirk Merrit's lawyer fell into the hands of the police, he would make the top ten of the FBI's most wanted. Luckily, while Carl had been trying to figure out a foolproof exit strategy, Erik Grow had come up with a simple plan to take control of their boss's last real income stream. As soon as everything fell into place and he had his hands on the money, Carl was going to deal with Dirk Merrit, change his identity, and find somewhere off the beaten track where he could settle down. Brazil looked good. Or Argentina. Carl had heard that you could live like a king in Buenos Aires on a few hundred US dollars a month.

Mind you, he'd been about ready to walk out last night, after Dirk Merrit had not only tried to outwit the two cops but had also explained his latest crazy plan. But then, later that evening, Erik Grow had called, told Carl that at long last Dirk Merrit had altered the percentage he was skimming off the credit-card subscriptions to the game he'd once owned.

'He pushed it up to one per cent for exactly two hours. He took this tremendous risk, exposing what he's up to, and raked off less than five thousand dollars.'

'Can you cover it?'

'A blip like that, it'll be hard—'

'Find some way of covering it for as long as possible. Should I pull the keystroke thing right now?'

'Why not? He changed the percentage on the skim, so he must have accessed the program. Assuming your keystroke-capture device is still in position and still working, it will have recorded the password he used.'

'If it isn't working, the bloke who sold it to me is going to be feeling very sorry for himself.'

'You have to get down here right away. I can't cover up what he did for long.'

'I'll be down in a couple of days. Keep a lid on things until then,' Carl had said, cutting the connection when Erik Grow had started to complain.

He'd sat in his bleak little room, working things through. Things were moving faster than he had expected. First the girl, then the wild plan to lure the sacrifice's partner to Portland, now this. Dirk Merrit was off on some wild jag. Maybe he *wanted* to be caught. Meanwhile, Carl needed to work up some excuse for making another trip to Los Angeles, something that wouldn't make Dirk Merrit suspicious; in his present state, there was no telling what he might do if he suspected that Carl was up to something. Carl thought long and hard about this. Maybe he could tell the man that the credit cards he'd just delivered were compromised, he needed to go back, sort things out. Or maybe there was a way of using this thing with Frank Wilson and Patrick Metcalf . . .

Much later, two in the morning, Carl had snuck over to the library, opened the casing of Dirk Merrit's computer and unplugged the keystroke-capture device. It was a square of printed circuit wired to a memory stick that contained a record of everything Dirk Merrit had typed into his computer in the past three weeks, a little package not much bigger than a .303 round, neatly wrapped in black duct tape. Carl had it in the pocket of his denim shirt right now. No two ways about it: as soon as this was done, and as soon as he'd shown Mr Patrick Metcalf what happened when you stepped on another man's turf, he was out of here.

The ultralight's buzz blew across the playa, rising in pitch as the little aircraft fell in a steep stoop, skimming so low above the dry lake bed that its prop stirred up a long trail of dust before it rose again, skinny white wings heliographing a flash of sunlight straight into Carl's eyes. If the man didn't make the kill soon, Carl thought, the kid would collapse of sunstroke or heat exhaustion and spoil all the fun.

Dirk Merrit must have realized that too. The ultralight was turning, coming back in a straight run and losing altitude, dropping down to make a short, bumpy landing. Carl raised the field glasses to his eyes, saw the sacrifice's naked figure running away from the skinny little aircraft, jiggling and breaking apart and reforming among layers of heat burning off the playa as it ran headlong, and then seeming to trip, tumbling over, lying still. Dirk Merrit's triumphant cry crackled faintly on the radio, and Carl saw him stalking through creosote bushes towards the spot where the sacrifice had fallen.

Carl gave the man ten minutes to enjoy his triumph, then picked up the plastic jug, kicked the trail bike into life, and rode straight out towards the spot. Dirk Merrit was stalking around the mutilated body with his little DV camera glued to his face. The sacrifice lay on its back, blood soaking into the dry sand around it. The ribcage had been opened and the heart removed:

Dirk Merrit liked to take a squirt of hot blood the way a tourist in Spain drinks from a wine sack, a baroque flourish that Carl thought cheap and distasteful.

The man turned his red smile on Carl and kicked the body onto its side, revealing the arrow buried to its black fletching in the small of the back.

'He gave me a good run, didn't he? As a matter of fact, he was still trying to crawl after I shot him,' Dirk Merrit said. He let the body flop back, pulled a hunting knife from the scabbard on his belt, offered it hilt-first to Carl. 'He was a brave boy. And in consideration of his bravery, I'd like to have his eyes. What's in the jug?'

'Liquid detergent and polystyrene mixed up in gasoline.'

'I don't want to ruin the moment with something as suburban as a barbecue. And don't you think a fire would attract attention, even out here?'

'We should burn him and bury what's left.'

'He's too noble for the worms.' Dirk Merrit gestured grandly at the north quarter of the sky, where a couple of buzzards were circling with a lazy grace that no human pilot could hope to equal. 'We'll leave him for my friends, once you've done me the favour of removing his eyes.'

'Maybe you should learn how to do that.'

'But then you might forget that we are both part of this.'

'I'm not likely to.'

Carl refused the knife. He used his thumbs.

It took an hour to dismantle the ultralight and lash it to the trailer. Carl drove fast along Route 140, heading due north towards Oregon. It was a dead straight, well-made stretch of road, a good place to test the mettle of your vehicle. Carl pinned the speedometer to seventy-five miles an hour and the powerful diesel engine made an unending roar as the RV ate up the blacktop. Behind him, Dirk Merrit had not yet exhausted the details of his triumph. Unconsciously, Carl was trying to outrun the man's boastful babbling.

The wind had gotten up. It rocked the big vehicle as it sped through the desert, blew skirls of alkaline dust and bowled balls of sagebrush across the two-lane blacktop. When the RV smashed into one of the rolling bushes the sage burst in a cloud of fragments that held its shape for a moment before the wind snatched it away.

Carl saw the dispersion in the big side mirror and felt a shiver of anticipation.

Two more days, three at the most, he'd be leaving all of Mr Dirk Merrit's shit behind. He could hardly wait.

13

Summer met with Hal Brockman, Edie Collier's probation agent, early Friday morning, before he began to deal with his slate of appointments. They sat either side of his metal desk in his tiny cubicle, a shelf packed with case files hanging over Summer's left shoulder. After Summer had explained why she was there, Hal Brockman said, 'I saw on the news that the creep who did it killed himself. Please don't tell me the police got the wrong man.'

'I'm doing a follow-up,' Summer said. 'Do you have an address for Ms Collier?'

Randy Farrell had told her that his stepdaughter and her boyfriend had been living out of a van; now, Hal Brockman said that as far as he knew she'd been staying in a motel on Southwest Jefferson.

'Did you ever visit her?'

Hal Brockman was a slim African-American in his late thirties, with a shaven head and a patient, deliberate manner. He said, 'How it works, detective, *they*'re obliged to visit *me.*'

'When was her last appointment?'

'I last saw her three weeks ago. She turned up on time, as always, and she didn't give any indication of being in any kind of trouble. She was working regularly, making plans to enrol in a secretarial course . . . I wish all my clients were as easy to deal with. I was supposed to meet with her again Friday last. When she didn't turn up, I called her cell phone but got an out-of-service message. I called her place of work too, they told me she hadn't showed up there either. I admit I was worried, she'd never before missed a meeting, but what happened – it was a shock.'

'She was at work Thursday?'

'I believe so.'

'And where was her place of work?'

'The Rite Spot. R-I-T-E. It's a truck stop off Portland Highway, over by Maywood Park. Several of our clients work there.'

Summer copied the address into her notebook, and wrote down Edie Collier's cell phone number too.

Hal Brockman said, 'May I ask what exactly this is about? The Cedar Falls police asked me the same questions, and I know they wanted to check out her place of work because they got the phone number off me.'

'As I said, sir, I'm doing a follow-up. Edie's stepfather told me that she was living with a young man, first name Billy, last name unknown. Do you know anything about him?'

'I handle more than a hundred clients, detective, many of them drug-dependent, almost all of them with unstable, chaotic lives. If they want to tell me about their personal business, I listen. If they don't want to tell me, I don't pry. Frankly, I don't have the time to do any kind of in-depth profiling – and besides, about half the time they flat-out lie.'

'Half the time is pretty good going,' Summer said.

Hal Brockman smiled. 'A few of them actually want to be helped. That's about the only thing that makes this job worthwhile.'

'Edie Collier was one of them?'

Hal Brockman's gaze softened. 'She was a very vulnerable young lady. Intelligent but naive, in my opinion easily led. A follower, not a doer. She'd sit there sort of hiding behind her hair, never looking you in the eye.'

'Otherwordly,' Summer said, picturing the girl in the shabby basement office of Meier and Frank. The poetry book in her bag.

'I'd ask her about work,' Hal Brockman said. 'Was she getting on with her parents, was she staying clean, was she seeing any of her old friends – she fell in with the wrong crowd at high school. At best I'd get one-word answers, or a shrug.'

'She didn't volunteer anything?'

'It wasn't because she had an attitude, or because she was a space cadet. It was as if she had better things to think about. You asked about a boyfriend. It's the first I knew she had one.' Hal Brockman paused, then said, 'The boyfriend. Is he implicated in . . . what happened?'

'We need to eliminate him from our inquiries.'

'Right. Well, if he was into something bad, I wouldn't be surprised to find that Edie went along with it. It's a goddamn shame,' Hal Brockman said. 'She showed every sign of wanting to make something of herself, which is why, between you and me, I didn't violate her when she failed to show up. I was hoping that she'd stop by, give me some bullshit reason why she'd missed her appointment, and that would be an end to it. It was a shock, believe me, when the Cedar Falls police called me with the bad news.'

In the moment of silence between them, Summer became aware of the murmur of conversations in the rest of the room, in other cubicles identical to this one.

She said, 'Do you have a photo of her in that file? I'd like to borrow it.'

'No problem,' Hal Brockman said, and unclipped a full-face mugshot and passed it across his desk. 'Good luck, detective. I hope you can do right by her.'

'Thank you, Mr Brockman. I hope so too.'

Summer bought coffee at a nearby Starbucks, sat at one of the sidewalk tables, and called one of the secretaries in the pool on the thirteenth floor of the Justice Building. Ryland Nelsen had agreed to her request for a personal day with considerable reluctance, and she believed that it would be a good idea to stay out of his way. She gave the secretary the number of Edie Collier's cell phone and asked her to find the name and office number of the service provider. The woman called back with the information a few minutes later, and after negotiating several levels of an automated switchboard Summer reached an actual human employee of the service provider, who after some discussion transferred her to a manager, who told her that she would need a warrant to check Edie Collier's call log.

'This is in relation to a homicide investigation. Can you at least tell me when she last used her phone?'

'If you can bring a warrant down to our office, ma'am, we'll be happy to cooperate.'

Fat chance of that. Summer was operating in her spare time on a case that wasn't hers, and she knew that most of Portland's judges required very good reasons for issuing warrants to access phone records or authorize wiretaps. She called Denise Childers and gave her what she had learned from Hal Brockman, asked if Denise could get a warrant to gain access to Edie Collier's cell phone records.

'It might be our best shot at tracing the boyfriend.'

'No way,' Denise said. 'It would have to go before the judge above Sheriff Worden's signature, and as far as the sheriff is concerned the case is down. Do you have any other leads?'

Summer said, 'I talked to one of the guys in the methamphetamine task force after I got back yesterday. He knows of one dealer called Billy, but the guy is doing jail right now. He said he'll ask around, see if anyone on the street knows anything. Meanwhile, I'm going to check out Edie Collier's place of work. And I'll stop by the motel where she had a room, too, see if anyone remembers anything.'

Denise said that she hadn't made much progress either. 'I did have one of the crime-scene people look at that padlock. He told me the scratches could well have been made by lock-picks, and that they're fresh, no more than a week old. So you could be right, it's possible someone broke into Kronenwetter's cellar. The problem is, it doesn't mean anything by itself.'

Summer felt a little kick of satisfaction. 'Did he find any prints?'

'He did that thing with superglue, but if someone did pick that padlock – and we don't know for certain that anyone did – either he was wearing gloves or he wiped it clean afterward. I checked up on Joe Kronenwetter's time in the county jail, too, but it was another dead end. The guard I talked to said that Joe was a loner, kind of pathetic for a big guy, out of his depth. There's no evidence that he associated with anyone in particular, let alone white supremacists. If you want to convince me that this had something to do with drugs, you're going to have to come up with something solid at your end.'

The motel on Southwest Jefferson was the kind of low-rent joint where room keys were automatically handed over to police armed with arrest warrants, no questions asked, because it was easier to cooperate than to replace locks on doors kicked in after the occupants of targeted rooms refused to open them. When Summer flashed her badge and asked for the register, the clerk behind the armoured-glass window handed over it over and went back to his crossword. Summer flipped back through the crowded pages and found out that Edie Collier had checked in on 8 February, had stayed for a little over three weeks. The clerk thought that he recognized her from the mug shot Summer had borrowed from Hal Brockman, but didn't remember any boyfriend; the only long-term resident Summer found, a tired young African-American woman who stood in the door of her room with a baby in her arms and two small children clinging to her legs, didn't remember Edie Collier at all.

Summer had better luck at the diner where Edie had worked as a waitress. There were trucks and tractor-trailer rigs drawn up in the diner's big parking lot, and an even dozen motorcycles lined up along the brick and glass frontage, including two full-dress Harley-Davidsons and a rakish three-wheeler with *Easy Rider*-style handlebars. Inside, most of the central booths and the tables along the windows were occupied, and the place was full of the clatter and bustle of the lunchtime rush.

The manager was a skinny dude with a greasy comb-over, a pencil moustache, and a petulant, harried manner. When Summer asked him what kind of employee Edie Collier had been, he shrugged and said, 'She turned up on time, didn't break too many plates or hack off too many customers, and didn't cop an attitude. That's about all I can tell you.'

'Did you happen to notice anyone unusual hanging around in the past couple of weeks? Did Edie mention that she was planning to go on a trip, and why?'

The manager shook his head.

'How about her boyfriend? Do you know anything about him?'

'Their private lives I could care less about, as long as they don't bring their problems to work,' the manager said.

He and Summer were standing next to a big stainless-steel refrigerator at one end of the narrow, noisy kitchen area. Two men were working at smoking hot plates and a third was chopping vegetables, while waitresses appeared and disappeared at the service counter to the curt jangle of finished-order bells.

Summer said, 'When did you last see her?'

'The end of last week. I'm pretty sure Thursday. I know she left me short-handed over the weekend,' the manager said, and told the man cutting vegetables to slice the onions thinner, for Chrissake.

'She didn't call in sick, or hand in her notice?'

'Are you kidding? She just didn't turn up. Yeah, the last day I saw her was definitely Thursday. She didn't even stop by to get her pay packet Friday.' The manager gave Summer a speculative look. 'Will anyone be looking for that, you think?'

Summer said, 'One of your employees failed to collect their pay, and you didn't think anything of it?'

'To be frank? I thought she was another no-good piece of jail-bait who couldn't hold down a steady job, that's what I thought.'

'Did she have any friends you knew of?'

'How would I know? *Thinner*, Harold. Nice and even and thin. Jesus Christ, if I have to come over there and show you how to do it, you'll be out of a job and back in the joint before you can catch your breath.' The manager gave Summer a sour look. 'Are we done here?'

'Not quite, sir. Was there anyone who used to hang out back, waiting for her at the end of the shift?'

'If there was, I didn't notice.'

'Did anyone stop by in the past week, asking after her?'

'Not to my knowledge.'

'I see you have a little video camera over the register there.'

'The insurance company insisted on it last year, after we got stuck up twice in one month. Not that it stopped half my staff from quitting after the second time. Your people took twenty minutes to respond to the emergency call, too.'

'I'm sorry to hear that, sir. Would it be possible to review the tapes from your camera, and any others you may have? It's possible the boyfriend visited her here.'

'That's the only camera. And the tape loops around, lasts only twelve hours.'

'You don't store tapes?'

Summer had never seen anyone smirk before, but that was exactly what the manager did now. Saying, 'Look around you, lady. This is a diner, not Blockbuster.'

'Was there anyone working here who was especially friendly with Edie?'

'She mostly kept herself to herself.'

Summer was beginning to tire of the man's attitude. She squared up to him and said, 'If you can't point me to anyone in particular, then I guess I'll have to take the time to interview your staff one by one.'

'In the middle of lunch?'

'Now that I'm here, why not?' Summer said, taking out her notebook and flipping it open to show him that she meant business.

'Jesus Christ. Look, you see that girl there? The blonde? She was friendly with Edie, why don't you go talk to her? But keep it short.'

The blonde waitress, Janice, was a tall and big-boned young woman, with acne in the corners of her mouth and too much blue eyeshadow. She said that she'd heard about what happened to Edie on the TV news, just about everyone was cut up about it, and confirmed that Edie had been at work last Thursday but hadn't turned up on Friday. 'It's a fucking shame what happened to her, excuse my French. She was a real darlin'. Everyone but Sneaky Pete liked her.'

'Sneaky Pete?'

'Mr Schopf, the manager? I don't suppose he was much help to you.'

Janice had an accent from someplace three thousand miles
south and east of Portland that lifted every other sentence into a
question. She wore a candy-striped cotton dress and a white
apron with a scalloped trim. Her dirty blonde hair was pulled
back in a ponytail fastened with a rubber band, and there was a
ballpoint pen tucked behind her ear.

Summer said, 'Mr Schopf thought you might be able to help
me.'

'I don't know how I can, but I can try.'

The girl was shifting from foot to foot in her trodden-down
flat-heeled shoes, easing the weight on her ankles. Summer suggested that they sit in an empty booth. When they were settled,
she said, 'Did you know Edie socially, or just here at work?'

'Just at work. We talked when we snuck cigarettes out back?
I know she was on probation, and she wanted to go straight. Her
big idea, she wanted to go work in one of those big offices
downtown. Excuse me.' Janice pulled a handkerchief from her
sleeve and dabbed at the corners of her eyes and said in a
pinched voice, 'I thought she was sweet, y'know?'

Summer said, 'Did she have a boyfriend that you knew of?'

Janice blew her nose with surprising delicacy. 'She sure did.
Real nice boy, name of Billy.'

Summer felt a quick flare of hope. 'Did you ever meet this
Billy?'

'Just the once. He came by on Edie's first day. I think he
wanted to see where she was working?'

Garrulous, sharp-eyed Janice, every cop's idea of a dream witness, gave Summer a description of Edie Collier's boyfriend: six
foot nothing, brown eyes and cheekbones to die for, shoulder-
length black hair, rangy, wearing Hi-Top sneakers, blue jeans out
at both knees and a raggedy old T-shirt. 'And he had a couple of
fingers missing from one of his hands.'

'Which hand?'

'The right.'

'Can you remember which fingers were missing?'

'The little finger, and the one next to it.' Janice wrinkled her
nose, remembering. 'They were cut off at the knuckle? He kept

his hand behind him, or in his pocket, like he was ashamed of it, but I saw it when he lit a cigarette.'

'Did Edie ever tell you how her boyfriend lost his fingers? Was it some kind of industrial accident, for instance?'

'Uh-uh.'

'How about his last name?'

Janice looked up at the ceiling for a moment, thinking. 'I don't believe it ever came up. Like I said, I only met him that one time.'

'Did Edie mention what he did for a living?'

'I believe it was something to do with computers. He played games in competition, something like that? I know when he came in that time he had one of those laptop cases. But whatever he was into, it can't have earned him much money – the two of them were living out of his van.'

Confirming Randy Farrell's story. Summer figured that Edie Collier had taken a room at the motel right after she'd left home, and then she'd moved out of the motel after she had taken up with this boyfriend, Billy no-last-name.

She said, 'Do you know what kind of van it was?'

'A Ford, one of those old boxy ones.'

'An Econoline?'

'Yeah. My first husband, he had one just like it? Put the same kind of window in the side, too, which is why I noticed it straight off.'

Janice remembered that the van had had a bad bright red paint job, but couldn't remember its licence number. 'It was a California plate, I know that. Old style, yellow lettering on a blue background?' She had a nice, open smile that lit up her face and took ten years off her age. 'You get to recognize just about every kind of licence plate working in a place like this.'

'Did Billy stop by here after Edie went missing?'

'Not while I was on shift. I guess I could ask around if you like.'

'I'd appreciate it. Did Edie always work the same shift, by the way?'

Janice nodded. 'Same as me.'

'If I asked a police artist to come out here, do you think you could give him an idea of what Billy looked like?'

'I guess I could try. I thought you caught the so-and-so that done it.'

'I need to find Billy, to make sure he's safe and well.'

'My Lord. You think he could have been murdered too?'

Summer said, 'I want to find him and talk to him. That's all there is to it.'

'They were in love,' Janice said. 'Just last week Edie showed me a cute tattoo she'd had put on her arm. A little red rose with a kind of banner with his name in it? And she said Billy had one on his arm, just the same, only with *her* name.'

Summer went over the boyfriend's description and the description of his van, then took out the front page she'd torn from a copy of yesterday's edition of the *Macabee Bugle and Courier*, Cedar Falls's local paper, folded to the photograph of Joseph Kronenwetter below the headline. 'Do you recall seeing this man? He could have been driving a beat-up old pickup.'

Janice took a good long look at the photograph, then shook her head and said she was sorry, she would surely remember a mean-looking scudder like that.

'That's okay,' Summer said. She wrote her cell phone number on the back of one of her business cards and told Janice to call her if she thought of anything else.

Janice promised she would, hesitated, then asked, 'Did she suffer?'

'I don't know,' Summer said. 'I hope not, but I don't know.'

The manager had been watching them from behind the cash register. Summer walked over to him and said, 'I've been think-ing about Edie Collier's pay packet, Mr Schopf. I believe it would be best if you gave it to me.'

'Can you do that? I mean, is that legal?'

'I'll pass it on to her family. And while you're at it, you can put back the twenty per cent you took out as kickback.'

Sitting in her car outside the Rite Spot, Summer called the Traffic Division and talked to a Ms Ada Simmons, asked her if a red Ford Econoline van had been issued with any tickets in the past year.

'That won't be easy if you don't have the licence number,' Ada Simmons said.

'I'm trying to find the licence number,' Summer said. 'There can't have been too many tickets issued to red Econoline vans in, say, the past year.'

'You'd be surprised,' Ada Simmons said. 'I'll do a global search and email you the results. When you come to print it out, detective, make sure you have plenty of paper in the hopper.'

14

Although he still hadn't reached the save point in the ruins of downtown Los Angeles, Daryl was feeling pleased with himself. He'd closed out bids on three items he was selling on eBay, drawn from the store of gadgets, maps and other valuables he'd acquired during Seeker8's adventures in *Trans*, and the deals had fattened his PayPal account by just over four hundred dollars. Even better, his partner, Ratking, finally had reached out to him, explaining that he'd had to attend to some urgent business out in the world, but now he could devote his attention to the final stage of the treasure hunt.

> *I've developed a new strategy. I can't come with you, but I'll be watching over you. I'll be your guardian angel.*

> *Lay it on me*, Daryl typed.

They were instant messaging, East Coast to West Coast and back again. It was one in the morning in Brooklyn, just after Daryl's latest attempt to get Seeker8 to the save point had failed.

> *I purchased a hack that lets me watch anyone in the game. I've become a point of view, pilgrim. I'm the eagle that dwells on the rock. Wherever you go, I'll be right there with you. I'll be the voice in the burning bush. I'll speak to you out of the whirlwind.*

Daryl, reading this, hunched over the glowing screen in his hot dark cell in Brooklyn's unsleeping anthill, wondered what had happened to his partner while he'd been out of the loop. Previously, Ratking's messages had been terse and clipped, pure business and always straight to the point, but now he was on fire with self-importance and a Biblical fervour.

After a moment's thought, popping gum with machine-gun rapidity, Daryl rattled out his reply:

> *I'd rather you were watching my back, helping me knock down the warewolves.*

Strictly speaking, Seeker8 had been taken down by tar babies this time, but it had been a pack of warewolves that had driven him into the broken channel of the Los Angeles River, with its smoking cinder cones, fields of congealed lava, and asphalt pits from which dozens of tar babies had clambered, lumbering stiff-legged towards him from every direction like giant teddy bears dipped in sump oil, eyes glowing red, stubby arms spread wide. He'd killed thirty or forty with incendiary bullets and grenades before he'd been caught from behind in an unbreakable embrace and carried off and drowned in a deep pool of oily water. The night before that, warewolves had chased him howling through the ruins, playing with him, nipping at his heels, harrying him with balletic coordination until they'd finally closed in and taken him down.

Each attempt to reach the next save point had been harder than the last. It wasn't just that the warewolves were making things difficult. The game itself constantly evolved as players roamed across it and interacted with each other, finding treasures, trading secrets and weapons, making alliances, building or destroying fiefdoms. The game learned from players' moves, adjusted itself to their strategies, messed up their plans by throwing storms and earthquakes, bandits and monsters into their paths. Daryl had been worrying that he had reached a no-win stalemate, reloading time and time again to try to make progress from a hopeless position, but now his partner was back with the promise of fresh information and this weird new mystical slant. Telling Daryl now:

> *The eagle dwells and abides on the crag of the rock, and the strong place. That's me.*

Daryl massaged his forehead with one hand, and with the forefinger of the other hit the Caps Lock key and pecked *?*

> *Read the Book of Job, pilgrim. Meanwhile, you need to reach that save point. Let me make some suggestions.*

Ratking might have started to have sound like the preacher at the church Daryl's mother attended each and every Sunday, but his advice was as detailed and sensible as ever. After some back and forth, he told Daryl to wait until tomorrow evening before he tried to move on.

> *I'll be watching then. And when you reach the next save point, we'll work out what to do next.*

Friday morning, then, Daryl woke full of optimistic energy. He washed up a week's worth of dishes, swept the kitchen floor, lugged a sack of garbage to the chute. He rinsed the counter and drainer with clean soapy water and dried them with paper towels. He scrubbed blackened dots of burned grease from the cast-iron grill of the stove with steel wool and Johnson's Force. He scrubbed coffee stains from the sink with bleach, cleaned the toilet and the sink in the tiny bathroom, and in a kind of ecstasy of mad energy used a toothbrush to attack the black mould in the grouting of the tiled shower stall, scrubbed mould from the hem of the shower curtain too, and rinsed it all away.

By now, his mother was stirring. Daryl filled the kettle and put it to boil on the stove, set up the jug and filter, and tipped in a generous heap of coffee. He poured boiling water on the grounds, set the jug, two cups, a pitcher of milk and a bowl of sugar on a tray, carried the tray across the living room, and knocked on the door of his mother's bedroom.

Irene Weir was sitting up in her disordered bed, looking small and brittle inside her quilted dressing gown, her hair in corn-rows, her face several shades darker than Daryl's. The shelf above the quilted bedhead was crowded with her collection of dolls in all kinds of national costume, bookended by Daryl's two gymnastic trophies. He'd thrown them out when he'd quit school, shortly after DeLeon had been killed, but she'd rescued them from the trash, telling him that she was proud of what he'd done, she wasn't going to see it go to waste, and besides, he'd want them again one day. Daryl wasn't so sure. As far as he was concerned, that part of his life was over, and the trophies stirred up painful memories of DeLeon cheering him on under the bright lights of the gymnasium, his big brother always there for him, sitting on the top row of the bleachers in his puffa jacket and baggy jeans and Timberlands, singing out *'Way to go, Daryl!'* over the noise of the crowd.

As Daryl poured the coffee and stirred in milk and sugar, his mother asked him what all the noise had been about. 'All this banging and crashing, and it ain't even ten yet.'

'I was cleaning up, momma.'

'I was going to do that over the weekend.'

'I don't mind it. I guess you don't have any work today, sleeping in like this.'

'Just Mr Campbell. And he doesn't like me coming around until the afternoon, he has to get his writing done in the morning.'

Irene Weir had lost most of her private clients after she'd gone into hospital last year with an infected kidney. She had taken a long time to recover from the operation that had removed it, and afterwards no longer had the energy to work twelve or fourteen hours a day, cleaning a string of private homes before starting on her regular job at the bank offices.

Daryl said, 'Do you want me to run down to the store? I can get you one of those cinnamon muffins you like so much.'

His mother speared him with a suspicious look. 'It isn't my birthday, so I have to ask why all the fuss.'

Daryl sat on the end of her bed and told her about the sales on eBay.

'That's nice, honey, but when are you going to get a real job?'

It was what she said just about every time Daryl had some good news – he didn't even get angry any more.

'Drink your coffee, momma. I'll go get you that muffin.'

Later, he rode downtown in the sooty heat and roar of the subway, bought a sack of White Castle burgers and a soda and had himself a late lunch in Washington Square Park, sitting near the fountains and watching the endless parade of NYU students and professors, skateboard kids, panhandlers, tourists, drug dealers, transvestites and for all he knew aliens dressed up in human skins. Then he strolled across to Broadway, where his friend Bernard worked as a salesman in an electronics store owned by two Iranian brothers.

Bernard Parrish lived in the same building as Daryl and his mother. He was only three years older than Daryl, but he had his own apartment, a beat-up Datsun, and a steady girlfriend. Bernard had given Daryl a good deal on his latest box, had shown him how to overclock it and install the heavy-duty heat sink that kept the processor cool when it ran at twice its normal speed. He was also Daryl's connection to a supply of military-grade amphetamine, the kind used by soldiers in the war over in Iraq.

They got that out of the way first, in the stockroom in back of the store. Fifty bucks for ten tiny bright yellow pills in a twist of Saran Wrap.

'I don't want you to be taking more than one a day,' Bernard told Daryl, 'so don't be coming back to me for more in less than two weeks. I'm not going to be the one turns you into a speed freak.'

'I just need an edge for a few days.'

'You still chasing after that shit? Shit,' Bernard said, pushing out his lips to show his disgust. He was perched on a big box that contained a widescreen TV. Tall and rangy, all elbows and knees. A big red badge clipped to the breast pocket of his white shirt: *I'm Bernard. How May I Help You?* He aimed a forefinger at Daryl and said, 'How much longer you gonna be wasting your life on that game?'

Daryl said, 'The money I just gave you? That was from the game. I made four hundred thirty bucks selling a map and a couple of energy guns.'

'To, I bet, rich white kids in some Middle America 'burb who got more cash than sense, spending their pocket money on stuff they should be winning for themselves.'

'As long as they got the money, I don't care who they are. Man, why are you giving me a hard time? I could swear you and my mother been talking behind my back.'

'The point is, to those white kids it's a game. Entertainment. Something they do for fun. But to you, it's how you earn your living. It's a way of life.'

'If you're going to tell me it ain't real, let me tell you all over again I just now paid you with real money I earned from it.'

'You're just about earning a living from white boys' pocket money, but where are you going?'

'I'm close to something that's worth a lot more than pocket money,' Daryl said.

Bernard dismissed this with a flick of his hand. 'Nothing you do in the game, none of your skills, none of the shit you win, not even your reputation as a stone-cold gamer, counts for anything in the real world. I mean, what are you going to do when it finishes?'

'It isn't about to—'

'Dog, when it comes to computers, you *know* nothing lasts long. These online games, how long has the oldest one been running? Five years? Ten? In ten years, do you think *Trans* will still be all that?'

'So what if it isn't? There'll be something better.'

'Yeah, and you'll have to start again from the very bottom, as a slave or whatever. Because what you do in *Trans*, all the respect and skills you earn, they only count in *Trans*. See what I'm saying? It ain't like the real world, where what you do really does count for something.'

'This is about me coming to work for you, isn't it?'

Bernard had been scuffling for a year now, scrimping and saving, trying to salt away enough cash to rent a storefront and turn his computer-repair sideline into a full-time business. He told Daryl, 'You can fix computers, hardware and software. You know your bios from your boot. That's the kind of thing I'm talking about. That's the kind of thing counts for something in the real world.'

'I'll think about it,' Daryl said, which was what he always said when Bernard got down on him. The truth was, he got an awful suffocating feeling just thinking about going to work in the back room of some little store, debugging recalcitrant programs, installing hard drives and graphic cards. He could live an ordinary life, for sure, but what was that compared to the dangers and glories of *Trans*? In *Trans*, he was a hero, engaged in heroic ventures. Out here in the world, he was a geek living in a Brooklyn project, the only surviving son of an office cleaner, with a dead brother and a father he'd never known.

Bernard said, 'If this big score is all you say it is, if you do pull it off, I want you to seriously think about your next move. You know that you could come in with me. We've talked about that enough times. Maybe it's time to make it happen.'

'Oh, *now* you like the money.'

'Let me ask you something, dog. What's more real, your own life or your so-called avatar?'

'I'm nearly there. After the next save point, all we have to figure out is how to reach the observatory, and then it's down.'

'As long as this Ratking doesn't cheat you.'

'We're partners. I'm the muscle, the skill. He's the brain, the secret knowledge. Together, we're the perfect team.'

'You never even met him.'

'Sure I have.'

'In the game.'

'So?'

Bernard said with exaggerated patience, 'Dog, you can meet all kinds of fourteen-year-old hard-bodied honeys begging for hot sex in Internet chat rooms, but every one of them is either an undercover cop or a pervert. You see what I'm saying?'

'We have an agreement, a fifty-fifty split,' Daryl said stubbornly. 'And trust cuts both ways. Right now, my partner's kind of disembodied. I'm in the game, and he's floating above it, giving me advice. Whatever we find, I'm the one who has to grab it and go.'

Bernard shook his head. 'Man, you're so innocent it's a wonder you can cross the street without getting ripped off. What we're talking about, it's a *computer* game. You're at one computer, tied into the game's server via the Internet. This Ratking, he's at another computer, thousands of miles away. He could enter a couple of lines of code, and the prize would be downloaded to his hard disk, and there'd be no way you could ever find him. Didn't you ever think of that?'

15

Now that her search for Edie Collier's boyfriend was heating up, and because more than half of the first of the three days she'd given herself to find him was already gone, Summer decided that she needed to check out the Traffic Division reports on red Econoline vans as soon as possible. No way around it, she'd have to pay a visit to the thirteenth floor before the end of the shift, and risk a confrontation with Ryland Nelsen.

When she reached the Robbery Unit's cube farm, she found a dozen enlarged photocopies of a Monopoly *Get Out Of Jail Free* card scattered across her desk. As she'd suspected, how she'd fouled up in Cedar Falls, letting Randy Farrell get into a fight that had put his behind in jail, had become common knowledge.

She thanked everyone in the vicinity for their thoughtfulness, saying, 'Only problem is, these are too late to do any good. The guy in question is already out.'

'Save them for the next time,' Jesse Little said. He was the unit's joker, a lanky guy with brush-cut black hair and a long pale face. Telling her, 'If you want, I can design you a nice business card too.'

Summer switched on her computer. 'I already have a business card.'

Jesse Little winked at Jim Jacklet, who sat at the desk that butted with his. 'She thinks we don't know.'

'She underestimates our powers of detection,' Jim Jacklet said, cracking his wide smile under his bandit's moustache. 'You're busted, Ziegler. We know all about it.'

'I bet. Where's Andy, by the way?'

'In court again – that British tourist who got stabbed outside a bar when he wouldn't give up his wallet,' Jesse Little said.

'And don't change the subject. You watch any crime shows on TV?'

Summer fired up her email browser and said warily, suspecting that she was being set up, 'I don't watch TV.'

'Bullshit. Everyone watches TV,' Jesse Little said. 'Even Searle, once he's put down the phone for the night.'

Dick Searle put his hand over the mouthpiece of his phone. 'You guys leave me out of this,' he said, and turned away, reaching for a pen and a legal pad.

Summer deleted three emails from reporters and found that Ada Simmons, bless her heart, had sent her a hundred and twenty-two reports about incidents involving Econoline vans in the Portland metropolitan area in the last twelve months.

Jesse Little said, 'I like that one with the guy who has obsessive-compulsive disorder. *Monk*. You ever watch that, Jacklet?'

'Uh-uh.'

'You should, it's pretty good. Funny and weird, like real life. One of his problems, he has a bug about neatness, gets upset if things aren't just so. Every time he discovers a fresh crime scene, he has to struggle real hard against this impulse to straighten it up.'

'I know what you mean,' Jim Jacklet said. 'I turn up one time at a convenience store robbery, the clerk got shot? The uniform who responded to the nine-eleven is sitting in the clerk's chair, reading the clerk's comic book.'

'That's not exactly what I meant,' Jesse Little said.

'It's a funny story – isn't that the point?'

'The point is,' Jesse Little said, 'this guy Monk has a quirk. They all have to have quirks, don't you think, Ziegler?'

Summer was trying to skim through the reports as quickly as possible. 'They do? Who do?'

'She's still pretending we don't know,' Jesse Little told Jim Jacklet.

'Oh, we know all right,' Jacklet said, aiming his forefinger at Summer, cocking his thumb.

'You do?'

'The days you take off,' Jim Jacklet said. 'The long road trips to the back of beyond. You're moonlighting, Ziegler.'

'As a private investigator,' Jesse Little said. 'But see, the PI business, it isn't just about solving crimes. If you want to get ahead, get yourself noticed, you got to have some kind of quirk. What you might call a unique selling point, to distinguish you from all the other PIs. What I can do for you, Ziegler, a two-for-one Jesse Little special, is figure out a good quirk *and* design a nice business card. What do you say?'

'I'd say thanks, but no thanks. For one thing, this isn't anything to do with a private investigation. And I've already seen your Photoshopping skills.'

After Ryland Nelsen's crack about Lycra on Summer's first day at the unit, Jesse Little had pinned a picture, Summer's face superimposed over Helen Slater costumed as Supergirl, to the unit's noticeboard.

'If you aren't moonlighting, what *are* you doing?' Jim Jacklet said.

'You can tell us,' Jesse Little said.

'You *should* tell us,' Jim Jacklet said. 'A rookie like you shouldn't have any secrets from veteran detectives like us. It's against regulations. So come on, spill.'

'What am I doing? I'm helping the police with their inquiries,' Summer said, and sent the traffic reports to the laser printer with a click of her mouse and stood up.

'Any time you need help,' Jesse Little called after her, 'I'm right here. And my rates are very reasonable.'

Summer was watching the report sheets emerge one by one from the laser printer when Ryland Nelsen wandered over, a cup of coffee in his hand and a gleam in his eye.

'I understood you were taking a personal day,' he said.

'Yes, sir. I am.'

He pulled one of the report sheets from the printer and studied it while Summer waited for the axe to fall. Because she knew that she was pushing the edge of the police bureau's tolerance, she'd asked Denise to sort of make their deal official by calling Ryland Nelsen and telling him how much she appreciated Summer volunteering to help out in the investigation into Edie Collier's kidnap and wrongful death. Now she realized that

Ryland Nelsen could have found out that Denise's investigation had been shut down by making just one call to the Cedar Falls Sheriff's office.

But when at last he gave her back the report sheet, all he said was, 'I don't recall seeing your request for transfer to the traffic police, Detective Ziegler.'

'No, sir. I'm trying to find Edie Collier's boyfriend. He owns a red Econoline van, and I was wondering if it had ever been in a fender-bender or gotten a parking ticket.'

'I heard the local police got the doer,' Ryland Nelsen said, his gaze locked with Summer's, his expression impossible to read.

Summer gave it right back to him, cop to cop. 'Yes, sir. But there are some loose ends.'

'I also heard that this creep had the girl's clothes and her ID stashed away in his cellar. And he hung himself in his cell, didn't he? Left some kind of confession behind.'

'As I said, sir, there are some loose ends. That's why I need to find Edie Collier's boyfriend, see what he has to say about the circumstances of her disappearance. But if I don't have any luck by the end of the weekend, I'll drop it in a drawer and forget about it.'

Ryland Nelsen shook his head. 'No, you won't. You know why not?'

'No, sir, but I believe you're about to tell me.'

'I'm going to let that pass, Detective Ziegler, because I feel sorry for you. Because you have a hungry look that tells me you aren't going to forget about this when Monday rolls around. Oh, maybe you'll *try* to forget about it, but it'll keep nagging at you, and pretty soon you'll find yourself working on it in every moment of your spare time. You'll work nights, you'll spend every weekend chasing down leads. And if you're not careful, it'll eat your soul. You'll end up like Jake Lee over in Homicide. You know Jake Lee?'

'I've heard the name.'

'He's a good cop, highest clearance rate in the unit, but the only life he has is his work. He's a loner, and my little family in the Robbery Unit doesn't have room for loners or super-heroes.'

'I promise there's not a scrap of Lycra anywhere on my person, sir. If I don't find the boyfriend by the end of the weekend, that's it, I swear.'

'I can't order you to forget about it,' Ryland Nelsen said. 'I'm not even going to make a comment about misuse of the Bureau's limited resources. But your card is marked, Detective Ziegler. If I find you working on this when you should be working for me, you'll be back in a patrol car. Understood?'

'Yes, sir.'

Summer felt that she'd got off lightly. She bought a late lunch, a cheese-and-black-bean taco and a can of soda, at the Mexican stand in the parking lot across the street from the rear of the Justice Building, and worked through the stack of reports that Ada Simmons had sent her. She checked the most recent reports first, and almost immediately found something that grabbed her attention: a van found burning on a patch of waste ground near the airport last Thursday, half past ten at night. The day before Edie Collier had failed to turn up for work at the Rite Spot. There was no mention of the van's licence tag or colour in the brief report, but the timing was right on the button, that was for sure.

The uniform who'd first attended the scene was off duty. Summer left a message on his voicemail, got through to the fire marshal who'd written up the incident.

He told her that the person who had set the fire had known what they were doing. 'Gangbangers and joyriders usually don't do much more than splash gas over the front seats when they want to set fire to their ride, but this was torched professionally. I found the remains of a plastic two-gallon canister and a simple alarm-clock igniter in the back. Gas chromatography of the residue showed that he used a mixture of unleaded gasoline, polystyrene and detergent. Basically, home-made napalm. It creates a fireball when it lights off, and the burning polystyrene sticks everywhere it touches.'

'I guess everything inside was pretty much burned up.'

'What's left of the van is sitting out at the reclamation yard, waiting to be cubed. You're welcome to poke around, but if you were hoping to find something in particular I'm afraid you're out of luck. But there was something else that provoked my interest, apart from the professional torch job. The van was cold-plated – it was equipped with a set of cloned licence plates.'

'Cloned plates?'

'Yeah. You know how they do it?'

'Perhaps you could remind me.'

'It's pretty simple. You use a commercial database company like Car Data Check to find details of another vehicle identical to yours, and then you get a chop shop or a crooked dealer to knock out a set of fake plates. These particular plates belonged to a red Econoline van all right, same year and model as the one torched, but the registered owner lives in San Francisco, and she still owns her vehicle.'

'So the van could have been stolen,' Summer said. It fitted with her idea that Edie Collier's boyfriend had been involved in something illegal.

'Luckily, whoever changed the plates didn't think to change the vehicle identification number,' the fire marshal said. 'The sticker on the door jamb had either been burned or ripped off, but the metal plate they put on the driver's side of the dashboard was sticking out of a chunk of melted plastic. I cleaned it up, fed the number into AutoTrack, but as I recall it didn't really go anywhere.'

AutoTrack, a database run by a private company, was used by law enforcement agencies, insurance companies and debt recovery businesses to locate the past and current addresses and other personal details of people, and identify the registered owners of vehicles.

Summer said, 'Anything you can give me will be useful. I'm running on fumes.'

The marshal told Summer to hang on while he pulled the case file, came back on the line and told her, 'The VIN belongs to a 1989 Ford Econoline model E350, title registered to a Mr Bruce Smith, last known address Apartment 6, 1090 East Spruce Street, Denver.'

'Bruce Smith?' Summer said, writing all this down. 'Not Billy?'

'Here's the interesting thing,' the marshal said. 'I checked out Bruce Smith on the databases. Not only does he have a conviction for shoplifting, but his prints belong to someone by the name of William Gundersen, who racked up a couple of convictions for the same offence a year earlier, in Los Angeles. Think he's the guy you're looking for?'

'Was this Mr Smith missing a couple of fingers on his right hand?'

'Let me take a look at his card . . . What do you know, the ring and little finger.'

Bingo. William Gundersen, a.k.a. Bruce Smith, had to be Billy no-name, Edie Collier's boyfriend.

The fire marshal asked why she was looking for him; she gave a brief account of Edie Collier's kidnap and death.

'You think this guy had something to do with it?'

'I know that I need to talk to him.'

'Well, good luck. I tried to trace him, but he moved out of his last known address, the one in Denver, last year. No one there knows where he went, and that's as far as I took it. He doesn't have anything serious on his record, he isn't currently wanted for anything, so I figure he decided to ditch the van for whatever reason, torched it, that's all she wrote.'

'Do you happen to have a phone number for his last address?'

When Summer called the number, a young woman answered, said that she'd been getting mail for Bruce Smith but she didn't know who he was.

'This building's mostly students. I guess he graduated or moved on or whatever.'

Summer said, 'Do you happen to have kept any of his mail?'

'I pass it on to the old guy who manages this place.'

'Could you give me the manager's phone number?'

'I don't know it, but he lives just two doors down.'

'The problem is, I can't go knock on his door myself,' Summer said.

'Excuse me?'

'What I mean is, could you do me a big favour? Could you

knock on the manager's door, ask him for his phone number, then come back and tell me what it is?'

Three minutes later, Summer was talking to the apartment building's manager, who told her that Bruce Smith had run out last year, leaving two months' rent owing and no forwarding address.

'He still gets letters from a collection agency. I told them he's long gone, but they keep sending them. If you can do something about that,' the manager said, 'I'd appreciate it.'

'I'll try my best, sir. Was Mr Smith missing a couple of fingers on his right hand?'

'Yes ma'am. He used to keep that hand in his pocket most of the time, like that old-time French fella. Napoleon.'

'Did he ever tell you how he lost those fingers?'

'If he ever did, I don't recall it.'

Summer dug a description of Bruce Smith out of the manager. White, early twenties. Brown eyes, skinny, cropped brown hair he could have grown out and dyed since, maybe five ten in height, which was as close to Janice's six feet as made no difference.

Summer said, 'Do you know what he did for a living?'

'I believe it was something to do with the university, but I don't recall what.'

'What kind of vehicle did he own?'

'A van, an old one.'

'A red Ford Econoline?'

'Not red, but it was an Econoline all right. White, if you cared to look under the dirt. He never washed it that I recall. Have you found him?'

'Not yet, sir. That's what this is all about.'

'When you do, you could remind him that he owes one thousand eight hundred dollars in back rent, plus another five hundred it cost to clean up the place. He left the refrigerator open and unplugged with a pound of shrimp in it – took me a week to get rid of the stink.'

'When did he leave, sir?'

'He ran out last year, it was September I believe. Luckily, it was the beginning of the Fall semester, I was able to rent the apartment straight after it was cleaned up.'

'And when did he move in?'

'Let me see . . . I believe it was maybe six months or so before he skipped. Six months or thereabouts. If you want, I can go check my books.'

'Did he pay his rent by cash or cheque?'

'Cheque. The last one he gave me bounced.'

'Do you happen to have kept that cheque?'

'I always make photocopies of cheques my tenants pay, so there's no fuss about lost paperwork. You'd be surprised at how many try to pull that particular trick. You want I should go look it out? Might take a few minutes, I'm a little behind on my filing.'

'I'll stay on the phone,' Summer said.

She waited ten whole minutes while the manager looked for his photocopies of Bruce Smith's cheques, wrote down the name of the bank and the account number, asked the manager if he had kept any of Bruce Smith's mail.

'You want me to send that on to you?'

'If you could open one of those letters from the collection agency, I can try to get them off your back.'

Summer felt a tight, hard excitement, but believed that she had it under control. After she had finished talking to the apartment manager, she called the reclamation yard, confirmed that the van was still there, and made the foreman promise that it wouldn't be pressed into a cube before she'd had a chance to look at it. She called Bruce Smith's bank in Denver, learned that he had opened the account in March last year, the same month he'd taken up the lease on his apartment. By June, the account had been some five hundred dollars overdrawn; by July, it had been frozen, and the bank had started chasing him for the debt. The bank officer told Summer that she couldn't supply copies of Bruce Smith's statements without a warrant, but the account manager of the credit-card company's collections centre was more helpful, telling Summer that Bruce Smith had exceeded his credit limit by more than four thousand dollars before disappearing off the map. Summer promised the account manager that she would notify him as soon as she had located Mr Smith, and the man agreed to fax her details of Bruce Smith's credit-card purchases as soon as he had confirmed that she was working for the Portland Police Bureau.

Summer went back up to the thirteenth floor, ran Bruce Smith, a.k.a. William Gundersen, through NCIC, the National Crime Index Computer, and printed off his record. Then she called the Denver Police's record department and asked them to fax her a copy of his custody report. She stood over the laser printer while it crawled out of the machine. Here were photographs of an ordinary-looking young man, front face and right and left profiles. Here was his fingerprint card, with blank spaces for the last two fingers of his right hand and a scrawled annotation noting that the fingers were missing.

'Gotcha,' Summer said.

The reclamation yard that had the contract to dispose of abandoned, wrecked and unroadworthy vehicles impounded by the city bordered the Willamette River to the north of the docks – ten forlorn, gull-haunted acres of rusting carcasses stacked in long rows. Bruce Smith/William Gundersen's burned-out van was stored in a far corner, squatting on the rims of its wheels, windshield gone, paint scorched from metal already patched orange with rust.

Summer took a pair of vinyl gloves from her purse and snapped them on. She was determined to do this right.

The door on the driver's side groaned open on stiff hinges, releasing a strong odour of seared plastic. The seats had been burned down to metal framing and springs. Scabs of melted plastic clung to the bottom of the steering wheel's braided wire. There was nothing but char in the gaping hole where the glove compartment had been, nothing but gritty ash under the seats. The lock on the rear doors was broken; someone had looped wire around the handles to hold them shut. Summer unwound the wire carefully, making sure that she didn't touch the handles, wrenched open one of the doors and switched on her little Mag-Lite and swept its beam over the charred remains of what had once been a cheap stuffed mattress. Flakes of ash shivered in the draught. A single scorched shoe lay on its side.

Summer climbed inside, moving as carefully as she could, the acrid stink searing her nose and throat as she felt under the edges of the burned mattress, explored every corner. She found blackened pennies lying among the cracked shards of a jelly jar. She found a belt buckle and a cheap silver chain discoloured by heat. She found several charred lumps that had been paperback books and carefully cracked them open one by one, checking pages scorched but not completely burned. One of the books was a copy of Billy Collins's *Nine Horses*.

She stripped off her vinyl gloves and did her best to dust ash from the knees and cuffs of her pants, took the roll of duct tape from the trunk of her Accura and used it to fasten plastic bags over the van's door handles. Firefighters and reclamation-yard workers had probably smudged any prints that might have survived the fire, but she wanted to have a crime-scenes officer come out and check the handles anyway, just in case.

When Summer climbed into her car, she got a glimpse of her face in the rear-view mirror and spent a couple of minutes wiping off smudges with tissues and a bottle of spring water. She drove through heavy rush-hour traffic to the Justice Building. The credit-card company had faxed copies of Bruce Smith's statements. She put them in an envelope and called Denise Childers to give her the good news.

Later that evening, Summer's mother said, 'So after all your work, you still don't know if this boy is alive or dead.'

Summer said, 'Edie Collier was asking about him when she was found. So I guess she thought he was still alive.'

Her mother said, 'She'd been badly injured by a blow to the head. She must have been in a lot of pain, and she could have been confused. The simplest explanation is that he was murdered, she was kidnapped, and the people who did it set fire to the van to cover their tracks.'

They were sitting at the kitchen table. Summer was eating take-out from the local Italian place again. A thin-crust pizza with fresh tomato and oregano sauce, buffalo mozzarella and green pepper and pepperoni, and sipping from a big glass of red wine.

She said, 'Whether he's alive or dead, the boyfriend was definitely in some kind of trouble. He'd run up bank and credit-card debts in Denver under a false name, he owed rent, and he had a shoplifting charge hanging over him. So he moved here, he resprayed his van and changed its licence plates, he was living rough . . . My guess is that he tried to make some fast money, he pissed off the wrong people, and it came back to bite him.'

This was the scenario that Summer and Denise Childers had agreed they liked best. Bad people had come looking for the boyfriend, and whether or not they'd found him, they'd definitely found Edie Collier.

'If this Billy Gundersen is dead, his grave isn't on Joe Kronenwetter's property,' Denise had said. 'We didn't turn up anything when we checked the immediate area with dogs and a methane probe, in case Kronenwetter had snatched other girls we didn't know about. But we have a whole bunch of woods out here. His body could be anywhere. Maybe some hiker or hunter will stumble over it, but don't hold your breath.'

'I checked with the Multnomah County morgue. None of the bodies of young white males brought in during the past week lacked two fingers from the right hand.'

'I guess I should write up a missing-person report for Mr Gundersen. Send it to every police department and Sheriff's office I can think of.'

'As long as it doesn't get you in trouble,' Summer had said, trying to keep the relief out of her voice. She knew that posting a missing-person report was the obvious next step, but she also knew that it was Denise's to make because Denise was the primary investigator.

Denise had said, 'We need to find out what happened to Edie Collier's boyfriend because his disappearance may have something to do with her kidnap and subsequent death. Who could argue with that?'

Neither of them had mentioned Dirk Merrit, but Summer knew that Denise wasn't about to give up her idea that the millionaire, with or without the help of Joseph Kronenwetter, had something to do with Edie Collier's death. Right now, Denise was probably trying to work up a link between Dirk Merrit and Edie's boyfriend.

Her mother said, 'Here's another idea. Edie Collier and her boyfriend were both kidnapped, they both managed to escape, but they became split up. For all you know he could still be wandering around in the woods. Are you going to eat that last slice?'

'Knock yourself out.'

'I shouldn't, but I can never resist Carlo's pizza,' her mother said, and neatly bit off the slice's drooping tip.

Summer said, 'I know the boyfriend's name, I know he was into credit-card fraud and shoplifting, and I know he put false licence plates on his van and resprayed it. But you're right – there's still a lot I need to find out. For instance, I need to know if it was Joseph Kronenwetter or someone who knew Kronenwetter who torched the van and snatched Edie Collier, or if it was someone from her boyfriend's past. Someone he crossed in Denver, or even in Los Angeles.'

Her mother said, 'I don't think that it was Mr Kronenwetter. Why would he have come all the way to Portland to kidnap a random girl? And why would he have set fire to her boyfriend's van?'

'That's right. Whoever torched the van came prepared. He brought along home-made napalm. He had a plan.'

'So what are you going to do next?'

'Since there's no evidence that the boyfriend was killed, I guess I'm going to carry on looking for him.'

'Don't forget our dinner party tomorrow night,' her mother said.

'I have a lot of ground to cover tomorrow. I'll try my best to make it, but—'

'I told our guests to turn up any time after seven,' her mother said. 'Some help in the kitchen before then would be lovely.'

16

Frank Wilson lived in a trailer park in Central Point, a wide spot in the road fifteen miles east of Dirk Merrit's estate. His shift wasn't scheduled to end for a couple of hours and there were no lights showing in the windows of his trailer, but just in case the man was shacked up with a pal or some piece of skirt Carl knocked on the door and waited a whole minute before snapping back the tongue of the lock with a thin strip of metal. The kitchen/living room had the stale smell and casual untidiness of a man living alone. A short corridor led past a filthy bathroom with a folding door to the bedroom. A box-spring mattress on the worn grey carpet; Polaroids of different women in various stages of undress stuck to one wall; several sets of clothes hung from hooks fixed to another. Chinos and shirts, a leather jacket and blue jeans, a suit in a dry-cleaner's plastic sleeve. Carl found a Beretta M9 with a full clip and one in the chamber tucked under the mattress; found a cassette tape in the inside pocket of the suit jacket.

He shoved the Beretta into the waistband of his combat pants and took the cassette into the living area, where he'd seen a cheap boombox standing next to the brand-new TV. Listening to what was on the tape didn't take more than two minutes. He fast-forwarded through the rest of the side, ejected the tape, turned it over and fast-forwarded through the other side. When he was certain that there was nothing but the brief muffled conversation on the tape, he slipped it into a pocket, then shrugged off his daypack, shook out a large sheet of plastic and spread it in front of the door, and sat in the dark in a greasy armchair.

He thought about what was on the tape, how he could best make use of it. One thing was certain: it was definitely a way out. If he could get Pat Metcalf to confess everything, he'd have the perfect excuse to head off for Los Angeles. He'd have to tell Dirk Merrit what had been going on, of course, but he was pretty sure that he knew how the man would react, that he'd want his loyal soldier to tidy up this little mess. Carl examined it from every angle, until he was certain that he knew how to play it. Thinking now about Joseph Kronenwetter's suicide, about Dirk Merrit's flat denial that he'd had anything to do with it. Carl didn't believe that for a moment, didn't believe that it was just one of those things that happen, as the man had claimed, when luck is going your way. The question was, how had Dirk Merrit reached out to Kronenwetter when he'd been banged up in a cell on the fourth floor of the Justice Building in Cedar Falls? It had to have been an inside job, Carl thought – one of the guards or one of the prisoners. Most likely one of the guards. Set aside the question of how Dirk Merrit happened to know a prison guard, he must have talked to him, explained what needed doing, handed over money . . .

Looking at it for the sixth or seventh time, Carl couldn't see how it could have gone down any differently.

Dirk Merrit and his giant ego, his stupid conviction that he was a new breed of human, smarter than anyone else in the world.

As far as the local cops were concerned, though, the man's luck seemed to be holding. According to the local TV news, they believed that Kronenwetter had topped himself out of remorse and they wanted to forget all about him and the dead girl, move on, nothing to see. On the other hand, that detective from Portland and her pal from the Sheriff's office clearly thought that Dirk Merrit was dirty, while the person Dirk Merrit had paid to murder Kronenwetter would come back for more money, sure as eggs were eggs. And Carl couldn't begin to guess what kind of damn fool stunt the man would try next.

Well, screw him. Carl had his own kind of luck – the luck he'd made for himself. He had the tape, he had Pat Metcalf in his sights, his work here was almost done. All he had to do was deliver the keystroke-capture device to Erik Grow, rape *Trans*'s subscription service, and move on. He still had the fake passport he'd used to get into the States. He'd catch a random flight to a random destination in South America, buy himself a new identity, and if the cops still hadn't caught up with Dirk Merrit, he'd drop them a line, let them know where all the bodies were buried . . .

Carl smiled in the near-dark. Everything was working out very nicely indeed. He could allow himself to relax a little while he waited for Frank Wilson, his thoughts dipping into the past, a dungeon full of blood and screams lit by flashes of black lightning, scenes where he'd shed his camouflage and expressed his true nature . . .

He snapped awake when he heard the sound of a car engine. Headlights flared through the frosted glass of the trailer's door, went out. A key scraped in the lock. The door opened. The light came on overhead.

Frank Wilson stood in the doorway in his cheap blue shirt and black pants. He stared at Carl, started to say something, and Carl raised his .22 Colt Woodsman and shot him twice in the chest. Carl had fitted a home-made silencer on the pistol, a length of TV-antenna pole stuffed with steel wool. The shots were no louder than party balloons popping. He was out of the armchair as quick as thought, catching Wilson as he collapsed, easing him onto the plastic sheeting. Saying gently into the dead man's ear, 'Was that real enough for you, pal?'

Outside then, a fast peek. Wilson's Blazer sat nearby in the warm dark. A TV was making noise in a trailer across the way, lights showed here and there through spindly eucalyptus trees the park's owner had planted in a vain attempt to give his property some class, but no one was about. Carl checked Wilson's body for exit wounds and didn't find any: he'd used light loads and frangible rounds that would break up on entry. He picked up the two casings that the Colt had ejected and the keys Wilson had dropped, wrapped Wilson's body in the plastic sheeting and dragged it out to the Blazer, drove at just under the posted limit out of town to the old logging trail where he'd left his pickup truck. He pitched Wilson's body into the pickup's load-bed, covered it with lengths of timber, and drove off. He'd left the keys in the ignition of the Blazer. Maybe someone would take it, maybe not. It didn't really matter. By the time the cops had worked out that its owner was missing, Frank Wilson would have vanished off the face of the earth.

It took Carl more than an hour to wrap the body in a set of old chains, drive around the lake to the boathouse, load the body into the Zodiac and motor out to the middle of the lake, roll the weighted corpse over the side. Splish-splash-splosh, gone. Hard work, but necessary.

It was a little after two a.m. Carl walked back to the mansion along the edge of the lake, savouring the quiet dark, one hand in the pocket of his combat pants, gripping the Ziploc bag and the souvenir he'd taken. In his spartan room at the top of the half-finished tower, he showered, lay down on his narrow bed, set his wristwatch alarm to go off in four hours, and fell asleep while thinking of the conversation he would soon be having with Mr Patrick Metcalf.

Carl planned to snatch Metcalf on his way to work and take him to a quiet place where they could focus on the matter at hand, but it didn't quite work out that way. Just before nine, Saturday morning, Carl was sitting in the pickup truck, parked across the street from Metcalf's Californian-style house in a new development in the hills east of Cedar Falls – red tile roof, white stucco walls and a dying yucca in the gravel front yard – when his cell phone rang.

'I need to talk to you right away,' Dirk Merrit said.

'I'll be there as soon as I can,' Carl said. 'I'm in the middle of something.'

'What part of "right away" don't you understand? Meet me in the solar,' Dirk Merrit said, and rang off.

For a second, Carl thought about calling back and telling Dirk Merrit where to stick his orders, but he knew that he had to keep the man sweet, pretend to be the loyal soldier, until the delicious, much-anticipated moment when he took down Powered By Lightning.

As Carl folded up his cell phone, the front door of Metcalf's house opened and a German shepherd galloped out. Metcalf appeared in the doorway, stuck his fingers in the corners of his mouth and gave a sharp whistle. The dog bounded back to him, barking and wagging its tail; an olive-skinned woman, a little plump but not bad, bare-legged in an oversize T-shirt, black hair loose around her shoulders, appeared behind him. In his pickup, Carl watched Metcalf fuss with the dog and kiss the woman goodbye, watched him climb into his black Range Rover as the woman stood by the door, holding the dog by its collar, watched the Range Rover reverse out of the short drive and move away down the sleepy suburban street.

It would be so easy to pull up beside the Range Rover at a stop light, roll down the window and smile at Pat Metcalf from behind the sharp end of a sawn-off shotgun before blowing him away . . . Trouble was, Carl needed some information from the man first.

'Soon,' he said, and waited until the woman had pulled the German shepherd inside before he started the pickup.

17

Saturday morning, while her mother was out shopping for groceries, Summer sat at the weathered cedarwood table on the deck her father had built in the backyard, sifting through copies of William Gundersen's credit-card statements. It was already warm, the sky a rich cloudless blue beyond the trees and rooftops. Birds singing, children shouting to each other off in the distance, the neighbourhood stirring around her.

Summer loved the big old Victorian house, its long front porch and spacious backyard, its fairy-tale turret, its richly decorated gables, every room full of battered, comfortable furniture, books, pieces of art, and curios. She loved the neighbourhood, too: the deep shade of its tree-lined streets, the family houses with their steep little front yards crammed with hostas and ferns, notices about yard sales or missing cats tacked to utility poles, the vacant lot where she'd played as a kid . . . Moving back here after she'd split up with Jeff had been like flopping into an old, familiar couch, but she really had to start looking around for a place of her own and get on with her life. Next week, she'd study the property pages of the *Oregonian* to get an idea of what the market was like, and register with letting agencies. A couple of real-estate brokers, ex-cops, advertised in the *Rap Sheet*, the newsletter of the Portland Police Association. Maybe they'd give her a good deal.

Meanwhile, she had to try to figure out what kind of shape Edie Collier's boyfriend had made, out there in the world. She felt that she had plenty to go on. Her mother had once told her that Sherlock Holmes could build up a picture of a man from his cigar ash. Billy Gundersen, a.k.a. Bruce Smith, had left behind a lot more than that.

He'd obtained his credit card in March last year, just after he'd moved into his new apartment, and had immediately used it to purchase items worth over two thousand dollars at a store in Denver called Abe's Bytes and Bits. In the next couple of months he'd made several other purchases in the store for lesser amounts, spent more than five hundred dollars at Apple's online music store, and taken out subscriptions to several online computer games.

One of the games was *Trans*, the game that Dirk Merrit had developed. Denise was going to love that particular detail.

In June, when Billy Gundersen's bank account had become overdrawn, small purchases at convenience stores and gas stations began to appear on his credit-card statements, ten dollars here, twenty there. By the time the card had been shut down he'd owed more than six thousand dollars in unpaid charges and accumulated interest.

Summer made a call to Abe's Bytes and Bits, and after five minutes and a lot of prompting, the surly clerk who'd answered located the records of Billy Gundersen's first credit-card purchase: a fully loaded Toshiba laptop with a WiFi-compatible network card and extra memory, and a carrying case. Later purchases included an iPod, several models of computer game joystick, and external speakers and an upgrade of his laptop's soundcard. These acquisitions and the subscription charges suggested to Summer that Billy Gundersen had a serious jones for computer games played over the Internet. Possibly there was a connection with Dirk Merrit, possibly not, but it gave her an idea about where to start looking for him. The WiFi card in his laptop would enable him to connect to the Internet anywhere there was a wireless network, and Summer bet that someone who'd been sleeping in his van would have taken advantage of places that offered free Internet access.

She went into the front room that served as her mother's office and fired up the computer. It shared the trestle table, set in one of the bay windows, with a tall stack of printed pages – the heavily annotated manuscript of the twentieth or thirtieth draft of her mother's novel. At the back of the big room, with its white-painted floorboards and metal stacking shelves stuffed with books, were unframed paintings of every size stacked along one wall, the sculpture of a bull's head made of welded piping on a stand of rough concrete, an easel propping up a half-finished painting, her father's battered metal desk still covered with his papers and tools . . .

Another reason for moving out. There were things that Summer's father had owned or made all over the house, little reminders of his presence that snagged her soul like thorns at every turn.

After just a few minutes on the Internet, she realized that tracking down Billy Gundersen was going to be harder than she'd first thought, because Portland was at the forefront of free public WiFi access. There were more than a hundred coffee shops, bars, hotels and restaurants where you could use a wireless-enabled laptop or other wireless device to connect to the Internet. Public and college libraries had their own WiFi networks too, and so did Portland International Airport . . .

After some thought, Summer decided that libraries and the coffee shops were her best bet. If you were short of funds, you could sit for as long as you wanted in a coffee shop for the price of a small latte, and not only were the libraries free but Summer remembered that Edie Collier had owned a reader's card for the Multnomah County Central Library – it had been found with her clothes and other possessions in Joseph Kronenwetter's basement.

Summer was getting ready to go out when her mother returned. She helped carry bags of groceries from the car to the kitchen, told her mother that she would probably be out and about for the rest of the day but she would be back in good time for the dinner party.

'As long as you're back before seven,' her mother said.

'I'll do my best.'

Her mother opened the fridge, started unloading salad makings into its crisper. She was wearing blue jeans and a yellow T-shirt; her hair was pinned up in a loose French braid. A little broad about the hips, but still slim . . . Summer hoped that she would look half as good when she reached her mother's age. She said, 'How long have you had your hair like that?'

'It seems like for ever. Why?'

'I was thinking maybe you should get a different style. Shorter, layered. It would suit your face.'

'I'd look like a lesbian librarian.'

Summer mimed shock.

'It's what men would think,' her mother said blithely.

'Are you thinking about dating, like that?'

'Thinking about it but not doing anything about it, not yet.' Her mother turned from the refrigerator, a bottle of spring water in her hand. 'So, as you're going out, do I take it that you have a hot lead on this boyfriend?'

'I know he was into computers and online computer games.'

'You mean MMOs?'

'I'm sorry?'

'MMOs. Massively multiplayer online games. You play against other players rather than against computer-controlled opponents. Strictly speaking, *Trans* is an MMORPG – a massively multi-player online *role-playing* game, because each player takes on a particular character before they start playing.'

'And you know this because . . .?'

'Tony is a big fan.'

'I didn't know that.'

Tony Otaka was one of her mother's graduate students.

'I'm sure he would be more than happy to help out,' her mother said. 'Players talk with other players all the time – in the games of course, and on bulletin boards where they exchange tips and tricks, gossip . . . In fact, MMOs are as much online communities as games. If this boyfriend you're looking for was an active player, he would have been a part of that world. Perhaps Tony knows him, or at any rate knows *about* him.'

Summer checked her notes. 'The boyfriend was into *Everquest*, *Trans*, and *World of Warcraft*. Or at least, he bought subscriptions to them last year, I don't know if they're still current.'

'I'm sure Tony will know how to find that out.'

'Okay. But don't tell him that it's because I'm looking for someone involved in a suspicious death.'

'Tony knows how to keep a secret.'

'I'm sure he does. But I shouldn't have told you about this, much less anyone else.'

Her mother sipped her spring water. 'All right. I'll think of a suitable excuse.'

'Something believable,' Summer said. 'This isn't one of your mystery stories.'

18

The solar was a small geodesic dome set at the end of the broad terrace behind the mansion's three towers, enclosing a Jacuzzi and a desert garden of sand, rocks and cacti. Most of the cacti had been genetically modified: bright red cacti; cacti mottled with white or yellow splotches; cacti that grew tufts of hair instead of spines. In the middle of this garden of curiosities, beside the fizzing Jacuzzi, Dirk Merrit lay naked on a black leather couch, resting his chin on his folded arms while the masseur who came by once a week worked on his shoulders. Elias Silver sat beside him in a canvas chair, pointing to something on his laptop's screen.

'Listen to this,' Dirk Merrit told Carl. 'It's a new breakthrough in genetic engineering, very exciting.'

Elias Silver clicked through PowerPoint slides on his laptop, talking about zinc-based enzymes that could be primed to target specific genes, unzip them from the chromosome, and replace them with engineered versions. Talking about how this could be used not only to replace defective genes with working copies, but also to insert genes that would express novel characteristics, riffing on the idea that the new technique meant that genetic modification was no longer confined to what he called germ cells – sperm or eggs. Instead, genes could be inserted in any kind of cell of anyone or anything.

'Imagine a virus that's engineered to infect only one kind of somatic cell. The epidermal cells that grow hairs, for instance. The virus carries this enzyme, and the enzyme inserts an engineered gene into every cell the virus infects. It could be used for something as trivial as altering hair colour, or it could be used for more radical transformations. For growing scales, for instance, or feathers.'

Carl sat on a rock and waited impatiently, sweating in the fierce heat trapped by the dome, while Dirk Merrit and Elias Silver batted nonsense back and forth for a couple of minutes. Dirk Merrit loved this castles-in-the-air science-fiction bullshit. He was passionately interested in personal immortality, and had squandered much of his fortune sponsoring charlatans who promised various kinds of life-extension treatments, IQ boosts, protection against cancer and symptoms of ageing, and radical redesigns of the human body. He'd once said, in an interview for *Wired*, that it didn't matter if he was down to his last dollar as long as he had used the rest of his money to buy eternal life. For if you could live for ever, you could stick just one dollar in a bank account and in an eye-blink of relative time – ten thousand years, say – simple compound interest would turn it into billions. Wait only a little longer, and you would own everything on Earth. And that was just the start. If you had all of time to play with, there was nothing that you could not do.

And while he had been waiting for one or another of his protégés to hit pay dirt, he'd not only had his body restructured by cutting-edge surgical techniques, but had also played with various side projects, such as the genetically engineered cacti, or the stunted apple tree in the little greenhouse on top of the main tower. Samples of Dirk Merrit's DNA had been chopped up and added in random sequences to the chromosomes of cultured apple cells, and one of those cells had given rise to the tree. He liked to say that anyone who ate one of its fruits would be eating his flesh. In the distant future, according to him, genetic engineers could extract his genome from the tree, or from one of its offspring, and use it to grow clones of himself.

At long last, Dirk Merrit sat up and dismissed Elias Silver and the masseur. Because the rest of his body had been so extensively altered, it was always a shock to see that he had normal male equipment. He was tall but oddly proportioned – he'd had lengths of titanium inserted in his thigh bones – and skinny too: the cage of his ribs, the articulation of his shoulder blades and the crests of his pelvis were all clearly visible under his powdery white skin. His scalp was hairless, his lips were blue-white, like the lips of a corpse, and his ears, elaborated with drooping lobes in which silver hoops were strung, were like strange pale fungi. Only his eyes had colour. Dirk Merrit had dozens of pairs of contact lenses and wore different ones according to his mood. Today his eyes were a dark gold, with slitted pupils. The eyes of a snake, or of a bird of prey.

These uncanny eyes stared at Carl; Carl stared right back. When Elias Silver and the masseur had left them alone in the hot, dry little garden, Dirk Merrit said, 'Is something worrying you?'

'Not really.'

'You seem a little distracted.'

Carl shrugged. He wasn't about to ask why Dirk Merrit wanted to see him. Let the man tell him in his own good time.

Dirk Merrit put on his silk kimono, showing Carl the chrysanthemum embroidered on its back, red against faded green, when he walked to the edge of the dome. He stared out through one of the big hexagonal panes of glass at the drop down to the white boulders of the dry creek at the bottom of the valley, saying at last, 'Did you see the news this morning?'

'I was out.'

'On one of your mysterious errands.'

Carl didn't say anything.

'It was on all the local affiliates,' Dirk Merrit said. 'CNN picked it up too.'

Carl waited.

'State troopers in Nevada stumbled upon the body of our last pilgrim,' Dirk Merrit said, and turned in a sudden flare of green silk. 'They've identified him, too. They know that he was the girl's boyfriend.'

For a moment, Carl was tempted to kill the man. His .22 was tucked in his belt under his denim jacket, its grip square against his back. He could kill the man right now, grab what he could, and make a run for it. He let the impulse roll through him and fade away, listened carefully while Dirk Merrit told him that the local cops had identified the body from fingerprints that

matched those on a missing-person report posted by a cop in
Cedar Falls, that the FBI had become involved . . .

And it came to Carl right there and then what he had to do.
A reason for heading down to Los Angeles, and a way of keeping Dirk Merrit out of the hands of the cops until Powered By
Lightning had been taken down, was coming together as smoothly
as the wards of a well-oiled lock.

Dirk Merrit was saying, 'I find it all very exciting. I'm a
hunter, but now I find that I'm being hunted. It adds a whole
new dimension to the game.'

'The prison guard you bribed to kill the guy we framed for
the girl's death – how is he holding up?'

There was a silence. At last, Dirk Merrit said, 'Did you find
out about him? Or was that a guess?'

'I worked it out. It wasn't difficult. The cops probably won't
have much difficulty working it out either.'

Dirk Merrit shrugged. 'Well, don't worry about it. Whatever
happens, it won't get back to me. Everything was done by phone
and a cut-out.'

'It won't take long for the cops to work out that the man supposed to have kidnapped the girl was in their custody when her
boyfriend was killed. When they do, you can bet that they'll be
taking a close look at his so-called suicide, and that's when your
guard is going to come back to you, ask for more money. A *lot*
more money. Not only that, he'll probably start to wonder if he
can make a deal. He'll start to wonder if he can hand you over
in exchange for immunity.'

'So I should take him out before he takes me out,' Dirk
Merrit said, clearly liking the idea.

'We can do it when I get back,' Carl said.

Dirk Merrit said, 'When you get back? You aren't going anywhere, Carl. I need you here. I need you to help me deal with
this situation, I need you to set up another hunt—'

'First of all, before anything else, you need me to get the FBI
off your back,' Carl said, letting himself smile now because he
had the man, he had him right in the palm of his hand. 'You
need me to draw their attention away from Cedar Falls before

they start to think about the girlfriend, how she ended up here. You need me to give them something else to think about. And I know just how to do it.'

Dirk Merrit studied him, then said, 'You have my attention.'

'Let's start with one of your security guards, Mr Frank Wilson, and what I caught him at a couple of days ago.'

19

Summer set out on the trail of Edie Collier's boyfriend with a good, positive feeling, but by the middle of the afternoon, after showing Billy Gundersen's mugshot to staff at every one of Portland's public and college libraries, she had come up with nothing but shrugs, headshakes and apologies. She stopped for a break in the big Starbucks that anchored a corner of Pioneer Courthouse Square, and spent a couple of hours trawling the spots in the city centre where Portland's young runaways and indigents hung out, making a loop south on SW Broadway, north on SW Fourth Avenue, showing the mug shots of Billy Gundersen and Edie Collier to the staff of every WiFi-enabled coffee shop, to needle-and-ink artists in tattoo shops. Late in the afternoon, at the fifth tattoo shop on her list, she finally lucked out: the shop's owner recognised the couple, said that she'd inked a pair of matching designs on them three weeks ago. A chunky middle-aged woman with short hair dyed bright red, wearing a denim vest that displayed arms gleaming with multi-coloured ink-work from shoulders to wrists, she told Summer that the boy hadn't had any other tattoos she could see, but she remembered his maimed right hand, and also remembered that he'd been carrying a laptop computer.

'Remind me again, what kind of trouble are they in?'

Summer believed that the woman was a straight-shooter and decided to get right to the point. 'I'm afraid that the girl is dead, ma'am.'

The woman blinked, then said, 'I'm sorry to hear it. What about the boyfriend?'

Summer said, 'Well, that's why I'm here. We need to find him, make sure he's safe. Can you remember what they talked about while you were working on them? People they hung out with, places where they hung out, anything at all.'

'The girl was pretty quiet. Quite a few of my first-timers are. See, a good tattoo artist rarely hurts a client,' the woman said. 'There's some tingling and prickling, sure, but it's nothing like as bad as your average injection. But some people, their first time, they anticipate pain, they go quiet and tense up. That's how the girl was.'

Summer thought of Edie Collier after she'd been arrested for shoplifting, her quiet untroubled otherworldliness. 'What about her boyfriend?'

'One thing I can tell you, he didn't kill her.'

'That's not why I'm looking for him.'

'They were sweet kids. Real sweet with each other. They asked for matching Rose-and-Banner tattoos with each other's names on their shoulders. Corny, but it's what they wanted and it's what I gave them, with some nice shading on the roses. A standard design like that, the shading makes all the difference. He held her hand while I worked on her, and then she held his hand.'

'Did you talk to the boyfriend while you worked on him?'

The woman thought for a moment, stroking the big, whiskery blue-green carp wound around her left arm. 'We talked about science fiction. Yeah, and computer games. He told me about this game he was playing over the Internet, how he was tracking down something that would make him rich and famous.'

'Did he mention what the game was called?'

The woman thought again, said, 'If he did, I don't remember.'

'Was it *Everquest*, *World of Warcraft*, *Trans*, one of those?'

The woman shrugged.

'Did he tell you exactly what he was looking for in the game, what was going to make him rich?'

'Some kind of treasure . . . Come to think of it, he was pretty vague about it. Maybe he thought I was going to rip him off. I don't know why, it's only a game, but he was very serious about it.'

They went over it for a couple of minutes. Summer gave the woman her card, told her to call if she remembered anything else.

It wasn't much to show for a day's work, but at least Summer had confirmation that Billy Gundersen definitely had been Edie Collier's boyfriend, that he was still using a laptop, and was still involved in role-playing games. She was on the way back to her mother's house, driving over Burnside Bridge, when her cell phone rang. It was Denise Childers, and she came straight to the point.

'The FBI have cherry-picked our case.'

Summer felt a muscle clench in the middle of her body. 'How did they get involved?'

'They found the body of Edie Collier's boyfriend.'

The end of the bridge was coming up. Summer told Denise to wait a moment, drove across the intersection with 1st Avenue and pulled over by a row of decrepit shops, picked up her cell phone again. 'You better start over.'

Denise explained that an anonymous tip-off yesterday afternoon had alerted state troopers to the presence of a body in the middle of a dry lake bed in northeast Nevada. 'Same deal as the tip-off we received about Joe Kronenwetter's cellar. It was made to a secretary's extension, and the voice was electronically disguised.'

She said that the FBI had taken up the investigation because there were parallels with two recent unsolved murders: Ben Ridden, a twenty-eight-year-old insurance salesman whose skeletal remains had been found in the Mojave Desert six months after he'd last been seen, checking into a motel in the northern Californian town of Yreka; and a German tourist, Tomas Stahl, whose badly decomposed body had been found in Christmas Lake Valley, Oregon, six weeks after he'd disappeared from his motel room in Redding, some eighty miles south of Yreka. Billy Gundersen, Ben Ridden, and the German tourist had all been shot by crossbow bolts and killed by close-range *coup de grâce* shots to the head; Billy Gundersen and the German tourist had been missing their hearts, and notches on

Ben Ridden's ribcage suggested that his chest had been cut open.

Summer remembered the crossbow that Dirk Merrit had shown off, and waited for Denise to mention it.

Instead, Denise said, 'The feds matched the body's fingerprints to Gundersen's AFIS record. Then they discovered the missing-person report I put out, and sent a couple of agents to talk to me. I would have called you earlier, but I only just finished with them. Right now I'm waiting on one of their forensic investigators. He wants to take a look at Edie's body.'

Summer said, 'Do they have any idea when Billy Gundersen was killed?'

'Sometime between late Thursday and the middle of Friday.'

'He was killed where he was found, or killed somewhere else and dumped?'

'It looks like he was killed on the spot. And from footprints and tracks at the scene, he was chased quite some way before he was killed.'

'If Billy Gundersen was killed in Nevada, Thursday or Friday—'

Denise said, 'I know. It means that Joe Kronenwetter couldn't possibly have killed him, because Kronenwetter was arrested on Tuesday and killed himself in his jail cell the next day.'

Summer took a moment to get it straight in her head. 'Billy Gundersen's van was found on fire here in Portland early Friday morning. Edie Collier didn't turn up for work Friday, she wasn't seen again until she was found in the forest near Cedar Falls, the following Tuesday, and her boyfriend didn't report her disappearance. It's possible that he was involved in something that meant he couldn't go to the police, but it's more likely that he was kidnapped at the same time she was.'

Denise said, 'And that means he was kept somewhere other than Kronenwetter's shack, and was taken out to the desert and killed by someone else. The feds didn't tell me everything, but they did let slip that there were tracks from some kind of RV at the scene.'

'Either Joe Kronenwetter had nothing to do with any of this, or he had an accomplice.'

Denise said, 'The feds are working on the idea that this travelling man and Kronenwetter are good buddies. They could have met up in the army, during Kronenwetter's spell in jail last year, or even at some gun show. They kidnapped the two kids, Kronenwetter got the girl, and his friend the travelling man got the boy. They went their separate ways and did their separate things, and then the travelling man ratted out Kronenwetter. They'll probably get around to interviewing you, in due course. Don't expect it to be in any way interesting. When these guys come in and take over a case, they leave everyone else out of the loop.'

'Who's in charge?'

'Section Chief Harry Malone, Behavioural Sciences. I was given to understand by the two suits who interviewed me that he's a good man, very experienced and very meticulous.'

'There's something I need to tell you,' Summer said, and explained about the credit-card bills that proved that Billy Gundersen had liked to play online computer games. 'He had subscriptions to three different games. One of them was *Trans*.' When Denise didn't say anything, she added, 'It's a possible connection with Dirk Merrit. After you first told me about him, after we met him, I have to admit that I wasn't convinced that he had anything to do with Edie. I guess I've changed my mind.'

Another pause. Summer heard children's laughter, a water splash, and guessed that Denise was calling from her backyard.

Summer said, 'I spent the morning canvassing WiFi hotspots here in Portland – places where you can connect to the Internet for free? I didn't have any luck there, but I did find the woman who gave Edie Collier and Billy Gundersen matching tattoos. She remembered that Billy Gundersen was carrying a laptop, said that he told her he was looking for some kind of treasure, something valuable, in an online game. So I definitely think it's worth pursuing Dirk Merrit, and the computer-gaming angle.'

Denise said, 'Can I ask you a straight question? Now that the feds are involved, do you want to give up on this?'

Sitting in her car, her hand sweating on her cellphone and traffic rumbling past, Summer knew that she had reached a crossroads, and none of the choices were promising. If she cooperated with the FBI, they'd take everything she had and cut her out of the loop. And if she and Denise continued with their unofficial investigation, the FBI could cause them all kinds of grief . . .

She said, 'I know one thing. Edie Collier didn't deserve what happened to her. Someone has to make it right.'

Denise said, 'It isn't going to be the feds. They told me they believe that what happened to Edie was, quote unquote, "collateral damage".'

'They have a nice turn of phrase.'

'Don't they just? They've been interviewing Kronenwetter's neighbours and the tradespeople he had business with. Fat lot of good that'll do, Joe Kronenwetter hardly ever talked to anyone unless it was to bitch about some imaginary grief. They trampled all over his property, stripped everything out of the shack, took his pickup and his broken-down tractor. If he'd ever owned a library ticket, I have the feeling they would have taken away every book he'd ever borrowed in case he'd scribbled something incriminating in one of them. Right now, like I said, I'm waiting on one of their forensic investigators to turn up. He wants to take a look at Edie's body, and I'm supposed to introduce him to our ME. But all this activity isn't because they're interested in Edie. It's because they're hoping that Kronenwetter's good buddy the travelling man left some trace when he paid Kronenwetter a visit.'

'What about Dirk Merrit?'

'I told them about him. They said they'd look into it, but it was clear that they weren't very interested.'

'They're fixated on this travelling man.'

'Exactly. So, you want to stay in the game?'

Summer said, 'I have one more day I can work on this, then I have to go back to the Robbery Unit. I think we should focus on Dirk Merrit, try to find out where he was when Edie was kidnapped, where he was when her boyfriend was killed. His security guards must know about his movements – we should talk to them. And we should try to find out more about that game of his. *Trans*. Actually, I may have a lead on that already.'

Denise said, 'The feds took everything we found in Kronenwetter's cellar for analysis at their labs in Quantico. Can you get hold of something that Edie wore?'

'I'm pretty sure Randy Farrell would have kept anything she left behind after she moved out. What do you need?'

'A topcoat or a scarf. A shoe or a sneaker, something that wouldn't have been washed.'

'You have an idea, don't you? What is it, something to do with DNA?'

'We need to talk this over face to face. Whatever you get from Edie's stepfather, can you bring it down here tomorrow morning?'

20

If he was going to make Pat Metcalf confess all his sins as quickly as possible, Carl knew that he would have to give the man a bad scare at the start and keep him scared and off balance, convince him that his nearest and dearest would suffer unless he did the right thing, make sure that he didn't get a chance to assert the authority he believed was his God-given right. Having seen the man at home, it wasn't hard to work out how to do it.

A little after six in the evening, Carl watched as Metcalf and an overweight young woman in a flower-print dress came out of the storefront office of the security firm. The young woman, probably the office receptionist, climbed into an old Buick and drove off, and Metcalf hooked down and padlocked the steel security shutter over the door and plate-glass window.

The office was in a mini-mall on the commercial strip strung along the highway north of the city centre. The other businesses – Cedar Falls's only Internet café, a dry-cleaner's, two law offices and a florist's – had already closed up for the night. No one saw Carl step from the cover of a Dumpster and walk up to Metcalf as he was unlocking his Range Rover. Carl showed the man Frank Wilson's Beretta, told him they were going to have a little chat.

'I don't think so,' Metcalf said, staring at Carl rather than the gun.

Carl put the Beretta in Metcalf's face, thumbed back the hammer, and said, 'You think I won't do this if I have to?'

Metcalf kept his cool. 'Son, you just stepped into a world of shit.'

'You're not any kind of police now. You're on the other side, just like me,' Carl said. 'Turn around and lock your hands on top of your head. I'm sure you know how it's done.'

Carl kicked the man's feet apart, grabbed hold of his interlaced fingers with one hand and patted him down with the other, pulled a black Colt .45 from a leather holster in the small of his back, a rat-tail sap in one of the side pockets of his sport coat, a cell phone in the other. He took Metcalf's car keys, too, told him to get into the Range Rover, on the passenger side. Told him to slide over behind the wheel and rest his hands on the dash, and then got in beside him and tossed a set of handcuffs into his lap.

'Put these on. One around your left wrist, the other around the steering wheel.'

Metcalf tried to reason with him. 'What you're doing here is kidnap. That's a Federal beef, and you don't want the feds on your tail. They go hard after people, hand down tough sentences, and put them away in maximum-security jails.'

Carl smiled into Metcalf's face and let him see a little of the person he usually kept hidden. 'Put on the fucking cuffs.'

'I should put my seat belt on first.'

'No, you leave it off. But I'll put on mine, so we know who'll come off worse if you happen to run off the road.'

After Metcalf had cuffed himself to the steering wheel, Carl gave him the Range Rover's keys and told him to head east. Sat with his back against the door and the Beretta aimed at his prisoner, the man driving nice and quietly, obeying Carl's directions without question. Metcalf slowed when they neared the gateway to Dirk Merrit's estate and Carl told him to keep going, told him after a mile to turn off the road onto a gravel track shaded by leaning trees.

Metcalf slowed again as they came up on the gate across the track. Carl told him that it wasn't locked. 'Just nudge it open and drive straight through.'

Two minutes later, the Range Rover pulled up beside the ruin of the small, single-storey house that way back when had been the home of the caretaker and general handyman of the lodge and camp grounds. A new barn stood on the other side of the clay yard, a big square building with unpainted aluminium walls, like a small factory dropped into the woods.

Carl told Metcalf to take the keys from the ignition and drop them out of the window, then got out and walked around the Range Rover, opened the door on Metcalf's side, and tossed him the handcuff key. Metcalf unfastened himself and climbed down, looking all around.

'It's a nice quiet place. No one will bother us,' Carl said, and walked him through the back door of the ruined house into the kitchen.

Sheets of hardboard nailed across the windows made it as dim as a cave. Teenage trespassers had spray-painted tags and obscenities across every inch of the crumbling plaster-and-lath walls. Crushed beer cans and cigarette butts were everywhere underfoot. A stained sleeping bag was crumpled in one corner. Earlier in the day, Carl had cleaned the sturdy pine table and set it in the centre of the room. Now he told Metcalf to sit in the kitchen chair in front of the table and stood behind him, enjoying his power over the man. Smiling when Metcalf asked what this was all about.

'Lean forward,' Carl said, 'and stick your left arm straight out behind you.'

Carl handcuffed the man's wrist to the back leg of the chair, then stepped around to the other side of the table and lit the two fat church candles in the iron spike holders he'd bought from the Christian bookshop in Cedar Falls. They stood at either end of a long bundle wrapped in yellow oilcloth on which a few fat black flies were crawling. A small brushed aluminium tape recorder and a framed photograph of Metcalf's young daughter were set in front of the bundle. Carl had stolen the photograph from Metcalf's house that afternoon. It held the man's attention and made him afraid and angry all over again, and he demanded to know what the fuck this was about. Carl pressed the PLAY button of the little recorder and watched Metcalf's expression change when he heard his own voice telling Frank Wilson that the bracelet would give him access to the main tower of the mansion, that the CCTV cameras would be switched off for half an hour which should be more than enough time to check things out.

Carl switched off the recorder and said, 'Your inside man taped one of your little get-togethers. Either he didn't trust you, or he was working for the cops. Not that it matters now.'

Metcalf denied having anything to do with it.

'I have Mr Wilson's cell phone. You called him twice today – why was that?'

Metcalf didn't answer. His face shone with sweat in the flickering candlelight.

'I also have a couple of souvenirs,' Carl said, and dropped Frank Wilson's driver's licence and the Ziploc bag containing Frank Wilson's forefinger on top of the yellow oilcloth. Flies rose and settled.

Metcalf started up from his chair but was brought up short by the handcuff biting into his wrist. Carl ordered him to sit back down, said, 'As long as you do right by me, I won't kill you.'

'You killed Wilson. Or you want me to think you killed him.'

Carl picked up the Ziploc bag, swung it to and fro. 'When we're through, you're welcome to take a print from this. You'll find it matches the right forefinger in the set of prints in Mr Wilson's police file.'

'If you don't let me go *right now*, you're gonna be in such deep shit you'll never find your way out.'

Carl fast-forwarded the tape, keeping an eye on the counter, pressed PLAY again.

Metcalf's voice again, halfway through a sentence. '—Nothing to worry about. Absolutely nothing. First, the security system will be programmed to ignore you. Second, the cameras will be switched off, it'll look like a genuine glitch. You can walk right in and make a list of everything worth taking. He's been selling off a lot of his stuff because he's more or less broke, he's been having trouble paying his bills. But I reckon he's kept back some favourite pieces, old Japanese shit and the like, and that's where you come in, Frank, because you know all about that kind of stuff. Make a list of pieces worth taking, and the next time you go in, you'll be able to take every piece on that list. The system will have been fixed so that it ignores their alarm-chip things. You can pick them up and walk straight out – it'll be as if you're invisible.'

Frank Wilson asked what would happen if Merrit noticed that something was missing.

'Don't worry about him. He's so zonked he barely knows what year it is. Anything you take, he'll probably think he already sold it.'

Carl pressed STOP. 'What puzzles me is how someone like you knows how to fix the security cameras and the computer that keeps track of the RFID tags, what you call the alarm-chip things.'

'I don't know where you got that,' Metcalf said, 'but it has to be some kind of fake.'

Carl pressed REVERSE, pressed PLAY. Metcalf's voice again, explaining about the security system and the alarm chips and the catalogue entries. Carl pressed STOP.

Metcalf stared at him, stubborn to the last.

'You're gonna talk,' Carl said, flipping the edge of the oilcloth bundle up and down, flies buzzing up around him as he smiled across the table at the man. 'Want to know why?'

'I worked LAPD twenty years, man. I've seen it all, so don't you try to frighten me. And don't you dare make threats to my family, either. Just tell me what you want, okay? Let's see if we can't work out some kind of deal.'

'Once Mr Wilson had picked out the best pieces, you were going to have their RFID tags inactivated so that he could steal them. Don't waste time denying it. Just tell me who you were going to use to get into the security computer.'

'You want my job, don't you? That's what this is all about. Well, fuck you, buster, it isn't for taking.'

'You're the one who's fucked.'

Carl was enjoying himself immensely. Everything was going exactly as he'd planned. He felt like an actor dominating a stage in front of a rapturous audience, felt that he could do anything he wanted.

Metcalf shook his head. He was recovering from the initial shock, was beginning to try to think his way around the situation.

'Why don't we stop playing around? Tell me what you want, I'll see what I can do. I can't put it fairer than that.'

'I'm not here to bargain with you,' Carl said, and grabbed hold of two corners of the oilcloth and pulled it out straight and fast, unwrapping the corpse of the German shepherd like a conjuror, the dead animal rolling to the edge of the table in front of Metcalf. There was a neat hole between its eyes. Its muzzle was covered in dried blood. Metcalf pushed to his feet, bringing the chair with him. Carl told him to sit down. Told him, when he began to bluster again, that what had happened to his dog could easily happen to his girlfriend, or to his pretty young daughter in Los Angeles.

Metcalf reared up again, swung the chair in front of him like a circus lion-tamer. Carl had to tell him twice to sit down, had to take a few seconds to compose himself after the man obeyed him. Metcalf's fear and anger were intoxicating.

Flies buzzed and droned around them in the dancing candle-light, settling on the dead dog, on its bloody muzzle and the hole punched between its eyes.

'If you don't behave,' Carl said, 'I'll fetch your girlfriend and do her here, right in front of you.'

He'd watched the girlfriend that afternoon as she stood by the back door of the house, calling the dog's name in a high sing-song voice. 'Bella! Bella, where *are* you? Bella!'

Bella had been lying dead at Carl's feet. He'd brought the dog to him by offering it a scrap of liver, and killed it with the captive-bolt pistol. Later, after the girlfriend had given up on the dog and driven off on some errand, Carl had broken into the house and swiped the photograph of Metcalf's daughter. It had taken less than a minute.

'All right, all right.' Metcalf's face was pale and gleaming in the candlelight. 'Just tell me what you want.'

'To begin with, I want you to tell me why you let Mr Wilson into the trophy room. He was looking for valuable items, wasn't he?'

After a moment, Metcalf nodded, jerking his head up and down.

'You were going to split the proceeds with him.'

Another nod.

'Why do you need the money?'

'I have . . . debts.'

'Who do you owe?'

'It doesn't matter. I just need some ready cash. This—'

'Who do you owe?'

Metcalf's head came up. 'The fucking Cardinals fumbled the last two games. Okay?'

'You owe a bookie.'

'A sports book.'

'Is it legitimate? Does it work out of Las Vegas, somewhere like that?'

Metcalf shook his head. 'Somewhere in Florida. Marathon.'

'How much do you owe?'

'That's none of your business.'

'How much?'

'Let's just say a lot, okay?'

'Are they threatening you?'

Metcalf looked at Carl, his eyes darkened by anger. 'I was warned that my clients would be informed about the debts. I told them that if I lost my clients I wouldn't be able to pay them back.'

'You promised to pay them back.'

'By the end of the month.'

'Does Mr Wilson work for them?'

'No.'

'So you already had Wilson in mind when you made that promise.'

'I had several guys in mind. He was the one available.'

'It was your idea to rob Mr Merrit.'

Metcalf shrugged.

'The people who own the sports book, they don't know how you were planning to get the money to pay them back. They don't know about Frank Wilson, they don't know that you were going to rob Mr Merrit.'

'I told them I'd pay them back – that's all they cared about.

Merrit has a ton of shit. Wilson spotted a few pieces that would get me out of the hole and leave plenty over, and I bet Merrit wouldn't even miss them,' Metcalf said, striving to hit a friendly note. 'If you want, I could cut you in. I could give you what Wilson was going to get.'

'If that was an even split, that would be a third, wouldn't it?' When Metcalf didn't say anything, Carl added, 'Why you're here, I want you to tell me who else was in on this.'

'It's just me and Wilson.'

'You hacked the camera system and the RFID system all by yourself?'

'Why not?'

'Why not? Because you're a broke-down cop whose dick cost him his career. Because you don't know one end of a computer from the other, that's why not. I want you to think about some-thing, Mr Metcalf. I want you to think about who's more important to you. Is it the guy who helped you with the security system, or is it your daughter?'

Metcalf's stare was hot and full of hate. 'If I give him up, will you let me go?'

Carl put the muzzle of the Beretta to his lips, breathed in the calming smell of gun oil. 'Mr Frank Wilson is dead, your dog is dead . . . it's only natural you should be wondering who's next. Well, I'll tell you. It won't be anyone you know as long as you tell me who was going to fix the security system.'

Metcalf said, 'It's a computer geek by the name of Erik Grow. He lives in Los Angeles. He's—'

'I know who Erik is. That's very good, Mr Metcalf. All you have to do now,' Carl said, ejecting the tape from the machine and inserting a new one, 'is to make a confession for the machine. It doesn't have to be long or fancy. Just the facts. Give it up, save your girlfriend and your daughter.'

Metcalf swore at him at length and with some considerable imagination.

'Do you need a moment to compose your thoughts? No? Okay, then,' Carl said, and pressed play and RECORD. Metcalf gave it up in half a dozen sentences. Carl pressed STOP, stuck the

Beretta in the waistband of his jeans, and said, 'You can come in now.'

Dirk Merrit stepped into the kitchen, wearing his camo gear, saying, 'Hello, Pat. Surprised to see me?'

Patrick Metcalf jerked up his head, eyes rolling as he tried to get a glimpse of the man, becoming very still when Dirk Merrit pressed the muzzle of his weapon against the soft spot on top of his head.

'There was just one problem with your little plan,' Dirk Merrit said. 'Carl and I are much smarter than you, and we've been having fun together for quite some while now. Carl heard your confession, and now I'm here to pass sentence. Any last words?'

Metcalf said quickly, 'Listen to me, man. *Listen*. I bet there's a lot you don't know about Erik Grow. I'll tell you everything, I promise, but you're going to have to make some promises too. I have to have your word that you'll keep that animal away from my daughter. That this is between you and me—'

The captive-bolt pistol made a sharp click. Metcalf shuddered, jerked and slumped forward. Blood welled from the neat hole on top of his head, ran down his face and dripped on the table, dark and glossy in the candlelight.

Dirk Merrit smiled at Carl. 'We found a use for your little gadget after all, didn't we? That was well done, Carl. Very well done indeed. I assume that you will deal with Mr Grow, while you're in Los Angeles?'

'I'll take care of everything,' Carl said. He pocketed the tape recorder, then took several photographs of the body with a digital camera the size of a pack of cigarettes, the flash bright and sudden in the ruined kitchen. 'We'll dump the body in the lake before I set off,' he told Dirk Merrit. 'But first I need to take a souvenir.'

21

No one came to the door of the Farrells' dilapidated bungalow when Summer rang the doorbell. She heard staticky washes of laughter and applause from the TV inside and leaned on the bell again, then banged on the door with the side of her hand and called out her name.

'You know I won't go away, Mr Farrell. So why not make things easier for both of us and open up?'

At last a light came on behind the door's three stepped panes of glass. Randy Farrell opened it on the chain, glared at her through the narrow gap. 'We don't have anything to talk about.'

Summer offered him the envelope she'd prised from the manager of the Rite Spot. 'This is Edie's pay. I figure you should have it. Also, I have some news.'

She started to explain about the discovery of the body of his stepdaughter's boyfriend, but Randy Farrell cut her off, telling her that he'd seen it on the TV news, and started to close the door.

'Hold on, Mr Farrell,' Summer said. 'I have to ask you a favour. I need you to loan me a piece of Edie's clothing.'

'Are you working with that redneck son of a bitch who set me up?'

'Do you really think that?'

Randy Farrell didn't say anything, but he didn't close the door either.

'Look, Mr Farrell, I agree that it was a rotten rap, but you shouldn't have lost your temper.'

'Yeah? What would you have done if it had been you instead of me?'

'You mean if I'd been provoked like you were, and couldn't

keep my temper under control? I would have swung at Detective Hill rather than Joseph Kronenwetter. I'd still have been arrested, but at least I would have had the satisfaction of seeing that stupid grin wiped off his face.'

'Yeah, I would have liked to have seen that too.'

'How about fetching something of Edie's, Mr Farrell? Help me out here.'

'They got the son of a bitch that did it, and he killed himself. So what's this about?'

'Joseph Kronenwetter couldn't have killed Edie's boyfriend. The timing is all wrong – the boyfriend was killed sometime on Thursday or Friday, after Kronenwetter had been arrested. And because we think the boyfriend was kidnapped at the same time as Edie, that means someone else was involved. We want to find out who.'

Summer watched Randy Farrell think about that. His pallor had a yellowish tinge to it, and there were liverish scoops under his eyes, as if he hadn't had any sleep since she'd last seen him. At last he said, 'What kind of thing do you need?'

'Anything that hasn't been washed since Edie last wore it.'

'Wait there,' Randy Farrell said, and shut the door.

Summer waited five minutes. She was ready to ring the doorbell again when Randy Farrell opened the door, this time off the chain. He handed her a pair of Converse sneakers, red with green laces, and said, 'I guess you aren't going to tell me what this has to do with anything.'

'Did Edie ever tell you what her boyfriend did for a living?'

'No, and I didn't care to ask.'

'She didn't mention anything about computers or computer games?'

'Like I told you before, when we talked that one time after she ran off it was mostly about how she was doing, her plans. I didn't care to know about her boyfriend, and she didn't care to talk about him. I did ask her was he looking after her properly. Well, it was more a threat, I guess. I said I'd smack the son of a bitch into the middle of next week if he wasn't doing right by her. She said that he'd been knocked back, but he was doing all right now. I do know they barely had enough money, even with Edie's job. They were living in the van, parking in different places. I told her it was no way to live, asked her to come home, but she wasn't having it.'

'When you and Edie talked, did she mention anyone other than her boyfriend? Friends she and her boyfriend had, people they hung out with?'

'She talked about people at the diner . . . She had this way of describing people, what they said, how they said it. It made you think you could see them, right there in front of you. She was funny too, but not at the expense of the people she talked about. She didn't have a mean bone in her body,' Randy Farrell said, with a desolate look.

Summer felt a pang of sympathy. After her father had died, she'd quickly learned how bittersweet it is to remember the dead. Even the happiest memory is tinged with sorrow and regret, because memory is all you have of them now.

She said, 'I appreciate your help, Mr Farrell. I'll bring these sneakers back as soon as I'm done with them, and tell you how it worked out.'

Randy Farrell hesitated, then leaned towards her and said, 'I think there's something else we need to talk about.'

'Sure.'

'The morning that bastard was found dead, while I was waiting for my court appearance? I heard talk that maybe he didn't kill himself.'

Summer tried not to flinch from the foul odour of Randy Farrell's breath. 'If he didn't kill himself, who did? One of the other prisoners?'

She could just about believe that Sheriff Worden, alert to the potential damage to his PR rating, might have organized some kind of cover-up if his star prisoner had been shanked in jail, but why hadn't Denise Childers heard anything about it? And if she had, why hadn't she said anything about it?

Randy Farrell was shaking his head, saying, 'No, nothing like that, although there were definitely people in there crazy enough to kill you for the fun of it. The place was full of crack fiends, glueheads, methheads, you name it. A guy was in there for raping a goat. I mean, no lie, he really was. But Kronenwetter, he was in a cell on his own. You know, one of the isolation cells. You want to know what happened, I think you should talk to the people in the cells close by.'

'I think you should quit beating about the bush, Mr Farrell, and tell me everything you know. I'm not going to waste my time chasing down a jailhouse rumour unless I know exactly what it is.'

'This won't come back on me?'

'You know I can't promise you that. If I find out that there's some basis of truth to this rumour, if the investigation turns into a prosecution, I'll have to explain how I heard about it in the first place.'

'And then maybe they'll throw my ass back in jail.'

'That's a separate matter, Mr Farrell. I can promise you they won't do that. Come on, tell me what you know. Let go of it.'

There was a long pause. At last, Randy Farrell said, 'You have to appreciate that I didn't see anything of it myself. All I know is that when Kronenwetter was brought up to the holding cells that night, he was bawling like a baby. He was shouting and screaming, making wild threats . . . It got pretty noisy. Anyone starts cutting up wild in the joint, the whole place gets stirred up. Men in the cells along the corridor, they were banging on the bars, on pipes, they were shouting, they were cheering the poor fucker on, making all kinds of noise. And then the guards came along, hitting the cell bars with their sticks, telling people to be quiet, making even more noise. I was in the other side of the block, but I heard some of it.'

'That part I can believe,' Summer said, remembering Joseph Kronenwetter at the end of his brutal session with Jerry Hill, his face screwed up, his eyes and cheeks shining with tears of fear and self-pity. 'Okay, what happened next?'

'The guards put Kronenwetter in one of the special cells where they keep the sick people,' Randy Farrell said. 'You know, guys detoxing, the drag queens, the crazies . . . Well, he was crazy, all right. They shut him away and got everyone quieted down, but the men in the cells near Kronenwetter, they were all stirred up, a lot of them couldn't sleep. The regular cells are just cages, bars in front, cement walls, you know what I mean. Four, six bunks in each one. But the special cells are off to one side, and they have sheet-steel doors, and just one bunk apiece . . .?'

'I get the picture. So Kronenwetter was locked up on his own, in one of these special cells. Then what?'

'He was still making noise, and it kept at least one of the guys in the cells nearby awake. According to what I heard the next day, he heard the door of Kronenwetter's cell being unlocked, and then things went quiet. He looked through a crack in the hatch where they slide in the food tray, saw someone leave. He thought at first, all it was, one of the guards had decided to get some licks in, the way they do when someone causes trouble. Anyway, the guard comes out, and about ten minutes later another guard finds Kronenwetter dead and raises the alarm. That I do know about. Everyone in the block knew about it. A siren went off like it was World War Three, and all the lights came on.'

'This is a serious accusation you're making here, Mr Farrell.'

'I'm not accusing anyone. I'm just telling you what I heard.'

'You're saying that one of the guards might have had something to do with Joseph Kronenwetter's death.'

Randy Farrell shrugged inside his baggy shirt. 'All I know is what I heard. And now I told you all I know. What you do with it, that's your call.'

'Do you have a name for the prisoner who saw the guard go into Kronenwetter's cell? Do you know if he can identify him?'

'All I heard, someone saw someone else go into Kronenwetter's cell just before he was found dead. I got the story second-hand, third-hand. You know, someone says that he got it from someone else. No names, nothing like that. If I had a name I guess I'd tell you straight out because I want whoever snatched Edie to pay for what he did,' Randy Farrell said. He was as out of breath as a marathon runner at the finish. Red spots the size of quarters were burning through the yellow-paper skin over the hinges of his jaw. 'If it was Kronenwetter did that to her and no one else then fine, the motherfucker is dead and that'll do for me. But you said you think someone else was involved, and now I can't help thinking that maybe they got to Kronenwetter, to stop him talking.'

That was exactly what Summer was thinking, too. She said, 'Before I can take this any further I need the name of that guard, or at least some kind of description. And I need to know who claimed to have seen all this, too.'

'If I had a name, I'd give it you. Jesus Christ, there must be a record of who was locked up in the special cells, and what guards were on duty. You're the detective — it shouldn't be hard to figure out.'

They went around it a couple of times, but Randy Farrell was adamant that he had told Summer all he knew. At last she said, 'I'll see what I can find out, but I can't promise anything. And I want you to think hard about this, too, and give me a call if you remember anything else. Okay?'

'Okay,' Randy Farrell said. But he wouldn't meet her gaze.

She said, 'Have you talked to Lucinda about any of this?'

'Yeah, but I don't think she took it in.' Randy Farrell paused, and then added, 'I know you think she's a heartless bitch, but I worry about her. If this takes a long time . . . I mean, if I'm not around when you've worked everything out, will you tell Lucinda? It'll ease her mind.'

Back in her car, Summer phoned Denise Childers and told her that she had a pair of Edie Collier's sneakers. 'You're going to use tracker dogs, aren't you? You want to try to follow her path back through the woods, find out where she came from.'

'It's something we were planning to do all along,' Denise said. 'But then we got the call tipping us off about Joe Kronenwetter, and there didn't seem to be any need. Are you still on for tomorrow?'

'You bet.'

'Bring hiking gear, if you have it. We'll be doing some serious walking.'

'We need to talk about something Randy Farrell just now told me,' Summer said, starting her car. 'But we'll have to talk while I drive. It's way past seven, and I'm running late for something.'

22

Daryl Weir reached the final save point at half past two, Sunday morning. Ratking had told him to look for it under one of the overpasses that took surface streets across the jungly trench of the Hollywood Freeway, and that was exactly where he found it: the icon of an old-fashioned computer disk spinning slowly in mid-air, between two support pillars. Daryl walked Seeker8 into the rotating disk and the screen went black, then presented him with the save option, *Y/N?* He typed *Y* and did a slow backwards roll into a headstand, held it for a few seconds and then flipped to his feet, dizzy, tired, and completely happy.

Before Daryl had started out on this latest run, Ratking had pointed him towards a tanker parked in the ruin of a gas station. Seeker8 had driven it straight at the lair of the tar babies in the trench of the Los Angeles River, bailing from the cab at the last minute, already moving north as the first of several huge explosions lit up the sky, taking a route that wove around the roving packs of warewolves. Now that he'd reached the Hollywood Freeway save point, he wouldn't have to endure the long dangerous trek down Wilshire Boulevard to the freeway ever again. Now he was poised for a final assault on the jungle of Griffith Park, and the search for the tunnel under the observatory that was supposed to lead to the treasure. One more push, and it would all be over. He sent Ratking an email, decided to heat up a slice of last night's pizza. He'd been immersed in *Trans* for five hours straight. A big hit of fat and carbs would calm him down.

His mother was passed out on the couch, snoring open-mouthed, her face stark in the flickering light of the TV, which was recycling an ancient episode of *Friends*. A tumbler lay on its side by her feet, ice-water and the milky dregs of a White Russian soaking into the carpet.

Daryl knew there was no point trying to wake her. He covered her with a throw from her bedroom, then turned off the TV, picked up the glass and set it on the kitchen drainer, and heated the last slice of pizza in the toaster oven. He was back at the computer, peeling a stray anchovy from melted cheese (his mother loved anchovies; he hated them), when the Internet browser beeped.

It was Ratking, asking him to go to instant messaging.

> *Now you've reached the last save point, we have to kick our game up a notch.*

> *Right.*

> *The next stage will be like nothing you have done before.*

> *I'm ready.*

> *No. No, you're not. We must make an appointment together. We must meet face to face.*

Daryl paused. This was so out of left field he hadn't seen it coming. He typed a question mark, pressed *Enter*.

> *I have been here before. I know what we face. It is difficult and dangerous. We can only win if we work together, side by side. I will have to react at once to what is happening in the game and you will have to follow my instructions at once. Working by email or by instant messaging will be too slow.*

> *What do we face?*

> *It will be like nothing you have seen or done before. We will have only one chance to solve it. If we don't, our avatars will die and we will have to start over as slaves.*

> *I'll die, you mean. I'm the one taking the risks.*

> *My present Godlike viewpoint does not make me immune. If you die, I die too.*

> *Say I agree. How we going to work this? Are you coming to New York? Or wait, you live here?*

> *I will book you a flight.*

> *I have to come to you?*

> *I will pay all your expenses – don't worry about that. I need a*

stone-cold killer like you at my side, and the fame and glory we will win together is worth the trifling cost of an airplane ticket.

Daryl thought about it. One thing was certain: Ratking wasn't some kid from the 'burbs in flyover country. He was a serious player with serious money, probably some rich yuppie deeply into *Trans*'s fantasy trip and hungry for kudos. Daryl had seen people like that at pro-gaming events: they sponsored the best players, paid them to endorse their companies or their product. He thought about Bernard, his jibe that nothing you ever won in *Trans* would do you any good in the real world. He thought about his brother, DeLeon, shot on his corner in a drive-by, dead at nineteen. He thought about his mother, passed out on the couch, dirt-poor, exhausted at the end of each and every week. If you don't chase your dreams, she liked to say, you'll never know if you can catch them. With a falling feeling, he typed:

> *What do I have to do?*

> *First of all, you tell me your real name, and I'll tell you mine. You can check me out on Google and we'll move on from there. Cool?*

Definitely a white boy, Daryl thought, and typed a single word.

> *Cool.*

23

Carl had Erik Grow down as a wannabe bad boy right from the start. Erik liked to believe that he lived life on the edge, mouthed off about knowing all kinds of dangerous people and having all kinds of connections, was full of bullshit gossip about this or that big score, who was up and who was down in Los Angeles's crime scene, but he didn't have the balls to get into anything more serious than cloning credit cards and a little light industrial espionage. He owned a stack of books on serial killers, one of John Wayne Gacey's awful clown paintings, a scanner permanently tuned to the LAPD channels, and a small collection of guns and knives, but all that was strictly for show. He'd probably never once used any of his guns outside of the shooting range, or any of his knives in anger.

How Erik Grow was: the first time Carl had met him, in a café on the beachwalk in Venice, Erik had made some remark about a passing beach bunny in a bikini top and short-shorts, fake tits, tanned legs up to here, and Carl had told him that if he liked her so much, why didn't he make a move on her?

Erik had said, 'There's no point, man. Chicks like that go for looks, not brains.'

'There are plenty of ways to persuade someone to do what you want. If charm doesn't work, you can always use a blade,' Carl had said. 'You cut someone, show them you're serious, after that they'll do whatever you want.'

Erik had stared at him, blinking behind his glasses. Then his cheesy smile had come back and he'd said, 'You're kidding, right? Man, you almost had me.'

Carl hadn't been kidding. If you wanted something, you took it, simple as that. And if someone tried to take something from you, you put them down and made sure they wouldn't get up again. That was how things worked in the real world, but Erik didn't get it. He talked the talk, but he never, ever walked the walk.

Erik Grow was not only Dirk Merrit's inside man at Powered By Lightning; and he also had access to a supply of high-quality cloned credit cards. One of Carl's jobs was to drive down to Los Angeles every two or three months, stop off at Erik's apartment, and pick up a new batch of cards. As far as he was concerned, Erik Grow was a useful idiot, mouthy but harmless. A tourist. But then, a couple of months ago, out of the blue, Erik had asked him if Dirk Merrit was still paying him his salary.

'That's none of your business, sonny.'

'You think? The man hasn't paid me for the last batch of cards, not to mention all the juicy nuggets of hot info I've been feeding him the past couple of months. He owes me. And I bet he owes you too.'

'If you have a problem with Mr Merrit, Erik, you should take it up with him.'

'You and me, we have some sort of relationship, don't we? I mean, I guess we're not what you could call friends, but we're business associates. We've come to sort of trust each other over the past couple of years.'

Carl didn't trust Erik to buy a newspaper and bring back the right change. 'What's your point?'

'Maybe you don't know it, but Mr Merrit has a serious cash-flow problem. Did you know that he owes Bank of America more than a million dollars? Did you know that they're getting ready to foreclose on his property? When that happens, you'll not only be out of a job, you'll be homeless too. So we both have kind of the same problem with him, don't we?'

Erik Grow leaned back in his chair and smiled, a pale, nervy twenty-six-year-old boy in baggy shorts and a faded Foo Fighters T-shirt, brimming with secrets that he was dying to share. He and Carl were sitting in the outdoor section of a café on Santa Monica's busy, pedestrianized Third Street. It had been Erik's idea to meet at the café instead of at his apartment, and now Carl realized why. The kid wanted to make a business proposition and felt safer doing it in a public place. No doubt the very large bloke a few tables over, the one who was doing a bad job of pretending not to watch them, was supposed to make Erik feel safe too.

Still, it took Erik a while to get to the point. He talked for ten minutes straight, telling Carl about the clandestine sale of assets that Carl hadn't known Dirk Merrit had owned, telling him about a shell company the man used to sell valuable items to players of *Trans* – weapons, gadgets, property, all kinds of shit that didn't exist outside the game. At last he paused, looked left and right as if checking that the people at the tables around them weren't listening in, then leaned forward and said, 'You know who Don Beebe was?'

'Mr Merrit's business partner.'

'His *former* business partner, and his best friend, too. The guy died a couple of years back. Actually, he was murdered,' Erik Grow said, watching Carl nervously, his pale blue eyes magnified by the fat round lenses of his glasses.

Carl didn't say anything, returning Erik's stare until the kid ducked his head, took a quick glance at the big guy several tables over, and said in a rush, 'Don Beebe wrote the core codes of *Trans*. Without him, it wouldn't exist. And it turns out, what I want to talk to you about, the only steady source of income Merrit has left comes from something Don Beebe set up a couple of years ago . . .'

Erik Grow's glasses had slipped down his nose. He pushed them up, wiped his hands on his T-shirt, and said, 'Before we go any further, I need to know that this is just between you and me, okay?'

'If you're worried that I might tell on you, Erik, you've already said too much.'

'But you aren't going to tell on me, are you? I mean, I know you *should*, you'd be doing your job, protecting Merrit's interests. But you aren't going to do it because in the present situation, with Merrit's finances in the toilet and his creditors closing in, you have to think of your own interests too.'

'Spit it out, Erik.'

Erik Grow took a breath. 'Back when Merrit's financial problems started to bite and he was forced to sell his controlling interest in *Trans* to Powered By Lightning, Don Beebe helped him set up a system designed to rip off the new owners. What Beebe did was patch a subroutine into the accounting system that handles the monthly fees players pay for access to the game – a very neat little program that skims one-tenth of a cent from every dollar that's paid in, sends the money to an offshore bank account, and disguises the loss in income by altering records of the numbers of subscribers. It's actually a lot simpler than it sounds,' Erik said. 'It's like having two sets of account books. One to show to the taxman, the other to record what you actually earn.'

'How do you know this?'

'Because I'm the man's inside man. I work for Powered By Lightning's accounting department because he put me there. It's my job to snoop around the company offices and turn up useful information, right? Well, this is one of the things I turned up. But it gets better,' Erik Grow said, growing more confident now that he was over the hump and there was no going back. 'As soon as the skim was up and running, Don Beebe and his wife were murdered. The cops think it was some sort of gay thing, that Beebe was killed by a male prostitute in this apartment he was using as a fuck-pad: the prostitute used Beebe's keys to break into his house, was surprised by Beebe's wife, and killed her. Which is kind of a neat story, except I know someone who knew Beebe at college, and he told me that not only was the man definitely not gay, he wasn't really interested in sex of any kind. He only married his wife because she was a ball-breaking, money-hungry bitch who claimed she was pregnant, and then suddenly turned out not to be pregnant after the happy day. So, what I think is, given the timing, it's possible that Merrit killed Beebe, or had him killed, in case he decided to go to the police about the skim.'

While he listened to this, Carl had been making the kind of calculation he'd made at least once a day in combat, in Africa –

the kind that in one sharp, intense moment determined the course of the rest of your life. Even before the mess with Billy Gundersen and his girlfriend, Carl had known that his relationship with Dirk Merrit was coming to an end. The man was growing more and more erratic, clearly believing that he was a superman who would never be caught. And Carl also knew that he himself wasn't getting any younger, that he couldn't work as a mercenary all his life. For some time now, he'd been dreaming of buying a place and settling down, taking road trips when he needed to have some fun. So it wasn't hard to work out how to play this, and for the first time in months he felt eager and alive, leaning across the café table, smiling into Erik Grow's face.

Saying, 'I know he killed Beebe. Matter of fact, he told me all about it.'

It had been after their first hunt together. Dirk Merrit, sprawling on the recliner in the RV, high on adrenalin and a couple of snorts of crystal meth, talking a mile a minute, had told Carl how he'd stalked Don Beebe, a keen hiker, in the San Bernadino Mountains. He'd killed Beebe with a single shot from his Winchester Custom Sharpshooter, hitting his moving target in the right lung with a special ball-118 round from a shade over four hundred yards. He'd taken Beebe's heart as a trophy, and humped the body to an apartment he'd rented a month earlier in Beebe's name. Later the same day, he'd shot Beebe's wife dead in her home and staged the murder so that it looked like a botched burglary. Details of the discovery of Beebe's mutilated, decomposing body amongst louche leather equipment and gay pornography had the tabloids and local TV news channels frothing with excitement. The general consensus was that one of Don Beebe's Pico Boulevard pick-ups had shot him dead, and then had murdered his wife while searching for cash and jewels in their West Hollywood house.

'I asked him what happened to the heart. He said that it shrivelled up like an apple left in the sun too long and he had to throw it out,' Carl said. 'What he didn't tell me was that he killed Beebe because he was skimming money from the game. So what were you thinking of doing with this, Erik? Blackmailing him, what?'

He had to give the kid credit. Erik came right back, saying, 'Blackmail was my first thought, but about the only income the man currently has is from the subscription scam, and whatever he gets from selling shit to players. Plus, if I did try to screw him, he'd probably send you after me.'

'He probably would.'

'Then I thought, he's using a hack to divert money from *Trans*'s subscription base into his bank account. Why not hack the hack, divert the cash flow somewhere else?'

'So why didn't you?'

Erik smiled. 'That's what I want to talk about.'

He told Carl that because Don Beebe's program was password-protected, he couldn't hack into it directly – only the system administrators of *Trans*'s computer cluster could do that – and he hadn't been able to hack into Dirk Merrit's personal computer either, because it was protected by too many layers of security. So he needed an inside man. He needed Carl. And all Carl had to do was install a simple device that would record everything typed into Dirk Merrit's computer. Dirk Merrit had been fiddling with the parameters of Beebe's program recently, briefly increasing the percentage it sucked from *Trans*'s subscriptions. That was how Erik had spotted what was going on in the first place.

'There'd be this sudden steep dip in the number of subscribers, and a day later numbers went right back to normal. I did some forensic accounting and found that the number of people signed up was always smaller than the number of payments, and then I discovered this neat little program embedded in the coding, and found out where it was sending the money.'

Once the keystroke recorder was in place, Erik said, he would monitor the flow of income from *Trans*'s subscription base to Dirk Merrit's offshore account 24/7. As soon as there was a change, Carl would pull the keystroke recorder and bring it to Erik, who would use the precise time the change had been made to identify the password for Beebe's program.

'And then you use the password, and send the money some-where else,' Carl said, to show that he had been keeping up.

'That's one way we can go, but it would take a while to yield anything useful. See, around two hundred thousand people play *Trans*, and every player pays a subscription fee of thirty dollars each and every month. Skimming one-tenth of one cent from every dollar, the default setting, yields around two hundred dollars a day, seventy-two thousand dollars a year. That isn't bad—'

'But we're splitting it two ways, and in any case it takes a year.'

'Well, we can talk about the split in a minute. But yeah, the big problem is that the default percentage is very low. It would take a long time to accumulate anything worthwhile.'

'So how much would you take, if you had the password?'

'Everything,' Erik Grow said. 'I work in accounts, I know that if I made the change over the weekend, I could divert at least two days' worth of takings before anyone noticed. A minimum of a cool two hundred thousand dollars. All you have to do is get into Merrit's personal computer. You open the case, and you plug this little device between the keyboard input and the CPU. It'll take you about five minutes to put it in, and another five minutes to remove it when the time comes. Ten minutes' work, and I'll give you twenty per cent of the take.'

'No,' Carl said. 'The split will be fifty-fifty. And before you say one more word, I want your friend over there to take a walk.'

Erik Grow started to bluster, so Carl stood up and walked over to the table where the big man in the sleeveless blue denim jacket had been pretending to read the same page of the *L.A. Weekly* for the past thirty minutes. When Carl suggested that he should take off, the man shook a lot of blond hair back from his gap-toothed smile and told Carl to calm down and go finish up his business with Mr Grow, everything was cool.

'You bet it is,' Carl said, and grabbed the man's little finger and twisted hard. The man came up from his chair off-balance, and Carl kicked him under his right kneecap, moved inside a flailing roundhouse punch that he took on his shoulder, and smacked his forehead against the bridge of the man's nose. When the man went down, taking two tables with him, Carl kicked him on the point of his jaw and laid him out, grabbed hold of Erik Grow and marched him into the street, cutting through the crowds of shoppers to an alley that led into one of the parking structures, where he slammed the kid against the side of a minivan.

Telling him, 'If we're going to do it, we're going to do it my way. The split is fifty-fifty, and I'll find someone who can sell me one of these keystroke-capturing things.'

Carl wasn't about to plug anything that Erik Grow gave him into Dirk Merrit's computer – he had a pretty good idea that it would squirt all the information it collected across the Internet, straight to Erik Grow. He told the kid how things would go down, and Erik, pale with shock, agreed to everything.

They went over the set-up until Carl was satisfied that he had it all straight in his head. When they were finished, Erik Grow had regained his composure, telling Carl, 'I'll keep a close watch on the flow of funds. We can move on him as soon as he uses the password and fucks around with the program. If you need to talk to me, call my cell phone. And don't waste your time looking for me at the old address – I just now moved.'

'Just in case, huh?'

Erik Grow managed a smile. 'As long as we keep a healthy sense of mutual mistrust, I think we'll get along just fine.'

Carl paid a guy in Seattle five thousand dollars cash for a key-stroke-recording device and step-by-step instructions on how to use it. Plugging it in was a doddle; Dirk Merrit didn't suspect a thing. And now Carl was on his way to Los Angeles with the device in his pocket, a complete history of everything the man had typed into his computer in the past six weeks, including the command string that two days ago had made the small, temporary adjustment to the cash flow skimmed from *Trans*'s subscriptions. The information that Erik Grow needed to take control of Don Beebe's program, and make both of them some serious spending money.

The problem was, Erik Grow hadn't bothered to tell Carl that he'd been working on another scam with Pat Metcalf. Carl had been right not to trust the little shit, and now he had to decide how to handle him. And there was also the small detail of keeping the FBI off Dirk Merrit's back until the fix was in.

Like his first boss used to say, back in London, it never rains but it pours.

Carl usually drove straight down the I-5 to Los Angeles. This time he took a diversion into Nevada, to Reno. He didn't get there until one in the morning, but the strip of casinos and hotels along Virginia Street was still busy. He left Pat Metcalf's Range Rover in a parking lot, walked a hundred yards down the street to a hotel, and crossed to the rear of its lobby. No one took any notice of him. He was wearing a baseball cap, blue denim jacket, and tan chinos. Apart from a couple of tasty items in his pockets he could have been a tourist from anywhere in the USA. He let two elevators go, the first boarded by an elderly couple, the second by a boisterous pack of college kids, followed a lone man into the third.

The man smiled vaguely at Carl, his face glazed with drink, and pressed the button for the fourth floor. Carl got off with him, turned left when he turned right, then doubled back, pulling on a pair of vinyl gloves. His target was fumbling his key card into the slot of the door to his room. He didn't look up as Carl went past, didn't see the rat-tail sap that swung in a short arc and clipped the top of his skull.

Carl took the man's weight as he collapsed, swung him through the door into a chilly room lit by orange light falling through an uncurtained window. He dumped the man on the bed, stuck a pillow over his face and shot him in the head with the silenced Colt Woodsman. A pop, a brief flash and a flutter of feathers, that's all she wrote.

Three kills in twenty-four hours. Not a record, but not bad.

Carl stood in the dark by the door until he was sure that the shot hadn't disturbed the muffled calm of the hotel. Then he switched on the bedside light, stripped naked, took out his knife, and went to work.

Half an hour later, dressed again, his hair wet from the shower, Carl took Pat Metcalf's right hand from the Ziploc bag in his jacket pocket, pressed its fingers on the PLEASE MAKE UP

ROOM sign, hung the sign on the door, and left the hotel with his trophies in a plastic laundry bag that he'd found in the closet. He drove west, taking the I-80 towards the mountains and California. Ten miles beyond Reno, the window of his car powered down. A white bag flew out and skittered away across the gravel and broken glass of the shoulder.

The coyotes could have the man's eyes and heart. The rest of him, back in the hotel room, was for the FBI.

24

Early Sunday morning, Denise Childers made a batch of peanut butter and banana sandwiches and stuck them in her daypack along with a waterproof jacket, two bottles of spring water, maps and a compass, her Glock 17, badge and handcuffs, and a five-cell Mag-Lite. She made sure that her daughter had everything she needed for the day and drove her to the home of her best friend, Susie Thompson, turned down the Thompsons' offer of coffee as politely as she knew how, kissed Becca and told her to have a fun day, and headed into Cedar Falls, where she had a rendezvous with a dead body.

She arrived at the morgue ten minutes late. The FBI forensic investigator, Gary Delgatto, was waiting for her in the parking lot. An alarmingly young, slim guy with a mop of black hair, he was leaning against the flank of his hire car, a white Lincoln Town Car, and wearing a check shirt, blue jeans and yellow Caterpillar boots, a city boy's idea of hiking gear.

Denise apologized for being late and thanked him for agreeing to help out; he told her that it was his pleasure, he was looking forward to field-testing his technique.

'Well, let's get this done,' Denise said.

They met with the county's medical examiner, Dr Alan Sandage, in his cluttered office. The ME's manner was brisk and aggressive. He hadn't been happy when Gary Delgatto had re-examined Edie Collier's body yesterday, and he wasn't happy now, despite all the balm that Denise had tried to smooth on last night, when she had told him that the FBI's forensic investigator wanted to take a look at the body of Joseph Kronenwetter.

'I cut him myself,' he told Gary Delgatto. 'The face was pale above a shallow furrow in the form of an inverted V, and there was a hairline fracture in the hyoid. Early traces of lividity in his legs and forearms showed that he had died in the position in which he was found. Sitting down, leaning slightly forward, supported by a noose. Entirely commensurate with a hanging death.'

Gary Delgatto, studying the autopsy file, said, 'Did you do a tox screen?'

'Why would I have wanted to do that?'

Gary Delgatto had a quick smile that made him look about fourteen. 'Good point. You believed that you were examining a simple hanging death, so why waste time and money looking for toxins?'

Denise said, 'But now we have to look at it from a new angle.'

Dr Sandage, who had been the county's ME for more than thirty years, said, 'I believe I know a hanging death when I see one. This is a small town, but we get our share of violent death or death by misadventure, and a good number of suicides. Especially out in the country, among the farming community. If you're not satisfied with the report, perhaps you would like to view the video of the autopsy. We had the system put in last year.'

Gary Delgatto said, 'I'm sure it's a hanging death, Dr Sandage. But the question is, did he hang himself, or did he have help?'

'As far as I'm concerned, the question is why you would choose to believe a cell-block rumour,' Dr Sandage said.

Denise said, trying to apply more balm, 'I'm sure you understand why we have to check it out, Doc. And I wish we could have kept it in the family, but it's the FBI's case now. On the upside, they can expedite whatever lab tests need to be done.'

Gary Delgatto said, 'All I need are a few samples, and I'm out of here.'

Dr Sandage looked at him and said, 'You want to do a tox screen. Blood and liver suit you?'

'You bet. Plus brain tissue, if it isn't too much trouble.'

'I found no needle marks when I examined him. If he was sedated, it was either a vapour anaesthetic or something in his food or drink. So you'd best take a look at his stomach contents, too.'

'Good idea.'

'Very well, young man. Let's get this done.'

Denise had been present at more autopsies than she cared to remember, and she'd hated every one of them. The sight of what had once been a person being messily dismantled was bad enough, but the sounds and the smells were worse. She'd thrown up the first couple of times, but had always forced herself to come back and watch until the end. She felt the usual visceral apprehension now, as Gary Delgatto and Dr Sandage put on green gowns and plastic gloves and hair covers, opened the square steel door of the walk-in refrigerator where the unclaimed dead were kept, and trundled out Kronenwetter's sheet-draped body on a gurney, but she also felt a fierce excitement plucking at her heart. Last night, after Summer Ziegler had told her Randy Farrell's story about the clandestine visitor to Kronenwetter's cell, and Gary Delgatto had explained why he thought that Edie Collier and Billy Gundersen had been kept in the same place, Denise hadn't been able to sleep, trying to fit all this new information into what she already knew. She was convinced now that Joe Kronenwetter had nothing to do with the deaths of Edie Collier and Billy Gundersen, which meant that either he'd killed himself because he'd been crazy, or someone else had killed him, and had scratched that note on the wall to make it look as if he'd committed suicide out of remorse. She believed that re-examination of his body would prove it one way or the other.

The two men locked the wheels of the gurney and rolled Kronenwetter's body onto the steel cutting table. He looked bigger in death, his bulk uncontained by any clothing. His beard had been roughly trimmed back to his jawline. He had a farmer's tan that stopped at his neck: apart from his face, hands and forearms, his body was as white as the tiles of the floor, and was marked here and there with patches and swirls of black hair. The livid Y of the autopsy incision, two cuts from his shoulders to the pit of his stomach and one down to his pelvis, was neatly stitched with green thread.

Gary Delgatto set his aluminium case on a counter, snapped it open and sorted through its contents. Dr Sandage switched on the cluster of lights over the body, adjusted the focus of the video camera, and switched on the video and audio tapes. Light gleamed on the pink scalp under his thin white hair, on the lenses of his glasses.

'Let's take blood first,' he said.

He fitted a plastic syringe with a long large-gauge needle, probed the inside of the body's thigh, plunged the needle deep and from the femoral artery drew blood so dark red and thick it was almost black. He handed the hypodermic to Gary Delgatto and began to cut the stitches that held together the incision in the body's belly.

'I excised the liver,' he said, 'noted that it was somewhat swollen and exhibited signs of incipient cirrhosis, and put it back in the body cavity. The brain is in here, too. I usually stuff the skull with paper after I've taken out the brain for examination – it minimizes leakage and keeps the funeral director happy.'

The sound of the heavy scissors cutting through the thread gave Denise a twinge of unease. She knew that the trick was to see what was on the table as evidence rather than the remains of a human being, but she was finding it hard because she'd had several run-ins with Joe Kronenwetter over the years, and had sat with him in the interrogation room only four days ago. Nevertheless, she forced herself to watch as Dr Sandage rooted inside the body cavity, punching out samples from the liver and the brain that went into separate tubes that Gary Delgatto sealed and labelled.

Dr Sandage said, 'I have samples of the stomach and intestinal contents in the refrigerator. About six hours before he died, he was given a meal of chilli and rice, with a banana for dessert. Also chocolate milk. He ate in his cell, so it's possible that someone could have adulterated his food. A barbiturate would be my guess.'

'Mine too,' Gary Delgatto said. 'Before we put him away, I want to examine his hands.'

Dr Sandage's glasses flashed when he looked up. 'If you hope to find skin fragments or traces of blood under his nails, there aren't any.'

'I don't expect there are. I agree with you that if someone had assisted him there wouldn't have been a struggle. And I noticed that there aren't any scratches around the mark left by the noose.'

'He didn't have second thoughts, if that's what you mean.'

'What about his hands? What was their position when you pronounced him?'

'Lying free. They weren't in his pockets, and they weren't tied. He wasn't sitting on them, either.' Dr Sandage looked at Denise and told her, 'Many people who hang themselves restrain their hands in some way, so that they can't free themselves at the last moment. That wasn't the case here.'

Gary Delgatto took a small digital camera from his briefcase and said, 'With your permission . . .'

Dr Sandage told him to go ahead. 'Before you ask, I didn't bag the hands because he was found in a locked cell and there was no sign that he had been assaulted or otherwise involved in a struggle with someone else.'

'Was he right-handed or left-handed?'

'Right-handed,' Dr Sandage said. 'At least, there's a writing callus on the forefinger of the right hand.'

'Waddya know,' Gary Delgatto said. He took several photographs of the body's right hand and then bent close to examine the fingers, noting that the nails were notched and irregular and that there were particles of grit under them.

'From the floor of the cell. He probably picked it up when he went into cadaveric spasm,' Dr Sandage said, making a claw of his own hand inside his bloodstained plastic glove.

'You're probably right,' Gary Delgatto said. 'I think I should take a scraping or two, just in case he picked up something microscopic but useful. Give me a hand here, Denise – you should excuse the pun.'

He used a cotton swab moistened with distilled water to swipe under each fingernail, placing each cotton bud in a separate vial that Denise labelled. Then he pulled open the dead man's mouth, swiped the inside of his cheek with a dry swab and placed that in a vial too.

'That's it,' he said, and peeled off his gloves and shot them into the waste basket under the steel table. 'Thanks for your help, Dr Sandage. It's greatly appreciated. Can you point me toward a place where I can get some dry ice? I'd like to send these samples off right now.'

Outside, once the package had been made up and they had thanked Dr Sandage all over again, Denise said to Gary Delgatto, 'What was it with the fingernails? You spotted something, didn't you?'

'It's more a question of what I didn't find,' Gary Delgatto said.

Denise said patiently, as if dealing with her daughter, 'And what didn't you find?'

'Fibres,' Gary Delgatto said. 'Kronenwetter was hung with a noose made from strips torn from his clothing. If someone rips up cloth, they usually get fibres under their nails, especially if their nails are as badly notched as his were. But there were no fibres. Also, there was grit under the fingernails of his right hand, but nothing under the fingernails of his left. Kronenwetter was right-handed, so that's the arm he would have tried to free if he was being restrained.'

'You'll have to explain that to me. I thought he was doped before whoever it was hung him.'

'It's possible he was sedated but not completely unconscious. In which case he could have got his right hand free for a moment or two and tried to push up to take the weight of his body, to stop himself strangling.'

'It doesn't sound like the kind of thing you could use in court.'

'Maybe not,' Gary Delgatto said. 'But there is also the question of the hyoid bone. You know what it is, the hyoid bone?'

'It's in the throat. If it's broken, it's an indicator of strangulation. We may be hicks, but we know most of the stuff you city folk know.'

'I don't doubt it. The point is, you usually don't find the hyoid bone cracked or broken in someone who died in a simple sit-down hanging. There's not enough force involved. No drop.'

Denise tried to picture it. 'Kronenwetter started to come around, he tried to get up. So his assailant pushed him down, anxious to finish the job, and that cracked the hyoid bone.'

Gary Delgatto flashed his quick smile. 'There you go.'

'It's a nice story, but any competent defence lawyer would dismiss it as unfounded speculation. How about those samples? How long will it take your lab to process them?'

'A good friend of mine will screen the blood and tissue samples as soon as possible. I should have the results by tomorrow morning. She'll also look for foreign DNA in the fingernail scrapings, but I have to warn you, that could take a couple of weeks. On the upside, although there was no visible material beneath the nails apart from the grit, all we need are a couple of skin cells. PCR can amplify up the DNA for identification.'

'He could have picked up almost anything from the floor of a jail cell.'

'That's true. But if you have a suspect, and if his DNA is found under Kronenwetter's fingernails . . .'

'I'll remember that when I have a suspect.' Denise checked her watch. 'Do you drink coffee?'

'Who doesn't? But so far I've only found coffee-like substances around here.'

'If it was any day but Sunday I'd take you to one of the good places, a cop hangout. As it is, I can treat you to a mug of Denny's finest reboiled while we wait for Summer Ziegler. Also, there's someone I want both of you to meet. He has an interesting story to tell you about Joe Kronenwetter's schooldays.'

25

Wearing dark glasses and a baseball cap with its bill pulled low over his face, Carl Kelley drove out of LAX airport in a dented red Honda with more than a hundred thousand miles on the clock, a bad crack in the windscreen, and a tendency to pull to the left. The owner, Julia Taylor, a forty-three-year-old stewardess who worked for a small outfit that shuttled package tourists between Los Angeles and resorts along Mexico's Californian Gulf Coast, was in the trunk.

Carl had driven most of the night, taking the I-5 straight down California's central valley, following the San Diego freeway through Los Angeles to LAX, where the pickings would be easy. He'd left Pat Metcalf's Range Rover in a long-term parking lot and loitered among the rows of vehicles in one of the parking structures across from the terminal building until he'd seen Julia Taylor pulling her flight case on its wheeled frame towards her Honda. Carl came up behind her as she lifted the case into the trunk of her car, and killed her with a precise thrust of his knife, severing her spinal cord between the third and fourth cervical vertebrae.

The Honda's air-conditioning spat warm water on his hands as he merged with the heavy mid-morning traffic on the San Diego freeway. He'd snatched a couple of hours' sleep in a rest stop outside Stockton, and afterwards had dropped a couple of amphetamines to keep his edge. Apart from a fluttering at the edges of his vision and a tight ache in the muscles of his jaw, he was feeling fine – he could work for a week on catnaps and speed.

He was stuck in a traffic jam, hot sunlight glittering off

hundreds of stationary vehicles ahead, around and behind him, when his cell phone rang. It was Dirk Merrit.

'I'm expecting the arrival of another package shortly. I need somewhere to put it.'

It took Carl a moment to realize that the man was talking about the kid from Brooklyn, the ace game-player. Jesus, the man was actually going ahead with his stupid plan. 'This isn't the kind of thing we should talk about right now.'

'I may be taking delivery before you get back. When is that, by the way?'

'Soon. I don't know exactly.' This wasn't the time to tell the man that he wasn't planning on ever coming back, not quite yet, but in a couple of days he could call him from LAX just before he boarded his flight . . . The thought lifted Carl's mood. 'I'm in the middle of something right now. I'll call you back when I'm done.'

'You sound happy,' Dirk Merrit said. 'Things must be going well.'

A horn sounded behind Carl. A gap of about two yards had opened up between the Honda and the car in front.

'You'll see soon enough. Got to go,' Carl said. He cut the connection and edged the Honda forward.

Although Erik Grow had taken the precaution of moving out of his old apartment in case the plan to rip off Dirk Merrit went bad, a skip tracer hired by Carl had found his new address inside a day. It was in Palms, a scruffy area between Westwood and Culver City popular with research students working at UCLA: an undistinguished two-storey apartment building on a short street near the Santa Monica freeway. Carl parked in back, used his picks to open the lock of the wrought-iron gate that led into the central courtyard, with the usual faded sunloungers, tubs of bird-of-paradise plants, and small swimming pool with its rain-bow skin of suntan oil. Erik Grow's apartment was on the first floor, in a corner. Carl squared off and gave the door a hefty kick just beneath its cheap lock, splintering the striking plate from the frame, and barged through it into the L-shaped living room.

Blinds were pulled down over the windows, and the dim air stank of stale marijuana smoke. A stained couch faced a wide-screen TV, several cardboard boxes were stacked along a wall, and Erik Grow stood by the cheap pine dining table where he'd been working at his laptop, wearing only his glasses and a pair of boxer shorts, his mouth open and his eyes wide. Carl told him to sit back down, walked into the bedroom, which was empty apart from a mattress and piles of clothing, and walked back out, saying, 'Don't be stupid, Erik. I'm here to deliver the password. I can't do that if you shoot me dead.'

Erik Grow was standing in the middle of the room now, pointing a pistol at Carl. The pistol was matt black, a Chinese or East European knock-off of a Sig-Sauer. Erik said, his voice pinched by fright, 'Something's gone wrong. Tell me what's gone wrong.'

'Everything is fine,' Carl said, looking straight into the kid's pale face, his blue eyes swimming behind his thick glasses.

'If everything's fine, why didn't you call, set up a meet?'

'My car's parked out back. There's something in it you need to see,' Carl said, and walked out of the apartment, through the wrought-iron gate into the little parking lot.

Erik Grow came out two minutes later, wearing a T-shirt over tan chinos. Carl unlocked the trunk of Julia Taylor's Honda, raised the lid, beckoned to him. Erik Grow slipped one hand under the hem of his T-shirt as he stepped up to the car to take a look, recoiling with a bat-squeak of fright when he saw Julia Taylor's body curled up on its side. Carl grabbed Erik's right wrist and yanked it up behind his back, pulled the knock-off Sig from the waistband of his chinos and kicked it under the Honda. Saying into the kid's ear, 'I don't know her. I never saw her until about an hour ago, and I killed her because I needed her car. I killed her quickly, but you, Erik, unless you tell me the truth right now, I'll do you so slow you'll thank me when I finish you off.'

Erik Grow fell on his ass when Carl pushed him away. He got to his feet slowly, folding his arms across his skinny chest, trying to look cool. 'We're partners, man. Of course I'll tell you the truth. What do you want to know?'

'What was your cut?'

Erik Grow tried out a smile. 'I don't know what you mean.'

'The thing you had going with Pat Metcalf,' Carl said. 'What was your cut?'

Erik Grow gave a little jump; Carl turned around, saw an African-American woman come out of the gate, carrying a basket of laundry on her hip and trailed by a little boy in a blue T-shirt that hung to his knees.

'Close it up before someone sees,' Erik Grow said in a furious whisper. His gaze was darting about, from the body in the trunk of the Honda to Carl to the woman and her child and back to the trunk again. 'I mean, I get the point, okay?'

'Do you, Erik? I wonder.' Carl was riding the swell of his tremendous calm, like a surfer on the ultimate wave. 'You like to play games so much, you must think everything is a game. You think that you can screw around without consequences.'

'I didn't—'

'You did, Erik. I know you did because Pat Metcalf told me all about the deal you'd made with him. We had a very crunchy conversation. If you want, I can play you a tape of his confession, but it would be better for you if you do the right thing and give it up now.'

The little boy turned to take a last look at Carl Kelley and Erik Grow as he followed his mother around the corner of the building towards the laundry room.

Erik said, 'Where is he?'

'Pat Metcalf? You don't have to worry about him, Erik. You have to worry about yourself.'

'You killed him, didn't you?'

'Of course I killed him.'

'Oh Jesus.'

'Whose idea was it, yours or his?'

'His. He wanted me to hack the surveillance system and the RFID catalogue.'

'Why you?'

'He knew me from when I had my problem at UCLA.'

'That would be when you were fired from your nice little job in the Information Technology Department because you were running porn sites from its computer system.'

'He didn't have anything to do with my case, but he knew about me. He introduced me to Dirk Merrit when Merrit was about to sell his interest in Powered By Lightning. Merrit wanted a man on the inside, someone who really knew computers—'

'Someone bent, just like you. We're supposed to be working together, Erik. We're supposed to be partners. Then I find out that you're playing around with Pat Metcalf too. What else are you into?'

'Nothing. Really. Listen, Metcalf threatened to drop the dime on me. He threatened to tell Powered By Lightning that I was working for them under false pretences. I had to do what he asked so I could keep our thing on track.'

'Did Metcalf know about "our thing"?'

'I asked him if he could get into Dirk Merrit's personal computer, and he said he couldn't. That was as far as I took it. Listen,' Erik said, 'it wasn't my idea to steal that shit. Really. It was his.'

'Why didn't you tell me about this, Erik? A problem shared is a problem solved. I could have helped you to deal with it.'

'I *was* dealing with it, okay? Look, I'll tell you everything about what he wanted me to do, but for Christ's sake close that trunk. You want someone should see her and call the cops?'

'You still haven't told me how much you were in for.'

'I'm sorry?'

'What percentage of the take did Metcalf promise you, Erik?'

'Oh, right. It was fifteen.'

'Fifteen per cent.'

Erik Grow jerked his head up and down. He was hugging himself, his eyes twitching behind his big glasses.

Carl said, 'Fifteen per cent of whatever he got when he sold the stuff. That's a very small price to sell me out, Erik. I feel insulted.'

'I went along with it to protect our thing. Now you tell me the guy's dead. Okay, fine, problem solved. Except, how is that going to play with Merrit?'

Carl had to hand it to the kid, he was making a fast recovery, already trying to work out the angles. He stared at Erik, letting a silence lengthen. A transformer buzzed on one of the utility poles, barely louder than the surf of traffic on the nearby freeway. The fronds of a palm tree leaning over the wall of the parking lot clattered in the hot breeze.

Erik said, looking everywhere but at Carl, 'I've offended you. Look, I'm sorry, maybe I made a mistake. Maybe I should have told you. But now you know all about it, you have to see that it doesn't affect our thing. I swear I didn't tell him one word about that.'

'You've lived in Los Angeles all your life. I guess you know it pretty well.'

'Sure.'

'How would I get to the San Gabriel mountains from here?'

'I'm sorry?'

'I thought I'd take her out to the San Gabriel mountains. I bet there are plenty of places where you can dump a body up there.'

'Are you crazy? It's the weekend, man.'

'So?'

'There are bound to be plenty of people out and about, that's why. Walking, cycling, having themselves picnics or whatever. Why not just leave the car somewhere in town?'

'The San Gabriel mountains,' Carl said, giving Erik a hard look.

'Right. Well, I guess you could take the 10 through downtown and San Bernadino, then go north on 39. There's plenty of little roads off there.'

'Get in.'

'I'm sorry?'

'Say that one more time, you will be. Get in the trunk.'

'Oh no.' Erik Grow was shaking his head.

Carl reached around behind his back, pulled out his Colt Woodsman and said, 'If I wanted to kill you, Erik, I would have done it when you aimed that gun at me in your apartment. But like you said, we have a thing. I need you, just like Metcalf needed you.'

He racked the slide and pointed the pistol at the kid's right knee.

He said, 'I'm not going to kill you, Erik, but I promise you that I will fuck you up very badly if you don't get in the trunk right now.'

26

It was cool and damp in Portland early Sunday morning, low cloud stretching across the city, brief showers freshening the air. Summer rolled down the window of her Accura as she took the 205 north and west. By the time she had hooked into the flow of traffic heading south on the I-5, the slipstream had blown away her headache.

She'd drunk a little too much wine last night, but the dinner party had been nowhere near as bad as she'd feared. Her mother had been mollified by the bunch of white roses she had bought at a gas station as a peace-offering for turning up too late to help with the preparations. And she'd dealt with her mother's crazy notion that she could go work for Ed Vara by telling the lawyer straight out that she'd heard that he was looking for a contract investigator.

'I already have a couple of good candidates,' he'd said, with a smile that let Summer know that he was privy to her mother's machinations. 'But I'll be glad to add you to my list.'

'I bet your candidates are way more experienced that me, Counsellor. I know I wouldn't stand a chance against them, but it's flattering to be asked.'

With that out of the way, Summer could relax with a couple of glasses of Chilean Shiraz, enjoy her mother's famous lamb-and-prune tagine, and chat with the other guests – Ed Vara's wife, David and Cindy Gerace, architects who specialized in homes that fit tiny, odd-shaped city lots and had helped Summer's father with the plans for his house in the Columbia River Gorge, and a British archaeologist and his brittle, porcelain-pale girlfriend – about university funding, grass-weaving traditions in various Native American tribes, the use of recycled materials in house-building, Prince William's girlfriend, the best coffee shops in Portland. Summer told a couple of choice war stories from her days in uniform, and promised to arrange a ride-along in a cruiser for the archaeologist.

It was a nice evening. At the end of it, after the guests had left and Summer was rinsing the plates and silverware and glasses and loading the dishwasher, her mother said that she had some interesting information about William Gundersen.

'So you talked to Tony Otaka?'

Her mother smiled. 'Actually, I did something that *you* should have thought of doing.'

'Are you going to tell me, or are you going to drag it out?'

'There's nothing *to* drag out. All I did was google Mr Gundersen's name,' her mother said, and told Summer that she'd been right to think that William Gundersen was into computer games: the search engine had pointed her to a very interesting story in the archive of the *Los Angeles Times*. 'It seems that he competed in tournaments against other players for cash prizes. Apparently, he was good, but not of the first rank – he never won any of the big prizes. So he supported himself by selling things he won in online games.'

'Wait a minute. Let me see if I'm following this,' Summer said as she closed the door of the dishwasher and switched it on. 'People pay real money for things that exist only inside computers?'

'It's just like any kind of intangible asset, such as copyright or some other form of intellectual property,' her mother said. 'Or money. How much is a dollar bill really worth?'

'You're going to tell me it isn't worth a dollar.'

'It's worth what everyone agrees it's worth. When it comes down to it, money is just a set of zeroes and ones in a database at a bank: it has value only because everyone agrees that it has value. It's the same with the virtual currencies in these games, or the virtual weapons and magic potions and spells. They're ones and zeroes in databases too, and they have value because people agree they're valuable.'

While her mother explained that players controlled characters who had adventures and won all kinds of things – weapons, money, magical power, even land – and could trade with each other inside the game using the game's virtual currency, or auction the things they'd won outside the game for real money on eBay and elsewhere, Summer decided against finishing her glass of wine, her third, and poured herself a glass of water instead. After the dinner party, and her long day tramping the streets of Portland, she was bone-tired and more than a little woozy, and felt that she needed to pay close attention to her mother's account of the virtual economics of these online games. Saying, when her mother had finished, 'What it boils down to, Billy Gundersen won stuff, and sold it for real money to other players. So how did he make the newspapers?'

'He cheated some people out of something they'd won by working together in one of the games. Apparently, he teamed up with three other players to win the title to some kind of castle, and the mining rights to the land around it. Then he sold the title via an online auction and pocketed all the money.'

'I bet this was something to do with a game called *Trans*.'

'It was, actually. How did you know?'

'Billy Gundersen had a subscription to it.' Summer decided that this wasn't the time to mention Dirk Merrit.

Her mother said, 'According to the newspaper story, the three players who had helped him win the title of this castle tracked him down and cut off two of his fingers with a pair of pruning scissors. A very symbolic punishment, don't you think? A kind of emasculation, especially for someone who made his living using a computer keyboard.'

'Did it go to trial?' Summer was wondering why she had missed this when she had checked William Gundersen's record.

Her mother shook her head. 'They were all juveniles, their parents could afford good lawyers, and William Gundersen agreed to drop the charges in exchange for an out-of-court settlement. Anyway, I don't know whether this helps your investigation, but there it is.'

Summer said, thinking aloud, 'Whatever Gundersen got as a settlement, he must have used it all up by the time he moved to

Denver, because he took to shoplifting and credit-card fraud more or less straight away. And when he moved here, he was so broke that he was living out of his van. I think that he was desperate to make some quick money, and he became involved in something that got him and his girlfriend killed. At first, I thought it was drugs, but now I'm convinced that it was something to do with this online game, *Trans*. He was looking for some kind of treasure, I guess he was planning to sell it on eBay . . . I don't suppose Tony Otaka could find out what it was?'

Her mother smiled. 'As a matter of fact, I was thinking of asking Tony if he or any of his friends have heard of Mr Gundersen.'

Summer smiled too. 'Ed Vara should forget about the two good candidates he has for that contract-investigator position and hire you instead.'

After Summer got onto the I-5, it took just over three hours to reach Cedar Falls. Denise Childers and a detective from the Sheriff's office, Jay Sexton, were waiting for her in the Denny's across the street from the Travelodge where she'd stayed the night after Randy Farrell's arrest. So was one of the FBI's forensic investigators, Gary Delgatto.

Summer said, 'What's he doing here? I thought the FBI weren't interested.'

She had the unsettling feeling of being one step behind, of being left out of the loop, and she was flushed with anger too, ready to get up and walk away if Denise or anyone else at the table said the wrong thing.

'Why I'm here, it's kind of unofficial,' Gary Delgatto said.

'*Kind of* unofficial?'

'Take it easy,' Denise said. 'We'll talk about it in a minute. First, Jay has a story you and Gary need to hear, and he can't stay long – he has a church service to get to.'

'And then you'll explain what's going on.'

Denise met Summer's hot gaze without flinching. 'Absolutely. Go ahead, Jay. Tell them what you told me.'

'It isn't much,' Jay Sexton said. A tall, awkward guy with sandy hair thinning back from his forehead, he wasn't much older than Summer. He folded his big hands around his coffee mug as he explained that his brother had been at high school with Joe Kronenwetter and Dirk Merrit in the 1980s.

'Kronenwetter was on the football team, a typical jock, and Merrit was a typical nerd. Clever, but no good at sports, and not at all sociable – my brother said that even the other nerds didn't like him. Anyhow, their last year in school, Merrit and Kronenwetter were like cat and dog. Kronenwetter was always ragging on Merrit, the usual stupid little tricks, knocking his tray out of his hands in the cafeteria, sticking his head down the john and flushing it, one time stealing his clothes from the gym locker room and shoving him out into the middle of an eighth-graders' class. A whole bunch of stuff like that.'

'I know you're thinking that we aren't going to get to this guy just because he was bullied at school,' Denise told Summer. 'But we're getting to the good part.'

'It's kind of sick, actually,' Jay Sexton said. 'Kronenwetter had this big old dog, some kind of cross between a German shepherd and a red setter. He loved that dog so much that when he got himself a car he'd drive around town with the dog in the front seat. Anyone else who rode with him had to ride in back. Anyhow, just before graduation, the last week of school, the dog went missing, and the next day it turned up in Kronenwetter's locker. Someone had killed it and done all kinds of real nasty stuff to the body. The rumour going the rounds was that Merrit had done it, but although Kronenwetter tried to beat the truth out of him Merrit didn't talk.'

Denise said, 'This was in 1988. Joe Kronenwetter joined the army straight from school, and about six months later, around Christmas, his parents were killed in a house fire.'

Summer felt a chill walk down her backbone, remembering that Kronenwetter's neighbour, Rhonda Cameron, had told her about the house burning in the middle of a snowstorm.

Jay Sexton said, 'Officially, the fire was put down to accidental causes. Kronenwetter's father drank heavily, his body was found in a chair near the seat of the fire, and the fire marshal concluded that he'd fallen asleep with a lit cigarette in his hand. But according to my brother – and this is hearsay, I'd appreciate it if he was kept out of this . . .'

'Just like we agreed,' Denise said, looking at Gary Delgatto.

'It's your investigation,' Gary Delgatto said. 'I'm not going to make any waves.'

Denise said, 'All this is, Jay, is deep background. I'm not even going to write it up.'

Jay Sexton ducked his head and said, 'Well, as long as you all remember this is just kids talking. The story went around that it was Dirk Merrit who set the fire. That like Kronenwetter's dog, it was part of some sick scheme for revenge. And if that's true, well, Merrit got what he wanted. Kronenwetter joined the army, he was in Kuwait during the First Gulf War. He saw that road full of burned-out vehicles, between Kuwait City and Basra, and then he had himself a nervous breakdown and was invalided out of the army, came back here and became a recluse.'

'He mentioned a monster when I interviewed him,' Denise said. 'It could be that after Joe Kronenwetter returned home, Merrit was tormenting him, on and off.'

Gary Delgatto said, 'You think this high-school shit is motivation for Merrit wanting to frame Kronenwetter for the kidnap of the girl? I have to say, it's a stretch.'

'So do I,' Summer said.

Denise said, 'I'm not big on motivation myself. But I know that if I was Merrit, and if I happened to be looking for someone to take the fall for something, Joe Kronenwetter would be the first person I'd think of.'

'Well, I don't know if I've been any help,' Jay Sexton said. 'But I'm going to have to hustle out of here if I'm going to make it to church.'

After the young detective had left, Denise told Summer and Gary Delgatto to drink up, they were going to meet a friend of hers, J. D. Sawyer, out in the forest where Edie Collier had been found. 'J. D. owns one of the best tracking dogs in the state. Most trackers can't distinguish between one person and the next, but Duke, J. D.'s dog, can. Once Duke's been primed with those sneakers you brought along,' Denise said to Summer, 'he won't hit on any trail but Edie's.'

'Which should lead back to Merrit's property,' Gary Delgatto said.

Denise gave him one of her tight little smiles. 'Well, let's hope so.'

Summer said, 'We talked about Mr Sawyer and his tracking dog last night, I have no problem with that. But before we go anywhere, maybe you could explain how Mr Delgatto fits into this.'

The first flush of her anger had cooled, but she still felt a little unsteady. She'd stayed with the case after Kronenwetter had killed himself because she and Denise had agreed that there was more to Edie Collier's death than the random savage impulse of some crazy loner. And she'd come here today because they'd agreed that the FBI were chasing off in the wrong direction, and she'd been bushwhacked. Denise was older than her, more experienced, and this was her turf, but Summer felt that as far this case was concerned they were equals. She felt that she had to assert herself, make it clear that she wouldn't be sidelined.

'Gary has agreed to help us out,' Denise said. 'I talked to him when he examined Edie Collier's body yesterday, and he had an interesting idea about how we might be able to tie her to Dirk Merrit.'

Summer said, 'Is his boss happy for him to help us out?'

Gary Delgatto said, 'I don't work directly for Mr Malone's team. After 9/11, any investigation that doesn't have anything to do with security or terrorism is always short-handed. I was asked if I could help out on a temporary basis, and here I am.'

Summer said, 'But you work for the FBI. Anything you find goes straight to them.'

Denise said, 'You're sore because I didn't tell you about this. Well, it can't be helped, I've been organizing things on the fly.'

'My understanding is that we're working on this together.'

'My understanding is that I'm still the primary.'

'Not after your boss closed down your investigation,' Summer said.

They were staring at each other across the table, cop to cop.

After a moment, Denise said, 'That's a low blow, but you have a point. Maybe I jumped the gun this one time.'

Gary Delgatto said, 'I'm happy to help out in any way I can, but if it's going to cause a problem . . .'

Summer said, still staring at Denise, 'The problem is, I didn't know we were working with the FBI now. But if you think it'll help us do right by Edie, then I guess it's okay.'

'That's why we're all here,' Denise said. 'Dr Delgatto can expedite any forensics, and as long as he's riding along with us, we're officially including Malone in this.'

'All right, then,' Summer said.

Gary Delgatto said, 'It's very flattering to be mistaken for a doctor, but I am not quite there yet.'

Summer said, a little more sharply than she'd intended, 'So what are you, exactly?'

Gary Delgatto said, 'I'm doing research towards a Ph.D in my spare time, but I'm also a qualified forensic investigator.'

Denise looked at her watch and said, 'We can continue this in the car. I don't want to keep J. D. waiting.'

'Fine,' Summer said. 'Just don't spring any more surprises on me.'

27

As they drove east in Gary Delgatto's rented Lincoln Town Car, towards the steep hills and valleys of the Umpqua National Forest, Denise told Summer that she hadn't been able to identify the prisoner who claimed to have seen someone going into Joe Kronenwetter's cell just before he was found dead.

'There were only two other people in the special cells that night. One was occupied by a vagrant picked up for panhandling customers outside a restaurant – the next day he was given a fine and told to get out of the city limits, so right now he's in the wind. The other guy is a local drunk, a wetbrain. I tracked him down and talked to him, but he doesn't even remember being locked up.'

'So we don't have a witness,' Summer said.

'I've put out a warrant for the vagrant. And I'll think up an excuse to take a look at the tapes from the security cameras, and check the register too, see who paid a visit to the holding cells that night. Everyone who goes in – police, attorneys, whoever – they have to sign the log, show ID, and stick their thumb on an electronic scanning device. If it comes to it, will Randy Farrell testify?'

'I think he would if it led to a conviction. But all he has is hearsay.' Summer felt uncomfortable talking about Randy Farrell in front of Gary Delgatto, and added, 'He's a sick man. The last thing he needs is the FBI giving him a hard time.'

Denise said, 'I'm taking his story seriously. I'm going to work all the angles. Especially now that Gary has found some evidence that Joe Kronenwetter didn't hang himself.'

'It's more what I didn't find,' Gary Delgatto said, looking at Summer in the rear-view mirror. 'If Mr Kronenwetter had made the noose, he should have picked up fibres when he ripped up the leg of his coveralls. I didn't find any.'

'So it's possible that he didn't tie the noose himself,' Denise said. She was sitting sideways in the shotgun seat.

'Absence of evidence isn't evidence of absence,' Summer said. It was what her mother sometimes said when talking about archaeological work.

'Also, Gary found that Joe's hyoid bone was cracked,' Denise said. 'Which means that there may have been a struggle, that someone may have pushed down on him, made sure he strangled on the noose. Gary took a blood sample, to see if Joe had been sedated, and he took scrapings from his fingernails, too. We might be able to use DNA to nail the son of a bitch that killed him.'

'*If* someone killed him,' Gary Delgatto said.

'We need to bring Summer up to speed on everything,' Denise said. 'Tell her why you think that Edie Collier and Billy Gundersen were kept in the same place.'

'In a cellar or cave somewhere above two thousand feet, in a valley bottom or a west-facing slope, to be exact,' Gary Delgatto said, smiling at Summer in the rear-view again.

He explained that he had developed a technique to extract particles of air-borne material from the lungs of the recently dead. With every breath, he said, we take in microscopic particles – dust and soot, bacteria and fungal spores, pollen grains – that are trapped in mucus continually produced by ciliated epithelial cells in our nasal cavities, windpipes and lungs. People who live in cities have a higher concentration of the kind of soot particles emitted by diesel vehicles than people who live out in the countryside; metalworkers, carpenters, workers in the construction industry, factory workers, farmers and librarians breathe in particles unique to their trade and place of employment. Gary Delgatto believed that analysis of these particles could be used to track the movements of the deceased prior to their death. Pollen grains were particularly useful, because the overall shape and the thorns, horns, spines, and other decorations of the highly resistant outer coat of pollen grains could be used to identify the species of plant that produced them, and different species or groupings of species were diagnostic of specific locations.

With that in mind, he'd taken samples from the lungs of both Edie Collier and Billy Gundersen, refluxed them with hydrochloric acid to remove mucus and tissue debris, and examined the residue under the microscope. Both samples had contained spores of a sooty fungus that thrived in damp places, as well as various kinds of pollen from conifer trees. The fungal spores suggested that their place of incarceration may have been a damp cellar or somewhere similar, and he'd emailed photomicrographs of the pollen grains to a specialist at the Missouri Botanical Garden, who had identified pollen from a number of tree species, including sugar pine, larch, and alpine fir.

'There were pollen grains from other plants, too, though my guy says that pollen grains from those three kinds of tree are the most useful for determining a specific location,' Gary Delgatto said. 'Sugar pine and larch are found in moist situations, such as valley bottoms and west-facing slopes where precipitation is heaviest, while in this latitude larch and alpine fir are found at elevations above two thousand feet.'

Summer said, 'You mentioned that you were working towards a Ph.D. So I guess this isn't what you'd call an established method.'

'Not yet, no. It takes a long time to prove the value of a new forensic technique. There have to be extensive tests in the field and in the laboratory, it has to stand up to cross-examination in court . . . Bottom line, it's still in development, but I'm hoping to publish a paper soon. My supervisor is very keen.'

Denise chipped in, saying, 'The pollen and the mould show that Edie Collier and Billy Gundersen were kept in the same place, and that it wasn't Joe Kronenwetter's cellar. And that means that either Kronenwetter had help kidnapping them, or he had nothing to do with it. And if he didn't have anything to do with it, he was set up to take the fall for someone else.'

'Dirk Merrit,' Summer said.

'He and Kronenwetter have a history,' Denise said. 'And

Merrit's property is at the right elevation, it's close to where Edie Collier was found, and her boyfriend was not only into computer games, he *stole* stuff from them.'

By now they were driving up a long straight road climbing between steep slopes crowded with Douglas firs. They were near the top of the rise when Gary Delgatto's cell phone rang. He pulled over onto the gravel shoulder, flipped the cell phone open and listened to someone speak, saying yes and no several times, saying that he would drive there at once. Then he folded the phone away and told Summer and Denise, 'I'm very sorry, ladies, but I am afraid that we will have to go back to Cedar Falls. I have to meet a National Guard plane at the airport and fly straight away to Reno. It appears that the travelling man may have struck again. A man was found dead in his hotel room an hour ago, missing his heart and eyes.'

28

Erik Grow's directions to the San Gabriel mountains were straightforward enough, but traffic became heavy and hectic as Carl approached downtown. He nearly missed the junction where the Santa Monica Freeway swung north and then west and turned into the San Bernadino Freeway, and didn't relax until he was driving up a steep, winding two-lane blacktop into the mountains and the forest. They had some kind of reverse tree-line here, starting instead of ending high up on the mountain slopes.

Vehicles were parked along the shoulder of the road and at picnic areas where families were having cook-outs in the shade of pine trees, but at last Carl found a deserted trail that went past a Forest Rangers' hut and wandered for half a mile through trees, ending at a steep drop with a view across a box canyon to a ridge of bare rock.

When Carl popped the Honda's trunk, Erik Grow clambered out white-faced and panicky, fell to his knees and threw up. Carl found a bottle of mineral water and a box of tissues in the glove compartment, told Erik to clean himself up, then played the taped confession and showed Erik the photographs of Pat Metcalf's body. 'Metcalf is dead. Frank Wilson, the man who was going to steal the stuff, he's dead too. As for Mr Merrit, he's going down. He's involved in some heavy stuff, and it's starting to catch up on him. So we have to make our move now. I can't risk leaving it any longer.'

Erik had calmed down a little, but he was still pale and shaky. 'I know I fucked up, and I'm sorry for it. Really and truly. But I want to make up for it. I'm ready to do this thing.'

'We'll do it as soon as we get back to your apartment. We'll take Powered By Lightning for all we can, then you go your way, I go mine, and if I never see you again it'll be too soon. All right?'

'Yeah. I mean, of course. Absolutely.'

Erik couldn't meet Carl's gaze.

'Good. Now you can give me a hand with the woman,' Carl said. 'I'll take her heart, but before I do that I want you to take her eyes.'

'You're kidding.'

'Do I look like I'm kidding?'

'No, no. Of course not. What I mean is, why would you even think about something like that? Excuse me for saying so, but it's sick.'

'When I told you that I killed her because I needed her car, that was only partly true. I also need a dead body, and it has to be found without its heart and eyes.' Carl stared at Erik and the kid flinched and looked away. 'Think of it as a test. You're not a tourist any more, Erik. You've gone native.'

The kid threw up again halfway through digging out the first eye, he was crying and shivering and got blood all over himself, but he did all right in the end.

Carl told him to go sit in the car, and cracked open the woman's ribcage with the dispatch of an emergency-room doctor. He was cutting out her heart when he sensed movement somewhere behind him. He threw himself to the left, rolled once, came up in a crouch. Erik Grow yelled wildly and ran straight at him, raising a tyre iron above his head like an axe. He must have found it in the trunk of the Honda. Carl came up under Erik's wild swing and punched the kid in the throat with his right hand – the hand holding his Spyderco knife.

A thread of blood pulsed into the air when Carl jerked out the serrated blade; he'd severed one of Erik's carotid arteries. Erik dropped the tyre iron and sat down and clutched his throat, blood running out between his fingers, spreading across the front of his T-shirt. He stared up at Carl through glasses knocked askew, then his gaze lost focus and he fell over sideways.

Shit.

For a moment, Carl thought of giving up the idea of ripping off Powered By Lightning right there and then; without Erik Grow, the keystroke recorder was a useless lump of electronic crap. He could hit the road and be in Mexico by nightfall: there was always plenty of bodyguard work and the like to be had south of the border. And then he remembered that there was another way to get the password, even if it meant going back to Dirk Merrit's mansion . . .

Carl carried Erik Grow's body to the edge of the steep drop and heaved it over. It fell bonelessly, smashing into a jut of rock about thirty feet below, rolling down a steep brush-covered slope in a small dust storm, faster and faster, rolling over an edge and spinning out into the air, arms and legs spreadeagled, gone. Carl propped the woman's body against a treetrunk close to the Forest Rangers' hut and drove back down the two-lane blacktop into Los Angeles. By the time he had reached the apartment at Palms, he had worked out exactly what he had to do.

He took a shower to clean Erik Grow's blood from his arms and chest, called Dirk Merrit, told him that he was heading back.

'About time. I trust that it all went well.'

'More or less. Do you still want me to scout out another location?'

'Very much so.'

Carl hesitated, wondering if his next question would give too much away. Fuck it. 'When are you expecting your visitor?'

'Wednesday morning. Speed is of the essence, Carl.'

Carl felt something relax deep inside himself, like a muscle uncramping. He could get to Dirk Merrit before Dirk Merrit got to the kid: the timing was just right. He said, 'I'll be back sometime Tuesday, unless you need me for something else.'

'Tuesday will be fine. Take your time, Carl. Choose well.'

Carl wiped every surface he might have touched, took Erik Grow's laptop, and in the parking lot behind the apartment building dipped the fingers of Pat Metcalf's hand in blood from Julia Taylor's heart and left a good print on the catch of the trunk of the Honda. He walked a few blocks to a mini-mall anchored by a Von's supermarket, tossed the hand and Julia Taylor's heart and eyes in a Dumpster, hot-wired an anonymous Dodge Neon, and headed north.

29

J. D. Sawyer picked up Summer and Denise in his old but scrupulously clean Ford Ranger just ten minutes after Gary Delgatto had left them at a pull-off by the side of the road. His tracker dog, an eager young black Labrador by the name of Duke, was chained to the jockeybox on the load-bed and watched inquisitively as Summer climbed into the cab. Denise squeezed in beside her on the bench seat.

'You must be the detective come all the way from Portland,' J. D. Sawyer said.

'Yes, sir. Summer Ziegler.'

'Pleased to meet you, Summer.'

They shook hands. J. D. Sawyer's grip was firm and dry. He was a lean, leathery man in his late forties, with a grey crew-cut and sharp blue eyes. He wore a canvas hunting vest and a green check shirt whose sleeves were folded back to his elbows. There was a Marine Corps tattoo, an eagle with raised wings in faded blue ink, on his left forearm. Summer liked him at once – he reminded her, just a little, of her father.

He made a neat three-point turn and asked Summer what she had brought along to prime Duke.

'I have a pair of the victim's sneakers,' Summer said.

'Sealed in a bag?'

'An evidence bag.'

'Keep 'em sealed in there tight. That way Duke won't get confused before we get to where you want to start searching.'

As they drove along the river-valley road, Summer learned that J. D. Sawyer worked for a hunting outfit, guiding clients who used bows or old-fashioned muzzle-loaders to take down whitetail or blacktail deer, mule deer and elk, mountain goat and javelina. He said that javelina were the trickiest to hunt: they were smart and quick, and didn't hesitate to charge you if cornered. He took clients on pheasant shoots too, and photography trips. He had used dogs to hunt cougar until it had been made illegal in Oregon, and now he was campaigning to make it legal to use dogs to track wounded deer.

'If you hurt a deer and it gets away from you, you have a responsibility to finish the job. You put a radio collar on the dog, the dog finds the deer, and you find the dog.'

He said that he and Duke were called out about ten times a year to help search for tourists who got lost in the woods. He'd bought Duke's sire from the litter of a bitch owned by an army buddy who'd worked with tracker-dog team handlers in Central America, searching for coca plantations hidden in the hill-forests. In fact, J. D. Sawyer said, Duke was descended from the same line that had produced the dogs used by the Australian Army to search for booby traps and enemy troops in the jungles of Vietnam.

'None of those in service made it back home, but the original line was kept going back in Australia, and our government took on some of them to use in Central America back in the 1980s, when there was the trouble with the Sandinistas.'

Summer said, 'Were you part of that? Running with the *Contras?*'

'No, ma'am. I was in the Marines. The Marines prefer straight fighting. The only action I ever saw in that part of the world was my first tour of duty, in Panama City.'

'When we decided to get rid of the dictator we'd been propping up until he got too greedy,' Summer said. She was still a little pissed off at Denise and it gave her a devilish impulse to try to get a rise from this dry, imperturbable man, get inside his cowboy cool.

'She's from Portland, J. D.,' Denise said. 'They think differently up there.'

'I wouldn't know about the politics,' J. D. Sawyer said amiably. 'I do know that music they used, to get Noriega out of the embassy where he was hiding? You could hear that all over town; hearing it wail over the rooftops put us on edge when we were out on patrol, especially at night. They said that the man was corrupt, but he was strong-willed, too. He held out against that music for an awful long time.'

They turned off the road and drove down a rutted dirt track that tunnelled between tall trees to a small campground with a drop toilet and a few cooking grills. They left the pickup truck there and hiked along a well-marked trail that followed a creek upstream. Stands of black cottonwoods and maple grew along the edge of the creek among outcrops of rock. Douglas firs grew thickly up the slopes on either side.

The place where the two fishermen had found Edie Collier was a ladder of pools and muscular rapids that ran between grey volcanic rock split into squarish blocks. Footprints left by the police, Forest Rangers and air-ambulance crew who had attended the scene were still visible in a broad crescent of gravel along the edge of the largest pool.

J. D. Sawyer told Summer and Denise that if they'd brought lunch they should eat it now; if Duke picked up a trail, they wouldn't stop until he ran it to ground. As she sat on a square boulder, eating one of Denise's peanut butter and banana sand-wiches, Summer tried to imagine Edie Collier, pale and naked, limping over the uneven blocks at the edge of the creek. Leaning on a splintered branch, badly hurt inside, determined to find her way out of the woods but sitting down for a moment to rest and discovering that she didn't have the strength to get up and go on. Summer wondered how far Edie had managed to travel through the night-time woods, saw again her face, her expression of serene indifference when she'd been confronted in the stuffy office in the department store with evidence of her shoplifting. Amazing what people were capable of doing when they came up against it.

Denise was examining the gadget that Gary Delgatto had given her as a parting gift. Designed to filter microscopic parti-cles from the air, it looked like a lunch box strapped with black duct tape, with an on/off switch sticking out of a hole in one corner, an inlet with a brass fitting to which a length of plastic hose could be attached at one end, and an outlet at the other. Gary Delgatto had told Denise that if her friend's dog did find a trail that led somewhere interesting, perhaps she could run it for ten minutes or so. If they were lucky, it would collect a sample of pollen similar to those he'd taken from the lungs of Edie Collier and William Gundersen.

When Denise saw that Summer was watching her, she said, 'It's pretty foolproof. Not much different from a vacuum cleaner.'

Summer said, 'I guess it won't hurt to give it a try.'

'I get the feeling you think Gary's technique isn't worth much.'

'He seems to know his stuff, and he made it sound plausible.'

'He's cute too, isn't he? Don't deny it, I saw the way you were looking at him.'

'He has a nice smile.'

'And those dark eyes,' Denise said, making a pass through the air with the gadget's plastic hose.

'I don't want to sound negative, but if you do happen to collect a sample of pollen that matches the samples he took from the lungs of Edie Collier and Billy Gundersen, what does it prove? There could be a thousand places where you can find the same kind of stuff floating around in the air.'

'Personally, I don't have much time for fancy forensic techniques. And I admit that Gary is young and eager, he wants to make a name for himself with this pollen thing of his, and whatever this gadget of his finds, it probably won't do us much good. But despite all that, I believe him when he said that because Edie Collier and Billy Gundersen had exactly the same kind of crud in their lungs they had to have been kept in the same place.'

'Do you also believe that it proves they were kept somewhere above two thousand feet?'

Denise smiled. 'That's what the botanist said, not Gary.'

Summer smiled too. 'Even if it's true, it doesn't mean that they were kept somewhere on Dirk Merrit's estate.'

'Not by itself, no. But if you have another suspect, I'd like to hear about it.'

'I don't. But – and again, I don't want to sound negative – I can't see how the random murder of some guy in Reno fits in with what we know about him.'

'If the guy in Reno was killed by a crossbow bolt it won't be a problem,' Denise said. 'And if J. D.'s tracker dog can pick up Edie Collier's trail, and if it leads back to Merrit's property, he's definitely going to have some explaining to do.'

'And if it doesn't?'

'Since we're in the vicinity, I think we should drop by in any case. You know how he likes to talk. Maybe he'll let slip something we can use.'

'Push the envelope a little.'

'Oh, I think we're way outside the envelope now.'

J. D. Sawyer fitted Duke with a long hunting leash and let him snuffle at the sneakers that Summer had brought, feeding him a Kibble and following him to and fro as he cast about. It took a little while. Duke was confused by the scents left by all the people who had attended the scene, several times starting back down the trail towards the campground. J. D. Sawyer knelt down and whispered to him, calming him down, allowing him to nose the sneakers before letting him loose again.

At last, the Labrador scrambled up a chute of ferny rocks beside the rapids and stopped at the beginning of the trees, one foreleg raised, head cocked forward. J. D. Sawyer fed him another Kibble, and Summer and Denise followed them past the rapids, clambering through trees and rocks beside the creek.

The channel that the creek had cut through layers of ancient pumice and lava grew deeper and narrower, white water brawling over wet black rocks at the bottom. The trail meandered up and down between trees and rocky outcrops. It was a hard scramble. They took two hours to travel two miles. Summer took off her windbreaker and tied it around her waist. They reached another series of rapids, a steep thickly forested slope rising on the far side, and Duke lost the scent trail.

While J. D. Sawyer and his dog ranged back and forth across the flat rocks beside the rapids, trying to pick up the trail again, Denise unfolded a map and showed Summer that Kronenwetter's property was way off to the northwest, showed her that they weren't far from the edge of Dirk Merrit's estate. At last, J. D. Sawyer came over and said that he believed the trail had gone cold.

'Duke's getting tired, and we need to get back while it's still light. I'm thinking that we should call it a day.'

'Let's try up there,' Denise said, pointing to the slope that loomed above them.

They had to make a wide diversion before they struck a logging track that climbed the slope, emerging at the edge of a long, rough meadow that stretched along the top of a ridge, falling away to trees on either side. Someone had mowed a wide strip right down the centre of the meadow very recently. The cut grass had been left where it had fallen, and was still green.

J. D. Sawyer refreshed Duke's memory with another whiff of Edie Collier's sneakers, followed the Labrador here and there until Duke settled on a spot midway along the ridge. When Summer and Denise walked over, Duke was chewing on another Kibble. J. D. Sawyer kicked at a steel ring welded to a steel stake hammered into the ground.

'Can't say I know what to make of this, but Duke's very taken by it.'

Denise took off her rucksack and pulled out a small digital camera. She took a picture, squinted at the camera's LCD screen, held it up to show Summer. 'Good enough, I guess. If I didn't know any better, I'd say someone anchored something here. An animal, or maybe a person.'

'You have a gruesome imagination,' J. D. Sawyer said.

'I know, and I wish I didn't,' Denise said. 'How's Duke holding out?'

'We'll give it one more go,' J. D. Sawyer said.

He and the dog worked around the edges of the meadow. Duke kept coming back to a stand of birches in a pocket of scrub at the far end of the meadow, but the Labrador seemed uncertain, twice beginning to point but then shaking his head and casting around again. There was a narrow track a little way beyond the spot, a pair of ruts with a mane of grass between them leading off into the trees.

'Maybe she came down there, maybe she didn't,' J. D. Sawyer said, shading his eyes with his forearm as he squinted down the track.

Denise discovered a tyre mark at the edge of a dried-out puddle, pulled out her camera, and took several photographs.

Summer said, 'You think someone drove her here?'

'It's possible.'

J. D. Sawyer said, 'If the poor girl was brought here in a vehicle, Duke won't be any help finding out where she came from.'

'He's already been a real help,' Denise said. 'I owe you big time, J. D. How I see it, someone brought her here and tied her to that stake for some reason, but she got free and ran off and ended up by the creek. She followed the creek downhill as far as she could, and if she hadn't hurt herself so badly, or if she'd just kept going until she reached the road, she might have been able to tell us exactly what happened to her.'

Denise seemed very happy to be there, happy with how this had gone. Her face flushed, a spray of freckles showing across the bridge of her nose, her auburn hair bunched back in a rough ponytail and loose hairs stirring around her face in the fresh breeze. Smiling at Summer, saying, 'Before you ask, this is Dirk Merrit's property. Or it was, until he sold it off last year. His mansion is about a mile away. All we have to do is follow this track.'

30

Denise's plan was simple: while she and Summer paid a call on Dirk Merrit, J. D. Sawyer would hike back through the woods to the campground where he'd left his pickup truck, drive to the entrance on the western edge of the estate, and wait for them there.

'If we don't turn up by six o'clock, call my cell,' Denise told J. D. Sawyer. 'And in the unlikely event that I don't answer, you might think to call the Sheriff's office.'

J. D. Sawyer considered this for a moment, then said, 'If you think Mr Merrit is going to give you trouble, you could walk back with me and I'll give you a ride straight to the front door of that mansion of his. I admit to being curious about seeing what it looks like. I've seen photographs, but never had an excuse to see it in the flesh, so to speak.'

'I appreciate the offer,' Denise said, 'but I figure that we have a better chance of surprising him if we come in the back way. We'll explain how we came to be there, and see what he has to say.'

So J. D. Sawyer doubled back towards the campground, and Denise and Summer went in the opposite direction, discussing how they'd handle Dirk Merrit if they got the chance to talk with him as they followed the track that ran downhill in the deep shadow of old-growth Douglas firs. It ended at a T-junction with a gravel fire road, where they turned east and soon reached a gate of welded metal pipe set in a tumbledown wall of unmortared stones. A laminated notice attached to the gate warned of armed response and dog patrols. The road beyond it curved away between dark trees.

Summer felt a little chill of caution as she followed Denise over the gate. Half expecting floodlights to snap on, the wail of sirens . . .

Nothing happened. The silence under the trees was so profound that Summer could hear her blood sing in her ears as she and Denise walked on. The trees on either side of the road thinned to scrub salted with saplings growing out of yard-high pieces of plastic tube that protected their tender stems from deer. The track made a sharp bend, and there was a wide stretch of hardpan clay with a low, stone-built house falling into ruin on one side and a large, industrial-looking barn on the other.

'That's where the caretaker who looked after the campgrounds used to live,' Denise said, pointing to the house. 'I don't know about the barn – it looks new.'

The building was constructed from pressed-steel panels on concrete footings, walls and roof painted rust red. As Summer and Denise approached it, a security light came on above a big sliding door at the top of a short ramp. Denise rattled the door, but it was chained and padlocked. She took her five-cell Mag-Lite from her rucksack, aimed it through the cut-out where the chain looped through the door, and said that she could see a big vehicle inside, it looked like an RV.

'It's parked right in front of the door, I can't see anything else. I should have brought along a pair of bolt-cutters.'

'You're kidding.'

'The FBI found tracks left by an RV near Billy Gundersen's body.'

Denise had a serious and determined look on her face as she peered through the gap, angling the flashlight this way and that.

Summer said, 'Maybe this is a good time to use that gadget Gary gave you.'

Denise switched off the flashlight and put it away. 'Not yet. If Merrit kidnapped those two kids, I reckon he would have kept them close to his mansion. And since that's where we're headed . . .'

'Lead on, then.'

'Cheer up. The worst that can happen is that he'll refuse to talk to us.'

They climbed the low ridge behind the house, cutting through a scatter of pines and emerging above the end of a lake that stretched away in a long vee under the late-afternoon sky, narrowing towards a dam at its northern end – a brief white dash pinched between rocks and trees. Denise pointed out the remains of holiday cabins on the far side of the water and a wooden boathouse.

'The lodge was on top of the ridge,' she said. 'See the notch in the tree-line? It had a view of the lake on one side and the mountains on the other. My mother and father were working there when they started dating. She was a chambermaid, he was a waiter in the restaurant. They could tell you a lot of stories about this place.'

A dirt track ran alongside the shore of the lake for half a mile, then veered away and plunged down through trees, curled around a massive shoulder of rock, and ended in a concrete stairway that descended beside the tall wedge of the dam. The narrow valley stretched beyond the dam, the three towers of Dirk Merrit's mansion standing halfway up the far side, looking more than ever like a fairy-tale castle. Denise said that this was as good a place as any to try out Gary's gadget, and she was rummaging in her rucksack when Summer spotted two men coming up the stairway towards them: security guards in blue shirts and black pants, one pot-bellied and balding, the other a skinny kid with flamboyant acne. By the time they had reached the top of the steps, Denise had clipped the long hose to the inlet of the filter unit and switched it on.

'I don't think you should be doing that,' the skinny kid said.

'Police business,' Denise said, aiming the business end of the gadget's hose at him. Inside the plastic box, the fan made a fat hum as it sucked air through the 0.22-micron filter.

'You have to come with us,' the balding guard said. 'Mr Merrit wants a word with you.'

Denise kept the filter unit running, sweeping the hose left and right, vacuuming the air, as she and Summer followed the two guards down the steps to a kind of Japanese garden of bamboos, rhododendrons and white boulders on the floor of the valley.

Summer asked the guards if Mr Merrit had taken any trips recently; the balding man told her that what Mr Merrit did was none of his business.

Flat stones stepped across the small stream that ran out from the boulder-fringed pool at the foot of the dam, and there were more steps climbing up the other side of the valley. When the balding guard stopped halfway up to catch his breath, Denise switched off the filter gadget and stuffed it into her rucksack. They crossed a wide terrace, going past a kind of domed greenhouse containing sand and rocks and oddly coloured cacti, and went around the foot of the biggest of the three towers to the road and the castle door. The door swung open as they approached and Summer and Denise followed the two guards across the foyer into the trophy room.

As before, Dirk Merrit was waiting for them in front of the big TV screen. This time he was wearing forest-camo combat pants and a matching jacket over a black T-shirt, looking even stranger in this military costume than in his kimono. He was as tall and skinny as a fashion model, his eyes black holes in his white skull-face, bars of black camouflage greasepaint under his eyes and his lips painted black. Summer realized that he must be wearing contact lenses that fitted over his eyeballs, but it didn't make his gaze any less spooky. He looked like some primitive mask from the pages of *National Geographic*, or Marilyn Manson's reflection in a smashed mirror.

The TV was showing what Summer supposed was a view from the game, *Trans*. The skeleton of a man lying amid rubble under a blood-red sky. Ghastly things like lopsided cartoon vultures, with scaly necks that were way too long, glowing eyes and hooked beaks, perched here and there on broken lengths of wall or girders poking up from the rubble.

After he'd dismissed the guards, Dirk Merrit said to Denise, 'What does that thing do? The thing with the hose that you put back in your rucksack just now? Oh, don't act surprised. I have an extensive security system. It has been tracking you ever since you triggered the security light at the barn. That device, I don't believe it's standard police-issue.'

Denise squared up to him. 'It belongs to a friend of mine, sir. A forensic investigator who works for the FBI.'

Dirk Merrit smiled, sharp white teeth peeking between black lips. 'Mmm. I heard that the FBI has taken over your case – the mystery of the girl in the woods. Am I a suspect, detective? Are you trying to intimidate me?'

'Not at all, sir. We were doing some follow-up work, and it happened to lead us to the south side of your estate.'

'And you thought you'd pay me a visit, is that it? Well, there was no need to trespass, detective. I would have been happy to let you through the front gate.' When Denise didn't reply, Dirk Merrit said, 'Did you see anything interesting in the barn, by the way? I saw you taking a good long look through the door.'

Denise said, 'I believe I saw an RV in there.'

'That's right. I use it for my hunting trips.'

'Have you been hunting recently, Mr Merrit?'

'As a matter of fact I *have* been on a trip, just last week. I believe I told you about it the last time we met.'

Denise said, 'Was this trip in Nevada? The desert there?'

'Nevada? I can't think what I would want to hunt in Nevada. No, it was right here in Oregon, in the Cascades. I have a permit, if you care to see it.'

'It won't be necessary. Did you have any luck?'

'Alas, no. But it's always good to get out and about, don't you think?'

'Did anyone go with you?'

'My driver. He accompanies me on all my little trips. But I'm afraid that he isn't here right now. If you want to talk to him you'll have to come back another time.'

'Where were you last night, sir?'

'Last night? I was right here, going through some architectural plans. I'm thinking of making some radical modifications to my home.'

'Can anyone verify that?'

'My cook, and my personal physician. Would you like to talk to them?'

'Do you think I should?'

'Perhaps you could tell me, Detective Childers, what you and your friend Detective Ziegler, of the Portland Police Bureau, are doing here. Is this an official visit, or some sort of desperate fishing expedition?'

'We'll get to that in a moment,' Denise said, touching her ear, the prearranged signal for Summer to step in.

Summer said, 'The FBI has become involved because the body of Edie Collier's boyfriend turned up in Nevada. William Gundersen – does that ring any bells with you?'

'Not especially.'

'How about Bruce Smith?'

'Are you fishing too, Detective Ziegler?'

'The reason I ask, sir, is because it turns out that William Gundersen, also known as Bruce Smith, was a keen player of *Trans*.'

'So are about two hundred thousand other people. And I sold my interest in the game two years ago.'

Summer said, 'But you still play it, don't you? That's a scene from it right there on your TV.'

Dirk Merrit said, 'I *watch* it. I don't play.'

On the screen behind him, a vulture-thing hopped onto the skeleton's back, and started to tug at a flap of skin attached to an arm bone.

Summer said, 'William Gundersen was looking for some kind of treasure hidden in the game.'

'I expect he was. There are all kinds of treasures and marvels hidden in the game. That's one of its attractions.'

'The treasure William Gundersen was trying to find is hidden somewhere in the ruins of Los Angeles. And maybe it's only a coincidence, Mr Merrit, but the last time we were here your TV was showing a scene set in those ruins – a hunter on a quest to find some kind of treasure.'

Dirk Merrit stared at Summer, the black holes of his eyes and the white mask of his face unreadable. Her blood hummed.

She said, 'I can't help wondering if that dead guy there on the TV is the hunter we saw before.'

Dirk Merrit turned to look at the TV. Giving himself time,

Summer thought, to think of a reply. He'd been playing with them last time, teasing, dropping hints, and she'd touched a nerve by giving one of those hints right back at him.

He said, 'Do you know, I'm not sure who or where that is, precisely. But it looks like that particular pilgrim has suffered some especially bad luck, hasn't he?'

Turning back, his smile in place.

Summer met his gaze and said, 'He's definitely had the same kind of bad luck as William Gundersen.'

'You're confusing the game with the real world, Detective Ziegler.'

'I don't think I'm the only one to make that mistake.'

Dirk Merrit left that hanging in the air.

Denise said, 'Why we're here, we used a tracker dog to follow the scent trail left by Edie Collier. You'll remember that she was found a few miles south of your property, at the edge of a creek. It turns out that she followed the creek downstream, starting from a spot not very far from here. There's a nice-looking meadow on a ridge, perhaps you know it.'

'No, I don't think so.'

Denise said, 'I'm surprised you don't remember it – it's part of the land you sold off last year. What we're wondering is how did she get there in the first place? She didn't walk there, because the tracker dog would have picked up her scent, so I guess someone drove her. We found fresh tyre-marks on a track leading off through the woods, we followed the track, and that's how we ended up here. Any idea how that could be?'

'Perhaps you should ask Mr Kronenwetter. Oh, but he's dead, isn't he? He killed himself and left a note saying how very sorry he was about what happened to the girl.'

'About Joe Kronenwetter,' Denise said. 'After we last talked, I heard you had quite a bit of trouble with him back when you were at school together. I find it odd that you didn't mention that he bullied you at school. In fact, you told me that you didn't remember him.'

'I prefer to look forward, detective. I don't dwell on the past.'

'He humiliated you every chance he got, didn't he? He'd

shove your head down the toilet, one time I believe he stole your clothes and pushed you naked into a class of young kids in the gym. I don't know about you, sir, but I'd definitely remember something like that if it had happened to me.'

'I made a success of my life, detective, and what happened to him? He became a crazy loner, a rapist and murderer who took his own life rather than face up to what he'd done.'

'He beat you up pretty badly one time, too,' Denise said. 'Something to do with his dog, wasn't it?'

'I do remember something about his dog. Someone killed it, didn't they?'

'It was badly mutilated, and left in his high-school locker.'

'That's right. He wailed like a baby when he found it.'

Summer could see that Denise's dogged frontal assault wasn't getting anywhere. Dirk Merrit was too sly, too nimble. But Denise wasn't about to give up, saying, 'Joe Kronenwetter believed that you killed his dog. That was why he beat you up.'

'He took his anger out on me, and broke my jaw in several places. He was expelled from school, and I had my first taste of the wonders of plastic surgery. If you think I still hold a grudge against him for that, detective, you're mistaken. In fact, in a roundabout way, I owe him a debt.'

'Perhaps you don't hold a grudge because you know that you deserved that beating.'

'Because I killed his dog? Is that what you think?'

'It's what other people think,' Denise said.

'Joe Kronenwetter was a bully, detective, and I was not his only victim. There were plenty of people who had reason to hate him back then. Even some of his so-called friends. Ask Charley Phelps, for instance.'

'Charley Phelps?'

Summer saw that the name meant something to Denise.

'Two weeks before the incident with the dog, Joe Kronenwetter started going out with Charley Phelps's girlfriend. Although "going out" isn't really the right way of putting it. They were fucking, mostly in Joe's car. Charley caught them at it one night, he and Joe had a fight, and Joe bested him. If you don't believe me, ask Charley, or his former girlfriend. Jenny Zirkle, formerly Mackee.'

'Maybe I will,' Denise said.

'This is the second time you and Detective Ziegler have visited me, asking all kinds of impertinent questions, making all kinds of wild and baseless accusations. I'm beginning to believe that you're waging some kind of personal vendetta against me.'

'I'm following up some loose ends, sir.'

'Under whose authority? Sheriff Worden's, or the FBI's?'

'I'm the primary on the investigation into Edie Collier's death.'

'I saw my good friend Sheriff Worden on TV, announcing that the case was closed. And the FBI is investigating the murder of her boyfriend. So it doesn't have anything to do with you, does it?'

'As I said, there are some loose ends—'

Dirk Merrit held out his hands, wrists together. 'Why don't you arrest me? Take me in for questioning? Oh, but then Sheriff Worden would find out, wouldn't he? Perhaps I should give him a call, ask him if he knows that you've been persecuting me.'

'That's entirely up to you,' Denise said, her face reddening, her jaw muscles tightening. 'And maybe you can explain why we tracked Edie Collier back to your property—'

'Not my property, not any longer.'

'And maybe you can explain why her boyfriend was found dead with a wound consistent with being shot with a crossbow arrow, just a few days after you boasted about using a crossbow on your hunting trips.'

'I don't have to explain anything to you,' Dirk Merrit said, his black gaze moving past Summer and Denise, his smile widening. 'Detective Hill. Thank you so much for coming here with such dispatch.'

As Jerry Hill drove Denise and Summer out of the main entrance of the estate, Denise said, 'You can stop right here and let us out.'

'No, I can't,' Jerry Hill said, turning sharp left onto the highway with a screech of tyres.

'I don't care what Merrit told you to do, you can let us off here.'

'It isn't anything to do with Merrit, Denise. Worden wants a word with both of you, and I'm not about to keep him waiting.'

'We already have a ride.'

'From J. D. Sawyer, I bet. I saw his truck parked down the road a ways, that tracker dog of his in back. Mind telling me what you and your friend have been up to?'

'Working the case.'

'It isn't yours to work any more,' Jerry Hill said. 'You should know that: you talked to the FBI most of yesterday, just like me.'

Summer, sitting behind them on the rear bench of the Dodge Ram's crew cabin, said, 'Detective Hill? One thing has been bothering me since we last talked. I know you set up that confrontation between Randy Farrell and Joe Kronenwetter, but how did you manage to arrange it for the TV crew to be there too?'

31

Summer's mother said, 'I don't suppose he took that too well.'

Summer said, 'Actually, he laughed it off, told me I had a vivid imagination that I needed to get under control if I wanted to have any kind of career as a police detective. He's not as dumb as he wants people to believe. Anyway, he drove us straight to the Justice Building in Cedar Falls, where the sheriff spent ten minutes explaining just how little time he had for Portland police who swaggered in and caused trouble in his town. It wasn't the finest moment in my career.'

Monday, half past twelve, Summer and her mother were sitting in one of the wood-panelled rooms of Jake's Famous Crawfish. White-coated waiters were hurrying to and fro between the tables as they served the lunchtime crowd. It was the beginning of the crawfish season. Summer had crawfish Creole style; her mother crawfish in a Cajun stew over rice.

Her mother said, 'He really said "swaggered"?'

'He really did. I thought of telling him that there were plenty of good reasons why someone needed to stir up trouble over the death of Edie Collier, but I managed to bite my tongue. At the end, he had two deputies escort me out of the building – they were nice guys, apologetic – and follow me to the county line.'

'He was making the point that it was his town.'

'Well, the deputies didn't turn on their lights, but I suppose so.'

Summer's mother took a sip of her white wine. She was wearing a buttercup-yellow jacket and a white roll-neck sweater. Her grey hair was brushed back and held by a wood and leather barrette. She looked at Summer over the rim of her glass and said, 'I heard you come in at about one, and then you went out early.'

'I wanted to talk to Ryland Nelsen before word about my little adventure got to him. He was pretty nice about it, took me out for coffee and sat me down and listened to the whole story. He said that as I had been working the case on my own time, at worst it was a question of whether or not I had harmed the good name of the Portland Police Bureau. I apologized for causing trouble after he'd given me a personal day at short notice, and he said he blamed himself for not checking that I'd been wearing Lycra, but was nice enough to add that he believed my heart was in the right place.'

'Lycra?'

'It's a long story about a silly little joke. So then I had to go see Lieutenant Powers, because Sheriff Worden had made a call to the chief's office. The lieutenant had me stand to attention while she told me that I was lucky that Sheriff Worden hadn't made an official complaint, reminded me that I was part of the police family here in Portland and any misjudgement on my part reflected badly on everyone else, and sent me on my way. I guess I got off lightly.'

'I don't suppose that your superior officer was very happy about having some self-righteous policeman from another part of the state telling her what to do,' her mother said, and neatly ate a forkful of crawfish stew.

'One good thing about having fucked up,' Summer said, 'the guys in the Robbery Unit have been a lot friendlier. A couple of them asked me out to lunch because they wanted to know all about it, every sordid detail. Luckily, I already had a date with you.'

'What about your friend?'

'Denise has been suspended, pending an investigation. I first heard about it from Dirk Merrit: he found out my cell phone number and called me to gloat. I hung up on him. Then Denise called. Not to bitch about her suspension, although I could tell that she was as mad as hell about it. She wanted to tell me that Dirk Merrit had invited Sheriff Worden to inspect his property.'

June Ziegler thought for a moment. 'That's a crafty move.'

'It gets better. He invited a TV crew too, and made a little speech about not holding any grudge over what he called police harassment. Said something to the effect that as someone at the forefront of experimentation in new expressions of human lifestyle he expected a certain amount of hostility, but he was always happy to confront it head on.'

'He's attempting to take the moral high ground.'

'That's what Denise said. Well, she actually said that he was trying to make himself a martyr, which I guess is roughly the same thing. She told me that Sheriff Worden backed him up by explaining how he supported a number of local charities and had made valuable contributions to civic life in the county. The sheriff also said that he had taken up with reluctance the invitation to inspect Mr Merrit's home, but felt that it was his duty to quote unquote "clear the air". He said that he had supervised the search personally, and had found nothing suspicious. Denise told me, you bet he didn't find anything, he had half a dozen officers with him and they were in and out inside an hour.'

'Your Mr Merrit does like to play games, doesn't he?'

'He likes to manipulate situations, try to take control. All the time he was talking with Denise and me, he knew that Jerry Hill was on the way. He must have called him as soon as his security cameras picked us up at the edge of his property.'

'Do you think that this man is working for your Mr Merrit?'

'Why not? Merrit may be weird, but he's also a rich guy from an old family in a small town. He has a lot of influence. Denise told me that Sheriff Worden is on the board of the town library, and Merrit made a sizeable donation to the library a couple of years ago, paid for installation of a dozen computers and broadband Internet access. Also, they know each other from charity balls and so on . . . And every year, Merrit holds a picnic out at his lake in aid of a charity that helps children who have congenital facial disfigurements, or who have had to have extensive plastic surgery.'

When Denise Childers had told her about the picnic, Summer had pictured Dirk Merrit stalking among family groups on a sunny grass slope, tall, skull-faced, and dressed in black, like a cartoon depiction of Death. She saw that picture again now, felt a chill climb her spine, and said, 'The first time I met him, I wasn't convinced that Merrit was capable of murder. Now I know that he is.'

Her mother said, 'Why do I have the feeling that this has become a personal crusade? That you aren't going to step back and let the FBI deal with this man.'

'As far the FBI is concerned, we have only circumstantial evidence linking Merrit with what happened to Edie Collier and Billy Gundersen. And there are a lot of holes in the story. We don't know why they were kidnapped in the first place, for instance, although I have a very strong feeling that it has something to do with *Trans*. Billy Gundersen played it, and Dirk Merrit developed it in the first place. He may not own it any more, but he's definitely still interested in it – he made a point of showing it on his TV both times Denise and I visited him. Which is why I was wondering if you'd invited me to lunch because your grad student had found something interesting.'

Summer's mother took a sip of wine and said, 'I realized something the other day – I haven't visited your father's house since he died. You and your brothers made an expedition to it last fall, to weatherproof it for the winter, and I know you've been there a few times since . . .'

'I like it there. It's a great place to chill, to think things through. If you want, we could go this weekend.'

'I've been wondering lately if I should sell it.'

'I'd be sorry if you did.'

The house was less than half-built, little more than a severe one-storey concrete bunker, and barely habitable, but it was perched on a raft of rock overlooking a white-water river, with woods rising behind it and a fabulous view towards Mount Hood. One of Summer's last memories of her father, a good one, was when she'd driven up to the place on a whim towards the end of July last year, a couple of weeks before he'd been struck down by his heart attack. She remembered that when she had arrived, her father had been working on the flagstone patio, using his power saw to cut supports for the sinuous kitchen counter he'd designed, barefoot in paint-spattered jeans and a faded black T-shirt, looking up when she called and waving, his rimless glasses catching sunlight, his smile wide and welcoming.

For a moment Summer saw him clear in her mind, and it pierced her through and through.

She said, 'We should go visit. I can show you how it stood up to the winter. Let's not decide anything until then.'

Her mother lit a cigarette. Taking her time, shaking out the match, placing it in the ashtray, saying, 'Ever since your father died, I've been worrying about all kinds of things I never used to worry about. Clearing the gutters of leaves, finding a tree surgeon to trim the cherry in the backyard . . . And now I see my daughter turning to the property pages of the newspaper first thing every morning.'

'When I moved back, you knew it was a temporary thing. I have to find a place of my own sooner or later, and I'll still be living right here in Portland. We can have lunch together all you want. Like I said, I didn't have lunch with those guys from work today because I wanted to have lunch with my mom.'

'And pump me for information.'

Summer smiled. 'That's a harsh way of putting it.'

Her mother said, 'We talk about what you do, but I sometimes feel that you live in another world. One with its own rules and its own language that only you and criminals really understand.'

'Like playing cops and robbers? You know it isn't like that.'

'You're playing a game with Dirk Merrit, aren't you?'

'He's trying to play *me*. If you're worried that this is a personal thing, that I want to get back at him after he got me into trouble with Sheriff Worden, you should know that all I'm interested in is making sure that he answers for what he did. And that's why I need to figure out if he had any kind of connection with Billy Gundersen.'

'You're here because you want to know what I found out from Tony.'

'The main reason I came here was to have lunch with you. But if Tony *did* find out something . . .'

June Ziegler stubbed out her half-smoked cigarette. 'You know that most graduate students are paid peanuts. They have to supplement their income with tutoring, teaching, all kinds of work . . . One of my colleagues has a student who does paintings of whales to commission. Tony is into virtual trading, but before that he was into grinding.'

'You'll have to explain that.'

'In most of these computer games, your character starts out with only a little money and not many skills. You have to work hard to move to the next level, and that means doing the same kind of thing over and over again. That's what the players call grinding, and some players are willing to pay for someone else to do it for them. They buy a ready-made character, or they pay to have their own character promoted to a more exciting level of the game.'

'This is what Tony does?'

'What he used to do, in *Trans*. He told me that it's set in a post-apocalyptic version of the United States where genetically enhanced overlords fight for territory. Players start out as slaves, and have to work at various menial tasks to gain fitness points, skills, money, and genetic enhancements to their bodies. Grinders spend all their time turning slaves into free citizens, and other players buy the resulting characters.'

'It sounds like cheating. Like bodybuilders taking steroids.'

'Tony says that there are click-farming sweatshops in Eastern Europe and Asia where kids spend all their time developing skilled characters for sale. They earn virtual currencies in the games, and exchange it over the Internet for real dollars, too. Or, like Tony, they win all kinds of virtual property, and sell it to other players.'

'Like the castle which cost Billy Gundersen two of his fingers.'

'Tony knows people who work for a click-farming company right here in Portland. I had him write down the details,' June Ziegler said, and rummaged in her purse and handed Summer a page torn from a notebook.

Written on it in her mother's neat, backward-slanting hand was an address in Northeast Portland and a name: Okay Soucek.

Summer said, 'So Tony thinks that this guy might know something about Billy Gundersen?'

'It's better than that,' her mother said. 'When I showed Tony the mug shots you gave me, he told me that Billy Gundersen used to work for Mr Soucek.'

32

Everyone in the Macabee County Sheriff's office knew that
Jerry Hill cut corners, and the man made no secret about his bad
behaviour, boasting, telling war stories and generally making a
lot of noise pretty much every night at the Hanging Drop, the
bar where cops and lawyers hung out after work. Most of it
wasn't serious – strong-arming suspects and witnesses, smoking
grass confiscated from teenagers and tourists, accepting the odd
freebie or favour – but Denise began to suspect that he was
into something really dirty after Summer Ziegler told her
about the rumour that someone had slipped into Joe
Kronenwetter's cell just before he'd been found dead. Her suspicion hardened into certainty when Gary Delgatto called and
gave her the results of the tests on Kronenwetter's blood and
tissue samples.

Something Denise hadn't yet told either Summer or Gary:
Charley Phelps, the guy who'd lost his girlfriend to Joe
Kronenwetter back in high school, worked as a guard in the
lock-up on the fourth floor of the Justice Building, and he was
also Jerry Hill's half-brother.

Denise wasn't the cerebral type. She nailed cases by working
the scene and gathering every scrap of evidence by every possible means, by interviewing witnesses and hassling likely bad
guys, looking for anything unusual or out of place, trying to
figure out who had the opportunity, who seemed evasive or
nervous, who told her a flat-out lie when they didn't need to.
She relied on instinct, a working knowledge of Macabee
County's lowlifes, and her ability to read the street. Luckily, most
criminals were as dumb as a bag of hammers, underachieving
high-school dropouts with chaotic lives who couldn't hack it in

a real, honest-to-God nine-to-five job. Most of them were so dumb they didn't even know how dumb they actually were. They believed that they were sly, streetwise guys who could out-smart police with their shuck and jive, but the plain fact of the matter was that Denise's twelve-year-old daughter was a lot smarter and a whole lot better at fabricating stories and excuses than most bad guys. Usually, it didn't take a lot of brainwork to figure out who was in the frame, and then Denise would bring them in, listen to what they had to say, and break them down by spelling out the inconsistencies and contradictions in their lame stories, and by telling them exactly how long they were going to spend in jail if they didn't cooperate. That was the only way she knew how to work, so after a long sleepless night Sunday, after all the excitement at Dirk Merrit's place and the aftermath, her first best thought was to roll over to Charley Phelps's place and see what he had to say for himself.

Monday morning then, after she'd been reamed out all over again by Sheriff Worden, this time in the presence of her shift commander and the police union lawyer, after she'd handed in her gun and her badge, Denise scooted up to the fourth floor of the Justice Building. The booking area and offices of the lock-up were either side of a central corridor with two pairs of short and long corridors at either end forming a lopsided H. The six special cells were on one of the short corridors, behind a locked door of steel bars with a security camera above it. Denise per-suaded the corrections officer at the reception desk to let her take a look at the tape made by the camera, but found that the camera had been knocked askew on the night in question, and the tape mostly showed a blank wall. She had more luck with the visitor records and the duty log, discovering that not only had Charley Phelps been working on the night when Joseph Kronenwetter had died but, lo and behold, he had been the first person to discover the body.

Right now, he was taking time off, claiming to be suffering from post-traumatic shock. Denise drove over to his house, stop-ping off at a gas station along the way to buy a six-pack of Henry Weinhard's. She knew all about Charley Phelps. The man was a drunk who'd gotten his job courtesy of his police half-brother, and had a habit of bringing his biker friends back to his place to party into the early hours. Denise figured that, since he'd been off work over the weekend, he'd probably been partying pretty hard and right now he'd be suffering from the excesses of the previous night. She planned to sit down and share a couple of cold ones with him, tell him she'd heard that he'd found Joe Kronenwetter's body. Sympathize about his trauma, keep him talking and see what he let slip. And if he didn't give up anything useful, she'd pull the rug out from underneath him, tell him that the FBI had taken a good look at Kronenwetter's body and con- cluded that he hadn't hung himself after all – that someone had given him an assist. Tell him about the cracked hyoid bone and the lack of fibres under the nails. Tell him about the results of the tests Gary Delgatto's friend had done. Tell him that right now a team of FBI technicians in snow-white lab coats were running all kinds of samples through their high-tech machines, analysing hairs and fibres and DNA and who knew what else. Then ask him if maybe he didn't want to go over his story again, see if he'd forgotten to mention anything.

Denise believed that she had herself a pretty good plan. The only problem was, Charley Phelps wasn't at home.

His house was a two-storey wood-frame in a run-down part of town between the railroad tracks and the river, its grey paint badly peeled, nothing but weeds and a rusted engine block in the front yard. No one answered when Denise banged on the front door, so she went around the back, found that the kitchen door was unlocked and went inside. Overflowing ashtrays, empty beer bottles and pizza boxes scattered around the living room, clothes all over the floor of one bedroom and a partly dis- assembled motorcycle in the other, a nasty stink in the bathroom, but no Charley.

As Denise was unlocking her Jeep, one of Charley's neigh- bours came over, a stout black woman who worked as a nurse at the medical centre – she'd syringed Becca's blocked ear last spring. The nurse told Denise that she hadn't seen Mr Phelps that morning, but his half-brother had come around early, banging on the door, shouting Charley's name and waking up people who'd been trying to sleep after a night shift, driving off at last in a bad temper in that big pickup truck of his, almost sideswiping the kid who delivered newspapers.

'I guess Charley is in some kind of trouble again,' the nurse said.

'Not exactly, ma'am,' Denise said. 'When did you last see him?'

'He was here yesterday evening,' the nurse said. 'Playing his heavy-metal music as loud as he could, and nothing the City Police cares to do about it. A couple of months ago, after I complained about one of Mr Charley Phelps's parties? I found my cat dead in my front yard, it had been shot with an air rifle. Other folk have had the tyres of their car slashed, stones through their windows—'

'I'm sorry to hear about your troubles, ma'am. One reason I want to talk to Charley is to straighten him out over things like that. If he comes home, I'd appreciate it if you could give me a call.'

Denise took out one of her cards, crossed out her phone number at the Justice Center, and wrote the number of her cell phone on the back.

Driving away, she wondered if Charley Phelps had gone on the run. Of course, it could be that he had nothing to do with any of it, that he was sleeping off a hangover in some bar-bunny's bed. But if that was the case, why had Jerry Hill come around this morning, banging on his door and speeding off when he didn't get an answer? If Charley Phelps and Jerry Hill had both been working for Dirk Merrit, and if Charley had found out that FBI agents were questioning the circumstances of Joe Kronenwetter's death, it was likely he'd panic . . .

Something was up. Denise didn't know what it was, but it occurred to her that she could plant a hook in Jerry Hill. Stir things up a little.

She stopped by the Justice Building, but according to the woman who manned the switchboard and just about ran the place, Jerry was out and about, checking out a couple of thefts from rooms in the Calico Country Inn. So Denise drove out to the Calico Country Inn, where the manager told her that Detective Hill had left just twenty minutes ago. She headed back into town, and there was Jerry Hill's cherry-red Dodge Ram angle-parked in front of the Hanging Drop.

He was at the far end of the counter, nursing a glass of beer and a bowl of chilli. Watching Denise come towards him down the length of the crowded bar, with its wooden booths and photographs of old-time legal officers and cops hung everywhere on the walls, saying loudly to the barkeep, 'Set one up for my pal here. She needs something to take her mind off her troubles.'

'Hold it back for another time, Hank,' Denise said to the barkeep. 'Jerry, you're a hard man to find.'

'If you're pissed at me for what happened last night, you should know I was only doing my job.'

'I'm not mad at you, Jerry, it's just that I'm not in the habit of drinking at lunchtime. Listen, there's something you can maybe help me out with. I hear you visited Joe Kronenwetter the night he died – is that right?'

She'd spotted the entry in the visitor records at once. Jerry had signed in at nine-thirty p.m., signed out at ten past ten.

He looked at her for a moment, then said, 'All it was, I wanted to ask the son of a bitch a couple of follow-up questions.'

'I'm the primary on the case. I should have been there.'

'If you'd been around, I would've let you know, of course I would. But I believe you and that pretty little girl from Portland were paying a visit to Dirk Merrit.'

'What kind of questions?'

'Huh?'

'You said you wanted to ask Joe Kronenwetter a couple of follow-up questions. I was wondering what they were.'

'It doesn't matter now. The sad bastard killed himself, and you're . . .'

'Suspended.'

Jerry Hill smiled. 'You're pissed off, and you're taking it out on me. That's okay. I understand how it is.'

'I'm not pissed off,' Denise said, although right at that

moment she wanted very much to land one good punch right in the middle of his stupid smirk. 'I was just wondering what it was you asked Kronenwetter, and what he said.'

Jerry Hill shook his head. 'The son of a bitch still wasn't talking, so after a couple of go-rounds I decided I was wasting good drinking time and got out of there. You can ask the guard who was present in the room while I tried to talk to Kronenwetter. It was Bill Porter, he'll tell you the exact same story.'

'I was also wondering, do you happen to know if Joe Kronenwetter needed any kind of medical treatment?'

Jerry's smile became a grin. He held up his hands and said, 'I swear on my grandmother's grave I didn't lay a finger on the man. Ask Bill.'

'The reason I ask,' Denise said, 'the FBI lab did some tests on Joe Kronenwetter's blood and found traces of sevoflurane. That's a surgical anaesthetic. Which is why I was wondering if he'd had medical treatment that evening.'

Jerry didn't say anything for a long moment, quiet and still behind his smile. Then he said, 'You should be asking the jail doctor about that, not me.'

Denise pushed away from the counter. She knew that she should come back with a killer quip, but all she had was, 'You know I can't do that, Jerry. I got suspended. But you can bet that the FBI will.'

Actually, thinking about it as she walked out, it seemed like a pretty good exit line after all.

33

Daryl said to Bernard, 'So after he told me his name, I looked him up. He has a website all about his business.'

'Yeah? And what's he into, this Hunter Smith?'

Daryl smiled: he had the perfect punchline answer. 'The future.'

'What, like *Star Trek*?'

'No, man. Not sci-fi. The *real* future. Looking at patterns, trends, lifestyles . . . Telling companies what people want to buy before they know it. Right now he's investigating something called "deep nesting", which is where people don't go out to movies or restaurants or bars but stay at home and watch their big TVs and invite friends around instead. The man calls himself an envisionist.'

Monday afternoon, Bernard's day off work, they were driving in Bernard's beat-up Datsun to the yuppie enclave of Cobble Hill, an emergency call-out to a client who had lost her broadband connection.

Bernard snorted. 'These white people invent some kind of service no one needs, then they figure out how they can make other white people want it. Like their New Age shit, crystals and Feng Shui, all that. What else did you find?'

'He has an office in downtown Portland.'

'So you think he's the real deal because he has a website and an office? Dog, *anyone* can put up a website and rent some cubicle. It doesn't make them any better than you or me.'

'He has a personal page, too. He's thirty, a geeky-looking white guy, has an MBA from Harvard business school.'

'Oh yeah? Did you look up his academic record, make sure it's for real?'

'I told you: I checked out the address of his office. I phoned it, too. A guy answered, his assistant. Told me that Mr Hunter was away in Los Angeles, on business.'

'What makes you think it was his assistant you talked to? I bet it was the man himself. And I bet he wasn't in any office, either. He was sitting around in his underwear in some basement full of pictures of naked black boys he fucked and stuffed in some freezer.'

'He rents a suite at the KOIN Center, Southwest Columbia Street and Southwest Third Avenue, Portland. He's the real deal, man – why are you giving me a hard time? I have to think you're jealous.'

The Datsun was crawling along now. Bernard was hunched over the wheel, looking left and right for a parking space. 'What it is, I don't want to feel bad when I read about your naked dis-membered body being found in some river.'

'There's a spot up ahead, past that Volvo,' Daryl said. 'Look, this guy is a player. I checked out his profile in *Trans*. He's sold all kinds of shit, all good stuff, and he has the best approval rating. I spent a whole month working with him on this thing, he booked me a return trip, first class, a hotel room . . . What kind of pervert would go to all that trouble?'

Bernard was easing into the tight space, cranking the wheel, driving backwards and forwards until he had the car straightened out to his satisfaction. Finally, he switched off the engine and looked at Daryl, his gaze serious. 'You're really going.'

'Why did this nice lady call you to fix your broadband? It's because you're good at what you do. Why Hunter Smith needs me, I'm good at what *I* do. I'm a star player. And if it ain't all that, well, the man gave me a return ticket. First sign of trouble, I'm coming straight back. How can I lose?'

34

Monday afternoon, Summer spent an hour going through the photo books with two young women who'd been robbed at gunpoint in two different vintage-clothing stores, one that morning, the other Sunday afternoon. The young women were eager to help, but maddeningly indecisive. After both of them had worked through the books without making a positive ID, Summer suggested that they try to pick out faces that resembled the doer, and after they'd done that she went over their statements again, thanked them for their help, and let them go.

Andy Parish said, 'Don't these people pay attention to their customers any more? We have a young white guy in a baseball cap and jeans and some kind of coat, perhaps blue, perhaps not, long hair that's either brown or blond, he's unshaven or he has a goatee beard . . . About the only thing they agree on is he was waving a big old knife. How much did he get from the last place?'

'Sixty bucks and change.'

'My guess is he's a dope-fiend with a little bit more get-up-and-go than most. Sixty bucks will buy him enough dope or coke for the day, but he'll be back on the street tomorrow, hungry for more.'

Summer said, 'Two stores in two days – he's definitely found something he likes doing.'

'Yeah, he's found his groove, all right. These places are soft targets. No alarms, no security cameras, a cute young woman behind the counter with the attention span of a goldfish . . .'

Andy Parish was perched on the corner of Summer's desk. A big guy in his fifties, with a florid face and snow-white hair in a crew-cut, he was a natural police detective of the old school, a thoughtful, dogged, meticulous investigator. He was a hard, critical taskmaster, quick to jump on any sign of incompetence or carelessness, but Summer considered herself lucky to be mentored by him. So far, he'd made no mention of her freelance investigation into the circumstances of Edie Collier's death, and she'd kept quiet about it too. If he gave her advice and she got into trouble, it could come back on him.

Dick Searle was telling his phone, 'That's what he said, huh? Well, it's bullshit. What happened, he asked me could I give him some advice, he took the damn thing out of his pocket and told me he'd bought it off a guy in the street the day before, he wasn't sure if it was legal. Laurie Chamberlain was standing right beside me, she'll tell you the same story, but you'll have to wait till she comes back from her honeymoon . . . Yeah, I'll hold.' Looking at Andy Parish and saying, 'Remember that guy who tried to hold up two gas stations with an automatic knife? His lawyer's trying to get it thrown out on improper search.'

Andy Parish said, 'This is the guy showed you the knife in question?'

'Six-inch blade with a pearl handle. He was coming down the stairs of the Beckett Hotel while we were going up with a warrant on another guy, he panicked and volunteered the knife because he thought I was about to throw him against the wall and pat him down. They got us outnumbered and outgunned, but thank God they're still as dumb as they ever were,' Dick Searle said, and went back to talking on the phone.

Andy Parish was in a playful mood; last week, a pawnshop robbery had finally made it to court after endless procedural delays, and the doer had gone down for ten years. He said to Summer, 'Maybe we should put you undercover. Put you in one of those 1920s cocktail dresses, a cute little black number with beads and shit, one of those bands around your hair, a twelve-gauge under the counter . . .'

'If no one else gives a good description or finds him in the books, I'll consider it.'

From the neighbouring cubicle, Jesse Little said, 'Hey, Summer? Don't let Ryland find out you're thinking about taking to costumes. Maybe, to be on the safe side, Andy should be the one dressing up. He's supposed to be mentoring you, he should show you how it's done. Plus, he'd look pretty good in a feather boa. Like that movie with what's-his-name, Jack Lemmon.'

Andy Parish said, '*Some Like It Hot*. And you've hurt my feelings. I like to think I'm more like Tony Curtis than Jack Lemmon.'

'Maybe the chat-show Tony Curtis,' Jesse Little said. 'Definitely not the younger, prettier movie version. Listen, if you had to, who would you boff? Tony Curtis or Jack Lemmon?'

Andy Parish pretended to take the question seriously. 'In drag, or straight?'

'In drag, naturally. I don't mean to imply you're gay.'

'Then it has to be Jack Lemmon. If I did Tony Curtis, it would be like sleeping with my twin sister.'

Summer caught up on paperwork until the end of the shift, was just unlocking the drawer where she kept her purse and her Glock when her phone rang.

Denise Childers said, 'He did it again.'

'Who did it again?'

'In Los Angeles. He must have driven straight down from Reno. First he killed Greg Yunis—'

Summer sat down and swung her chair around so that she had her back to the rest of the unit. 'Wait. Back up and start over. Who is Greg Yunis?'

'The guy they found in his hotel room in Reno, minus his eyes and heart. The reason why Gary dropped out of our little expedition, because he had to go work the scene.'

'I remember that part. I didn't know the victim had been mutilated.'

'Just like Billy Gundersen, and the German tourist, and that other guy.'

'Ben Ridden.'

'The point is,' Denise said, 'there's been another death. Gary just now called me, he had all kinds of news. The feds have linked Gary Yunis's death with the death of an airline stewardess, Julia Taylor, in Los Angeles. Her body was found in the San

Gabriel mountains this afternoon by a Forest Ranger. She was missing her heart and her eyes, just like Billy Gundersen and Mr Yunis. The LAPD were already looking for her because she didn't turn up at work, and her car was found in the parking lot of a supermarket with, wait for it, bloody fingerprints on the trunk. Her blood, someone else's fingerprints. Care to guess whose?'

'I don't suppose they're Dirk Merrit's. If the FBI had arrested him, that's the first thing you would have told me.'

'Not Merrit, no, but someone close to him. A man by the name of Patrick Metcalf, an ex-cop whose company manages the security at Merrit's estate. Greg told me that not only were his fingerprints found on the trunk of the stewardess's car, they were also found on one of those make-up-my-room signs left hanging on the door of Gary Yunis's hotel room in Reno. Metcalf's girlfriend reported him missing Saturday night, she hadn't seen him since he left for work, and his Range Rover was found in a long-term parking lot at LAX. The LAPD think that Julia Taylor was carjacked right after she got back on a flight from Mexico. She was last seen alive just after nine a.m. and her car was caught on a security camera as it left LAX at around nine-twenty: it was being driven by a man in dark glasses and a baseball cap. The video isn't good enough to make an ID, but the feds are hot for Metcalf. It seems that he has a history of violence, he left the LAPD on account of a third-degree assault on a prostitute, and before that he'd had a couple of disciplinary charges brought against him for being too enthusiastic with uncooperative suspects.'

'So it's possible that Dirk Merrit had nothing to do with any of this after all. Or wait – maybe he and Patrick Metcalf were working together.'

'It's possible, but why they would have wanted to kill two strangers? And why did Metcalf leave his fingerprints at both scenes? Not to mention his Range Rover.'

Summer thought for a moment. 'You think that Metcalf has been set up, like Joseph Kronenwetter?'

Denise said, 'It's all just a bit too convenient, isn't it? The fingerprints, the Range Rover, the fact that the two bodies were left where they could be easily found, while the other victims were dumped in remote locations. We found Dirk Merrit at home late Sunday afternoon, but he'd have had enough time to kill the stewardess, dump her body, and fly back from Los Angeles on a commercial flight, or in a private plane – he has a pilot's licence. I want to check passenger lists for flights from LA to Oregon, and also plane-rental companies. One advantage we have, if it *was* Dirk Merrit, anyone who saw him won't have forgotten it.'

'We should tell the FBI about this.'

There was a pause, then Denise said, 'Have they interviewed you?'

'I'm still waiting to hear from them.'

'There you go. I told Gary, and he's going to talk to his boss when he gets the chance, but like I said, the feds are looking for Metcalf. And his dog – the girlfriend reported that his dog is missing too. You want to take the rental companies or the airlines?'

'As a matter of fact, I want to check out a lead of my own,' Summer said.

35

The address that Summer's mother had given her was at 82nd and Division, a corner storefront with whitewashed windows. Inside, young men sat at two long tables, hunched intently over computer monitors. In T-shirts and denim, long hair or no hair at all, accessorized with all kinds of tattoos, piercings and juvenile attempts at beards or sideburns, they were wearing headphones, clicking computer mice, hitting buttons on keyboards. Several had rucksacks or army-surplus kitbags by their feet. None of them looked up as Okay Soucek, the middle-aged Turkish man who owned the place, took Summer into the office at the back. She handed him the mug shot of William Gundersen and said that she understood that he had been working here.

'Why do you look for him?'

Okay Soucek was polite but wary, a concerned expression furrowing his brow, black hair brushed back in a wave from his pockmarked face.

Summer said, 'I believe he went by the name of Billy Newman.'

That was the name by which Tony Otaka had known Edie Collier's boyfriend. When he'd left Denver, William Gundersen, a.k.a. Bruce Smith, had not only resprayed his van and changed its licence plates, he'd also given himself a new alias.

Okay Soucek said, 'I know him, but I don't see him for a while.'

Summer said, 'I'm afraid he's dead, sir. Someone killed him.'

There was a brief silence. Okay Soucek looked past Summer, considering something inside his head, then focused on her again and said, 'How you think I can help you?'

Summer asked him about the nature of his business, pretended that she didn't know anything about grinding, and got an explanation that wasn't very different from the one her mother had given.

Summer said what she'd said to her mother. 'It sort of sounds like cheating.'

Okay Soucek shrugged. 'It is the free market. In the free market, everything has a value. Even things that do not exist.'

'This is what Billy Newman did. He made these virtual characters.'

Okay Soucek said, 'Not made. What he did, he *improve* them.'

'Was he good at it?'

'Of course. He lose two fingers in an accident, but he was still faster than most of my kids.'

'I heard that his fingers were cut off by some people he cheated out of some kind of virtual gizmo.'

'That is not how he told it,' Okay Soucek said. 'He said it was an accident in a factory.'

Summer shook her head. 'His name wasn't Billy Newman, either. It was William Gundersen. He used to be a professional gamer until he lost his fingers. It was in Los Angeles, a few years ago.'

Okay Soucek thought about this, then said, 'If this is true . . . you think they killed him, the ones who cut off his fingers?'

'I don't believe so.'

'It would be worth looking into it, I think. Some of these boys take their games very seriously. A guy in China kill his friend because his friend borrow a sword they use in a game, and then he sell it.'

'How long had Billy been working here?'

'A year, something like that. He was very good. I even make him supervisor over the others, have him teach them what to do. Now you tell me he was a big player one time, I see why he was so good.'

'He didn't ever tell you that he used to play professionally?'

'He arrive one day, ask for work. When I see how good he is, he tell me he use to play the games for fun, and I don't think no more about it.'

Summer believed that she had the arc of Billy Gundersen's story entire and complete now. He'd been a hotshot gunslinger at one time, a rising star in his little world. But then a bad move had caught up with him, and at age nineteen he'd been crippled and over the hill. After the case against the kids who'd cut off his fingers had been settled out of court, he'd run through the money he'd been given, or what had been left of it after his lawyer had taken his bite, he'd moved to Denver for some reason and changed his name and tried to get by on credit-card fraud. And when that hadn't worked out, he'd ended up in Portland, living out of his van, with its respray job and cold plates in case the cops or someone else came looking for him, grinding for Okay Soucek and trying to devise a score that would set him back on his feet.

She said, 'Did Billy have any enemies here in Portland? Anyone like the kids who cut off his fingers?'

'I don't know of any. He worked hard, didn't talk much. If he got up to mischief in his spare time, I don't know anything about it. Those boys you say hurt him, I think you make a mistake if you don't look at them.'

'He owned a laptop computer with a wireless card. He was playing computer games in his spare time . . . Did he ever talk about that?'

'Not really.'

'Did he mention that he was looking for treasure, anything like that?'

Okay Soucek shrugged, his wariness back. 'What he did for himself, I'm sorry, I can't help you.'

Summer, convinced that the man was hiding something, said, 'The people who work for you – are they living on the streets too, like Billy?'

'I'm not sure what you mean.'

'Those kids out there, with their rucksacks and tattoos, is what I mean. They look like runaways to me.'

'How it is, I cannot pay much because I must compete against sweatshops in countries much less rich than America. These Internet games – anyone can play them, anywhere in the world.

In Mexico, the Philippines, Taiwan, in Romania, Bulgaria . . .
most of the countries of Eastern Europe. And in Russia too, of
course. I must compete with all those people, it is a global
market, so I must keep my overheads down.'

'By paying street kids very little to work in a sweatshop.'

'Is better they work than beg on the streets.'

'I'm sure you're a credit to the community, Mr Soucek. That
is, as long as you aren't dealing in marijuana any more.'

She had looked up Okay Soucek on the computer: two
counts of possession with intent to sell, the first dismissed, the
second going to trial and earning him thirty months federal
time. The detective who had handled the case, Debbie Pinches,
had told Summer that Okay Soucek's brother was in the middle
of a five-year sentence; the DEA had raided a house he'd
recently bought and had found every room full of marijuana
plants growing in hydroponic tanks under racks of lights.

Okay Soucek gave her a sleepy look and said, 'I am legitimate
businessman, detective, and this is legitimate business.'

'Maybe I should take a look around, just in case.'

The threat didn't put a dent in his smile. 'You come back with
a warrant, then sure, you can look all you like. But now I have told
you all I know about Billy Newman, we are finished here, yes?'

Summer waited outside Okay Soucek's storefront in her Accura.
When a bearded boy finally came out, she started the car and
followed him to the intersection, lowered the window and told
him to get in. 'I'll take you to where you want to go.'

The boy climbed into the Accura with an air of sulky resig-
nation, gave her the name of a motel on Lombard Street, told
her that his name was Lee. Told her, yeah, he knew Billy
Newman, but so what, everyone who worked there did.

'Do you know that he was murdered, Lee? That's what this is
all about.'

The kid shrugged.

'Do you play *Trans*, Lee?'

'What we do, it isn't play. It's hard work, is what it is.'

'Billy played *Trans*, didn't he?'

The kid shrugged again. He was slouched on his spine, slightly turned away from her, long blond hair hanging across his face, acne livid on his cheeks, his fingernails bitten to the quick. Summer had seen dozens like him when she'd been working in the Runaway Juvenile Unit.

She said, 'I'm not trying to make any trouble for you and your friends, Lee. I'm trying to find out who killed Billy. Also his girl-friend, Edie Collier. Did you know her?'

'She wrote poetry.'

'She and Billy were kidnapped, Lee. She escaped but was badly injured and died, and Billy was killed. I want to find out who was responsible for that.'

The boy shrugged.

'I promise that anything you tell me won't get back to Mr Soucek.'

The boy shrugged again.

'Tell me about *Trans*. Tell me about the treasure Billy was looking for.'

The boy looked at her through his hair. 'How much?'

'Lee, I've known you about ten minutes, and I'm already disappointed. One of your friends has been murdered, and you want to make money out of it.'

'You pay informers, don't you? How much?'

They settled on fifty bucks. Lee told Summer that Billy Newman had had a serious jones for *Trans*, that he had learned from gossip on bulletin boards devoted to *Trans* that there was some kind of treasure hidden in the ruins of the game's version of Los Angeles. No one knew what it was, but everyone agreed that it was very valuable and very difficult to get at.

'That's why he needed help,' Lee said, wiggling the fingers of one hand. 'See, when it came down to any action, he didn't have the moves any more.'

'Because of his accident. So what was his plan?'

'He wanted to get up a clan.'

'Like a gang?'

'Sort of. But working together inside the game, you understand?'

Lee told Summer that Billy had persuaded Okay Soucek to

lend him several computers in exchange for half of whatever he found. Using his own money, Billy had equipped them with high-quality mouse mats and computer mice, over-clocked the central processing units of the computers so that they ran faster, and installed heat-sink fans to keep the CPUs cool, because the faster they ran the hotter they got.

'He had four guys working with him,' Lee said. 'The plan was, he would help them build up the skills and weapons of their characters, and then their characters would help his character reach the treasure. Like a little army.'

'And they could do this because the game is interactive.'

'That's the point,' Lee said, with a sneer.

'Were you one of them?'

'I'm okay at grinding, doing the same basic stuff over and over, but I'm not really a player. I'm just doing it for the money. Billy and the other guys, though, they were really into it. I used to watch them sometimes . . . Anyway, they worked at it for a month, they got as far as Los Angeles, but it turned out there's this other clan guarding the place. Called themselves ware-wolves.' Lee spelled it out, said, 'You know, "ware" as in "software". There were a lot of them, and Billy and his guys couldn't get past. They kept trying until Okay said enough is enough, and pulled the plug.'

'Do you know who these warewolves are? Not in the game, in the real world.'

Lee shrugged. 'Could be anyone, anywhere. There are plenty of people who get their kicks by fucking up other people's shit. That's why I don't really like *Trans* – too many people on creepy power-trips, getting off on owning slaves and shit. That, and it's too twitch-based, there's too much fighting and not enough strategy. And the designers instanced the hell out of it too. A lot of the time it might as well be a single-player game.'

'Instanced?'

'Yeah, where the world is divided up into small instances for groups of players. Like rooms where no one else can go.'

'So this treasure-hunt of Billy Newman's, that would be an instance.'

Lee shrugged again.

'What happened after Mr Soucek pulled the plug?'

'Billy got mad at him, went away for a couple of weeks. But he came back because he needed the money, like we all do.'

'Was he still trying to find this treasure, or had he given up?'

'One time I heard him say he had this new plan. He'd teamed up with a player – a real one, a champion. Some kid went by the handle of Seeker8.'

'Seeker8?'

'With the number not spelled out,' Lee said. 'In the games, you don't play under your own name. You're always someone else. That's the point too.'

After she had dropped off Lee at his motel, Summer called Denise Childers and told her about Billy Gundersen's job in Okay Soucek's grinding shop, his failed attempt to reach some kind of treasure hidden in *Trans*, his alliance with Seeker8. Denise said she'd pass it on to Gary Delgatto, but she didn't think that the feds would do much with it, they were too busy chasing Patrick Metcalf.

Summer said, 'I'm wondering if Dirk Merrit is behind these warewolves.'

'He could be.'

'And I'm also wondering how I could find this champion player who went by the name of Seeker8. Lee told me to look on the bulletin boards, but I think I should call Powered By Lightning, the company that owns the game. Players have to pay a monthly fee, so there has to be a list of subscribers. Did you have any luck with the airlines?'

'No, but thanks for asking. And so far I've drawn a blank with the rental companies too. If Merrit flew back from Los Angeles yesterday, he didn't use his own name.'

Denise had been excited when she'd given Summer the news about Julia Taylor's murder, but she seemed distracted and on edge now. It wasn't surprising. Her theory that Dirk Merrit had killed Greg Yunis and Julia Taylor, planting evidence pointing towards Patrick Metcalf and flying back from Los Angeles, had run into a brick wall, and her suspension and the prospect of a disciplinary hearing must be hanging over her. When she rang off, Summer decided that after she'd talked to Powered By Lightning, she'd call Gary Delgatto and go over everything with him. She was convinced that she was finally getting somewhere, and believed that the best way to help Denise out of her jam would be to prove that Dirk Merrit and Billy Gundersen had been linked by the game. By *Trans*.

36

First thing Tuesday morning, Denise wanted to get an early start on the day: she had a long list of places where Charley Phelps might be hiding out. But Becca, getting ready for school, couldn't find her favourite pen.

'You have dozens of pens. What's wrong with them?'

'*Mom*, this is the best one, the pink one with sparkles in the ink. I use it in my special notebook – if I use anything else it'll make it look trashy and cheap.'

It took ten minutes to find the pen – it was under the cushions of the couch where Becca had done her homework last night while watching *Charmed* – and then Denise had to wait while Becca took her own sweet time packing her books, pens, cell phone, and special notebook, the one covered with a collage of photographs of pop stars, into her rucksack. And when they were finally ready to go, Becca had to know why they were using grandmom's old Honda Accord instead of the Jeep Cherokee. Denise told her what she'd told her mother when she'd borrowed the Accord, that the Jeep had a problem with its engine, she'd had to take it in to the shop to get it fixed, but she knew that Becca thought that something was up.

'We'll go on a trip this weekend,' she told her daughter, trying to divert her attention. 'How does the Wildlife Safari sound?'

'If I was like eight years old it would sound great.'

After a discussion that lasted the rest of the short trip, they settled on Medford and its shopping malls. Denise was parked outside the school, watching her daughter walk up the steps of the modern brick building among the other students, when her cell phone rang. It was Charley Phelps's neighbour, telling her that the man had just now come home on his noisy motorcycle.

Well, it was about time she had some luck. She waited until Becca had disappeared through the main door of the school in the press of other kids, then drove over to Charley Phelps's place.

The back door was unlocked. When she walked in, Charley Phelps, sitting at the kitchen table, bare-chested in blue jeans, picking at a plate of scrambled eggs, a joint smouldering in the tin ashtray beside his elbow, looked at her with sleepy confusion and said, 'Oh man.'

'I heard you've been tying one on, Charley, so I thought I'd bring along some hair of the dog that bit you,' Denise said. She used her penknife to uncap a couple of bottles of Henry Weinhard's, set one of them in front of his plate of eggs and sat down across the table from him. She raised her own bottle, took a sip, and said, 'It's warm, but it's beer.'

Charley Phelps looked at her, then picked up the bottle in front of him, took a long drink, breathed out and said, 'Oh man.' Looked at Denise again and said, 'Am I in trouble?'

'Why would you think that, Charley?'

He shrugged, picked up the joint and said with a sly smile, 'Well . . . am I gonna get in trouble for this?'

'Knock yourself out,' Denise said.

She watched him take a drag, his mouth pinched as he held in the smoke. He was handsome in a rawboned kind of way, black hair shaved to a greasy stubble, dark eyes bloodshot. One hand moving over the hair swirled across his bare chest as, still holding his breath, he stared at her from beneath his thick eyebrows, asking her in a pinched voice if she wanted a hit.

'I'll pass. How are you doing, Charley? Can you talk?'

He breathed out a huge volume of smoke and said, 'Oh man. I'm gonna have to get some sleep.'

'I bet you're still suffering over seeing Joe Kronenwetter dead in his cell like that.'

'Well, I knew him, you know? We were in high school together.'

'I know you were.' She let that hang for a moment, then said, 'I guess it must have been a shock, when you found him dead like that.'

'Yeah, it was. But I guess that isn't why you brought me beer, is it?'

'I need to get a few things straight about the way Joe Kronenwetter died, how he was found. I thought you could help me out.'

'I've already been through all this, you know?'

Charley Phelps sounded like Becca, that put-upon whine in her voice when she knew she'd been busted.

'If you've got your story straight this won't take long,' Denise said. She pulled another bottle from the pack, popped it open, set it in front of him.

He tried a smile that didn't quite take. 'I believe you're tryin' to take advantage of me.'

'Hell, Charley, if I wanted to take advantage of you I wouldn't bother with beer, I'd just deploy my full-on natural charm. So tell me about what happened that night. You were working the reception desk, I believe.'

'When Joe killed himself? Yeah.'

'Your shift started at ten p.m.'

'Ten till six, always a bitch,' Charley Phelps said, smiling at his silly little rhyme.

'And about an hour later, around eleven, you thought you'd go take a look at Joe Kronenwetter.'

'I already explained, I knew the man. That's why I looked in on him.'

'Is that why you opened the cell door? You wanted to talk about old times?'

'I thought I'd check up on him because he'd been upset, making all kinds of noise. I opened it because I couldn't see him.'

Charley Phelps saying this as if reciting something he'd learned by rote.

Denise said, 'Where was Jerry while all this was going on?'

'Jerry? What's Jerry got to do with anything?'

'I know your half-brother visited Joe Kronenwetter around nine-thirty that evening. He said he left just after ten. In fact, according to the register, he signed out at ten past ten. You didn't see him?'

Charley Phelps shrugged.

'I talked with the other guards, Charley. They remember that you came in half an hour early that day. In fact, a couple of them remarked on it, it was so unusual. I checked your time card, too. You punched in half an hour early, all right. So I guess you had to be on the reception desk when Jerry signed out that night, ten past ten.'

'Yeah . . .?'

'Everyone who goes up to the fourth floor, they have to sign in, they have to give their thumbprint, and if they're carrying, they have to check in their piece. And Jerry always wears his piece, even in the office. Pecking away at a computer with his gun at his hip like a big old cowboy . . . So if you were working on the reception desk, you would have given his piece back to him when he left at ten past ten.'

'Then I guess I did.' Charley Phelps was suddenly very interested in his beer bottle, picking at a corner of its label. 'What's the deal? You guys are in and out all the time — it's hard to keep track on an ordinary day, let alone when one of the prisoners hangs his self.'

'So you were on the desk when Jerry signed out.'

'I guess. If you say so.'

'How did he seem, when you gave him back his gun?'

'What do you mean?'

'Was he pissed off, excited, in a hurry, what?'

Charley Phelps looked up at a corner of the ceiling, then said, 'Just his ordinary self.'

Denise smiled. 'So you did see him.'

'You think I'm lying? Why would I lie?'

'I don't know, Charley. Why would you?'

'Well, I'm not. I'm just tired, is all. I got a killer headache, you come at me with all these questions, I don't know where I am.'

'You were at the reception desk the night Joe Kronenwetter died. You signed out your half-brother.'

'I guess.'

'Maybe you're confused because Jerry signed out but he didn't leave,' Denise said.

'He signed out, didn't he?'

'I'm just trying out a story, Charley, so bear with me. Around eleven that night, you left the reception desk to go check up on your friend Joe Kronenwetter. You unlocked his cell door, you found him dead, and you hit the nearest alarm. I'm right so far?'

After a moment Charley Phelps shrugged, still intent on shredding the label of the beer bottle.

'The alarm is ringing, everyone on duty comes running, the lights go on, there's all kinds of confusion. Prisoners banging on their doors, wanting to know what's going on, the other guards asking you what happened . . .'

'Yeah . . . ?'

'What I'm wondering, while all this was going on who was looking after the reception desk?'

'I don't know what you mean.'

'You were at Joe Kronenwetter's cell, people were coming and going, there was all kinds of confusion, so I guess someone could have slipped out of the fourth floor without being noticed.'

'Look, the man hanged hisself. That's all there is to it.'

For a moment, Denise felt sorry for him. She said, 'Here's the problem, Charley. An FBI forensic investigator examined Joe Kronenwetter's body. He found all kinds of evidence that showed that Joe didn't kill himself. The thing that most interests me is that he found traces of a surgical anaesthetic in Joe's blood. Someone knocked him out, tied him up, put a noose around his neck, and hanged him. It wasn't suicide. It was murder.'

Charley shook his head. 'Come on . . .'

'I think you were on the reception desk when Jerry signed the book at ten past ten, but he didn't leave. He borrowed your keys or he already had a spare set, and he hung around on the fourth floor, somewhere out of sight. Around eleven o'clock he found you and told you to go check on Joe Kronenwetter. And when everything kicked off, when the place was in an uproar, he slipped away.'

Charley was shaking his head, his mouth open, the poor guy trying to figure out how he'd ended up in this corner.

Denise said, giving him an out, 'It's okay, Charley. I'm not mad at you. I bet Jerry didn't tell you what he was about. You didn't realize what was going on until you found Joe Kronenwetter dead in his cell. But now the FBI is on the case, and when Jerry goes down he'll take you with him. Unless, that is, you tell me what happened that night.'

'I *told* you what happened.'

'That story doesn't work any more, Charley. You better tell me the truth before you get into real trouble. Before the FBI finds out that you and Joe fell out over a girl once upon a time.'

Charley Phelps stared at her, a silly smile on his face. 'Whoa. How did you hear about that?'

'Never mind where I heard about it. He stole her from you, and then he beat you up when you and him had a fight about it. Is it true?'

'More or less. It was so long ago, back in high school . . . Ancient history.'

'Are you still sore at Joe because of it?'

'What, because of Jenny Mackee? Naw, it wasn't like she was really my girlfriend. I mean, she screwed just about everyone on the football team one time or another. And now she's married to that real-estate guy, looks right through me when I see her on the street, sticks her nose in the air as if I don't know she can suck a golf ball through a garden hose.'

'But you and Joe had a fight over her.'

Charley Phelps shrugged. 'It wasn't anything, and it was a long time ago, you know? I ain't one for holding grudges.'

'You're saying that you and Joe were still friends afterwards.'

Charley Phelps shrugged again.

'I believe you, Charley, but other people won't. Other people will think you had a reason for killing Joe Kronenwetter. They'll pin the whole thing on you, when all you did was help out your half-brother when he asked you for a favour. So why don't you tell me what happened, and I'll figure out a way of helping you.'

For a moment, Denise thought that he was going to do it. But then he shook his head.

They went at it for twenty minutes, but Charley Phelps grew stubborn, retreating into himself, and Denise couldn't bring him

back. At last, she told him to think hard about what he needed
to do and left him with his plate of cold eggs and the bottle of
beer she hadn't touched, and sat in her mother's Accord down
the street, watching his house, waiting to see what would happen
next.

Nothing much did for more than three hours. Denise had
always hated stake-outs, and it was even worse when she was on
her own, with no one to talk to and the constant low-level
worry that her bladder would betray her at the wrong moment.
She wrote up the interview with Charley Phelps. Charley's
neighbour, the nurse, came out in her white smock and got in
a shit-brown Toyota and drove off. Someone was using a plane
saw, its plaintive cry nagging on and off, on and off. And then,
at last, Charley Phelps came out, climbed onto his black
Triumph motorcycle, and rode off down the street. Denise
started the Accord and followed him.

37

Summer called up the local FBI office and after some back and forth got through to a special agent, Arnold Carson. Special Agent Carson wouldn't give her the number of Gary Delgatto's cell phone, but said that he would be happy to pass on any message.

'Ask Mr Delgatto to call me,' Summer said, and gave her work number and the number of her cell phone, not expecting much.

Gary Delgatto called back a couple of hours later, twelve thirty. It turned out that, as Summer had suspected, Carson hadn't passed on her message; Gary was in Portland, supervising the transportation of Billy Gundersen's burned-out van to the garage under the Edith Green Wendell Wyatt Federal Building, where he planned to make a full forensic examination of it. 'I believe I'm right around the corner from where you work,' he said. 'Why don't I take you out for lunch and bring you up to speed on the latest developments?'

They bought burritos and cans of soft drink at the Mexican place in the parking lot across from the Justice Building, walked down to the Waterfront Park and found a bench. It was a nice day, the sky clear blue, a fresh breeze coming off the river, sunlight twinkling on the traffic moving along the raised highway on the far side.

While they ate, Summer described Billy Gundersen's work in Okay Soucek's storefront operation, explained how his failed attempt to capture some kind of treasure in *Trans* tied in with something Dirk Merrit had mentioned. 'According to my informant, he had a new plan involving a hotshot player who calls himself Seeker8.'

Gary Delgatto smiled. He was wearing black jeans and a

brown leather jacket just a shade lighter than his eyes, looking pretty cool for a lab geek. 'You don't like to let go, do you?'

Summer smiled back. 'It's my big fault.'

That's what her ex, Jeff Tuohy, had told her, anyway. They'd had a big row about it once, after she'd spent what Jeff believed to be too much of her own time trying to track down a hit-and-run driver who'd left a homeless drug addict in a coma. Jeff had thought that Summer too often confused police work with justice, told her that it was unprofessional to get, as he called it, too attached. Told her that she'd developed an obsession about seeing things through to the bitter end as a reaction to the way her parents never seemed to finish anything – her father's house in the Columbia River Gorge, her mother's novel. There was enough truth in that to sting. She'd tried to tell him what she'd learned from the sergeant who'd mentored her when she'd first gone on patrol in her scratchy new uniform: that good police work meant chasing down every lead no matter how trifling; it meant never forgetting or giving up on cold cases because there was always a chance that they'd catch the doer for something else, or something new would come to light; it wasn't about producing numbers to satisfy the bosses. Jeff had told her that she was good-hearted but naive. He'd meant it kindly, he'd been trying to help her career, but now she thought that it was amazing she'd stuck with the patronizing son of a bitch for so long.

Gary Delgatto said, 'Denise told me you wanted to do right by the girl, Edie Collier.'

'It's karma,' Summer said. 'I got into this because I arrested Edie for shoplifting last December, and that put me first in line to notify her parents of her death. I drove her stepfather to Cedar Falls so he could make the formal ID, he got into trouble and I had to stay overnight, which gave me the chance to compare notes with Denise. Edie didn't do anything wrong except fall in love with the wrong boy, and she had a lot of courage. She got away from someone who wanted to do something bad to her, she was badly hurt but she almost made it out of the woods . . .'

Summer paused, seeing Edie Collier clearly for a moment, pale and quiet, unknowably remote.

Gary said, 'You think there really is something to this computer stuff?'

'Doesn't the FBI?'

'Malone is thorough. He's probably had people look into it.' Gary paused, then said, 'You realize I have to tell them about this.'

'I know. I figured it would sound better coming from you. Also, I was hoping to find out Seeker8's real name from Powered By Lightning's subscription list,' Summer said. 'The problem is, they won't supply it unless they're served with a warrant.'

'And you're wondering if the FBI might have some leverage.'

'Might it?'

'Give me all the details,' Gary said. 'I can't promise anything: whether or not we get a warrant is down to Mr Malone. But I'll give it my best shot.'

He took out a reporter's notebook and wrote down the phone number and address of Powered By Lightning's offices, the names of the people Summer had talked to. His face was in profile to her as he bent over the notebook, a lock of black hair falling over his forehead.

'Billy Gundersen could have been kidnapped and murdered because he went after this so-called treasure,' Summer said. 'And Seeker8 was his partner. I have a bad feeling about him.'

'You think it's all about this game? If you don't mind me saying so, that's a pretty wild theory.'

'Billy Gundersen lost two of his fingers because of something he did in the game. And Dirk Merrit had himself made over to look like a character in the game, his mansion looks like something out of it too, and it's full of TVs playing scenes from the game. I'd say he is so obsessed with it that he wouldn't think twice about harming another player who was trying to steal something from him.'

Gary looked suitably impressed. He promised that he would pass the story to Harry Malone's team.

Summer said, 'I know you have strong evidence linking Pat Metcalf to the murders of the man in Reno and the stewardess in Los Angeles. But it's possible, isn't it, that they could be some kind of sick game, intended to divert your attention away from Dirk Merrit?'

'Denise has already been bending my ear about that. And as a matter of fact, we think there's something funny about those murders too.'

'You do? I saw a newspaper story about them this morning. According to the statement Mr Malone gave the press, the FBI is looking for Patrick Metcalf. But I think that Metcalf may be dead—'

'So do we – I'll explain why in a minute.' Gary gave Summer a serious look and said, 'You have to understand that this is kind of confidential. But we've already had to let the local police know what we're doing, and seeing as you've figured some of it out, and since I guess we're both on the same side . . .'

'I hope so.'

'Okay. Well, like you, we're fairly sure that the last two murders were an attempt at misdirection. But we want the killer to think he fooled us, which is why Mr Malone issued that statement to the press.'

'That's pretty smart.'

'Mr Malone has been working on this for a while,' Gary said. 'He has a good idea of how our man operates, and the last two murders don't fit the pattern. The first victims we know about, Ben Ridden and Tomas Stahl, were last seen in motels along the I-5, but their bodies both turned up a long way from where they disappeared. Ridden's was found in the Mojave Desert; Stahl's in Christmas Lake Valley, in Oregon. William Gundersen was probably snatched right here in Portland, but his body was dumped in the Black Rock Desert, in Nevada. All three locations are flat, wide-open spaces – the profiler working with Mr Malone thinks that's highly significant. There could be other victims, too: we're following up a number of unsolved disappearances from motels along the I-5 in the past two years. It looks like that's our man's main hunting ground. He's driven by some kind of fantasy, but he isn't impulsive. He's organized. He makes plans. He selects his victims, stashes them somewhere for a while, and then kills them in a specific way in a specific kind of place, a remote area where he can leave the body with little chance of it being found quickly.'

Summer said, 'Edie Collier and William Gundersen were definitely kept somewhere after they were kidnapped.'

Gary said, 'It was the same place. I'm sure of it.'

'Because of your trace analysis. I was wondering, what happened to the sample Denise took at Dirk Merrit's property?'

'I had her Fed-Ex the filter to my guy in the Missouri Botanical Garden. He says that it had trapped some of the same kinds of pollen that were in the samples I took from the lungs of Collier and Gundersen.'

'But not exactly the same mix.'

'I wouldn't expect *exactly* the same mix. As I told Denise, it doesn't prove that they were kept somewhere on Mr Merrit's property, but at least it doesn't rule it out. And the samples I took from their lungs show that Collier and Gundersen were definitely breathing the same air, over a period of several days.'

'If Edie Collier and William Gundersen were kept in the same place, I have to wonder why Edie wasn't taken out to the desert too.'

Gary shrugged. 'She doesn't fit the profile of the other victims, or the unsolved disappearances. They're all young white males, aged between nineteen and twenty-eight, all of them reasonably fit.'

'And Greg Yunis and Julia Taylor don't fit the profile either.'

'That's why we think the killer is trying to play us. Their hearts had been excised, like Ridden, Stahl and Gundersen, but whoever did it used a different knife, one with a short serrated blade. More significantly, they weren't abducted. They were killed on the spot, and left where they could easily be found. Greg Yunis in his hotel room, Julia Taylor near a Forest Rangers' hut in the San Bernadino mountains.'

'Someone wanted you to find William Gundersen's body, too. There was an anonymous phone call.'

'Our profiler thinks that after Edie Collier escaped, the killer decided to change up, to have some fun with the people hunting him. Bearing that in mind, finding Mr Metcalf's fingerprints in Greg Yunis's hotel room and on the trunk of Julia Taylor's car was altogether too convenient. And there was something odd about the set of prints on the card left on the door of Greg Yunis's hotel room. How do you pick up a piece of paper?'

'You mean how do I hold it?'

Gary tore off a page from his notebook and held it out. When Summer took it from him, he smiled and said, 'See? Thumb at the front, one or more fingers at the back. Or vice versa. How everybody does it. What I found were good impressions of the fingers and the thumb on one side of the card, nothing on the other.'

'Like a fingerprint record,' Summer said. She liked Gary's smile, the way it lit up his dark brown eyes.

'It's the same deal with the prints on the trunk of Julia Taylor's car,' he said. 'Someone put those prints there, a crude attempt to make us think that Patrick Metcalf was in both places.'

'Put them there? How?'

'Good question. The easiest answer, someone used his hand.'

'Someone killed Metcalf, cut off his hand, used it to place those prints?'

'It's possible. What we do know is that Patrick Metcalf definitely wasn't the man who rode up in the hotel elevator with Mr Yunis shortly before his murder. This was a white male of slender build and less than average height, five-four, five-five, around a hundred twenty pounds. Black hair cut short, his face obscured by a baseball cap. Of course, it is possible that this guy might not have anything to do with the murder, but another video camera in the lobby caught him leaving an hour later, carrying something in a laundry bag. Possibly the trophies he excised from Mr Yunis.'

'Jesus,' Summer said, feeling a little sick at the thought.

'I know. We're examining tape from every video camera at LAX, hoping to find one that took close-up footage of Julia Taylor's car. The guy driving it was wearing a baseball cap too. If we can get a clear shot of his face, Mr Malone wants to show it to Dirk Merrit and ask him if he knows who it is.'

'So the FBI definitely likes Dirk Merrit now.'

'Let's put it this way,' Gary said. 'We've been looking for a good suspect in the kidnapping/death of Edie Collier ever since I found some hard evidence that Joseph Kronenwetter had been murdered.'

That was when Summer found out that Denise hadn't told her about the results of the tests on the samples taken from Joseph Kronenwetter's body. That traces of someone else's DNA had been found under his fingernails, and a surgical anaesthetic, sevoflurane, had been found in his blood.

Gary said, 'Bad guys in books and movies often use ether or chloroform on their victims, but ether and chloroform can take two or three minutes to make a person fully unconscious, and meanwhile the victim will be putting up a struggle, trying not to breathe. Sevoflurane is highly effective, and it isn't hard to obtain. It looks like someone used it to knock out Mr Kronenwetter, probably by applying a cloth wetted with it over his nose and mouth, and then they hanged him. It's possible that he regained consciousness before he died, tried to get up, and was subdued. It would explain the grit under his nails, and the cracked hyoid bone.'

'What about the DNA?'

'My friend back at the lab amplified the sample and checked short tandem repeats on thirteen sites, good enough for court. She ran it through CODIS, but didn't get any hits. We plan to take samples from everyone who works in the Justice Building. It'll take a while.'

'I bet Sheriff Worden is going to love that.' Summer had a worrying thought and said, 'You explained all this to Denise?'

'Of course I did. I wouldn't have picked up on it in the first place if she hadn't pointed me in the right direction.'

'Then we might have a problem,' Summer said. 'You told Denise about this hard evidence of yours, but she didn't tell me. And I told her that Billy Gundersen was definitely trying to get at something in *Trans*, and asked her to pass it on to you, but she didn't.'

'Maybe she forgot, in all the excitement.'

'It's possible . . .'

'But?'

'I think she could be planning to use the information to confront Dirk Merrit again.'

'I'm returning to Cedar Falls tomorrow. I'll talk to her then.' Gary hesitated, then added, 'I'm staying right here tonight. I was wondering . . . would you like to have dinner with me?'

Summer thought about it for a moment. On the one hand, he was definitely cute, and he was smart, and easy to talk to. On the other, she didn't really know all that much about him: he could have a girlfriend back in Washington, D.C., he could even be married, the kind of guy who slips off his wedding band on trips out of town. And even if he was single, she wasn't about to start any kind of relationship with someone who lived on the other coast. She'd already broken up with one boyfriend because of that.

Gary misread her hesitation and said, 'Just dinner. No strings.'

Yeah, right. Summer knew, no matter how much they denied it, that at some level men were always thinking about sex. So she smiled and said, 'Why don't you come back to my place?'

Now Gary paused. Saying after a moment, 'I guess that would be cool.'

'I should warn you that I'm living with my mother right now, a temporary thing. But she's a great cook, and I know there's some of her famous lamb tagine in the fridge. Also, I know she'll be thrilled to meet a real-life forensic investigator. She's a big fan of detective stories – she'll want to know everything about your work.'

38

Denise followed Charley Phelps out of town on the 138, heading east. The old Honda couldn't keep pace with his motorcycle
and she soon lost sight of him, had no choice but to keep going.
She caught up with him at Argyle, spotting his motorcycle at
one of the pumps of the gas station as she went past. She made
a U-turn and came back, parked across from the gas station and
saw him come out of the little store, draining a soft-drink can
and lobbing it in the general direction of a trash basket before
climbing onto his bike. Denise made another U-turn and followed him across the old iron bridge north of the little
settlement, saw the brake lights of his bike flare, saw it turn down
the fire road.

    She drove slowly through the deep shade of the tall firs that
crowded either side of the fire road, the trees opening out on
her left, excitement sparking in her heart when she spotted
the motorcycle raising dust beyond the creek at the edge of
Joe Kronenwetter's property. Denise drove past, parked at the
beginning of an old logging track and remembered to turn off
her cell phone – she didn't want the damn thing going off
in the middle of a surveillance – then cut through the thick
woods. When she reached the saplings and thin brush at the
edge of the trees, she crouched low and edged forward until she
had a good view of the shack, about thirty yards away. She
couldn't see the motorcycle, it must have been parked in front,
but another vehicle stood a little way beyond, an old Ford
Ranger pickup it looked like, light blue paintwork, well-used
but clean.

    Denise was pretty sure that her ruse had worked, that Charley
Phelps was mixed up in Joe Kronenwetter's murder and he'd

panicked after she'd confronted him, had arranged to meet whoever else was involved. They must be in the shack right now,
arguing about how to fix up the holes in their story. Or maybe
Charley was asking for more money, the stupid son of a bitch.
She'd been certain that Jerry Hill had been involved, but now
she wasn't so sure – that definitely wasn't his pickup parked outside the shack.

She pulled out the digital camera her parents had given her
last Christmas, took a shot of the shack, used the zoom and took
a couple of close-up shots of the pickup. More than anything,
she wanted to sneak up to the shack and put her ear to the door
or peek through a window, but knew it would be too risky.
Okay, next best thing, get the licence tag of the blue pickup, run
it through AutoTrack. See if it was registered to Dirk Merrit, or
someone who worked for him.

Denise crabbed sideways through the scrub until she had a
good view of the rear end of the pickup. She made a note of the
licence tag and took a couple of pictures, was putting away her
notebook and camera when someone walked around the corner
of the shack.

It was Dirk Merrit.

It was a shock to see him walking in the open air, like a special effect escaped from a movie. He was wearing his forest-camo
jacket and pants, and an athletic bag was slung over one shoulder. As he walked towards the pickup, Denise switched on the
camera and started taking photographs, and the goddamn thing
started to make a thin beeping noise because it was almost out of
power. She switched it off and crouched low among the soft
new leaves of a young alder, shivering with excitement and fear.

Dirk Merrit was looking up at the tree-line, one hand shading his eyes. Something jumped in Denise's chest as his white
face turned towards her. She put her hand in her bag, and
remembered that she'd had to give up her gun and shield. Dirk
Merrit turned away, opened the door of the pickup and slung
the athletic bag inside. For a moment, Denise thought she had
gotten away with it, but then he turned back – and now he was
holding his big black crossbow.

He walked uphill quickly and purposefully. If he'd been an ordinary man, Denise might have held her ground and tried to tough it out, but Dirk Merrit was crazy and he was armed. She jumped up and made a run for it. Fallen cones and bits of broken wood crackled underfoot; trees plunged crazily in her vision. She smashed through a tangle of branches, plunged down the steep slope of a hollow, skidding on pine needles, losing her footing and sitting down hard with a shock that gripped her entire body. She grabbed up her bag and pushed to her feet, scrambled up the other side of the hollow, glimpsed the Honda through the trees – and a tremendous blow between her shoulder blades knocked her down. She tried to get up, but her back felt as if it had snapped in two and her legs kicked feebly, she couldn't get any purchase. Her bag lay right in front of her face, things spilled from it, and she grabbed the little camera and threw it away as hard as she could. She was searching for her canister of pepper spray when Dirk Merrit moved around the edge of the hollow, the crossbow in his left hand, his right pulling an automatic pistol from the waistband of his pants.

Denise closed her eyes. She had a moment to think of her daughter. Becca on the swing in the backyard, laughing with wild abandon, legs out straight as she rocked high, framed against a heavenly blue sky.

When he was certain that the woman was dead, Dirk Merrit went to look for whatever it was she had thrown into the undergrowth. It only took a couple of minutes to find the digital camera. Its battery gave out as he was studying the last photograph she had taken, a good shot of him walking towards the pickup. Good enough to send to a friend, he thought, and slipped the camera into one of his pockets before grabbing the woman's wrists and dragging her towards the edge of the trees.

39

Carl got back to the estate late Tuesday afternoon. He'd stopped at a Motel-6 on the outskirts of Santa Clarita on Sunday evening and had slept for twelve hours straight, and he'd made another stop in Sacramento on Monday, where he'd bought a Smith & Wesson thirty-eight and two boxes of hollow-points from a dealer who'd come straight to his hotel room. The man had given him a good price on a hooker too, five hundred dollars for the night but worth it.

At first, local and national TV news had been playing the same thirty-second clip of Dirk Merrit talking about being harassed by the police over the girl found in the forest near his property and having nothing to hide, but that had dropped out of the cycle as soon as the FBI announced that Patrick Metcalf was wanted for questioning about murders in Oregon, Nevada, and California. According to the guy in charge of the case, Metcalf was armed and highly dangerous, and might be attempting to cross the border into Mexico. There was no mention of Erik Grow: it looked like his body hadn't been found.

Perfect. The feds were looking for a dead man, and Carl was refreshed and ready for action. His plan was simple. Get in and out as quickly as he could. Kill Elias Silver and the cook, Louis Frazier, and put Dirk Merrit to the question. Carl had learned a lot about extracting information from reluctant prisoners when he'd worked as a mercenary in Africa, and he was certain that he could get the man to give up the password for Don Beebe's program. He'd get out of the country, use the program to rip off Powered By Lightning, and start laying the foundations of a brand-new life.

There were no guards at the main entrance to the estate.

Maybe they were all down at the Sheriff's office being questioned about Patrick Metcalf, or maybe Dirk Merrit had sent them away before his latest pilgrim arrived. Whatever the reason, it was a definite plus as far as Carl was concerned, one thing less to worry about. He used the little zapper on his keyring to open the gate, and after he'd driven through the gate he had to climb out of the Dodge Neon he'd stolen in Los Angeles to raise the pole barrier. There was no sign of the cook, Louis Frazier, either. Carl rooted around in the refrigerator and found a dish of raw beef sliced thin and swimming in olive oil and capers. He was standing at the central workstation, scarfing this down, when the phone on the wall rang. He let it ring out while he finished the tasty raw beef, but then it started up again and didn't stop. Carl wiped his oily fingers on kitchen paper, picked up the phone, and said, 'Louis isn't around.'

'I know,' Dirk Merrit said. 'Welcome back, Carl. I'm in the library.'

Coming out of the elevator into the big round room, Carl said, 'I saw you on TV, making a fool of yourself, claiming to be a victim of police harassment. I bet that was Elias Silver's idea – it's just the kind of stupid stunt he likes to dream up. Where is the little bugger, by the way?'

He could feel the grip of his brand-new Smith & Wesson in the small of his back. He was more than ready to whip it out, put it in Elias Silver's face and enjoy the moment of surprise before he blew the man's famous brains out of his skull.

Dirk Merrit stood in front of the big circle of the library's only window, skinny as a whip in a camo jacket and camo pants with loops and big thigh pockets. He said, 'As a matter of fact, that was *my* idea. Once the local police had inspected the property and satisfied themselves that there was no sign of any wrongdoing, it made it harder for other agencies to obtain a warrant. To give him due credit, though, Elias did help me work up a few soundbites. I've been wondering – should I ask for royalties? I bet the TV station made a mint from syndication fees. It's only fair that I should get a piece of the action.'

The man was in one of his whimsical moods, put there no doubt by one or more of Dr Elias Silver's magic pills and potions.

Carl said, 'If by other agencies you mean the FBI, I've drawn them off. The Black Rock Desert, Reno, LA – see how it works? A straight line, north to south. If you've been watching the TV, you'll know they think their killer is heading for the Mexican border.'

'Mmm. The problem is, Carl, not everyone believes that Patrick Metcalf is the bad guy. The reason why I went on TV and invited Sheriff Worden to search my home is because I had caught a couple of police snooping around the day before. Two women, one from the Sheriff's office, the other from Portland. Remember them?'

'They came back?'

Carl was tempted to take out his pistol and shoot the man dead there and then. One shot, straight through the ridged plate of his forehead. He could almost hear the hard pop of the gun, see that black hole appear, see Dirk Merrit's look of surprise fade to nothing, his long thin body collapsing like a bundle of sticks. But first, he needed to find out what had happened here, and he needed the password, too: he couldn't have his fun until the subscription money was flowing his way.

Dirk Merrit said, 'They told me that they had used a tracker dog to follow the girl's trail through the woods, and ended up close to my property.'

'They were probably lying. Trying to scare you into saying something.'

'Oh, I don't think they were lying – they told me the trail ended at the meadow up on the ridge. I told them I knew nothing about it, sent them on their way, and took action to make sure they wouldn't cause me any more trouble. And I can assure you that the detective from the Sheriff's office, the redhead, is definitely out of the picture. Everything has been sorted out,' Dirk Merrit said, walking over to his big desk, picking up the remote control, aiming it across the room. 'Just in time for our new guest.'

Carl turned to look at the rack of TVs. They all showed the

same thing, a blurred green figure hunched into itself at the bottom of a pit full of shadows. 'That's the kid, isn't it? I thought he wasn't arriving until tomorrow.'

'I lied,' Dirk Merrit said. 'Here's why.'

The TVs flickered in unison, showing now a view of the library in soft greens and blacks. A bright figure was stooping under the desk.

Carl turned back to Dirk Merrit, reaching behind himself for his Smith & Wesson.

'Don't do it, Carl.'

The man was pointing a gun at him, a Colt .45 it looked like, watching him over the sight, saying, 'They make cameras so small now that they're almost impossible to spot. Would you care to explain, Carl, why you are removing a keystroke-capture device in my computer? I assume Mr Grow put you up to it, because while you're very good at what you do you aren't a very technical sort of guy, are you?'

Carl met the man's gaze and said, 'I was going to tell you about that. Erik Grow was blackmailing me. He found out something about my past, said he would go to the cops unless I did what he asked.'

Dirk Merrit smiled. 'Very good, Carl. That's almost plausible.'

'It's the truth. But you don't have to worry about that now. Erik's dead.'

'You and Erik were planning to take control of a certain little program, weren't you? The one that lets me access the account system of Powered By Lightning.'

'It was Erik's idea.'

'I'm sure it was. He had you put in that device because he wanted to get the password, didn't he? He must have been watching Powered By Lightning's accounts, waiting until I used the program. When I did, he had you pull the device. No wonder you were so eager to get to LA.'

'I killed him. I did him the same time I did that stewardess.'

'It's funny that the FBI didn't mention finding his body.'

'I hid it. I knew that if they found it, it might have led them back to you, so I hid it.'

Dirk Merrit said, his gaze steady on Carl's face, 'What do you think, Elias? Should I give him the benefit of the doubt?'

Elias Silver stepped out from the archway that led to the stairs. 'Psychopaths are expert fabulators. They have to be. They spend most of their time constructing their own version of reality because they don't really understand other human beings.'

Carl remembered what he'd seen in the psychiatric report so long ago, and felt as if spiders were crawling over his brain.

Dirk Merrit said, 'It doesn't matter if you killed Erik or not, Carl. I changed the password right after you removed that little device. If the little shit is still alive, I'll find him and deal with him in my own time. As for you, I want you to handcuff yourself and sit down. Over there, in the armchair. Oh, but before you do, I think should you should get rid of the gun that you're wearing under your shirt-tail.'

'I don't get this,' Carl said, trying to stall, looking for a way out.

'Use your left hand, reach around behind you, pull it out using only your thumb and forefinger. Do you "get" that? If you do it any other way, I'll shoot you.'

Carl got rid of the gun. He put on the handcuffs that Elias Silver tossed him, walked to the armchair and sat down, looking at Dirk Merrit while Elias Silver moved behind him, out of sight. He still had his knife, in the scabbard strapped to his calf. If one of them got in range he'd stick him, use the body as a shield. He heard Elias Silver moving somewhere behind him, got ready . . .

Dirk Merrit shot him in the left shoulder, the impact punching him back against the chair, and something was pressed over his face, a wet cloth with a strong chemical smell.

When he came round, he was still sitting in the chair. He was shirtless now, and a bandage held a compress over his wounded shoulder. A hot wire ran through it, and the whole arm ached stiffly. Lamps had been switched on here and there in the big room. Dirk Merrit sat behind his desk and Elias Silver stood beside him. Both men were watching Carl.

Dirk Merrit said, 'In many respects, Carl, you have been a

good and faithful servant. But I can no longer trust you, and I can't afford servants any more, either. This place – I no longer own it. My bank has foreclosed on all the loans I raised against it. I've been given notice to quit the premises, turn my home over to my creditors, but Dr Silver and I have a much better idea. It's a shame you won't live to see it . . .'

The man waited to see if Carl had anything to say. Carl wouldn't give him the pleasure.

'They'll call me a monster, but they're wrong. I'm the latest thing. I'm the future. There isn't yet a name for what I am becoming.'

'We'll find it,' Elias Silver said.

'Yes, we will.' Dirk Merrit smiled his awful smile at Carl. 'I have an appointment in Mexico with a plastic surgeon. Dr Silver is coming with me. He will supervise the creation of my next avatar. Fortunately, most of my improvements are reversible. Implants that can be removed, bone grafts that can be planed away . . . We'll soon be far, far away. But you, Carl, my good and faithful servant, you aren't going anywhere. You're going to take part in our first true work of art.'

40

Six-thirty in the evening, Summer's mother called her. 'Have you checked your email recently?'

'What's wrong?'

'Someone just sent me an email addressed to you, with two photographs attached. I think you should check if they were also sent to your work address.'

'Hang on a second,' Summer said, and turned to her computer. Apart from a couple of people working over in the corner occupied by the Homicide Unit, she was the only detective left on the thirteenth floor.

Her mother said, 'It's from a hotmail account. The subject line says, "Happy hunting". The user name is Seeker8. With the number—'

'Not spelled out, I know.'

Summer clicked on the browser, found the email, opened it. There were two photographs attached. One was of the rear of Joseph Kronenwetter's shack, a light-blue pickup truck parked on the other side. The other was of Dirk Merrit in his camo gear, walking towards the pickup.

Her mother was asking if she'd found the email.

'Don't worry about it. I guess they weren't sure if I'd still be at work.'

Summer was trying to figure out who could have sent the photographs. Her first thought was that it had to be Denise Childers – she was certain that Denise was still working the case in spite of her suspension, and she'd given Denise her mother's email address as well as her email address at work, so that they could keep in touch day and night. But the cryptic message wasn't Denise's style. And anyway, why would she send it under Seeker8's name . . .?

Her mother said, 'I hope you aren't working too late. I'm looking forward to meeting this mysterious date of yours.'

Summer said, 'It isn't like that. Gary's visiting town, we're working together on this thing, he's at a loose end . . .'

'And he asked you out to dinner,' her mother said. 'That sounds like a date to me.'

'Listen, I have to make a couple of phone calls. Let's talk later.'

Summer called Denise's cell phone and got an out-of-service message; called her home number and got an engaged tone. With a widening sense of unease, she called Gary Delgatto and told him about the emailed photographs. 'They show Dirk Merrit at Kronenwetter's place, but I don't know when—'

'Has anyone seen them apart from your mother?'

'What's going on?'

'It looks like we'll have to reschedule our dinner. I have to get to Cedar Falls.'

'Something has happened. What happened?'

'There's no easy way to put this, so I'll tell you straight out, you deserve to know. Denise Childers is missing.'

Something huge and cold moved through Summer. She said, 'Where are you now?'

'In my room at the Marriot, packing. I have a car waiting downstairs.'

With three mouse clicks, Summer sent the email and the two photographs to the colour printer. 'I'll be there in ten minutes. Don't you dare leave without me.'

Gary Delgatto and a driver were waiting in a black Crown Victoria parked outside the hotel. As soon as Summer had climbed into the back, beside Gary, the driver started the car and pulled out into the traffic.

Gary told her that someone had made an anonymous call to the Sheriff's office at Cedar Falls, said there was a body in the shack on the Kronenwetter property. 'The caller used a vocoder to disguise their voice, and they called the detectives' office direct, so there's no recording.'

'Like the calls about Billy Gundersen and Joseph

Kronenwetter's cellar. You said Denise is missing, so what's this about a body?'

'Does the name Charley Phelps mean anything to you?'

Summer was breathless and numb. She had to cast about in her mind for several moments before she remembered where she had first heard the name.

'Charley Phelps was at high school with Joseph Kronenwetter and Dirk Merrit. When Denise and I last paid him a visit, Merrit told us that Phelps and Kronenwetter were best friends until they fell out over some girl. Is that who was found dead at the shack?'

'Did Denise tell you that Charley Phelps worked as a guard in the lock-up in the Cedar Falls Justice Building? That he was the one who discovered Kronenwetter's body?'

'No, she didn't.' Summer met Gary's gaze, her mind racing to process these new revelations. 'I'm not holding out on you. If Denise was chasing this guy, she was doing it on her own.'

Gary looked embarrassed. 'You understand why I had to ask.'

'I think you had better tell me what happened.'

'According to one of Mr Phelps's neighbours, Denise paid a call on his house yesterday. We think she was tailing him today. She borrowed her mother's car, presumably because Mr Phelps was familiar with her own vehicle. It was found on the fire road that runs past Kronenwetter's property. People from the Sheriff's office are combing the woods, but so far nothing has turned up.'

'They're looking in the wrong place,' Summer said, and handed Gary the prints of the two photographs. 'What I think happened is that this guy, Charley Phelps, met with Dirk Merrit at Kronenwetter's place. Denise was following Charley Phelps, she saw Dirk Merrit, took his photograph, and then something went wrong. I think he must have spotted her, he gave chase . . .' She didn't want to complete the thought. 'In any case, I'm certain that Dirk Merrit emailed these photographs. He could be holding Denise prisoner in that damn mansion of his, or somewhere on his estate. That's where the Sheriff's office should be looking.'

'Summer, relax a little, okay? Mr Malone was sent these photographs too, and he came to the same conclusion. He's probably writing up a warrant for Dirk Merrit as we speak.'

'What happened to Charley Phelps?'

'His body was found inside the shack. He'd been shot in the head and chest at close range. Blood spray and blood trails suggest that he was shot when he opened the door, he fell backward, and was dragged inside.' Gary paused, then said, 'His heart had been cut out.'

Summer thought of the photograph of Dirk Merrit, the athletic bag he was carrying. Dirk Merrit liked to hunt, and he liked to take trophies. He'd bragged about it. Sending those photographs was another brag, and a teasing invitation. *Happy hunting*. She took a breath and held it, looking out of the window at nothing in particular while she got her thoughts in order.

'I think Phelps was working for Dirk Merrit, and that he had something to do with Kronenwetter's death,' she said. 'He was in the right place at the right time, and both he and Merrit knew each other from high school. Merrit knew that Denise and I were gathering evidence that would prove Kronenwetter had been framed, he knew that we'd followed Edie Collier's trail back to his estate. So he decided to get rid of Phelps in case he decided to talk or cause some kind of trouble, and he arranged a meeting . . .'

'He also told you about Phelps in the first place.'

'He was playing us. Leading us to a place he wanted us to reach. He showed us a crossbow, too, talked about hunting people . . .'

'Why would he incriminate himself?'

'He likes to play games. When did all this happen?'

'Phelps's body was in rigor when it was found,' Gary said. He was cool and calm, and she liked him for that. 'The ME estimates it was likely he was shot and killed between noon and four p.m.'

'And the photographs were emailed to me just before six thirty. So Merrit has had plenty of time to do Christ knows what.'

'If he was the one who sent the email.'

'He sent it, all right. He's playing some kind of game. He's been playing it all along. That message is exactly his style, and so is signing it "Seeker8". I guess he learned about Seeker8 from Billy Gundersen. You need to find him, Gary. He could be in danger.'

Gary said, 'I have more bad news. We took out a warrant to examine Powered By Lightning's subscription base, found out that Seeker8's real name is Daryl Weir. He's a black male, age sixteen, lives with his mother in an apartment in Brooklyn. We also found out that he flew into Portland today – we have a record of an airline ticket issued in his name, first class on an American West flight that arrived at half past eleven this morning.'

'Jesus. Then what?'

'We don't know. According to his mother, he came here to talk to someone about a sponsorship deal, but she didn't know who he was meeting with. The Visa card that was used to purchase the ticket belongs to a gentleman by the name of Anthony Wise, but he lives in London, England. We're waiting for the police there to come back to us, but it looks like someone cloned Mr Wise's card.'

'Jesus.'

'The local field office is checking hotels, canvassing taxi drivers and bus drivers. They're also checking video footage from the security cameras in the airport.'

'Dirk Merrit couldn't have picked him up at Portland and got back to Cedar Falls in time to meet with Charley Phelps. He must have someone helping him – I bet it's the person who tried to lay that false trail, who killed those two people in Reno and Los Angeles.'

'It's possible, if Daryl Weir was met at the airport,' Gary Delgatto said. 'But we don't know that yet. We do know he was a high-school dropout who, according to his mother, was earning a living from playing *Trans*. He sold items that he won in the game to other players. Who knows what else he got up to? He could have cloned the credit card that bought the ticket, and flown to Portland to look for Gundersen. He took his laptop with him, but the agents found all kinds of CD-ROMs and Zip disks, they're going through them and they're interviewing his friends too. Hopefully they'll turn up something useful.'

'Let's hope so,' Summer said. But she had a bad feeling about Seeker8 – Daryl Weir – and an even worse feeling about Denise.

The car was on the 205 freeway now, stuck in heavy traffic about a mile from the turn-off for Airport Way. Summer leaned forward and told the driver, 'How about putting on your lights and siren?'

41

Daryl Weir sat on a dirt floor in darkness as complete as the end of the world. His back wedged against a wall of rough stones, his feet drawn up, his hands wrapped around his knees, trying like a child playing hide-and-seek to make himself as inconspicuous as possible. A shackle around his right ankle was tethered to a steel ring in the floor by a chain so short that it allowed him to take no more than two steps in any direction. The only things in reach were a couple of plastic buckets. One was half-filled with water; the other had a lid – Daryl supposed it was for when he needed to go to the toilet.

He didn't know where he was or how long he'd been there, chained up like a slave in one of those old-time ships. It was hard to keep track of time in the dark, and he believed that he'd zoned out a couple of times. He did know that it seemed a very long time, another life, since he'd arrived at Portland International Airport. He remembered walking onto the bustling concourse, past security gates where people were waiting in line to put their bags through X-ray machines, taking off their shoes, stepping in socks or bare feet through metal detectors. He remembered feeling nervous and exposed, his happy speculations about Mr Hunter Smith and all the money he was going to make from winning the treasure suddenly crowded out by the idea that this was some kind of horrible practical joke. He'd have to go home empty-handed, face up to his mother, to Bernard . . . But then he'd spotted a man holding up a laminated sheet of paper printed with SEEKER8 in bold letters a foot high, and he'd felt a rush of relief. Felt that everything was going to be all right.

The man had a cap of white hair and a collarless jacket that looked like some kind of uniform. He told Daryl that he was Mr Smith's assistant, asked did he have any luggage apart from the athletic bag? Daryl told him no, started to explain that he'd brought along his customized controller, his mouse and special mousepad, but the man cut him short and said that they were running a little late, please come this way. Daryl followed him out of the airport building, across several lanes busy with cars and buses and green taxis, into a parking structure. Climbed concrete stairs to the fifth level, where a black Mercedes SUV beeped and flashed its lights when the man pointed his key at it.

Daryl's good feeling surged up a notch when he saw the SUV. It was a top-of-the-line ride: Mr Smith definitely had money to burn. The white-haired assistant opened the hatchback door and got behind Daryl as he leaned in to put away his athletic bag, grabbing hold of him and after a brief fierce struggle pressing a cloth over his face. And that was all Daryl knew until he woke here, sick and dizzy, a headache thumping behind his eyes, chained to the floor in absolute darkness.

At first he'd been convinced that someone, the white-haired man or his employer, Hunter Smith, was standing there in the dark, watching him.

He'd ask if anyone was there, wait, ask again.

Saying, 'Mr Smith, is that you?'

Saying, 'There's something wrong, I don't mind talking about it.'

Saying, 'This ain't right. I came here to *help* you.'

Daryl had grown angry, shouted until his throat was raw, but no one replied, there probably wasn't anyone out there in the dark, he was all alone, perhaps he'd been left here to die . . . He'd close his eyes and try to think of what to say when the white-haired man came back, and then fear would lean over him, and he had to open his eyes again, straining to see something, anything at all.

He opened his eyes now, hearing a heavy door closing and

cloth stirring, layers of cloth moving over each other. His pulse jumping in his throat, cold spreading over his skin, as footsteps clicked through the darkness towards him.

Dirk Merrit, infrared goggles clamped over his eyes, watched the boy strain blindly this way and that, eyes wide in what to him would be pitch darkness, his face luminous green in the beam of the infrared lamp. He had to admit that he hadn't been sure that Elias Silver had been up to the task of snatching the boy: he'd half-expected that the man would lose his nerve and run away or fuck up somehow, fall foul of the authorities, but everything had gone down exactly according to plan. He had dealt with Charley Phelps and that pernicious detective. He had the boy. He had Carl Kelley. And very soon the FBI would arrive, and the real fun would begin. He was giddy with delicious anticipation.

'Seeker8,' he said.

The boy jerked like a fish when the hook bites.

'Please, I don't understand why I'm here. What have I done?'

'You've done many things. You've had great adventures, won many treasures. You're a brave pilgrim, Seeker8.'

'Listen, Mr Smith—'

'Mr Smith is a website and a rented office. A front for one of my little businesses.'

The boy closed his eyes, swallowed, then took a breath and said, 'Listen, I don't know who you are. Who you really are. You fooled me good, but that's okay, the joke's on me, right? You can let me go, and I won't tell anyone about this ever, I swear I won't.'

'The man who met you at the airport. The man who brought you here. Did you recognize him?'

'No. I don't know who he is, I don't know who you are—'

'That will disappoint him. He used to have a certain profile in the media, once upon a time. Do you run?'

'What?'

'Do you run?'

'You mean like jogging? Not really.'

'But I bet you could run if you had to . . . Do you play any sports?'

'Gymnastics, back at school. Why do you want to know this? What do you want?'

Dirk Merrit switched off the infrared lamp and set it on the floor, pushed his goggles up to his forehead and pulled the little flashlight from his pocket. He held it under his chin, savouring the moment, then switched it on and said, 'Do you know who I am now?'

The boy shook his head from side to side. His eyes were still squeezed shut.

'If you lie, I'll hurt you.'

'You invented *Trans*.'

The boy's voice small and squeezed, like a child admitting a transgression.

'Good. What's my name? The name I use in the world.'

'Oh God.'

'Say my name.'

'Please, what do you want from me?'

'Say it.'

'Dirk Merrit.'

'I made *Trans*. I am its god, and I am a jealous god. No one has ever won the treasure you were trying to reach. Now do you understand why you are here?'

Daryl sat still and quiet, hugging his knees, while Dirk Merrit knelt down and unlocked the shackle around his ankle and stood up again. Impossibly tall and thin in camouflage jacket and pants, his face stark white. Goggles with stalky lenses pushed up on his forehead, a pistol in a leather holster on the point of his right hip, a big knife with a bone handle in a scabbard on his left, in front of the cell phone clipped to his belt.

'Stand up, face the wall. Go on, turn around, I'm not going to hurt you as long as you do as I say. Put your hands behind your back. Hold them straight out, as far as they will go.'

Daryl did as he was told. Something snapped around his right wrist, his left. Handcuffs. Then Dirk Merrit seized a bunch of material at the back of his T-shirt, twisting it tight between his shoulder blades, turning him around and shoving him forward. Through layers of black cloth hanging in front of a doorway, up a set of stone steps into cold night air.

The low remains of stone walls starkly lit by the headlight glare of a pickup truck. Rough ground sloping down to a lake silvered by the light of the full moon that rode just above the trees on the far side. The far end of the lake was pinched between trees and lit by a trio of floodlights on top of a small bridge – no, it was a dam. Daryl remembered seeing pictures of Dirk Merrit's hi-tech residence in an article in *Wired*, the towers standing on one side of a narrow valley with a small dam in the background.

Dirk Merrit pushed Daryl towards the pickup, saying, 'You were down in what used to be the wine cellar of the old family home. Errol Flynn stayed here once, a summer weekend in 1941. My favourite movie actor.'

Daryl, who'd never heard of the guy, didn't say anything.

They drove away from the ruined house and the floodlit dam, swinging around the other end of the lake and rattling over a wooden bridge that crossed a creek, speeding past a ramshackle house and a big, new-looking barn, through a gate in a low stone wall. Turning onto a narrower, rougher track that climbed between tall trees, trees pressing on either side, caught in the pickup's headlights and rushing past, their branches scraping the sides of the pickup, the cold air full of their sharp clean Christmassy smell. Sitting in handcuffs beside Dirk Merrit, Daryl did his best to stay calm. He'd had no chance of escaping when he had been shackled down in the cellar, but he had to stay alert now, be ready to take any chance . . .

The pickup slowed, and trees fell away on either side as it drove into a long meadow exposed beneath the cold white eye of the Moon. A small, sawn-off airplane with a rear-mounted propeller behind its open cockpit was cocked at the end of a runway strip. Off to one side the black Mercedes SUV that Daryl had last seen in the airport parking structure aimed its headlights at a naked man sitting in a circle of trampled grass. The man got to his feet as the pickup pulled up, and the white-haired man came around the rear of the SUV, saying loudly, 'You cut it fine. Three cars from the Sheriff's office just pulled up at the front gate.'

42

Summer Ziegler and Gary Delgatto were flown to Cedar Falls in a twelve-year-old Cessna C-172 which had been confiscated from a marijuana farmer last year and was now shared by the Oregon State Police and the DEA. It was noisy and cold in the little plane, hard to talk. As it droned south above the forests and farmlands of the Willamette Valley, the sky darkening beyond the blurred circle of its single propeller, Summer had plenty of time to line up her facts so that she could present them to Section Chief Malone as clearly and concisely as possible. She also had plenty of time for her thoughts to stray back to Denise and the kid, Daryl Weir.

She knew that thinking about what might have happened to Denise at Kronenwetter's shack, thinking about what might be happening to her right now, would squeeze out everything else. She knew that she had to try to rise above her emotions, stay cool and calm. But as she sat hunched into herself in the cold, noisy dark, her hands locked together between her knees, trying to remember everything that Dirk Merrit had said to her and organizing her lines of evidence, her thoughts kept returning to worst-case scenarios as a tongue will keep returning to an aching tooth.

The plane touched down at the little airfield outside Cedar Falls just before eight p.m. A black Crown Victoria exactly like the black Crown Victoria they'd left back in Portland was waiting by the runway. The driver, Special Agent Buck Cole, drove at precisely ten miles above the speed limit, economically overtaking other vehicles and swinging around bends in slippery squeals of tyres. He told Summer and Gary that they had arrived just behind Malone and his team, and that there had been a major development while they'd been in the air.

'The Sheriff's office received a nine-eleven from a man who told them that he was being held hostage in the main tower of Dirk Merrit's mansion. He said that someone by the name of Carl had gone crazy, shot and killed Merrit, and rounded up everyone else.'

Summer, sharing the rear seat with Gary, had an airy sense of falling. 'Dirk Merrit is dead?'

'According to the caller,' Buck Cole said. He had a Texas drawl. 'We haven't confirmed any of his story yet.'

'What about Denise Childers and Daryl Weir?'

'We don't know. The guy didn't stay on the line long enough for anyone to ask him any questions. But here's where it gets interesting,' Buck Cole said. 'The Sheriff's office traced the call to a cell phone belonging to an employee of Mr Merrit by the name of Louis Frazier, and rang back. Someone else answered, we don't know who because he was using an electronic device to disguise his voice.'

Summer said, 'Like the person who called the Sheriff's office about Joseph Kronenwetter's cellar. Who's probably the same person who made the call about the location of William Gundersen's body.'

Buck Cole said, 'It's very likely. But we don't have tapes of those calls, so we have no way of making a voiceprint comparison. Anyhow, he demanded a helicopter and ten million dollars in cash, and said that if we didn't get him what he wanted by ten p.m. he would start shooting his hostages.'

Summer said, 'Did he say how many hostages he was holding? Did he mention any names?'

Thinking of Denise and Daryl Weir as hostages was so much better than thinking of them as victims.

'No, he didn't. He said he'd kill them all if anyone tried to get into the mansion, and he hung up. We've been trying to re-establish contact ever since, but so far he hasn't picked up. Like I said, we haven't confirmed any of this, but we have to assume this is a genuine hostage situation. The road that goes past Merrit's estate has been sealed off, and when I left to collect you guys, people were working their way towards the house. You know what it looks like, the house? I understand it's pretty weird.'

Summer said, 'I've been inside.'

Buck Cole said, 'From what I saw it isn't going to be the easiest perimeter to contain. Everyone on the team is out there, so is most of the local Sheriff's office. A bunch of state troopers too, Cedar Falls's fire department, some guys from the Park Police, I don't know who else. The Oregon State Police SWAT team is flying in from Salem. They're bringing a negotiator as well as marksmen and tactical operators. We're hoping to get this guy talking, persuade him to walk out.'

Gary said, 'Do we know anything about him?'

Buck Cole said, 'We believe he's Carl Kelley, a Brit who's been working for Dirk Merrit as his driver for just under two years. White male, thirty-eight, no criminal record in this country, although you can bet we're looking into what he might have got up to before he arrived.'

Gary said to Summer, 'Did you see anyone like that, when you visited the place?'

'No . . . but the first time Denise and I talked to him, Merrit mentioned something about his driver. He said that they'd been on a hunting trip together.'

Buck Cole said, 'Anything you can remember could be of use, Detective Ziegler. This is a tricky situation full of unknowns. We don't know the number of hostages, we don't know who's dead and who's alive – we don't even know if it *is* a hostage situation. It's possible the nine-eleven call was scripted, or that it was the bad guy who made it.'

'I'm not so sure that Merrit is dead,' Summer said. 'He likes to play games. It could be that he set this whole thing up, that he's sitting tight somewhere, waiting for your people to try to force entry.'

Buck Cole smiled at her in the rear-view mirror. 'If anyone is hoping to play games with us, he's about to find out that he's in the big boys' league now.'

43

Dirk Merrit and Elias Silver watched the siege unfold on a laptop computer they'd set up on the hood of the pickup. The laptop was cabled to a satellite phone that connected it to the estate's security-camera system. Dirk Merrit, all sharp angles in his camo jacket and pants, switched from camera to camera as vehicles kept arriving, first police and emergency services, and then the FBI. A scanner tuned to the police channel emitted staticky spurts of jargon.

The two men commented on the action as FBI agents shorted out the electronic lock of the main gate and pulled the gate open, crept down the main drive and checked out the gate-house, took up positions overlooking the mansion's three towers. Both of them growing more and more excited as their deadly practical joke unfolded, Dirk Merrit actually cutting a brief capering dance after he'd zoomed in on a pair of agents armed with sniper rifles creeping through trees.

It reminded Daryl of the times when DeLeon and his friends had watched basketball on the TV back in the apartment, lounging loose-limbed and languid on the sofa and armchairs, cheering on the play, whooping and high-fiving every time their team scored. He was standing hard against the driver's door of the pickup, his right arm thrust through the open window, his wrist handcuffed to the steering wheel, his shoulders and spine aching because of the awkward stance this forced him to assume. Cotton-mouthed, sweating in the cold night air. Whenever Dirk Merrit so much as glanced at him he felt his heart stumble and quicken. He was so tired, and so tired of being scared, that it took an effort to remember that the man could kill him at any time for no reason at all, that he wasn't going to survive this unless he did something to help himself. He'd had an idea about that ever since he'd noticed that Dirk Merrit had left the keys in the ignition of the pickup, but there was nothing he could do about it while the two men were whooping it up right in front of him . . .

Thirty or forty yards away, the naked man sat in the mingled headlight beams of the Mercedes SUV and the pickup, patient as stone. His wrists were bound in front of him by a dozen turns of thin cord knotted tightly, pressing into the skin of his wrists. His right ankle was shackled, fastened by a short chain to a stake driven into the ground. A pad of gauze spotted with blood was held in place by bandages that went over his right shoulder and around his chest. Dirk Merrit had introduced him to Daryl earlier, leading Daryl by the arm into the glare of the headlights, saying, 'Daryl Weir, meet Carl Kelley. Carl, this young man is the player I told you about. The good friend of our last pilgrim.'

The naked man, Carl Kelley, had ignored Dirk Merrit. Staring instead at Daryl, smiling coldly, saying, 'Don't worry, kid. I'm going to fuck him up. Him and his fairy boyfriend, they're both dead men walking.'

'That's the spirit,' Dirk Merrit had said pleasantly. 'How are you feeling, Carl? Any nausea or dizziness? Any numbness? No? Think you're ready for a little action?'

Carl Kelley wouldn't answer any of Dirk Merrit's questions and he'd remained silent and still ever since, sitting with his bound arms resting on top of his knees, only his eyes moving. Watching now as Dirk Merrit tapped the laptop's screen with a forefinger and said, 'There's the man in charge. See him? The one with the bullhorn.'

'Section Chief Harry Malone, Behavioural Sciences,' Elias Silver said.

'My nemesis,' Dirk Merrit said happily. 'I wonder what he's saying. Damn, I should have thought to wire us up for sound.'

'It looks like they're getting ready to go in,' Elias Silver said, squinting at the screen.

'Not yet,' Dirk Merrit said. 'They won't try to force entry before the deadline I gave them expires. Timing is the essence of drama, Elias. That's why I gave them the deadline. That's why bombs in movies always have clocks counting down to zero. You know, I should have thought of that. They burst in, and there's a package on the table with a big digital counter running backwards ... They wouldn't know whether to shit or run,' Dirk Merrit said, looking at his watch. 'Meanwhile, we have a little over thirty minutes before the deadline runs out. More than enough time to deal with our good friend Carl.'

'You're really going through with that right now?'

'Would you prefer to bring him with us?'

'Frankly, I'd prefer it if you shot him in the back of the head.'

'Carl has been a good soldier; he deserves a soldier's death. I'm afraid we don't have enough time for our usual ceremony,' Dirk Merrit said, addressing the naked man. 'This will be more in the nature of a duel. A very one-sided duel.'

The naked man stared up at Dirk Merrit but didn't say anything. After a moment, Dirk Merrit walked over to the SUV and pulled a kind of leather harness from its back seat. The man didn't have wings, but otherwise he was a pretty good replica of an overlord. It was spooky to see him standing there, buckling the harness across his narrow chest and hips, sliding a sword with a short curved blade and a hilt wrapped with red silk through one of its loops. He reached into the SUV again, brought out a big crossbow and plucked a single low note from its taut string. Smiling at Daryl, saying, 'Just like the game, isn't it?'

Daryl's heart jinked sideways, like a kicked dog. He didn't trust himself to speak, he didn't *want* to speak, to give Dirk Merrit the satisfaction of any kind of answer, but the man's gaze was compelling. He nodded once, up and down, and immediately felt ashamed of his weakness.

'You'll go free if Carl wins, so you might want to cheer him on,' Dirk Merrit said, and walked towards the naked man, holding the crossbow by the side of his leg. 'How about it, Carl? Think you can save the boy? Think you can redeem all your sins by saving his life?'

The naked man was standing up now. Staring at Dirk Merrit with stony contempt.

Elias Silver said, 'Let's get this done.'

'We're going to have a high old time,' Dirk Merrit said.

The inhumanly tall overlord and his naked prey: Daryl had seen this tableau so many times when he'd started playing *Trans*, when Seeker8 had been no more than a slave on an overlord's estate. The only way a slave could win its freedom and gain promotion to the next level of the game was to escape while being hunted by an overlord. Seeker8 had died over and over again before he had figured out the right direction to run, discovered the slab of rock where he could hide (after killing the snakes that nested there) and wait until nightfall, then head out into the desert towards the nearest settlement. But this was real . . .

Dirk Merrit told the naked man, 'I'm proud of you, Carl. Really. You're my first true test. The first time I've stood up against a righteous killer. And you should be proud too, because yours will be a noble death.'

Exactly the kind of lame speech overlords always gave before the hunt began.

Carl Kelley held up his bound wrists. 'Make it a real contest. Make it a duel, man to man. Free me. Give me a weapon.'

Elias Silver, standing off to one side, said, 'You know that isn't going to happen. Let's get this done.'

Dirk Merrit stood still, thinking, then said, 'On the other hand, it might be more fun to do it Carl's way.'

He drew his big hunting knife from its scabbard and flipped it in a quick arc, its hilt quivering in the grass at the feet of the naked man. Who dropped to his knees and wrenched the knife from the ground, worked its hilt between his thighs, and began to saw at the loops of rope that bound his wrists.

Elias Silver said to Dirk Merrit, 'This is no time for grandstanding.'

Dirk Merrit pulled the pistol from his waistband and tossed it to the white-haired man, who caught it in an awkward two-handed grip.

'If you have a problem with this,' Dirk Merrit said, 'feel free to shoot him. I'd advise a chest shot, it's a lot easier to hit the chest than the head. Oh, and you had better disengage the safety first.'

'Fuck you,' the white-haired man said, turning back to watch the naked man, the pistol held down by his leg.

Dirk Merrit pulled out his sword and cut the air with a cross-wise stroke. 'Errol Flynn against Basil Rathbone, my sword against your knife, how does that sound?'

'Right here, right now, motherfucker,' Carl Kelley said without looking up, his wrists jerking up and down against the knife. He'd cut himself, blood bright red on his hands and thighs in the glare of the headlights.

Daryl realized that no one was looking at him, told himself now or never, and climbed onto the footboard of the pickup. Dirk Merrit and Elias Silver had their backs to him, watching the naked man free himself, and Daryl took a breath – now or never – and gripped the sill of the open window with his left hand, lifted himself up and rammed his head and shoulders through, wriggling desperately, his right arm wrenching around as he fell head first onto the seat, a sharp tearing pain in his shoulder and the steel bracelet digging hard into his wrist bone, forcing him to twist onto his side. His legs were sticking out through the window and for a horrible moment he thought he wouldn't be able to pull them inside. He kicked frantically, one of his feet found purchase, and with a single hard push he was lying across the seats, the ball on top of the gearshift jammed against his ribs, his right arm pulled straight back, his wrist hurting badly where it had twisted against the handcuffs that secured it to the steering wheel.

He sat up, thinking, *Way to go, Daryl!* Cheering himself the way DeLeon had cheered him from the top row of the bleachers whenever he'd pulled off a good move on the mats. Through the bug-smeared windshield, he saw that Carl Kelley had freed his wrists and was standing up in the glare of the headlights, pale as a statue, the knife in his hand, its blade flashing when he drew his arm back as if to throw it.

Elias Silver was pointing the pistol at Carl Kelley, his arm thrust straight out and slightly shaking, but he was looking at

Dirk Merrit. Who stood with the sword held up to his face as if he was about to kiss it, telling Carl Kelley, 'If you miss, you won't get another chance.'

The naked man said, 'If you don't let me out of these irons, you're going to have to bring the fight to me.'

With his right hand cuffed to the steering wheel, Daryl had to reach across himself to release the handbrake, then couldn't remember which of the three pedals worked the clutch. Panic fizzed in his blood. Wait. Think. Slow down, dog, take a breath and think. He decided that the middle pedal, the biggest, had to be the brake, the gas pedal was to the right of the brake in Bernard's Datsun . . . He pressed down on the left pedal, awkwardly wiggled the gearshift with his left hand, his heart lifting when the stick slipped into the notch marked 1. *Way to go, Daryl!* Now get this thing started, run the crazy white motherfuckers down.

Dirk Merrit pulled something from a pocket of his combat pants, a key he tossed flashing through the headlights to Carl Kelley, who snatched it from the air.

Elias Silver said, 'Jesus Christ.'

Carl Kelley grinned at him. 'You don't like it, pal, you know what you can do.'

Standing there with the knife glittering in his right hand, blood dripping from his wrists, staring at Elias Silver, smiling his cold smile.

Dirk Merrit said, 'Don't worry, Elias. He's all mine.'

'I think Elias is more likely to piss his pants than shoot me.' Carl Kelley stooped over and unlocked his leg-iron, stepped out of it, and pointed the knife at Dirk Merrit. 'Let's do it.'

Not quite like *Trans*, Daryl thought, his thumb and forefinger pinching the head of the ignition key, getting ready to turn it. In the game, you were staked out in the desert and the shackle popped open and you knew then that you had to run for your life. But it was close enough.

What happened now:

The naked man walked straight at Dirk Merrit, and Dirk Merrit stepped to the left, moving his sword through the air in figure-of-eight arcs. Daryl turned the key, the engine made a horrible grinding noise, and the pickup jerked forward and stalled. The three men in the headlights turned to look at Daryl as he reached over and wrenched at the gearshift, trying to get it into neutral, remembering then that he had to press down on the clutch pedal.

Carl Kelley rushed at Dirk Merrit, the two of them tangling in a quick clash of steel on steel that threw them back from each other. Elias Silver swung around, straight-arming the pistol at the pickup, and Daryl started the engine, shifted into first gear and stamped on the accelerator pedal. The pickup lurched forward. The laptop and scanner slid the length of the hood, banged against the windshield and fell away; Dirk Merrit and Carl Kelley turned, faces white in the oncoming beams of the pickup's headlights and dodged left and right. Daryl barely saw them. He was trying to steer and change gear at the same time, and then there was a tremendous thump as the offside front wheel ran over an old tree-stump hidden in the grass. The pickup stalled and the steering wheel spun around, the handcuffs jerking hard at Daryl's wrist, throwing him sideways. His head slammed against the doorpost and that was all he knew.

44

Half a mile from the main entrance to Dirk Merrit's estate, lines of red flares narrowed the road to a single lane flanked by Sheriff's-office cruisers and state-trooper sedans. A cruiser reversed out of the way to let the Crown Victoria through. A TV van was parked off to the side; as the Crown Vic surged past it, Summer saw Sheriff Worden doing a stand-up interview with a perfectly tailored woman in the glare of a light clipped to a camera. More vehicles were drawn up outside the gate itself – cruisers, fire trucks, ambulances, unmarked sedans and SUVs, light bars flashing, gumball lights revolving, shadows and light dancing under the trees on either side. Buck Cole asked Summer and Gary to wait by the Crown Vic, but after the FBI agent crossed the road and passed between two SUVs someone called Summer's name.

'Detective Summer fucking Ziegler.'

It was Jerry Hill, walking quickly towards her through flickering red and blue light, his face flushed with anger. Two men followed him. One was the red-haired detective Summer had met last Sunday, Jay Sexton. The other was a uniformed deputy with sergeant's stripes.

'The fuck you doing *here*?' Jerry Hill said.

Summer had dealt with plenty of angry and unreasonable people in her time, often without back-up. Some of them had been armed, too, like Jerry Hill. She stood her ground, straightened her back, looked right at him, and said, 'What's your problem, Detective Hill?'

'My problem? Jesus Christ,' Jerry Hill said, appealing to Jay Sexton and the sergeant. 'Are you hearing this shit? The interfering bitch gets my little brother killed and she asks what my fucking *problem* is?'

'Take it easy, Jerry,' the sergeant said.

'It isn't her fault,' Jay Sexton said.

'The case was down,' Jerry Hill said. 'We had Kronenwetter locked away, we found the girl's clothes and ID at his shack, the miserable fuck killed himself and left a confession. It was *down*. Done and dusted. But that wasn't good enough for Denise Childers and this interfering do-gooding bitch. Oh no. They just had to start stirring the shit. And what happened? More people die is what happened. My brother dies. He's murdered. Shot in the head like a fucking dog. Because of you,' Jerry Hill said, sticking a finger in Summer's face.

Summer felt a jolt of shock. She said, 'Charley Phelps was your brother?'

'His half-brother,' Jay Sexton said.

'My little brother I always took care of,' Jerry Hill said. From three feet away Summer could smell the alcohol on his breath.

Summer said, 'Why I'm here, Detective Hill, I have information that may help catch the man who killed your brother. So why don't you back off and let me do my job?'

Jerry Hill stabbed at her with his finger again. 'Why don't *you* back off all the way to Portland before you get someone else killed?'

Summer said, giving it straight back to him, 'I'm sorry for your brother's death but he was into something bad and you know it. He was working in the lock-up the night Kronenwetter was murdered. That's right, Detective Hill, Kronenwetter didn't kill himself. He was murdered. We have hard evidence to prove it, we know your brother had something to do with it, and we know that he was connected with Dirk Merrit. That's why Denise talked to him. That's why she was following him. That's what got him killed. If you know anything about it, you should do the right thing. You should give it up.'

Jerry Hill swung at her, a wild roundhouse punch. She took a step back, felt the breeze of his fist past her face, and when he came at her again she kicked him in the right knee, the heel of her shoe connecting hard with the cap of bone. He went down roaring, groping for the gun holstered at his hip, and then Jay Sexton and the uniformed sergeant had him, pinning his arms, lifting him up, pulling him away from Summer.

'Fucking *bitch*,' Jerry Hill said. 'You better get out—'

'Don't threaten me,' Summer said, her throat parched with adrenalin, her pulse beating behind her eyes. 'And don't try to pull another stupid stunt, like you did with Randy Farrell, because if you do I promise I'll come looking for you. And you really don't want that, *Detective* Hill.'

Jerry Hill's glare was full of anger and defiance, but he was the first to look away.

'I'm here to do my job, so stay out of my way,' Summer said, and turned her back on him.

Garry Delgatto ran his fingers through his hair and blew out a breath. 'What was *that* about?'

He seemed more shaken by the confrontation than Summer. She was in the middle of telling him about the trick that Jerry Hill had pulled after she had brought Randy Farrell to Cedar Falls to identify his stepdaughter's body when Jay Sexton came back and apologized for what had happened.

Summer said, 'Forget about it. I guess he was looking for someone to blame.'

'We put him in his pickup, told him to go home. I think you should know, one reason why he was so angry, we had to interview him about Joe Kronenwetter's death.'

Jay Sexton explained that Denise's notebook had been found in the woods bordering Kronenwetter's property, along with her lipstick and her pepper spray.

'We figure they fell out of her bag when she was running for her car. She'd interviewed Charley Phelps and written it up. He was on the reception desk the night Kronenwetter died – I guess you know that. Well, from her notes, we worked out that Denise had a theory that Jerry Hill paid Kronenwetter a visit, signed himself out, but didn't leave. She thought that, with Charley Phelps's connivance, he hung around in one of the empty cells, waited until things got quiet so that he could sneak into

Kronenwetter's cell and, well, kill him. So we had to interview Jerry, but he had a solid alibi. He paid a visit to Kronenwetter all right, but for the rest of the evening he was drinking in a bar across the street.'

Gary Delgatto said, 'I have hard evidence that Kronenwetter was murdered. From what you say, it looks like it's down to Mr Phelps.'

'It's possible,' Jay Sexton said. 'Whatever happened, it's going to cause a big stink when it gets out.'

Summer was sick of thinking about Jerry Hill. She said, 'What's the situation here?'

'As far as I know, the hostage-taker is sitting tight. The FBI shut off the outside lines, you know, so reporters can't call in. They've been calling him on the cell he used, but he hasn't answered, he hasn't made any new demands. If Denise is in there, if she's able to talk to him, she could maybe persuade him to see sense and give it up. Anyone can survive this, it's Denise. She's tough and smart,' Jay Sexton said, with a bright, desperate look that plucked at Summer's heart. He was wearing a bullet-proof vest under his sport coat.

'She's all that and more,' Summer said.

Jay Sexton explained that the estate's gatehouse had been secured and the FBI had people in there ringing the internal phones, trying to make contact with the hostage-taker or anyone else in the mansion. 'Mr Malone is down near the house with a bullhorn, asking the guy to pick up the phone. Mostly, we're waiting on the SWAT team. If you want coffee, there's some over there, the car by the fire truck. The TV crew sent it up, hoping to win our affection.'

Flasks of coffee and foam cups sat on the back seat of the car. Summer held a cup between both hands. It was cold enough to hang clouds of breath on the air; she could feel the cold through her lightweight wool skirt suit, on her bare calves. Blue light from the fire truck's bar twirled across over the ground, over Gary's face as he took a sip from his own cup.

He said, 'I was thinking. If this hostage-taker, Carl Kelley, really is Dirk Merrit's driver, he could be the one who killed the guy in Reno and the stewardess in LA.'

Summer said, 'It's possible. When Denise and I paid Merrit a visit on Sunday, he made a point of telling us that his driver wasn't there.'

She remembered for a moment Dirk Merrit's smile, his stiff white face. A chill that had nothing to do with the cold night air pierced her.

Gary said, 'So the driver could have been in LA. He gets back, or he goes off to Portland to collect the kid, Daryl Weir, comes back here and finds out that Dirk Merrit has killed Phelps and kidnapped a cop. They have an argument, and it all gets out of hand. The driver kills Dirk Merrit. The cook sees something and makes a phone call, and it somehow turns into a hostage situation.'

'That's what I have a problem with. Why did it turn into a hostage situation? Why didn't Carl Kelley make a run for it?'

They kicked it around for a little while. Summer found it easy to talk with Gary. They could speak directly to each other without letting their emotions get in the way. Two people who knew a little about the bad ways of the world, and believed that they were looking at something they had never seen before.

Gary said, 'This is quite a first date.'

Summer felt that she could say anything she liked to him. 'I didn't realize it was supposed to be a date.'

Buck Cole came back, said that Mr Malone would talk to them as soon as he could and went away again. Around nine-thirty there was a stir among the people behind the cars lined across the road. Three men in bulletproof vests and FBI raid jackets were coming through the gateway.

'That's Mr Malone in the centre,' Gary said.

Malone was a short, vigorous man. He walked quickly towards a knot of men standing around a car with a large-scale map spread out on its hood and weighted with rocks, the agents on either side of him trotting to keep up. By the time Summer and Gary reached him, he was talking into a cell phone, saying yes several times, folding the phone away and telling the people around the car that they definitely had a live situation.

'The offices and workshop in the gatehouse are clear, but we spotted a body at the beginning of the drive, right here,' he said, stabbing at a large aerial photograph of the mansion pinned to a corner of the map. 'White male, wearing a blue shirt, black pants, a belt with equipment hooked to it. Probably one of the security guards. We couldn't get close because he's lying in sight of the towers, but it looks like he was shot in the back, it's possible he was trying to get away. I left Grosse and Morgan in the gatehouse, trying to make contact through the internal phone system – he still isn't picking up the cell. The others are up on the ridge above the mansion or setting up a barricade at the end of the drive. The SWAT team are flying in on a National Guard helicopter, they should be here inside fifteen minutes but they'll have to hustle if they're going to get set up before the deadline expires. You must be Detective Ziegler,' Malone said, looking at Summer, barely pausing for breath. 'Are you up to speed with what's going on here?'

'Yes, sir.'

'You have five minutes of my time. You were inside this place Sunday. You talked to Merrit. Tell me what you know.'

Summer looked at the map for a moment, pointed to the meadow where Edie Collier's trail had ended, traced the route that she and Denise Childers had followed to the farmhouse and the barn, from there to the mansion.

Malone said, 'You go in this barn?'

He had quick blue eyes behind steel-rimmed bifocals.

'No, sir. It was padlocked.'

'What happened when the security guards found you? Where were you taken?'

'Into the ground floor of the biggest tower. What Dirk Merrit called his trophy room. It's where we talked to him on our first visit.'

'I've seen photographs from style and architectural magazines. Did you go anywhere else?'

'No.'

'Who did you meet?'

'Dirk Merrit, and two of the guards.'

'Anyone else?'

'No, sir.'

'How did Merrit seem to you? Was he angry, guarded, what?'

'He seemed playful. Amused. On both occasions he made a point of mentioning that he liked hunting. He told us that his favourite weapon is a crossbow. He was playing with us. Teasing. Dropping hints.'

Summer gave Malone a quick summary of the two conversations. The man listened with his head cocked to one side, reminding her of the falcon that sometimes perched on the utility pole outside her father's half-completed house. Malone had the same drab coloration, the same quick, searching gaze.

She told him, 'My impression of Merrit is that he's vain, attention-seeking, self-centred. He also thinks he's smarter than anyone else, believes that he can manipulate any situation to his advantage. He's had plastic surgery to make him look like one of the creatures in his computer game, the ones who have evolved into a species superior to ordinary humans. His house looks like one of their keeps.'

'Did he seem hostile, make any direct threats?'

'He was too clever for that, sir. He did say, the first time we met, that it would be an honour to be able to hunt me. I called him on it, asked him if it was a threat. He said that it was meant as a compliment.' Summer could see that the brief interview was drawing to an end. She knew that Malone was far more experienced than she was, but she felt that she had to say it. 'I think you should be very careful. All this, it could be one of Merrit's games. He could still be alive. He could have set a trap for you down there.'

Malone studied her for a moment, then looked up. Summer heard it too – the fluttering roar of an approaching helicopter.

'Stay close, detective. The SWAT team is bringing a negotiator, he might want to talk with you,' he said, and started to walk away.

Summer called after him. 'There was an RV in the barn, sir. Dirk Merrit told Denise Childers that he used it on his hunting trips, and I believe you found RV tracks near Billy Gundersen's body. There could be other vehicles in there too. Shouldn't someone go check it out?'

45

Carl heard the bass throb of a big helicopter – it sounded like a Chinook – coming in a couple of miles away to the north, and hoped that it was bringing reinforcements for the feds who were laying siege to the mansion. It might distract Dirk Merrit and Elias Silver, make them careless, and give him the opportunity to make a move.

He was lying on his belly in a patch of scrub at the far end of the meadow. The moon hung huge and bright and unforgiving above black trees, painting the long ridge with pale light. The shallow groove of the fresh bullet-wound in Carl's right side hurt every time he took a breath. He bet that at least one rib was broken, his shoulder ached like a bastard, and the night was as cold as a witch's teat, but he felt alert and strong. Although a rough track plunged down through trees behind him, he had no intention of escaping. He still had the hunting knife. He was ready for some serious payback.

A couple of hundred yards away, Elias Silver hauled the unconscious boy from the pickup truck, dumping him on the ground, bending over him. Dirk Merrit stood off to one side, his tall skinny shape silhouetted by the glare of the pickup's head-lights. Looking up at the sky, his head turning this way and that, until the noise of the helicopter died away, then fitting his infrared goggles over his eyes.

Carl put his face in the dirt and covered the top of his head, the warmest part of his body, with his hands, keeping absolutely still and presenting the smallest possible profile. He counted out a minute and when nothing happened he risked raising his head. Dirk Merrit had crossed to the SUV, leaning in at the driver's door, turning with a short-barrelled Uzi in his hands, stepping forward and firing from the hip, full automatic, muzzle-flashes lighting up his white face as he sprayed three short bursts into the trees that bordered the meadow. Carl ate dirt again. Rounds struck tree trunks and whipped through foliage; a couple cracked through the air above Carl's head, kicking his pulse up a notch and making him smile. Dirk Merrit was trying to play soldiers, but he didn't know the first fucking thing about it.

In the ringing silence that followed the gunfire, Elias Silver's voice sounded thin and childishly petulant, telling Dirk Merrit to keep up the good work, by now every FBI agent and police officer in the area would know where they were.

Carl raised his head again. Dirk Merrit was walking back towards the pickup, saying, 'The FBI and the police are getting ready to storm the mansion. I bet that helicopter was bringing in a SWAT team.'

'That's why we should get out of here,' Elias Silver said.

'Be cool,' Dirk Merrit said. 'If we try to run now we'll probably hit a roadblock inside ten minutes. We have to stick to the plan.'

The two men were black shapes against the glare of the pickup's headlights, one much taller than the other, their voices carrying clearly in the cold air.

'I don't have any problems with the plan. The plan is good. But you can't be serious about going up now. Not while he's still out there.'

'Elias, there's absolutely no way I'm going to miss all the fun. I orchestrated this and I'm going to be right over their heads when I bring it all down.'

Carl smiled. The man was pumped up, unable to think about anything but playing his games, getting his kicks.

Elias Silver said, 'When things go awry, you can't carry on as if nothing has happened. You have to change your plan. You have to adapt to the new situation. You have to be flexible.'

'What are you worried about? Didn't you say that you shot Carl?'

'I said that I *thought* I did,' Elias Silver said, that childish whine coming back into his voice. 'I saw him stumble.'

'Well, I know *I* shot him.' Dirk Merrit shoved the Uzi against Elias Silver's chest; the white-haired man had to take it or let it fall. 'If he comes at you, shoot the fucker as many times as you can. It has a tendency to pull up when you fire on full auto, so aim for his knees.'

'I'm not sure if I'm ready for this.'

'There's no way to get ready for it. It happens and you deal with it. Look at me, Elias. At me, not at the fucking trees, you won't learn anything from them. Carl is either dead or badly wounded, or he's running as hard as he can toward the next county. But just in case he's stupid enough to stick around and try to cause trouble, you have your pistol, you have a top-of-the-line sub-machine gun that cost me three thousand dollars, and there's a bag of spare clips in the SUV, forty rounds in each clip.' Dirk Merrit turned away from Elias Silver and addressed the night. 'And what does he have? He has a knife. If he has any sense, he'll get out now, while he still has a chance of getting past the police and the FBI.'

Elias Silver said, 'Let's at least do the kid.'

'"Do the kid." Are you up for that, Elias? Can you kill him right now, in cold blood?'

Elias Silver said, trying to reason with a man beyond reason, 'He's an unnecessary complication.'

'How is he?'

'He hit his head. He's in and out of consciousness, but he isn't concussed.'

'That's good. He really is brave and resourceful, isn't he? Definitely worthy of my attention.'

'We don't have time to get into any kind of game with him.'

'Not here, of course not. But we'll make time somewhere on the road between here and Mexico. It won't take long. An hour, two hours. While I have my fun you can stretch your legs and admire the desert scenery, and then we can be on our way.'

'All right. Whatever. Now, can we get on with this?'

'That's more like it. Listen to me, Elias. We're the new thing, the coming thing. We're *Homo superior*. Everyone else, they're as good as extinct. They're no problem for the likes of us.'

'All right,' Elias Silver said.

'I believe it. I know you do too,' Dirk Merrit said, drawing on a pair of gloves. 'You're nervous, but that's understandable. You haven't learned yet that adrenalin is your friend. Any time you think you see something move, you just let rip. There's enough spare ammunition to take out an army of elephants, and pretty soon the police and the FBI will be too busy to worry about a little gunfire. Are you set?'

Elias Silver jerked his head up and down. Carl, watching all this from his nest in the scrub, smiled to himself, thinking that Dr Elias Silver didn't like any part of this.

'I'll be back before you know it,' Dirk Merrit said. 'All right, let's get this done. Light up the strip while I get ready.'

After a moment, Elias Silver gave another stiff nod. Dirk Merrit went back to the SUV and rooted inside it while Elias Silver drove the pickup along the top of the ridge, making a wide turn and parking behind the ultralight, the pickup's headlights throwing the shadow of the little aircraft down the long strip of mown grass. Now Dirk Merrit was striding towards it, wearing a fleece-trimmed flying jacket over his leather harness and hefting an athletic bag. The two men briefly embraced; then Elias Silver turned to stare into the darkness, pointing the Uzi this way and that while Dirk Merrit crammed his ungainly length into the ultralight's tiny open cockpit.

Carl lay quiet and still, pain in his left shoulder and right side pulsing in unison as he tried to work out his next move. Wait for Dirk Merrit to leave, then take down Elias Silver, that much was obvious. But then what? It was easy enough to guess that Dirk Merrit was planning some kind of spectacular, and of course the man had to be right there when it kicked off, getting off on it, having fun, behaving like one of those fucking overlords in his stupid game because that was how he saw himself. The question was, Carl thought, should he wait for Dirk Merrit to come back, or switch things around, use his stupid plan against him . . .?

Now Elias Silver was cranking the ultralight's propeller, stepping back when it caught. Dirk Merrit throttled up the engine and the ultralight trundled forward, bumping along the strip of mown grass, gathering speed, rising into the air, skimming above Carl's hiding place and climbing away into the starry night above the trees.

As the sound of the little aircraft faded into the distance, Carl watched Elias Silver turn off the headlights of the pickup and walk back towards the SUV, gripping the Uzi tightly, looking this way and that, even walking backwards for a few steps. Carl grinned. This part was going to be a piece of cake.

There was a big knot of pain above Daryl's ear and he felt oddly disconnected from the world; he didn't put up any kind of struggle when he was hauled out of the cab and left lying on his back. The pain was like a rock that he couldn't scramble over or around. All he could do was lie there and watch moths swoop through the long beams of the headlights while the lumpy ground beneath him tilted in an endless sickening slide. When someone fired some kind of machine gun, he barely flinched.

Dirk Merrit was talking now with Elias Silver, like a distant mumbling in another room, like his mother's TV. After a little while the pickup's engine started with a cough and its headlights swept over him as it turned and drove off, leaving Daryl in endlessly tilting dark.

He must have passed out. He jerked awake when Elias Silver grabbed hold of his shoulders, started to haul him towards the SUV. The man was breathing hard as he lifted Daryl up and dragged him three steps, stopped, dragged him three steps more. Finally, he got Daryl propped against the SUV's front fender, and pinched his cheeks until Daryl tried to bat his hand away.

'You have to get up,' Elias Silver said. He was holding a neat little sub-machine gun tight in both hands as he stood over Daryl, looking here and there at the night.

Daryl held on to the fender and managed to push himself to his feet. But his head hurt worse than ever, and then his knees gave way and he sat down again. Elias Silver swore and started to kick at him, but Daryl was too tired to care, too busy trying to keep his stomach from doing a backflip out of his mouth. Elias

Silver aimed one last petulant kick at him and said he'd had enough.

'If he wants to have fun, I can find him a hundred like you,' he said, and stepped sideways through the glare of the offside head-light and raised the sub-machine gun.

Daryl stared at the white-haired man and wondered why he didn't care. The man lowered the sub-machine gun after a long, long moment. He swallowed visibly and took a deep breath, raised his weapon again. Daryl stared up, unable to move. The man's eyes were tight shut, the sub-machine gun trembled in his grip, and a ghost rose up behind him, grabbed him around the chest and pushed a big knife under his chin. The gun went off with a brief ripping sound, things punching into metal two feet from Daryl's head, and the blade slid away from beneath Elias Silver's chin, followed by a long pulse of blood like a magician's red silk handkerchief, blood gurgling in the man's throat as he tried and failed to say something.

Carl lowered Elias Silver to the ground and put one foot between the man's shoulder blades, pinning him down as he twitched and jerked, blood running quickly from beneath his half-turned face. The twitches diminishing as he quickly bled out: there, all done, it had taken less than a minute.

'I'm going to do you another favour,' Carl told the dazed black boy, 'and get you out of here.'

He rolled Elias Silver's body over and patted it down, getting his hands all bloody before he found the cell phone in a holster on the man's belt.

'But first, I have to call the cops.'

46

A Sheriff's-office patrol car rode the Crown Victoria's rear fender, headlights glaring through the rear window, as Buck Cole drove at speed down the county road. Beside Summer in the back seat Gary Delgatto was listening to traffic on the two-way radio he'd borrowed. He reported that the National Guard helicopter had landed by the gatehouse and the SWAT team was setting up close to the mansion. Meanwhile, police and FBI observers were calling in their reports every two minutes. No one was seeing anything. And no one was answering the phones.

Buck Cole made a squealing turn onto the fire road that plunged through the darkness between fir and pine trees, said that he had a bad feeling about this one.

'In situations like this, when the guy isn't talking, it means that either he's dead by his own hand, or he wants us to come in and get him. A classic suicide-by-cop scenario.'

The clock glowing in the Crown Vic's dash was just a few minutes shy of the ten o'clock deadline, and Summer had her own bad feeling. A couple of years ago she'd helped back up an FBI team when it had moved in to arrest a bank robber hiding out at his mother's house. Agents had smashed down the front door and poured inside, shooting the robber dead as he was getting up from the sofa where he'd been watching TV, and wounding the robber's mother and his girlfriend – the mother was in a wheelchair now, suing the FBI and the Portland Police Bureau for fifty million dollars. Summer, three other uniformed police and two detectives had been covering the backyard when they'd heard gunfire inside the house, saw the robber's partner burst out of the back door. They'd piled onto him and subdued

him, and then had nearly been shot by a bunch of trigger-happy
FBI agents hard on his heels. Now she was worried that the FBI
and the SWAT team would turn the siege into a circus, smash
their way into the mansion with guns blazing, kill Denise and
everyone else. And she was certain that if Dirk Merrit was still
alive he wouldn't be planning anything as mundane as suicide-
by-cop. He was famous for wanting to live for ever. He would
have a plan to get away, a back door. And the FBI, intent on
locking down the mansion, hadn't thought to check the rest of
the estate.

The gate in the low wall was wide open. The Crown Victoria
and the patrol car blasted through it, braking side by side in front
of the barn. A black recreation vehicle the size of a school bus
was parked to one side, and the barn's big square door was wide
open, showing lights inside.

Summer said, 'Someone has been here. The first time I saw
this place, the RV was parked inside the barn and the door was
padlocked.'

Buck Cole switched off the Crown Vic's headlights and took
out his gun. 'We'll take this nice and slow. Gary, call this in, ask
if someone can send up a K-9 unit. If someone is lurking, we've
a better chance of finding them with a dog.'

As they climbed out, Buck Cole called to the two Sheriff's
deputies in the patrol car, told them to turn off their goddamn
lights before someone shot them out.

Gary, holding the two-way radio to his ear, said, 'Wait up.
Shots have been heard inside the main tower.'

Buck Cole said, 'That's it, then. He might just as well open
the front door and invite in the SWAT team.'

Summer said, 'Has he picked up the phone?'

If Dirk Merrit was alive, if he was inside the mansion and he'd
just shot and killed one of his hostages, he wouldn't be able to
resist boasting about it.

Gary listened to the two-way and after a moment shook his
head. 'Mr Malone is asking for radio silence.'

'The SWAT team'll be going in any time now,' Buck Cole
said, studying the dark, empty house on the other side of the

yard for a moment, then turning back to the floodlit barn. 'The sooner we get this done, the sooner we can get back.'

Summer asked Gary if he was armed.

'A lab rat like me? Are you kidding?'

'Then stay close,' she said, and pulled her Glock from her purse and followed Buck Cole up the ramp into the barn. A red John Deere tractor with a grass-cutting rig to the right; a power-boat on a trailer and a couple of trail bikes to the left; steel equipment lockers and a workbench set against the wall at the far end, the bench backed by a pegboard holding saws and hack-saws, hammers, a set of chisels. Buck Cole told Summer there was nothing here, he was going to check the RV, and Gary went past them and squatted on his haunches to study a chainsaw that lay on the floor. Looking at Summer, saying, 'I think this was used on meat – see these shreds? And that looks like a bloodstain on the concrete.'

Summer's scalp prickled. 'You thought that someone had cut off Pat Metcalf's hand . . .'

'It'll be easy to prove it one way or the other by DNA, but it'll take time. Right now, I think we should be careful not to con-taminate the scene.'

Summer stopped on the way out to look at the tractor, broke open one of the clods of brown grass caught in the blades of the grass-cutting rig and saw that it was damp inside, then hurried to catch up with Gary.

Buck Cole climbed down from the RV, showing Summer and Gary the keys he'd taken from its ignition, telling them that if the sumbitch expected to make his escape he was in for a sur-prise. The two deputies came around the side of the house, guns drawn, shining their flashlights this way and that on the rough ground as they walked across the yard.

Gary said to them, 'I hope you didn't touch anything in there. This could be a crime scene.'

'You might want to check the vehicle parked at the back,' one of the deputies said.

It was a cherry-red Dodge Ramcharger.

The deputy said, 'Unless I'm mistaken, that's Jerry Hill's.'

Summer told Buck Cole, 'He's the half-brother of Charley Phelps. Charley Phelps—'

'Is the guy who was shot,' Buck Cole said. 'The one who was working for Dirk Merrit.'

'We don't know that yet,' the deputy said.

'I know that Phelps and Merrit definitely had a falling-out,' Buck Cole said, meeting the deputy's gaze. 'That's how Phelps happened to get shot in the head.'

Summer tried to cut through the sudden testosterone-fuelled enmity. 'I think we can agree that Detective Hill shouldn't be here. He's probably looking for Dirk Merrit, and he can only cause trouble.'

Buck Cole said, 'Merrit is dead.'

Summer said, 'Someone claiming to be a hostage *told* us that Merrit is dead, but we can't be sure that he was telling us the truth. For all we know, he could have been Merrit himself.'

Buck Cole studied the darkness beyond the house and barn. 'Maybe you should break radio silence, Delgatto. Call it in.'

'Wait,' one of the deputies said. 'Listen up a minute.'

Summer heard it – the crawly whine of a small airplane moving towards them from the south.

Buck Cole said, 'I bet it's some damn TV crew, violating the no-fly zone.'

They were all looking up at the sky, seeing only the moon's cold disc above the jagged line of the treetops beyond the barn.

The deputy said, 'If I didn't know better, I'd say it was Mr Merrit's ultralight.'

Summer remembered with a jolt that Denise had told her that Dirk Merrit had a pilot's licence and it was possible that he'd flown back from Los Angeles after killing the stewardess, Julia Taylor. And she remembered something else Denise had said, too, when they had been on their way to pay their first visit to the mansion. Dirk Merrit had had extensive plastic surgery to make himself took like one of the overlords from his computer game, everything but the wings. And he always made the same joke when asked about his lack of wings, said he had to use a plane like everyone else . . .

The deputy was saying, 'He has this tiny little airplane, what they call an ultralight. He was cited last year for buzzing traffic—'

'Use your radio,' Summer told Gary. 'Tell your boss that Dirk Merrit definitely isn't dead. Tell him he isn't in the mansion, he's in the air. And I think I know where he came from.'

47

The bottom of the narrow road that switchbacked down the side of the valley to the mansion's three towers was barricaded by sedans and SUVs. Detectives, Sheriff's deputies, and special agents wearing blue raid jackets stencilled with 'FBI' in large yellow letters crouched behind the vehicles, armed with shotguns and rifles, watching for movement in the floodlit towers and terraces. At the edge of the trees, to the left and right of the main tower, two SWAT sharpshooters sprawled behind Remington 700 Standard sniper rifles, scanning lighted windows through ITT day/night scopes. Another SWAT team member wore headphones plugged into what looked like a small satellite dish made of transparent plastic, a Gibson parabolic microphone that he aimed at different parts of the main tower, trying to pick up any conversations or other sounds inside.

The ten p.m. deadline passed. Nothing moved at the windows or anywhere around the main tower. Then, at precisely five minutes past ten, the man with the parabolic microphone heard three spaced gunshots from somewhere inside the main tower. The SWAT negotiator spent ten minutes on the bullhorn, his amplified voice booming into the night, asking the hostage-taker to please pick up one of the phones. At ten-fifteen, word passed that Malone had given the SWAT team the go-ahead to attempt to enter the tower. Everyone checked their weapons and got ready.

The SWAT tactical team leader, Sergeant Robbie Tyler, crouched with five of his men at the base of the tower. Tyler and his team were veterans of numerous dynamic entries, but this was by far the strangest building they had ever faced. While flying to the scene in the National Guard Chinook, Tyler had studied plans of the mansion and discussed them over the radio with Malone. They'd agreed that the best entry point was a service door under the walkway that connected it with the kitchen in the smaller tower directly behind it. That was where Tyler was now, three men hugging the wall to the left of the plain steel door and Tyler and two others hugging the wall to the right, all of them wearing respirator masks and radio earpieces, black coveralls under body armour reinforced with ceramic plates that could stop a rifle bullet, armed with Glock 40s and Heckler & Koch 9mm short-barrelled sub-machine guns. One man carried a break-open 37mm gas gun loaded with CS rounds; a second, Bill Stanley, hefted a cut-down, pistol-gripped Remington shotgun loaded with magnesium TKO breaching rounds. On Tyler's hand signal, Stanley stepped up to the door and blew out the lock with a single shot.

Tyler was the first through the door, into a bare lobby with an elevator on the left, a concrete stairwell winding up to the right, another door straight ahead. Stanley blew open that door too. Tyler threw in a flash-bang grenade, flattening himself beside Stanley as the grenade went off with a blinding flare and a tremendous concussion, then slammed through into a big, high-ceilinged room with adobe walls and a central fireplace, the stock of his sub-machine gun against his shoulder, pointing it in different directions, seeing over the sight no movement but the swirling haze of smoke from the grenade, seeing three bodies, two men and a woman, lying side by side by the fireplace.

Stanley smashed open a door on the far side of the room, and he and two other men dodged through. Thirty seconds later, Stanley reported over the radio that the foyer was clear, asked if they should proceed up the stairs to the next floor. Tyler told him to secure the stairs and stand by. He was standing over the bodies. The woman had been shot through the forehead with a small-calibre weapon, but there was no blood on the stone flags on which she lay; clearly she had been killed somewhere else. One of the dead men was African-American, the other was wearing a rent-a-cop uniform: both had been shot in the chest with short steel arrows, heart shots. A boombox stood beside the bodies, emitting a staticky hiss as a cassette tape turned behind a clear plastic window, connected by a long cable that snaked across the floor to an electronic timer plugged into a wall outlet. Tyler very much wanted to rewind and play the tape, but he knew that the boombox could be booby-trapped. He unstrapped his respirator and spoke into his throat mike, was telling Stanley to check the next floor but to stay vigilant, he was pretty sure that the shots they'd heard had been taped, this could be some kind of set-up, when the FBI chief, Malone, cut in, asking Tyler if he'd located the hostages.

'Three on the ground floor, all dead. We're still checking—'

'Listen up, sergeant. I have two pieces of information. First, a nine-eleven call claimed that Dirk Merrit is alive, he's booby-trapped the place, and he's heading toward it right now in a small aircraft. Second, a team at the southern edge of the estate just now reported hearing an aircraft pass overhead. I don't want to take any chances. I want your men out of there right now, quick as you can.'

Tyler counted his men through the steel door, followed them at a run around the base of the tower, hearing the buzz of an aircraft somewhere in the darkness overhead. They were halfway towards the line of vehicles that barricaded the road when the valley lit up with a flash of yellow light, and the muscular crack of high explosive shivered the air. Tyler spun around, saw a ball of black smoke rolling up the floodlit face of the dam.

For a moment, nothing else happened.

Then a rope of water spurted from the dam's white wedge, glistening in the floodlights, falling in a fanning gush that doubled and redoubled in strength as a fissure widened above it, blocks of concrete collapsing away on either side of a foaming flood with a tremendous roar that muffled the sound of a second set of explosions that blew rings of black smoke from three different levels in the main tower. Tyler and his men huddled together, crouching with their arms over their heads as debris smashed down all around and thick dust rolled over them, and the tower sagged to one side and came apart in an arc of rubble that rained down into the flood.

48

High above it all, freezing wind whipping past the Perspex windshield of the open cockpit, the steady note of the engine vibrating deep in his bones and the last movement of Mahler's Second playing at maximum volume on his iPod (he'd agonized for days over the appropriate soundtrack before realizing that Mahler's masterpiece, with its theme of apocalypse and resurrection, really was the only choice), Dirk Merrit heeled the ultralight around. Bringing it back over the moonlit lake towards the dam, flying low above the frothing churn of water flooding through the breach, skimming above the cloud of dust and smoke that filled the narrow valley edge to edge, floodlights shining through it, the tops of two towers sticking out of it, the main tower gone.

Dirk's sharp teeth were clamped in a shark's grin. He had an erection, his first in months. The great march of the dead thundered in his ears.

Everything had worked perfectly. He'd circled over his mansion, spying out the circus of law-enforcement vehicles along the road at the edge of the estate, the men laying siege to the mansion itself, before reaching for the cell phone at his hip. He'd gone to a great deal of trouble to work out where to emplace the explosives for maximum effect, wiring up two sets of charges and linking the detonators to two different cell phones. He'd speed-dialled the first as he completed his turn above the mansion, seeing the smoke of the explosion darken the glare of the floodlights, seeing water suddenly spout from the widening breach. Turning high above the valley and making the second call as he swooped back towards the dam, the tower tottering and collapsing just as he shot past with the daredevil élan of an ace fighter pilot, so close that if he'd been a second late he would have been engulfed by the swooning arc of rubble and dust, so close that the great rush of air displaced by the tower's fall shoved his little craft sideways – there'd been a sticky moment when he'd had to make a sharp turn to miss the trees along the top of the valley ridge and the ultralight had almost stalled.

And now he was coming back over his great work again, with the soprano and choir soaring towards their climax, it really was too perfect. *O Tod! Du Allbezwinger! Nun Bist du bezwungen! O death! You that overcome all things, now you are overcome!*

He had overcome death.

He *was* death.

With one hand on the stick, keeping the ultralight level, he pulled a Mason jar from the athletic bag under his seat, dropped it over the side into the milky swirls of smoke.

On trial runs over the lake, he'd discovered that unless you got the height exactly right grenades tended to explode before they reached the ground. He'd solved that by pulling the pins from the grenades and fitting them into quart-sized Mason jars; the jars kept the lever from popping out until they hit the ground and shattered.

He dumped half his jars, made a sharp circle in the freezing dark and came back towards the dam again, thinking that this was how the angel of death must feel. Dropping a Mason jar over the side and seeing from the corner of his eye flashes along the dark ridge where the gatehouse stood, men firing at him.

The ultralight shuddered as rounds punched a row of ragged holes in the starboard wing and thumped into the engine cowling right behind his head. The pedal that controlled the wing's pitch came loose under Dirk's right boot, the stick jumped in his grip, and the little aircraft wallowed. He put the nose down, gaining a little speed as he lost altitude, fighting to keep the ultralight level as he skimmed over the dam, the black lake. The engine was making a ragged noise now, losing power, and the temperature gauge was rising – a stray round must have hit the coolant line – but he was riding high on adrenalin and bloodlust and the triumphant finale of the *Resurrection Symphony.*

He could not fail now. He would escape, and change, and rise again renewed.

Nothing could stop him.

49

Leaving the two deputies at the house and barn in case Jerry Hill came back for his pickup, Buck Cole, Gary Delgatto and Summer Ziegler headed for the ridge-top meadow to the south of Dirk Merrit's estate. They were speeding up the steep track, the Crown Victoria wallowing over ruts pinched between tall dark trees, when Summer glimpsed from the corner of her eye a flash of red lightning in the black land spread behind and below them. A moment later, Gary's radio came alive with a crackling cacophony of voices. He held it to his ear, reported after a moment that the dam had been breached by an explosion, that one of the towers had collapsed.

Buck Cole said that he had to be fucking kidding.

Summer felt the valves of her body open. 'The hostages. What about the hostages? What about Denise?'

Gary briefly listened to his radio, shook his head. 'Everyone is shouting at everyone else.'

'Dirk Merrit likes his games,' Summer said. 'He drew us into a fake hostage situation, he blew up his mansion after the SWAT team went in. He must be circling overhead in that little plane of his . . .'

'If he's alive,' Buck Cole said.

'He's alive,' Summer said.

She was certain of it. And she was certain that right now he was flying circles above the carnage, savouring the proof that he was smarter than anyone else. The two phone calls, one from a hostage, the other from the hostage-taker, they had been part of his plan. There never had been any hostages. Denise was probably dead, and the kid, Daryl Weir, was dead too . . .

The Crown Vic reached the crest of the track and Buck Cole

drove straight out into the meadow, braking sharply beside a pickup truck and killing his headlights. Summer cracked the door and tumbled out into fresh cold air, her Glock in one hand, her flashlight in the other. The pickup's load-bed was empty; so was its cab. Its headlights had been shot out and all four tyres were flat.

Buck Cole reckoned that they were too late, the sumbitch had fled the scene.

Summer said, 'Maybe not. Merrit has to land somewhere. He just might come back.'

A long strip of close-cut grass stretched away beyond the pickup and the Crown Victoria, pale in the moonlight. Rough grass sloping down either side of it to tall dark trees. She had forgotten about it until she'd seen the tractor in the barn, the blades of its mowing rig clotted with damp grass. And then she'd seen the ultralight heading away from the direction of the ridge where Edie Collier's trail had ended, and realized that someone could have mown a strip along the crest of the ridge so that it could be used as a runway . . .

She jumped when Gary touched her shoulder. He pointed and said, 'What's that?'

It sat off to one side of the strip of grass about a hundred yards away, long and low and skeletal, hard to make out in the stark moonlight. Summer kept her Glock trained on it while Buck Cole told Gary to stay by the Crown Vic, and pulled a little .38 revolver from an ankle-strap holster and handed it to him.

'If anyone but me or Detective Ziegler comes at you, tell them to stop. "Stop or I'll shoot." Sing it out as loud as you can. If they don't stop, shoot them. There's no safety, you just point and pull the trigger. Okay?'

'Okay,' Gary said. He looked scared but determined.

Summer followed Buck Cole as he walked towards the shadowy shape, stopping when he stopped, just ten yards away.

Buck Cole said, 'Stay exactly where you are, motherfucker!' and switched on his flashlight, illuminating a long, low trailer and a body lying in rough grass a little way beyond it. Summer's heart contracted, but then she realized that it wasn't Denise, it was a man she didn't recognize. He lay on his back with his arms outflung, a bib of blood dark and wet on the front of his collar-less blue jacket.

Summer followed Buck Cole to the body. The FBI agent held the beam of his flashlight on the man's face for a moment – a cap of white hair, unseeing eyes, a gashed throat – then switched it off.

'Elias Silver,' Buck Cole said. 'A house guest of Dirk Merrit's. My guess is that he helped Merrit get the ultralight off the trailer, and then Merrit killed him.'

'It's possible. But who shot out the headlights and tyres on the pickup?'

'What do you mean?'

They were speaking in low voices, standing back to back in the dark, scanning the long moonlit meadow, the trees falling away on either side.

Summer said, 'I think Dirk Merrit wanted to kill as many people as he could in some grand, stupid gesture, and he wanted to watch it happen. He took off from here in his ultralight, but he couldn't have done it in the dark. He must have used the pickup's headlights to illuminate that strip of grass, and that means someone shot out the headlights after he took off. And shot out the tyres too, so he couldn't use it to get away when he came back.'

'You think Jerry Hill?'

'It's possible. He could have killed this guy as well.'

Buck Cole thought about it for a moment. Then he said, 'Do you hear that?'

The drone of an engine somewhere to the north, coming closer.

Summer ran towards the Crown Vic, tripping on a hump of grass and falling full length with a tremendous shock, springing up again and running on. Shouting breathlessly to Gary, telling him not to shoot.

'We need some lights. He's expecting lights – he can't land without them.'

She yanked open the door of the Crown Victoria and leaned inside, her heart knocking against her ribs as she fumbled for the stalk that controlled the headlights. Turning it two clicks, the headlights coming on, illuminating the strip of mown grass. A moment later, the ultralight fell out of the night, skimming the tops of the trees at the end of the narrow meadow, passing overhead in a sudden blast of noise and wind, dropping into the glare of the Crown Vic's headlights, thumping down and running neatly along the mown strip. Its engine roared in reverse for a moment, then cut out with a sharp bang.

As the fragile little aircraft slewed sideways and stopped, its prop whirring down into silence, Summer grabbed Gary's arm, told him to stay by the car. 'Just in case he has a friend hiding nearby.'

'Jesus.'

'You're doing just fine, for a lab rat,' Summer said, and ran down the meadow towards the ultralight, angling away from the headlights, her Glock extended. Buck Cole caught up with her, saying, 'This is an arrest. No instant justice.'

'Don't worry. I want to find out what happened to Denise.'

The ultralight was tipped up, nose down in tall grass and weeds. A shadow was unfolding from it, everything black and white in the moonlight.

Summer put a little pressure on the trigger of the Glock, disengaging the bar that acted as a safety, stepping to the left as Buck Cole stepped to the right, both of them aiming their guns and flashlights at Dirk Merrit. He stood quiet and still, the intersecting beams stark on the angles of his face. He was wearing a flying jacket with a big fleece collar. Squinting into the glare, he said in his engaging baritone, 'Detective Ziegler, is that you? How did you like my little show?'

Buck Cole, putting everything he had into it, said, 'PUT YOUR FUCKING HANDS ON YOUR HEAD! DO IT RIGHT NOW!'

Dirk Merrit flipped his right hand up against his shoulder, a careless, insolent gesture. 'I can't move my left arm. I believe it might be broken.' He didn't sound as if he was in pain. He was smiling at Summer, showing his sharp teeth. Saying, 'You really do have a little more sand than most, Detective Ziegler. I meant it, you know, when I said that it would be fun to hunt you. Did you find the boy?'

Buck Cole stepped towards him. Summer stood still, just ten feet away, watching his left hand over the foresight of her Glock.

'I want you to kneel down,' Buck Cole said. 'Nice and slow.'

Dirk Merrit ignored him, said to Summer, 'If you and your friend put down your guns, I'll give you Daryl Weir, and the man holding him prisoner.'

'If you mean Elias Silver,' Summer said, 'he's lying back there with his throat cut.'

Dirk Merrit stared at her, his bone-white face showing nothing.

Summer said, 'You've run out of options, Mr Merrit.'

Buck Cole said, 'Kneel down. Do it slowly.'

'Certainly,' Dirk Merrit said, but instead of kneeling he brought up his left hand, displaying the grenade in his palm. 'I've pulled out the pin. All that's stopping it from going off is my thumb on the spring mechanism. Lay down your guns, both of you.'

Summer said, 'It isn't going to happen.'

'Then we'll all die.'

'I don't think so,' Summer said, and took careful aim and shot him.

He went straight down, dropping the grenade and clutching at his right thigh.

Summer ducked, half turned. The grenade didn't go off.

Buck Cole approached Dirk Merrit cautiously. The man was lying on the ground with his hand around his leg. Looking at Summer, his lips drawn back from his sharp teeth in a sharp grimace, saying in astonishment, 'You shot me.'

'You bet I did,' Summer said, and unhooked her cuffs from her belt.

Buck Cole shone his flashlight on the grenade, nested in the grass like a black egg. 'The pin's still in place. How did you know he was bluffing?'

'He isn't the suicide-by-cop type. He thinks he's going to live for ever.'

She and Buck Cole got Dirk Merrit to sit up, the man compliant now, in a lot of pain. There was a sweet moment of triumph when she put the handcuffs on him, ratcheting them tight. Buck Cole said that he'd fetch the car, and at the same moment Summer saw Gary coming towards them, silhouetted in the glow of the Crown Vic's headlights, walking stiff-legged with his hands clasped at the back of his neck and one wrist held by the man behind him.

It was Jerry Hill. The muzzle of his Sig-Sauer .38 was jammed behind Gary's ear. Summer swung her Glock and flashlight towards him, saw from the corner of her eye Buck Cole make the same move.

Jerry Hill's face was shotgunned with sweat and lit by a fierce wild expression. 'Drop your fucking guns,' he said. 'Do it now or I swear I'll do him.'

Summer remembered something she'd said to her mother about calling Jerry Hill out, like in the Wild West. His Sig-Sauer against her Glock. 'Jerry, wait up a moment and take a breath. Stay calm and listen to me. You know we're not going to give up our guns, and you know we're not going to let you do anything—'

Gary cried out when Jerry Hill screwed the muzzle of his pistol into the soft flesh behind his ear. Buck Cole took a step to the right, and Summer took a step to the left, saying, 'If you shoot him, Jerry, you know we'll shoot you. What good will that do?'

'He's a fucking monster. He deserves to die.'

'Help us bring him to justice, Jerry.'

'He deserves to die.'

'He deserves to answer for everything he's done. Help us bring him in.'

For a moment, she and Jerry Hill locked gazes, and she believed that she might be able to talk him down. Then, behind her, Dirk Merrit said, 'Take your shot, Detective Ziegler,' and she saw Jerry Hill's gaze harden. She started to tell him not to do it, but he was too quick, aiming the Sig-Sauer past Gary's face and firing, two quick shots that hit Dirk Merrit in the chest and knocked him onto his back.

Summer told Jerry Hill to drop his gun. He stared straight through her, then said, 'Fuck it,' and shoved Gary away. Gary falling to his knees as Jerry Hill jammed the muzzle of his gun into his own mouth. The shot lit up his face like a Halloween lantern.

50

On the phone to her mother, Summer said, 'Even with two guns aimed at him, Merrit tried to control the situation. He put everything he had into trying to work his way out of an impossible corner.'

Her mother's voice said, 'You sound as if you admire him.'

'If it had been anyone else,' Summer said, 'I might think that it was something like bravery. But he really was a monster. Monstrously vain, monstrously arrogant, monstrously cruel. He believed that he was always in control, that he was smarter than everyone else. He had to have the last word, and that's what killed him.'

'Perhaps he wanted it to happen. Perhaps he told you to shoot Detective Hill because he knew that it would goad Hill into shooting him.'

'I don't think it was suicide-by-cop. I think he told me to shoot Jerry Hill because that's what he did, ordered people around.'

Summer was sitting at a desk in a corner of the detectives' office on the third floor of the Justice Building in Cedar Falls. It was a little after midnight. Deputies, state troopers, detectives and FBI agents were coming and going, holding hasty conferences, sitting at desks and working phones and computers, leafing through stacks of files and photographs. A couple of half-pints of Scotch were being passed around behind the backs of senior officers. One desk was littered with the remains of pizzas and cartons of Chinese take-out. There was a buzzy atmosphere of relief and celebration.

Dirk Merrit's trap had failed to claim any victims. Two men had been hurt when the dam had burst and the tower had collapsed – one struck by flying debris, the other sustaining a broken wrist in the scramble to get clear – but no one had been killed. The siege, if that was what it had been, was over. The bad guys were dead or in custody. Elias Silver had been murdered by an unknown assailant. Jerry Hill had taken his own life after shooting Dirk Merrit, and Dirk Merrit had died of his wounds while being helicoptered to the hospital, just like Edie Collier.

Summer's mother said, 'CNN.com has a piece by a forensic psychologist. He says that your Mr Merrit exhibited symptoms of narcissistic personality disorder. Grandiosity and a need for admiration, preoccupation with fantasies of unlimited power and success. And, in extreme cases, the willingness to take violent action to protect a fantasy. Does any of that sound familiar?'

'He was living in a fantasy world, all right. If he hadn't been shot dead he'd probably be lawyered up right now, trying to put the blame on Walt Disney and enjoying every minute.'

'The psychologist said that people with this disorder also suffer from what he called heightened self-love. According to him, Dirk Merrit altered himself to match his imaginary ideal, and his computer game was a projection of his personal fantasies.'

Summer supposed that there would be a lot more of this kind of thing until the media had chewed the whole affair to pulp and moved on to something else. She said, 'The feds want *Trans* shut down, but I don't think they have a chance. The company that owns it has already put out a statement claiming it has nothing to do with Dirk Merrit.'

There was a brief pause. Her mother said, 'Did I say that the CNN report mentioned your name?'

'It was just about the first thing you said.'

'My daughter, the hero.'

'I don't feel especially heroic.'

Summer kept seeing the awful moment when Jerry Hill had turned his gun on himself, when she'd known what he was about to do and hadn't been able to do anything to stop him. And she knew now that Denise Childers really was dead, too. The leader of the SWAT tactical team had seen her body in the trophy room of Dirk Merrit's mansion, laid out between the bodies of Louis Frazier, the mansion's cook, and Charles Paulson, one of the security guards. So far, none of the bodies had been recovered from what was left of the main tower. Daryl Weir was still missing. So was Dirk Merrit's driver, Carl Kelley.

Her mother was saying, 'When are you coming home?'

'Some time tomorrow. I'll give you a call when I know for sure.'

Summer had already gone over everything with Section Chief Harry Malone, explaining that she had shot Dirk Merrit once in the thigh and Jerry Hill had shot the man twice before shooting himself. Malone had been satisfied with her story, but Sheriff Worden, out of spite, had insisted that she surrender her Glock so that his fatal-shooting investigation could establish the precise sequence of the events that had led to the deaths of Dirk Merrit and Jerry Hill. Now, after saying goodnight to her mother, she finished writing up a Use Of Force report and waited her turn to present it to Harry Malone. She was damned if she was going to hand it to anyone else.

'We're not giving the press anything until we know everything,' Malone told her when she finally got a few minutes with him.

He was sitting behind Sheriff Worden's desk, shirt cuffs folded back above his elbows, his suit jacket draped across the back of his chair. Sheriff Worden was closeted with the mayor, working up a strategy to cope with the media. A big TV set in the corner of the office was tuned to Fox News, the sound muted. A reporter was making a stand-up report in front of the jam of police and emergency vehicles outside the gates of Dirk Merrit's estate. Malone pointed at the TV with his chin and told Summer, 'Your name came up more than once. They'll want to talk to you.'

'I don't intend to talk to them, sir.'

'That won't be easy. They'll chase you for as long as this stays in the news. They'll phone you at work, at home, they'll doorstep you . . . You should consult with your department's press office as soon as you get back to Portland. They can help you work up a statement. You'll get a visit from the US Attorney's office, too: they'll want to go over your deposition. But don't worry about that now. How are you feeling?'

'Numb, mostly.'

Summer felt that she had screwed the pooch. She should have realized that Denise had gone after Dirk Merrit on her own. She should have stopped Jerry Hill before he'd shot Dirk Merrit. She believed that she didn't deserve any sympathy.

The TV cut from aerial footage of the breached dam, flood-water churning past batteries of lights set up by rescue and recovery workers, to a news anchor behind a desk.

'He almost had us,' Malone said. 'If it hadn't been for that nine-eleven call and your quick ID of the ultralight, people would have died.'

'There's no sign of Carl Kelley or Daryl Weir?'

Malone's working hypothesis was that Carl Kelley had fallen out with Dirk Merrit, killed Elias Silver and made the phone call that had sabotaged Dirk Merrit's plan, and had then escaped the scene with Daryl Weir as a hostage.

'We're looking everywhere,' he said. 'The fact he took a hostage means that he'll be easier to spot. And it'll slow him down.'

Summer said, 'If there's anything I can do to help, I'll be happy to stick around.'

'You've done more than enough for us. Get some rest, detective.' As Summer walked past two agents waiting outside the office, Malone came to the door and called after her. 'Dirk Merrit won't ever be able to kill anyone else. Try to feel good about that.'

A deputy drove Summer to the motel where the FBI had block-booked rooms for the night. As she was signing the register, another cruiser drew up outside the office and Gary Delgatto got out.

Gary had been to the hospital, getting treatment for powder burns to his cheek from the two shots that had fatally wounded Dirk Merrit. He was still deaf in his right ear, and he was still upset and angry. Like Summer, he blamed himself for what had happened: for having been taken hostage by Jerry Hill, for Denise Childers's death.

He said, 'Denise was right all along.'

'Yes, she was.'

'She suspected Dirk Merrit from the first. She kept at him when everyone else believed that Joseph Kronenwetter had kidnapped Edie Collier. She kept at him after she was suspended . . . I can't help thinking that if I'd been able to come up with evidence proving that Phelps killed Kronenwetter, she wouldn't have needed to follow Phelps to that meeting with Merrit. You know? I should have taken DNA samples from everyone in that lock-up, run them against the DNA under Kronenwetter's fingernails,' Gary said, looking through Summer, looking at something that wasn't there.

'Who would have authorized it?' Summer said. 'And how long would it have taken to process all those samples?'

'Well, I should have done *something*,' Gary said, looking stubborn and miserable.

'I've been thinking about it too. This is going to sound harsh, but in the end it was Denise's idea, no one else's, to go after Charley Phelps on her own.'

'That's one way of looking at it.'

Summer made a decision, said, 'Come with me.'

Gary focused on her.

Summer said, 'The gas station across the road sells booze, and it's still open. I think I should buy you a drink.'

They sat on the end of the bed in Summer's room, drinking Jack Daniel's and Coke from plastic cups, the TV tuned to CNN, sound turned down to a whisper. They talked about Dirk Merrit's grandiose plan, about what might have happened to Daryl Weir and Carl Kelley. Gary kept developing a thousand-yard stare and lapsing into silence; Summer was certain that he was playing over and over again in his mind different moments from the confrontation in the meadow. But he seemed to be holding up, more or less. He looked attractively dishevelled in the flicker of TV light, a pad of gauze taped over his right cheek like a duelling scar, and his hand was steady when he fixed fresh drinks.

Raising his plastic cup, saying with a weak smile, 'At least we stopped Merrit.'

'We did.'

They drank Jack and Coke, watched TV. Gary said, 'I'm not seeing anything I didn't see in hospital. That was weird. All these cops kept coming up to me, wanting to shake my hand . . .'

'You did all right, for a lab rat.'

'Maybe I should go,' he said.

They both stood at the same moment, they were standing thigh to thigh, they were kissing, and then they were on the bed, trying to get each other out of their clothes, only half succeeding before things got really serious.

'Wait up,' Gary said, and rolled over and snagged his leather jacket from the floor, found his wallet and extracted a condom.

Summer giggled, because he looked so boyishly solemn, and said, her mouth suddenly dry with desire, 'C'mere.'

Later, lying in each other's arms between the sheets, she said, 'I should explain that I've never before put out on a first date.'

'Is this a date?'

'It's as close as we've come.'

They made love again, slower now, taking their time, getting used to each other. Summer began to feel a little detached, as if she was watching herself, judging herself. Like in that movie, *Annie Hall*, where a ghostly Diane Keaton gets up from the bed where she's making out with Woody Allen . . .

Gary, moving gently on her, said in her ear, 'Are you okay?' and she kissed him and moved with him, starting to get into it, feeling it coming, almost there but not quite, almost there, almost, almost . . . *There*.

Afterwards, Summer used the bathroom. When she came back, Gary held up the covers so she could slip in, slip into his arms.

He said, 'You look sad.'

'I'm tired, is what it is.'

One of his hands was cradling her head, fingers in her hair, the other was stroking her back. It felt comforting, holding this man skin to skin, but strange, too. As if she'd been on a long journey and had arrived in a place she didn't know. She was tired and sad, knowing this couldn't go anywhere, knowing that she was going to have to talk to him in the morning.

Gary said, 'You think we can sleep?'

She said, 'I think we should give it a try.'

Summer woke with early-morning light defining the edges of the drapes. Gary's side of the bed was empty. The shower was running in the bathroom. The radio clock by the bed told her it was seven-twenty. She lay back, closed her eyes and tried to think things through. When Gary came out of the bathroom in his boxers, his hair wet and a towel around his shoulders, he said, 'This isn't what you think.'

'So you aren't running out on me?'

Trying to keep it light seemed like a good idea.

Gary said, 'Remember Julia Taylor?'

'The airline stewardess.'

'Her body was left in the San Gabriel mountains, close to a Forest Rangers' hut.' Gary sat down on the end of the bed to pull on his socks. 'Yesterday afternoon, Rangers turned up a body at the bottom of a cliff nearby. The news only just reached Mr Malone. He wants me to go to LA and assist with the autopsy.'

'Do they have an ID on this body?'

'Erik Grow. White male, twenty-six, and you'll love this,' Gary said, standing up, pulling up his pants. 'Not only does he have a conviction for misuse of computer equipment – he was fired from UCLA a couple of years ago because he'd been using their computers to run a porn site – but he also worked for Powered By Lightning, the company that runs *Trans*.'

Summer sat up, wound the sheet around herself. 'Julia Taylor and Gary Yunis were random victims, they were supposed to draw the FBI's attention away from Dirk Merrit. But Erik Grow must have had a connection with Dirk Merrit, Merrit wanted him out of the way . . .'

'So he sent Carl Kelley to kill him. And Kelley killed Greg Yunis and Julia Taylor along the way. We're pretty sure that Kelley was the guy in the elevator with Yunis. One of the security guards who worked at Merrit's estate identified him from the security-camera stills. We also think he's the guy who drove Julia Taylor's car out of LAX.'

'I don't suppose there's any news of him.'

'Not yet.' Gary finished buttoning his shirt, reached for his leather jacket.

'Maybe there's a reason why he took an ace game-player with him. After all, Dirk Merrit went to a lot of trouble to get hold of the poor kid.'

'Dirk Merrit was crazy.'

'Is that an official forensic finding?'

'It's based on eyewitness evidence of his behaviour.' Gary hesitated, then said, 'I really have to run. The car's waiting right outside.'

Summer said, 'It can wait a couple of minutes longer.'

'Uh-oh.' Gary's smile made him look like an awkward teenager.

Summer felt awkward too, but she also wanted to deal with what had happened sooner rather than later. She said, 'I don't regret last night, not for a moment.'

'I'm pleased to hear it.'

'The first time I saw you, I thought you were pretty cool.'

'For a lab rat.'

He wasn't making it easy, but she pressed on, holding his gaze. 'I still think you're cool. I want you to understand that I don't go to bed with just anyone. But I also think that last night wasn't just about you and me. Part of it, a pretty big part, was down to what happened. We'd come through something pretty intense. We were proving to ourselves that we were still alive.'

Gary said, 'I'm going to say something that might make you mad. But I want to say it anyway. Why I asked you out yesterday, I guess it was obvious that it wasn't just to talk about the case. I wanted to see you again. In other circumstances . . .'

She thought she knew what he was trying to say, and gave him an out. 'If we hadn't been thrown together.'

'And also – this is the part that might make you angry – if I wasn't seeing someone back in D.C.'

'I kind of guessed you might be. A cute guy like you.'

Summer did feel a little angry, but what she mostly felt was relief.

'If you're wondering why I carry condoms, it isn't that I'm on the prowl when I work in the field. She's not on the pill—'

'That's already too much information.'

'I'm sorry. I have this bad habit of trying to explain everything.'

'Come here,' Summer said.

When Gary leaned over the bed, there was an awkward moment, a slight hesitation, before they kissed. He hadn't shaved; his bristles scratched her cheek.

She said, 'Let me know what you find out in LA.'

'You bet.' He paused, then said, 'What are you going to do now?'

'I'm officially absent without leave. I have to go back to Portland and face the music. I guess it's down to your people to find Carl Kelley and Daryl Weir.'

51

Daryl Weir was in *Trans*, leaning into the screen of the laptop, working a controller with an annoyingly sticky left joystick, concentrating on guiding Seeker8 through tangles of writhing blood-red creepers but never quite unable to forget the room at his back, the dead man sprawled in a pool of blood in the doorway and the crazy man sat in an armchair, watching the TV news and eating a TV dinner, shovelling food into his mouth with his fingers, making all kinds of disgusting noises.

They'd arrived here early in the morning, while it was still dark. Daryl, lying dazed and scared in the wayback of the Mercedes SUV like a child in an adult-sized coffin, came all the way awake when the vehicle stopped and its engine cut off. A door opened and closed, and then there was a long silence before at last the rear door lifted up and Carl Kelley leaned in, smiling his death's-head smile, telling Daryl to get out.

The SUV was parked in an alley squeezed between the backs of two- and three-storey buildings. Carl Kelley shoved Daryl towards the building on the corner, through a steel door, up a narrow flight of unpainted wooden stairs, through a bead curtain into a big old-fashioned kitchen. Where a man lay face down in the arched doorway between the kitchen and the front room, a hole torn ragged and red in the back of his white singlet, his face turned sideways in a glossy puddle of blood creeping across dirty yellow linoleum.

Carl Kelley clamped a hand above Daryl's elbow and steered him around the body into the front room, forced him to sit down on a worn leather couch, and sat across from him in an armchair. This grim, deadly little man wearing clothes he'd taken from a suitcase he'd found in the back of the SUV, black leather shoes whose sides he'd slit to make them fit, black pants, a yellow collarless jacket that hung open and showed the bandage wrapped around his bare chest. Telling Daryl that everything was going to be hunky-dory. Saying, 'Want to know why we're here?'

Daryl shook his head, deciding that he'd be safer if he acted dumb.

'My friend there – you can look at him if you want, he won't mind – he's got all kinds of computers downstairs, all of them set up to play the game you're so good at. I thought, what should I do if I want this kid to show me what he's got? I could buy a computer, except I wouldn't know where to start. And I can't walk you into a shop and have you choose one . . . Then I remembered this guy.' He paused, then said, 'Cat got your tongue, huh? Do you find me scary?'

'A little.'

'You're trembling all over. Take a breath, try to calm down. I'm not going to hurt you. I *need* you. You and me, we're partners now. You understand?'

Daryl didn't, but he jerked his head up and down.

'I found this place a couple of weeks ago, when I was looking for your old pal William Gundersen. He also called himself Billy Newman, but I think you knew him as Ratking. Ratking, Seeker8 . . . Jesus. You really think those are cool names?'

Daryl shrugged.

'You would have been killed just like him if I hadn't rescued you,' Carl Kelley said. 'Mr Merrit would have taken you out to the desert and hunted you down and killed you. He would have cut out your heart and drunk your blood and left the rest for the buzzards. You owe me your life, and all I'm asking in return is you finish what you started. There's a bunch of computers downstairs, loaded up and ready to go, but it's our lucky day, I don't think we need to go downstairs after all. Look there, on the table. That's a nice-looking laptop, don't you think? It has one of those joystick things and a connection to the phone line . . . Start it up for me. Check it out.'

It was a nice new Toshiba with a titanium shell and a thirty-two-inch screen. After Daryl had fired it up, Carl Kelley leaned over his shoulder and studied the screen, which was tiled edge to edge with icons for about a hundred programs. Daryl flinched when the man pointed to the familiar cat's-eye-in-a-black-triangle, the icon for *Trans*.

'I reckon we're in business,' Carl Kelley said. 'But before you begin, you better tell me about this treasure.'

'I don't—'

'Don't play dumb. I know you know what I'm talking about. The treasure. The stuff Mr Merrit didn't want you to find. He went to a lot of trouble to get hold of you, so it has to be valuable. Tell me about it, and don't fucking lie, because I'll know.'

'I don't know what it is, exactly,' Daryl said, cold sweat starting all over his body.

'Bullshit.'

'Really, I don't. Some people think it's an evolution gun, it can turn a slave into an overlord with one shot? Or an overlord into a slave. Or it's something that makes you invisible. Or it's a hyperlink that allows you to jump from one place to another—'

'You went to all this trouble, but you don't know what it is?'

'It's something valuable,' Daryl said. 'It has to be, because it's so hard to get to. But no one knows exactly what it is.'

There was a long, terrible moment of silence. Then the man said, 'Mr Merrit knows what it is. And he definitely thinks it's valuable, because he doesn't want anyone to get hold of it. But that's what you're going to do for me. You're going to get hold of it, and then you're going to sell it. People who play this game will pay good money for it, right?'

Daryl nodded.

'Fuck it, the motherfucker changed the password on the subscription scam, so it's either this or rob a bank. And I need to rest up, too. So let's do it. Go online, log in, get moving.'

Daryl entered his name and password, and in less than a minute was under the virtual bridge that crossed the virtual Hollywood Freeway, looking over the shoulder of Seeker8 at the computer disk of the save point revolving in the dim air.

Carl Kelley, leaning close, his breath hot on Daryl's ear, tapped the screen of the laptop. 'How long will it take?'

'I don't know. Really. I have to walk about a mile, but the closer you get, the harder it becomes.'

'An hour? Two hours?'

'Maybe longer. It depends on what tries to stop me.'

'A day?'

'Maybe.'

'Yeah, but you don't have a day. You have until twelve o'clock. Noon.'

Daryl tried to swallow the taste of metal in his mouth. 'What happens when I get there?'

'If you get me what I want, I'll walk away. I'll have to leave you tied up, but I'll do it so you can get free without too much trouble. Then you can call the police, you can do what you want. How does that sound?'

'Fine, I guess.'

Daryl didn't believe the man for a second. He knew that Carl Kelley was planning to kill him whether he reached the treasure or not, but he also knew that he'd be killed if he didn't do as he was told. At least, while he was trying to get there, while he was in the game, he could buy some time . . .

At first it was hard to concentrate because Carl Kelley sat close behind him, watching as Seeker8 jogged through the ruins of Western Avenue. The man getting up whenever a buzzer sounded in the shop downstairs, peeking around one of the tan blinds pulled down over the windows, waiting until the buzzer stopped, settling back in the armchair in front of the TV to watch Fox News, where the story about Dirk Merrit's death and the destruction of his mansion was on heavy rotation. Daryl could more or less tune out the TV, but because he couldn't tune out Carl Kelley's restless, dangerous presence or the creepy knowledge that a man lay dead in the same room, he couldn't immerse himself completely in the game. Seeker8 felt like a clumsy puppet, and Daryl's reactions to the bloodbats and rabid coyotes, the mechanized zombies and all the other menaces that lurched at him were as panicky and frenzied as any tyro's. So far he'd managed to fight off everything, but each encounter left him sweating and more tightly wound – a single mistake, one little slip, would mean starting over from the save point. If Carl Kelley didn't kill him first, that was.

52

Summer flew back to Portland in the little Cessna, touched down at the airport just after nine a.m. Once she'd settled into the back of a taxi, she checked the calls that had stacked up on her cell-phone service while she'd been in the air. Five journalists had ferreted out her number and left messages. There were also messages from the Police Bureau press office and the office of the Chief of Police. There was a message from Ryland Nelsen, telling her to report straight to the Chief's office when she came in, reminding her that the Employee Assistance Program gave her free use of a counselling service if she needed it. And there were two messages from her mother. She called back, got her mother's answering service, and told it that she was all right, she would be home as soon as she could and was planning to sleep for about a week.

Her cell rang several times as the taxi sped along the freeway into the city. The Chief's office. Someone who worked in the newsroom of KOIN, the CBS affiliate. The reporter who covered the Portland crime beat for the *Oregonian*. She listened to the messages but didn't reply – for all they knew, she was still in the air, out of contact. And then, as the taxi was crossing the river on Morrison Bridge, Gary Delgatto called.

Summer answered, said, 'Tell me you found Carl Kelley.'

'Hey, I'm fine, thanks for asking. On my way to Parker Center, the LAPD headquarters. How about you?'

'I'm a little ragged, but I'm holding in there,' Summer said, knowing that wasn't what he meant. 'I'm back in Portland, about to find out what my bosses plan to do with me. It would really help if I could tell them that everything was wrapped up.'

'Right. Well, I don't know if we're any closer to Carl Kelley, but it looks like he definitely had something to do with that body the Rangers found yesterday.'

'Erik Grow.'

'The LAPD located his apartment. Their crime-scene people lifted several good prints that matched prints one of our guys took from Carl Kelley's room back in Merrit's mansion. Also, one of Erik Grow's neighbours says that a man fitting Carl Kelley's description visited him Sunday, around about Grow's estimated time of death. The neighbour remembers Kelley because the man gave her a look she didn't like at all. She said, I quote, "He had evil intent." It puts Kelley in Los Angeles on the day the stewardess was murdered, and it's just about possible he could have driven there from Reno after murdering Greg Yunis. The timing is tight, but it's possible. The apartment is being watched in case Kelley turns up.'

'Meanwhile he's in the wind. With Daryl Weir.'

Gary said, 'Erik Grow got a job in the accounts department of Powered By Lightning just before Dirk Merrit sold his controlling interest in *Trans*. Mr Malone thinks that he was Merrit's inside man. He had access to the details of people who subscribed to the game, their names and addresses and payment details – it could explain how Dirk Merrit was able to locate Daryl Weir.'

'Right.'

But Billy Gundersen hadn't had a street address; he and Edie Collier had been living in his van. Summer had the feeling that she was missing something in plain sight, something she had missed all along. She knew it was right in front of her, but she couldn't see it . . .

Gary said, 'Also, Erik Grow was into credit-card fraud. The LAPD found a batch of cloned cards in his apartment.'

'Someone used a cloned credit card to buy Daryl Weir's airline ticket.'

'Exactly. We're trying to make a solid connection right now.'

The taxi had pulled up outside the Justice Building. Summer told the driver to wait, she had to finish this call, and told Gary, 'It keeps coming back to the game. Dirk Merrit told me about this treasure someone was trying to reach, he hinted it might have had something to do with Billy Gundersen . . .' She remembered that both Billy Gundersen and Daryl Weir had made money by selling items they had won in *Trans*, remembered that Billy Gundersen had been maimed by players he'd cheated out of some virtual artefact, and said, 'Suppose this treasure is something really valuable. Billy Gundersen was trying to reach it and he was killed. And Daryl Weir was Billy Gundersen's partner, he was trying to reach it too . . .'

'You think this is why Carl Kelley kidnapped Daryl Weir?'

'If this is about something hidden in the game, something that Carl Kelley wants to get hold of, it's possible that Daryl Weir could be playing right now. That can't be difficult to check, can it? Powered By Lightning must have a way of monitoring who's online, playing *Trans*. His character is called Seeker8.'

'I'll see if anyone has thought of that. If he is online, do you think Powered By Lightning could give us his location?'

'That would be too easy, wouldn't it?' Summer remembered something that the kid from Okay Soucek's sweatshop had told her. 'Players in the game can talk to each other. Ask the people at Powered By Lightning if there's a way of getting in touch with him.'

Gary promised that he'd do it at once, said that he'd call her back as soon as he knew anything. Summer paid the taxi driver and, standing outside the entrance to the First Precinct, called her mother again. She wanted to talk to someone who knew about online games, was hoping that her mother would put her in touch with her research student, but her mother still wasn't picking up, she must be in a meeting, or giving a lecture or a seminar . . .

There was someone else who might help her, Summer thought. When she'd interviewed him before, she'd been certain that he had been hiding something. Now she wanted to ask him if he happened to have any idea about how Dirk Merrit might have found Billy Gundersen.

53

Daryl hunched over the laptop in a funk of misery and fear, his back aching, his hands cramped around the controller, jerking Seeker8 left and right as the avatar picked his way through the jungle knitted across the slopes of Griffith Park. Creepers snatched at his feet, his arms. Cacti spat volleys of poisoned needles. Bats with razor-edged wings dive-bombed him.

Carl Kelley stepped over the body as he went into the kitchen, opening the refrigerator, saying loudly, 'You want anything to drink, kid? There's milk, orange juice, peach juice, grape juice . . . Christ, sour-cherry juice. The man was looking after himself, probably believed he could live for ever if he drank enough of this stuff. Or how about a Coke, to keep your blood sugar up?'

Daryl said Coke would be good, just to get him to shut up.

Carl Kelley set the unopened can beside the laptop, leaned at Daryl's shoulder, breathing on his neck. He smelled of goatish sweat. 'What is this crap?'

'I'm getting close now,' Daryl said.

'You better be. Tell me the very second you get there.'

The man settled back in the armchair in front of the TV, and the buzzer sounded downstairs.

'Fucking kids,' Carl Kelley said.

The buzzer sounded again, a long ring like a bee trapped in a bottle, ringing on and on, suddenly stopping. Carl Kelley grunted, flicking through TV channels, searching for more news about Dirk Merrit, and then someone started to bang on the back door. The man swore, got up and went into the kitchen, stepping over the body. On the screen of the laptop, blood-red creepers snapped at Seeker8 with thorny teeth. Daryl lopped off their tips with a single sweep of his sword and glanced up, saw Carl Kelley framed beyond the archway, raised up on tiptoe as he looked through the window above the sink, peering down at something in the alley. Watching, watching, then coming back into the living room, moving quickly, twitching the edge of one of the shades, peeking out. After a long minute, he left the window and shrugged on the yellow jacket, tugging it down to cover the gun stuck in the waist of his pants.

'I won't be long,' he said. 'Don't even think of doing anything else but getting your man to where he needs to be.'

The door of Okay Soucek's storefront sweatshop was locked, the lights were out behind the whitewashed window, and no one came to the door when Summer rang the bell. She cupped her hands against the window and peered through a clear spot. Shadows, stillness. She rang the bell again, leaning on it for a full minute, then went around to the alley at the back, squeezed past a black Mercedes SUV and found that the steel fire door was locked too.

She used her best side-of-the-fist police knock on the door, rattling it, raising echoes up and down the alley. Nothing happened. She had a hinky feeling that someone might have been standing at the window above her, but it was blank and empty when she leaned back against the SUV to check.

The black paint on the side of the SUV was scratched. Long, thin, parallel lines, as if someone had driven it through a hedge . . .

Something ticked in Summer's head, like a card turning over. When Denise had driven her to Dirk Merrit's mansion, they'd parked behind a Mercedes SUV, a black one. Summer walked all the way around the SUV now, taking her time, scoping it out from stem to stern. She found what looked like bullet holes punched into the front quarter-panel, spotted something caught in the rear fender. The tip of a pine twig, the torn end still sticky with sap.

She felt a jolt of excitement, but she also felt exposed. Blank windows staring down at her, who knew what behind them.

She groped in her purse for her Glock, remembered that it was still with the forensic technicians at Cedar Falls. She jotted down the licence tag of the SUV in her notebook, then walked towards the mouth of the alley, taking out her cell phone.

It rang before she could switch it on. It was Gary. 'You were right. He's online. He's in the game.'

Summer walked around the corner of the building, heading for her Accura. 'Are you sure it's Daryl Weir?'

'Well, it's someone using his password.'

'Can you send him a message?'

'Apparently not. Players can only talk to each other when they're face to face inside the game.'

'Jesus. Can you get hold of a list of Dirk Merrit's vehicles? I want you to check a licence tag.'

'What's up?'

Summer gave him the SUV's tag, asked him call her back. She unlocked her car, started to punch in the number for the desk of the Northeast Precinct, and a man in a collarless yellow jacket came around the corner and looked straight at her.

As soon as he heard the steel door slam shut downstairs, Daryl pushed away from the laptop and stood up. His first thought was childish. Find a place to hide – under a bed, inside a closet – and stay there. His second: use the phone and call nine-eleven – but the phone was dead, its cable ripped out of the wall socket. His third: find a weapon, something that he could use against Carl Kelley.

He edged around the dead man, trying not to look at him, trying not to step in the puddle of blood, yanked open drawers one after the other, found a clutch of kitchen knives and took the biggest.

On the screen of the laptop, vines were coiling around Seeker8's arms and legs, his chest, lifting him up and strangling him, his health indicator sliding down towards zero.

Daryl went to the window and saw an ordinary city street, saw a woman standing beside a car parked in front of the building, saw Carl Kelley walking towards her, pulling his gun from the waistband of his pants.

The man was short and wiry, wearing unlaced shoes with the sides slit, pants with rolled cuffs, and a yellow jacket half buttoned up, clean white bandages peeking from underneath it. There were bandages around his wrists, too. At first glance he could have been a walk-on from Portland's extensive cast of street people, but his manner and gaze were too purposeful. When Summer pulled open the door of her car, putting it between herself and the man, he said, 'Don't even think of getting in that car, sweetheart.'

His voice was flat and calm, his accent from somewhere in London, where Summer had worked as an au pair years ago. A scruffy English guy: he had to be Carl Kelley, standing three or four yards away and aiming a pistol at her, traffic going past them as if nothing was out of the ordinary.

Summer looked past the pistol at Carl Kelley's face. His eyes were hard and unblinking and his jaw was clenched tight. A muscle jumped and jumped in his unshaven cheek. He was wired on something. He must have driven through the night to get here, had been staying awake to keep on top of Daryl Weir as he moved through *Trans* . . .

She said, 'I'm not going to give you any trouble.'

She was standing behind the open door of her car. Her right hand was inside her purse and her purse was wedged between her hip and the door, where she hoped he couldn't see it.

'You're police. No, don't waste time denying it, just raise your hands so I can see them and move away from the car.'

Summer said, 'We can work this out. We can talk about – whatever it is you want to talk about.'

Carl Kelley stepped closer. The black hole in the end of the pistol swallowed her attention for a moment and she flinched when a car sounded its horn, going past. Perhaps the driver had seen the pistol. Carl Kelley flinched too, the pistol twitching, coming back to centre on Summer's face.

'Put up your hands and step away from the car,' he said.

He was just a yard away now. The pistol was right in her face.
The hammer was cocked and his forefinger was curled tight
inside the trigger guard. He was getting ready to shoot her, she
couldn't do anything about it, and then there was the smash of
breaking glass above them and something, a chair, crashed onto
the sidewalk among a hail of bright fragments.

Carl Kelley turned, jerked his pistol towards the broken
window, ducked as something else, a laptop computer trailing
cables, flew at him. It slammed into the hood of the Accura and
fell into the street, and Carl Kelley came up and fired twice at
the window, the hard noise of the shots slamming off the side of
the building, then turned the pistol on Summer as she
straightarmed the little canister of pepper spray and emptied it
into his face.

Carl Kelley reeled backwards and his pistol went off; the
round punched through the open car door and struck Summer
in the calf. It was like being hit by a baseball bat. Her whole leg
went numb and she clutched at the edge of the door to stay
upright. Carl Kelley was bent double, clawing at his face, roaring. Summer levered herself stiff-legged behind the wheel and
rammed the key into the ignition. Her nose was running and her
eyes were streaming with tears, stinging from blowback from the
pepper spray. The engine started with a roar and she reversed
straight out into traffic without checking the mirror, brakes
screeching and horns blaring behind her. Her first thought was
to get away and call nine-eleven. But she was certain that Daryl
Weir was up there above the shop, so she put the transmission
into drive, stamped on the accelerator pedal and wrenched the
wheel around, bumping up over the kerb, seeing Carl Kelley
straighten up in front of her. He put a shot through the windshield and then there was a bang, much louder than she had
expected, and he disappeared.

Summer got out to a chorus of horns up and down the street.
Her leg wasn't hurting yet but she could feel strength draining
out of it as she limped over to where Carl Kelley lay on his side
curled into himself, looking up at her, dazed, unable to focus.
His pistol was on the sidewalk a couple of feet away. Summer

didn't dare bend to pick it up in case she fell over and couldn't get up again, so she kicked it under her car. Her right shoe was full of blood. She leaned against the side of her car and pulled out her cell phone.

The operator asked her which service she wanted. She said, 'All of them.'

54

Summer's surgeon told her that she had been lucky: the round had been slowed when it had punched through her car door but it hadn't spun or fragmented, and had missed the bone and major blood vessels. Pretty soon she'd be walking again, although she might be left with just the trace of a limp. Her mother was amazingly calm about it, only once mentioning that Summer was now eligible for early retirement because she had been wounded in the line of duty. Flower arrangements crowded the windowsill of her hospital room. Laura Killinger sat with her for a couple of hours. Several of Summer's friends from the Central Precinct and the detectives from the Robbery Unit came to stand by her bed. Ryland Nelsen said, 'I guess it's true. You really are slower than a speeding bullet.'

During the three days she spent in hospital, she was able to piece together Carl Kelley's history from the TV in her hospital room and the newspapers that her mother brought in every day. His real name was Stephen Thompson, a British citizen who'd been born in London's East End, the youngest of four children. When he'd been six, his father, a policeman and chronic alcoholic with a history of domestic violence, had committed suicide. His mother had died of lung cancer two years later. He'd spent the rest of his childhood in various foster-families and orphanages; a psychiatrist who had written a popular book on serial killers made much of the fact that one foster-family had returned him to social services after he'd killed the family's pet cat, and drew parallels with Dirk Merrit's alleged killing and mutilation of a classmate's pet dog.

He had joined the British Army at age sixteen and served for almost twenty years. His tours of duty included Northern

Ireland, former Yugoslavia, and the First Gulf War. He received several commendations for bravery, was promoted to the rank of sergeant, and quit the army after being implicated in a scandal at a training barracks where a number of recruits had committed suicide. After a brief spell with a security firm in South Africa, he fought with mercenary groups in the Congo, Liberia, and Uganda. In Uganda, he was involved in an incident in which more than twenty child soldiers of the Lord's Army were executed. The International War Crimes Tribunal in The Hague issued a warrant for his arrest and he went on the run, surfacing in Namibia under the name of Carl Kelley, working as a hunting guide. That was where he had met Dirk Merrit. A month later, travelling on a counterfeit passport, he arrived in the United States via Hong Kong and Vancouver. Soon afterwards he and Dirk Merrit killed their first victim near Wheeler Peak in northeast Nevada.

The FBI found out about the Wheeler Peak murder after it served a warrant on Dirk Merrit's bank and forced it to hand over material stored in a safety-deposit box, including a video that showed Dirk Merrit's ultralight chasing the victim across the desert, and the subsequent mutilation of the victim's body. Harry Malone told Summer about it when he visited her in hospital.

'It looks like Kelley obtained the victims, and then he and Merrit took them out to remote areas where Merrit killed them. The video shows that Kelley was present when Merrit killed the first victim, at Wheeler's Peak, but we can't use it against him until we find the body – his lawyer will claim it's staged. If Merrit was running true to form, he left the body out there; we're using satellite imaging to match landmarks on the video. And we'll be sifting through the wreckage of the mansion and searching the rest of Dirk Merrit's estate for at least another week so we may yet turn up something helpful. We're also fighting Merrit's lawyer through the courts; papers from the safety-deposit box suggest that he has material, too. But I have to tell you that at this point we don't know how many people Kelley and Merrit killed,' Malone said. 'And unless Kelley starts to talk, I'm afraid that we may never know.'

'Is Kelley holding out for a deal?'

'He isn't going to get one.' Malone sat stiffly in the chair by Summer's bed in a black suit and mirror-polished shoes. He had stopped off on his way to Salem, where he was going to supervise the transfer of Carl Kelley into federal custody. 'He's facing seven counts of murder, not to mention kidnap and wounding a police officer with intent to kill. We already have more than enough to put him away for four of the murders – Elias Silver and Okay Soucek, and Patrick Metcalf and one of Metcalf's employees, Frank Wilson. We have video footage from Merrit's security system that shows Kelley dumping the bodies of Metcalf and Wilson in the lake on Merrit's property, and we recovered the bodies, too. It wasn't difficult because the lake was mostly drained after Merrit blew up the dam. We're still working up the forensics on Greg Yunis, Julia Taylor and Erik Grow, but he's going to answer for them, too. He'll be in prison for the rest of his life, and because he killed three people that we know of in California and Nevada, he could get the death penalty.'

'What about Edie Collier and William Gundersen?'

'We think that Dirk Merrit tried to kill Edie Collier on his own; at the time of her escape, Kelley was in a motel in Los Angeles. As for Gundersen, we have good circumstantial evidence that Merrit killed him, but so far we haven't been able to put Kelley there.'

Summer understood. The federal prosecutor would commit Carl Kelley to trial on charges that had a good chance of conviction, but the FBI couldn't afford to investigate every one of his crimes in detail. The other murders would be hung on Dirk Merrit, who was conveniently dead.

Malone told her that Merrit had booked himself into a grey-market clinic in Mexico, that he had been planning to have some of his plastic surgery reversed so that he could disappear into the population and no doubt continue to have his special kind of fun. He also told her that DNA from scrapings of Kronenwetter's fingernails had matched Charley Phelps's DNA.

'It looks like Phelps killed Kronenwetter on his own. We rechecked Detective Hill's alibi, and it held up.'

'It was about the only thing that Denise got wrong. And even then she was half right.' Summer looked Malone straight in the eye and added, 'I hope that she'll get proper acknowledgement for what she did.'

She was worried that now the FBI had taken complete control of the case it would relegate Denise's contribution to a footnote.

'She died in the line of duty. She won't be overlooked. And if you're not satisfied, well, you'll get your day in court, Detective Ziegler. You can speak for her then.' Malone checked his watch, asked her if the hospital was treating her right.

'They're letting me go this afternoon.'

'Have you had any problems with the press, anything like that? I saw the uniform outside.'

'Nothing that the Public Information Office can't handle. The press is mostly interested in Dirk Merrit.'

'He'll be in the headlines for a while. I want you to know that I appreciate your help,' Malone said. 'You did good.'

'I wish I could have done more. I should have realized from the first that Dirk Merrit was deadly serious about his games.'

Because Denise Childers had died in line of duty, she got a hero's farewell. It was held the day after Edie Collier's funeral – a quiet affair attended by Randy Farrell, three people from the diner where Edie had worked, and Summer and her mother. Summer wanted to talk to Randy Farrell afterwards, thank him for the tip-off that had revealed Joseph Kronenwetter's death to be murder rather than suicide. But when she started towards him he turned and walked away, back to the overheated little tomb of the bungalow in Felony Flats and the living death of his marriage.

In contrast to Edie Collier's sparse send-off, Denise Childers got the full show, including two long lines of police motorcycles preceding the black limos, ranks of police in dress uniform, and an honour guard escorting the flag-draped casket to the grave, where Denise's daughter, a solemn, heartbreakingly beautiful little girl, sat with her grandparents amongst civilian dignitaries and police brass from all over the state. Summer was there in her dress blues, leaning on a pair of crutches, and so was her friend, Laura Killinger, who had driven her to Cedar Falls.

It was a beautiful summer day, the sky cloudless, bright sunlight accentuating the colours of the flowers heaped around the grave, sparkling on the polished badges and buttons of the ranks of uniformed officers, flashing off the river at the bottom of the cemetery's long slope. That Jerry Hill had gotten the same treatment – the Macabee County Sheriff's office had suppressed the events surrounding his death so that its image wouldn't be tarnished by a rogue cop who had shot a suspect before turning his gun on himself – didn't lessen the solemnity of the occasion. Sheriff Worden delivered a surprisingly touching eulogy, talking about how the best police officers, like Denise, would unstintingly give their all to uphold the law, protect the citizens of their community, and pursue their investigations with unflagging zeal. He mentioned several difficult cases she had solved, and said that being part of the investigation that had ended a string of murders had been her finest achievement, and he was sure that she would have been proud of all that had been done after her death to bring the tragic affair to a close.

It was better than Summer had expected, but she had to resist the temptation to limp up to the podium and take a swing at the white-haired little hypocrite with one of her crutches, smack him down and tell everyone there that his failure to back Denise and his readiness to pin Edie Collier's death on the nearest suspect had contributed to her death. But she let the moment pass and held her peace because she also knew that Denise had made her own choices, that she had pushed the envelope and taken needless risks in her pursuit of Dirk Merrit, and that her motives had not always been as pure as they could have been. Because nothing was ever simple in police work, and sometimes it was necessary to take refuge in the comfort of stories so that those left behind could make their peace with the world.

Seven of Denise's colleagues aimed their rifles at the blue sky and fired three rounds of blanks. The flag was removed from the casket and carefully folded by a white-gloved officer and presented to Denise's young daughter, who promptly burst into tears. Then the coffin was lowered into the ground. Summer waited with Laura while Denise's colleagues and family made their farewells, and the crowd slowly dispersed. When the cemetery was empty, she limped over to the fill mound on her crutches, and clumsily leaned down.

'Let me help,' Laura said, moving forward.

'It's okay. I can do this myself.'

Summer had to splay one crutch wide so that she could bend down and scoop up a handful of sandy dirt. She got herself upright again, and limped over to the grave under its white canopy. She looked down at the polished top of the casket, remembering the simple wicker basket in which her father had been buried, and let the handful of dirt sift down. She said, 'I hope I did the right thing.'

Summer was waiting for Laura to unlock the car when Gary Delgatto came across the parking lot towards them. He looked good in a black suit and black tie, his hair neatly brushed back. Solemnly shaking Laura's hand when Summer introduced her, smiling at Summer and saying that he was glad she had come.

'You guys want to talk,' Laura said. 'Take your time. I'll wait in the car.'

When they were alone, Gary said, 'I hope you don't mind this. Saying hi, I mean.'

'Why should I mind?'

'I thought you might want to know what's been happening. With the case.'

'Your boss stopped by and brought me up to date.'

'He did?'

'It was a few days ago,' Summer said, touched by his crestfallen look. 'What else is new?'

'Did Mr Malone tell you that Daryl Weir made it all the way to the end of his search?'

'In *Trans*?'

'Yeah, in *Trans*. We gave the kid a top-of-the-line computer and a tech to hold his hand, not that he needed it. It took him a while, but he got to the end of the road. It was inside a virtual replica of Griffith Observatory, behind a door guarded by a crazy-looking robot. He had to answer three questions to get past that thing – we helped him out there – and then find a hidden door in a corridor full of nasty surprises. He dealt with those, got the door open, and, well, care to take a guess what he found?'

'Nothing.'

Gary blinked. 'I thought you hadn't heard—'

'I hadn't. But I figured Dirk Merrit wouldn't leave anything valuable where anyone in the game could find it.'

'We think that he spread rumours about treasure to lure people in,' Gary said. 'So that he could have fun with them, perhaps use it as a way of choosing new victims.'

'How is Daryl Weir? The kid went through a lot.'

'He's back in New York, with his mother. We're giving him counselling, and he told us that he's ready to stand up in court and give evidence at Kelley's trial.'

'Good for him.'

'We did find out something else involving the game. It turns out that Dirk Merrit was skimming a tenth of a cent off the top of every dollar of the subscriptions people pay to play it. He'd inserted a viral program into the accounting software. It adjusted the books to cover its operation and sent the skimmed money to a bank account in Bermuda. It didn't add up to much,' Gary said. 'Just enough to pay for his utility bills. But I guess the amount wasn't the point.'

'He was proud. That was his fatal flaw. He was forced to sell off his controlling interest in his precious game, so he took revenge on the company that bought it by stealing from them.'

'We still haven't found out everything he was into,' Gary said.

It felt wrong, talking about Dirk Merrit at Denise's funeral. Summer changed the subject, asked Gary how his Ph.D work was coming on.

'I haven't had time for that. The case, and so on. I'll get back to it when things quiet down.'

There was a silence. Gary asked Summer if she was staying in town.

'I have a lift back to Portland.'

'Right.'

'In fact, I should go. I still think you're a cool guy, Gary.' She leaned forward on her crutches, planted a kiss on his cheek and said, 'I don't regret anything.'

In the car, Laura said, 'Man, if you aren't going to do anything about that, I will.'

'He has a girlfriend.'

'I bet he does. And I bet she wouldn't stand a chance if you went after him. I saw the way he looked at you. All you have to do is crook your little finger . . .'

'Yeah, and move to Washington, D.C. And you know why that isn't going to happen.'

'After this, I bet the FBI would take you like a shot.'

'Me become a fed? And I thought you were my friend.'

Summer got home at seven in the evening. Her mother was out on the deck, dozing on the chaise longue, a paperback book splayed open on her stomach. When Summer came through the French window, crutches rattling on the cedar planks of the deck, her mother sat up with a start and the paperback slid off and fell to the floor.

Summer said, 'What's wrong? Bad dreams or a bad conscience?'

Her mother was shading her eyes and staring at her with a strange, lost expression. Then her face cleared and she smiled and said, 'I'm a foolish old woman, and I've had a long day, up to his house and back. For a moment . . . I suppose it's the uniform, but for a moment I mistook you for your father.'

'You drove up to the Columbia Gorge?'

'I've been driving for longer than you've been alive, and I'm not quite in my dotage,' her mother said. 'I will admit that the round trip took it out of me, but it was a nice day, I had nothing better to do, so I thought I'd go take a look. It's beautiful up there, isn't it?'

'Yes, it is. I had a lot of happy times there.'

'I know I used to tease your father about his obsession with the place, but I had a lot of happy times there too. And I don't think I'm quite ready to let it go.'

Summer smiled. 'I'm pleased to hear it.'

'I think you should stay there while you're getting better. As long as I can come visit.'

'I'd like that. But until I'm fit to drive again, you're stuck with me for a little while.'

Her mother was still looking at her in an odd way, looking at her and through her at the same time.

Summer said, 'I guess I should go change.'

'You look very becoming in your uniform, dear. Just like your father. Sometimes I wonder if I would have noticed him at all if he hadn't been in uniform.'

'As I recall the famous story, you picked a fight with him because he was in uniform.'

'That's what I always told him. But the fact is, I picked a fight with him because he was the most handsome creature I'd ever laid my eyes on and I wanted to get to know him better. And quite frankly, I'm sure the uniform had something to do with it.'

'Still, I should go wash up.'

Summer still had dirt from the graveside under her nails.

Her mother patted the edge of the chaise longue. 'Sit down first, and tell me how your day went. Tell me everything.'

Acknowledgements

My thanks to all the members of the City of Portland Police Bureau who generously gave me their time and hospitality, particularly Officer Ryan Engweiler, Detective Matt Horton, Detective Sergeant Kelly Scheffler, and Sergeant Brian Schmantz. Michael Alkire MD answered an important question about anaesthetics, and Russell Schechter and Jack Womack read a draft of the manuscript and gave invaluable advice and encouragement.

Although this novel is set in Oregon and the city of Portland, the procedures described in it should not be mistaken for actual police practice in that state.